BROKEN WEB

by Ryan Alcock

BOOK ONE

THE KILLING LABEL

I

Bella North-Spectra was whining and it was, quite frankly, irritating Dana Spectra beyond belief. The younger girl was on one of her current pet peeves, that being Dana should really be doing better in her career. In truth, Dana had a relatively good life as a model, even despite the fact that winning the Miss Green Earth competition had not propelled her to the international stardom and success that her younger sister thought it should.

"If you spent a little less time fighting gun smugglers and helping thieves escape global crime syndicates, you'd be more popular. Your followers are still in the hundreds of thousands, which is totally ridiculous for someone who was Miss Green Earth. And involved in the scandalous death of a billionaire. More people should be taking notice of this," Bella pouted.

"I could get an OnlyFans page," Dana suggested, playfully.

"That's not going to increase your followers, is it?" she growled, and Dana was a little disappointed her sister wasn't more stirred by the lascivious suggestion.

"I'd sign up for it," Jeremy, Dana's best friend and confidante, grinned.

"Thank you," Dana said, as Bella rolled her eyes.

There are copious time travel stories in science-fiction that endlessly preach the idea that ripples spread out from even the slightest event, such that a simple and subtle action in someone's life can have consequences that are much further reaching that would initially appear.

Coming from a therapy session with her sister, Dana Spectra had had time to pause and look back to see the sheer enormity of how her life had changed with all the impact of a sledgehammer through a plate-glass window, thanks to meeting one person in a casino in Singapore. She was about to discover that something even simpler could have a more dramatic impact.

As they walked along Petrie Terrace, chatting to themselves, Dana blinked as she spied a black cat deciding to cross the road, with an arrogance that only a cat can possess. It watched cars zoom back and forth along Petrie Terrace, its green eyes deep in thought, and then it decided that it could possibly make it across the road. As soon as Dana realised what it was about to do, her heart dropped and she ran forward, her brain hoping desperately that cars would stop as she decided to cross the road.

She was not wrong, and the cars did indeed pull up, drivers shouting angrily as they blasted their horns at the blonde girl in the black mini-dress. But Dana didn't care. Traffic had been brought to a standstill, but she was able to get to the black cat, picking it up carefully and taking it across to where it wanted to go. The cat actually purred, contented that it didn't need to use its legs anymore as a human had decided to do that job instead.

As she came back to her friends, the smile on her face, dropped a little when she saw her sister and friend standing beside the occupants of one of the cars that had stopped. Dressed in dark blue, and wearing heavy vests with a number of pockets, Dana didn't need to see the "police" on their uniforms to know that she was in trouble. Well, she sighed, it wouldn't be the first time this year she had been taken into police custody.

She had got a surprisingly polite, Irish cop named Rosney who explained to her as a parent might to a three-year-old child, why it was important not to just randomly cross the road. They were going to let her go, not least because a number of drivers who had been there had spoken out for her when they discovered what she had been doing.

"And please, take the cat with you," Rosney said, shaking his head.

Less than an hour later, Bella raced into her room, holding the cat.

"Have you seen the headlines?" she demanded, sticking out her phone. **MODEL RISKS LIFE TO RESCUE CAT**.

"Wow," Dana murmured, as she saw the number of articles.

"Also I think the cat might be deaf," Bella added, dropping him beside Dana.

Within another hour it became **AUSSIE MODEL RISKS LIFE FOR DEAF CAT**, and Dana scowled at her sister who shrugged innocently. Looking at her IG account, which her younger sister kept for her, Dana saw a number of candid pictures of her and the cat. Bella, however, was more excited about something else, and she scrolled to the top of the account. Dana's followers had finally crossed the million mark. Thirty minutes later it was over two million.

#catmodel began to trend, along with #catsavior and #Danaspussy, the latter of which Dana rolled her eyes at, much to Bella's confusion, until she picked up on it. By the end of the day Dana's followers had crossed the five million mark. Almost the precise moment it did, her phone buzzed, and Dana saw that it was her manager, Christa Adams, and she wondered how much trouble she was in.

"Brilliant!" Adams said, though there wasn't a lot of excitement in her voice.

"What…?" Dana started, but Adams wasn't to be interrupted.

"I don't know which of you made sure your bracelet was included in some of those shots, but whoever it was deserves a medal."

"My bracelet?"

"It's Digné!" Adams said, as though Dana struggled to understand English.

"It was a present. It's a bit chunky, but I have to wear it when I go out with Jeremy because he gave it to me."

"I don't care about that! Your name is trending in association with Digné, and their people have only just bloody contacted my people. Clicks, Spectra! They love the story, they love your look, and they want you to be the

7

new face of Digné!" Dana dropped the phone as the news sank in. A brand ambassador for a major jewellery company? Oh my…

"Yeah, but what does that mean?" Bella said, having picked up the phone, and Dana snatched it away from her.

Adams replied with her usual steely composure "You're going to be fucking rich if *she* doesn't balls this up."

And so, one Thursday morning Dana had woken up and joined her best friend and sister on a trip into the city, dressed casually and ready for sun later, and the following morning she had awoken to being an overnight sensation. All thanks to a cat (whom Bella had named Dine – Dana wasn't quite sure why, and wondered if she had misheard Digné, but decided to leave it).

However, there was one more ripple that was to have an effect the following day.

"Hey, you know who's followed you on IG?" Bella asked out of the blue.

"Honestly no," Dana replied. "A lot of creepy people, I'm guessing."

"Err, yeah, that's true," Bella admitted with a little grimace. "Though to be fair they followed you already. No, this is way more exciting."

"Do tell," Dana grinned indulgently.

"Millie!" The indulgent grin turned to a blank expression. "Bong-cha Nam!" Bella said. "Millie from G'Star!" That rang a louder bell, and Dana sat up from the couch.

"G'Star the pop group?" she clarified.

"Yeah, Millie is following you. Oh, so is Mee. You have two followers from G'Star! Oh my god, you should be following them back!" Bella gushed.

"Well, fucking follow them back then!" her sister squealed, and Bella immediately began tapping away on the phone. "Wait, aren't there others?"

"Yeah, it's Millie, Mee, uh…" Bella paused, flustered, but Dana already had her phone out and was Googling.

"Bong-cha "Millie" Nam, Mee Bu, Soojin Sam and Aimi "Amy" Hirano," Dana supplied. "Follow them all. Oh my god, I can't believe famous people are following me!"

"I mean, Ophélie is not going to be happy," said Bella, raising an eyebrow pointedly.

"I mean more famous than me," Dana replied, a little annoyed. "Oh," she added, not looking up from her phone.

"Good oh, or bad oh?"

"Curious oh," her sister said. "Millie is the face of Digné in Korea."

"I mean," Bella began, a huge smile creeping across her face. "If that's not an excuse to go to a G'Star concert and meet and greet, what the actual is?"

II

Though she had a soft spot for Changi Airport in Singapore, Dana Spectra had to admit that Incheon Airport was mightily impressive. They had flown over it and Dana, sitting in a window seat, had the opportunity to see the airport from above, impressed at the symmetrical shape of the design, which looked to her a little like a claw hanging from a teardrop. Her flight having been booked by Digné (who had agreed with Christa Adams that Dana attending a G'Star concert would be brilliant promotion for the brand and create a lot of online chatter), Dana had to fly to Sydney to catch the Korean Air flight to Seoul. The consequence was reading an inflight magazine that outlined future changes to Incheon Airport which looked as though it was going to become considerably greener in the future.

Incheon was an airport that had won a number of awards over the previous years, and ranked in the top five airports for the past five years. More impressively it posted times of less than fifteen minutes for departure and arrival, and while it had followed the rest of the world with online booking and biometric check-ins, it was the AI robots named Airstar that were the revolutionary step forward. The short, squat, sleek white robots with touch-screens on their backs were multilingual and designed to assist passengers with a variety of services. Dana assumed that the plans to improve and update the airport would include more dependence on Airstar as time went on. As long as the system didn't crack under the pressure of the millions of passengers that went through the airport, it would be quite the revolution, Dana reflected.

She had spent most of the flight, however, catching on G'Star. It wasn't so much that she wasn't interested in the group; along with the likes of Blackpink and Twice, Dana very much enjoyed K-pop, but in truth G'Star was a new group she hadn't heard that much of. They were less the bubblegum pop of Twice and closer in style to the sexier, genre-bending Blackpink. Bella – who had more of an interest in K-Pop than she did – had told her that all K-pop groups have official colours, and their fans had their own names; G'star's colours were gold and white, their fans were called Glitter. Dana was a little sad she couldn't take her sister, but did promise her video messages and autographs.

"You are Glitter!" Bella intoned. "Don't forget it!"

Their music was catchy, but unexpected and some of the songs on their mini-albums (they had yet to release an album) were very different to what she thought the band would produce; moody, sensual stuff that defied the louder, in-your-face style of their A-sides. Songs like *Heol* and *Epic* had made the charts for obvious reasons, but it was *Wow* which captured her attention the most, and made her feel like she was in some strange, alien environment which unsettled her. A unique sensation, but one that made her fall in love with the group completely.

Millie, Mee, Soojin and Amy were also names she had forced herself to study. G'Star was not dissimilar to the mood of some K-Pop girl groups which utilised foreigners in their line-up. Aimi Hirano (or Amy) was Japanese and the youngest in the group. Bella had informed her that she was the *maknae*, literally the youngest who was generally regarded as the cutest, or perhaps sometimes the naughtiest. Certainly, from some of the online interviews it seemed that Amy had the cheekiest personality. She also seemed to share a close bond with Mee, a member who had been raised in London before moving back to Korea to join the group at the age of 14. Mee spoke the best English and was the "face of the group" when it came to interviews. Soojin, the oldest, was the main vocalist, and had a quieter, more background personality, though it was clear she cared about the other members deeply. That left Millie, the lead rapper of the group. The management team also deemed her the most beautiful of the group – she was the visual and centre. With her sharp features, surprising freckles and spiky short hair, she certainly caught the attention.

The Korean Air flight arrived at Terminal 2 of Incheon and Dana was forced to navigate through the long-carpeted corridors with the seemingly endless travelators in order to get to the actual Arrivals part of the airport. Here she was struck by how *white* the airport was. She wasn't certain whether that was just terminal 2 or if it applied to the entire structure, but with so much white – be it the speckled tiled floor, the reflective plastic around the shop fronts or light strips – she felt a little like she was on a spaceship in a science-fiction show. It didn't help that the entrances to the shops were rounded at the corners and designed to look as though they were on an angle. Add to that the random archways that were either mirrored or flashing multi-coloured lights, and Dana decided she was definitely on something that could be from *Star Trek*.

As she made her way through the terminal, she was surprised to see Airstar itself, moving along the corridor, chatting to itself in a variety of languages, including Japanese and English, and presumably Korean.

"Hello, my name is Airstar. Please come and say Airstar if you need any help from me." The robot was about the size of a teenager (probably Bella's height) and was essentially a white cylinder with a large screen on the front that flicked through a variety of different screens. On the top of the cylinder was a rounded head, also white, but with a black screen that had two big blue eyes picture on it. On its sides, two strips of lights cycled through a variety of colours, from purple to orange.

"Did you have a good time at Incheon Airport. Will you take pictures with me?" Airstar said, and Dana found it was now, inadvertently, directly in front of her. The screen showed two pictures, one of which indicated a photograph. Dana paused, and then lent forward and pressed the little Korean flag in the corner, which brought a menu that allowed her to change the text to English. She chose the photo option, and Airstar gave her the option of an email or SMS. Choosing the latter, the screen changed to a reflective image of herself, and Dana almost laughed out loud. She could see in the background other passengers looking curiously to see what she was doing. A large circle came up on screen, counting down from 3, and soon her picture was displayed, with *disagree* and *agree* options.

In truth, the picture wasn't that bad, so she agreed, and felt the vibration in her clutch as Airstar messaged her the photo.

"I love you dear. It is my gift. Please keep the memories. When you want to say goodbye to me, please press the goodbye button, or say Airstar." Dana looked around, catching the eyes of a wide-eyed little girl who smiled at her, entertained by the interaction. Dana lent forward and pressed the *goodbye* button that was now on the screen. "I'm returning home. See you later." With that, the robot rotated on its axis and then moved away from her. That was one for IG, she reflected.

It wasn't the most interestingly designed airport she had ever been in (it seemed that Changi had no competition here), but it was pleasant and reminded her in many ways of the Brisbane airport. She noticed that the white was broken up every so often by wood panelling and greenery and the roof in some areas had a curious triangle pattern that made up the skylights – though given that she had arrived in the evening it didn't look as impressive as it could. Nonetheless, looking out of the windows she could see the mighty city of Seoul throbbing away.

Dana had her various forms ready for submission and thanks to a mix of both these and the facial recognition the airport used, she was surprised to find that her arrival time had taken her roughly twenty minutes. After collecting her luggage from the baggage carousels, she exited into the greeting area on the first floor. There were surprisingly few people around, or to be more accurate, there were fewer people than Dana expected to be. She didn't feel crowded or forced into a flow of people. Instead, people quietly made their way to where they needed to be.

As in most airports, on passing through the Arrival exit, Dana saw groups of people standing around holding signs, which they waved excitedly as each new person exited in the hope that they would find the person they were looking for. Dana was slightly surprised to see some people standing around with cameras at the ready, and when they saw her and started snapping, she was even more surprised to find a large, burly Korean come up to her, bow and mumble her name.

"Err, yes?" she replied, not sure what to say, and the Korean

12

man took her luggage and started to move, shielding Dana from the photographers. He shoved a card into her free hand and she looked at it, seeing her name printed neatly with the word Digné below it. Dana nodded absently, sliding the card into her clutch and following the man. She tried to remember what her email from Christa had said regarding her trip into the city, but aside from *You'll be met at the airport by one of Digné's representatives*, it mostly escaped her. She could always check the email on the journey, she reflected, though briefly wished Bella was with her to keep her organised.

Once outside, the man released her and made his way towards a large, black Mercedes-Benz people mover. Dana was surprised to see that there were more photographers lurking around, and in the dark their flashes were far more obvious. However, it was when the man opened the door to the Merc that the flashes began in earnest.

He gestured to Dana to get in the car with some urgency, and she did, her mind logically reasoning that if that many people were taking photos of her getting into a car, it was unlikely that she was about to be kidnapped. Also, she was fairly certain that kidnappers didn't use Mercedes-Benzes. If they could afford that kind of car, they wouldn't need to ransom hostages.

Once inside, however, she realised that she wasn't really the target of the photographers. Seated in the car opposite her were two faces she immediately recognised, thanks to having spent an inordinate amount of time over the last few days looking at them. One was the oval-shaped, bright eyed face of Mee Bu, while beside her, looking as moody as always was Bong-Cha Nam, better known as Millie. Her sharp features were even more striking in real life and she could see the girl was wearing minimal makeup as her freckles were patently obvious. Both women bowed as she sat, but then Mee leapt forward and embraced her. Dana was a little astonished but happily hugged the other girl.

"I'm so happy to meet you," Mee gushed, her accent strangely English. "Millie and I were so impressed by everything you did for that poor little kitten. You're amazing!"

"I mean, it really wasn't that special," Dana said, spectacularly failing to comprehend quite what was going on.

"Can I hug you?" Millie suddenly asked, and Mee put her hand to

13

her mouth.

"I'm sorry, I didn't think," she started, but Dana interrupted her.

"It's fine, honestly. Of course you can hug me. I can't believe you'd want to…" But this time it was Dana who was cut off as Millie leaned forward and pulled her close.

"When Digné made you the Australian face of their brand, I thought it would be the perfect opportunity to get to meet you," Millie said, though she never smiled and Dana found her impassiveness a little unsettling. She was very difficult to read, and Dana couldn't work out if the body contact was something to make her feel welcome, or a genuine emotion. Given what she knew of Koreans, the latter seemed unlikely.

"And then we were told you would like to see us in concert, and we couldn't have been more excited," Mee continued. Her hug had seemed more a product of her English upbringing which also explained her more Western sensibilities.

"Guys," Dana grinned, unable to reject Mee's infectious enthusiasm any longer, "you're one of the biggest groups in the world. I'm just an Aussie model who rescued a cat!"

"Not just that," Millie said, and she seemed to smirk a little. "We met DJ Kabuki not so long ago."

"Oh, I wouldn't put too much stock in rumours," Dana waved her hand a little, though she tried to think back to what Kabuki could have told them. Certainly Karen Ichioka had been around when some of their friends had been murdered by a snake-eyed assassin, and she may have told her girlfriend some of that story. "We were in the wrong place at the wrong time," Dana added, hoping that she was right about what Kabuki had told Millie. The look on the Korean girl's face, however, didn't really suggest she believed it.

Dana was surprised at how easy it was to babble with the girls about mostly inane things, as they discussed Dine (the mere name of which sent Mee into gales of laughter, as she covered her face with both hands in a typical Korean gesture) and the sort of cat she was, as well as music that they liked in general. Despite appearing taciturn and rarely smiling, Millie had a cheeky sense of humour, but it was definitely Mee who had the most to say on the journey. Dana had noticed when she was watching videos of G'Star online that the girls' personalities appeared to be fairly close to what they presented – in interviews Mee and Amy tended to dominate the discussion, helped in no small part by Mee's fluency in English, while both Soojin and Millie would add in their own comment at various points. There was a playfulness to the foursome's public persona that was present in the real-life women in front of her. If they were putting on an act for her, it was a very good one.

Incheon was an island off the coast of South Korea, so to actually get to the city required travelling to get to the mainland. This brought Dana to mind of her relatively recent visit to Japan and travelling to Haneda Airport, though that certainly hadn't been as far away from the mainland as Incheon seemed to be which looked like it might take about an hour. As they crossed Yeongjong Bridge, Seoul opened up before them. At 7 pm at night, it looked like a piece of sci-fi anime, a futuristic city painted in gold and teal, with neon purples, pinks and oranges liberally splashed around. When Dana touched the window, a little in awe of what she saw, she felt the cold bite back at her and checked her phone to see that it was seven in the evening.

"How did you get time off from your rehearsals?" Dana suddenly realised, turning back to the singers in front of her.

"We've been at it all day," Mee grinned. "Trust me, when we arranged to meet you at the airport it was under strict instructions that we would be working our butts off during the day to make sure we are ready for tomorrow."

"Not that we don't work our butts off, right Nam Shik?" Millie turned to the front of the car where the large, burly Korean man who had first appeared at the airport turned and gave a wry smile. "He doesn't understand English," Millie continued, and Mee giggled.

"He probably thinks you're being mean," Mee said. She turned as well and spoke quickly in Korean to Nam, who furrowed his heavy brow and looked at Millie, though the older girl leaned over and slapped Mee on the arm.

"Unnie!" Mee exclaimed, and got another slap.

"She just told him that I said he needed to lose weight," Millie growled and Dana bit her lip to stop the smile. Mee was still laughing at her own joke.

The rest of the journey passed in much the same way, and all three took selfies which they posted on their social media; Dana noticing that the simple #glitter was enough to get the attention of hundreds of thousands. When she saw that both Millie and Mee were tagging her, Dana suddenly realised the unexpected depth of her new found popularity.

"Where are we going?" Dana suddenly asked, realising she had no idea what her night was going to hold. Millie shifted across to sit beside her, though kept a respectful distance, and pointed out the window to the neon dream the Mercedes was travelling through, to a tall juggernaut of glass and metal that reached up to the sky, leaving the rest of the city far behind.

"Lotte World Tower," Mee supplied. "You're staying at the Signiel Seoul, one of the best hotels in Seoul. Did you not get told?"

"Oh wow," Dana murmured, the height of the building overwhelming her momentarily. She wondered if she should pretend she'd been kept in the dark, but couldn't bring herself to do it. "I forgot," she admitted, shamefacedly.

"It's the tallest building in Seoul," Millie whispered. "Fifth tallest in the world. At the top you can walk from the one side to the other via a skybridge. You have to do it."

"It'll terrify you!" Mee gushed. "Well, it terrified me. We did it for a promotional exercise."

"You don't live here, do you?" Dana said, turning to Millie, surprised to see the woman had moved closer.

"No, but the press think we do," Mee said, and she moved back to her original seat. "We have been here before with guests and we have a little system because there are always press waiting out the front when we arrive. So we go in, then we slip out the back way and the press never see us leave. So, they think we live there. The hotel is around the hundredth floor…"

"I think it's the thirty floors leading up to the 100th," Millie

16

interrupted.

"And below that are apartments people can stay in," Mee continued, unperturbed by the interjection. "I guess that's where they think we live."

Dana nodded, her mind recalling Bella mentioning that the group all lived together, possibly in Lotte World Tower. Online, the "netizens" had argued it wasn't true, but one commenter had talked about how they often enter but never leave, which meant the set up was clearly working. She wondered if it was the girls' idea or someone else's. Perhaps the brooding Nam Shik, or was he simply security?

When the car had reached Olympic Road, an eight-lane highway that clung to the Han River, they had turned onto it and settled into the flow of traffic that eased along surprisingly quickly, all things considered. By the time that Millie had been able to point out Lotte World Tower, the Mercedes turned right into Songpa Road and continued forward, their destination now patently obvious.

Sitting in front of the tower was Lotte World Mall, a shopping centre which Mee described as amazing and promised they would go shopping at some point, though the obviously pragmatic Millie had warned her not to make promises she couldn't keep.

"We can barely go shopping anywhere these days," Millie explained, a little ruefully. "Do you get that?"

"Oh, no, not really," Dana said. "I mean, there are a few people who recognise me, but I don't get people crowding to get my autograph."

"I thought people might recognise you easier because of your favourite outfit," said Mee. "The little black dress with the white collar," she added.

"Oh," Dana exclaimed, a little surprised. "Yeah, I do like that style. And that dress in particular is a bit of a fave. I have a few," she admitted.

"I like it," added Millie, and she gave Dana a rare smile.

Two more lefts brought them firstly onto Jamsil Road, and then out the front of the Lotte World Tower itself. As the car pulled up, Nam Shik was the first to action, bounding out of the car and opening the door nearest the building, whereupon Millie and Mee got out, Millie grabbing Dana's hand on the way to help her down. The girls had been correct, and there were a number of photographers standing around, though unlike some paparazzi in other countries, these stayed a polite distance away, but began snapping regardless. Millie didn't let go of Dana's hand as the trio made their way through the glass doors into the lobby of the Tower, but even as they did, Dana noticed that Nam Shik wasn't their only company. Now they were joined by two more men in dark suits and turtlenecks, as well as a woman in an equally dark suit, but with a white collared shirt and round glasses, staring intently at her phone. A young man, in a less interesting grey suit, walked beside her, as obsessed with his tablet as his boss was with her phone. He kept whispering urgently to the woman, who nodded, but didn't seem able to reply.

By the time they were inside, Mee had linked her arm with Dana's, and Millie continued to lead the way, her hand never letting go of Dana's. The entourage that had formed around them had only increased the attention of the photographers outside, who continued to snap in an attempt to get something of interest from inside the lobby of Lotte World Tower.

Dana barely got a chance to take in the lobby, and had only glimpses of a curved ceiling and walls of glass as she was bustled towards an elevator. By now they had picked up a few more members for their entourage, one of whom was dressed in a neat, deep purple suit with a crisp white shirt that was buttoned to the collar, but had no tie. His grey hair was carefully styled, matching the equally grey mustache and pointed beard, while the bright white frames of his glasses ensured his face was the thing that grabbed the attention.

"Dana?" he purred with a smooth French accent, "how do you do? I am Mainard Descoteaux, I am the public relations vice-president of Digné, such a pleasure to meet you." He was able to talk and shake hands without breaking the stride of the team that they were with, as well as successfully not getting in between any of the girls to do it. "Millie, a pleasure as always," he added, and Dana noticed he gave a small nod to the woman with the phone, as though they too had already met. As he continued, the group all entered the elevator, which was a convenient size, given the amount of people who had gotten in. A woman in a long, deep blue dress, who seemed to be Descoteaux's assistant, pressed a button, clearly setting the destination for the group.

"Can I say how excited we all are at Digné with what is going to happen tomorrow night. A G'Star concert is, of course, one of the most exciting things that can happen, but to know that our two most recent ambassadors will be there, unveiling one of them, all of which is a massive thrill for everyone. The timing could not have been better, and the fact your Ms Adams came up with the suggestion is a master stroke. We couldn't have planned this better if we tried."

"I'm really excited to be here," she said, suddenly feeling that she could have come out with something better.

"Of course, we have sorted out everything that will be needed for your attendance tomorrow. Ms François and I have been working on your accessories, and I think I have something you will fall in love with."

"I have a few things prepared, and you are welcome to pick anything that suits you," the lady in the blue dress said, turning to Dana, a tablet in her hand. "Hair and makeup are ready to go. We have Sasha Song booked in for tomorrow at 4 to get your make up done, and we'll be here around 2 in order to have your outfit ready to go."

"*Parfait, non*?" Descoteaux gushed.

"The girls have to be ready for tomorrow. We can't keep them out much later," the woman in dark suit suddenly announced, and her grey offsider whispered something to her in Korean. "Millie, Mee," she said simply, and the girls looked a little flustered.

"We can settle her in, can't we?" Mee said. "She's new and doesn't know anyone. We can't just abandon her." The man in grey whispered again to the woman in the dark suit, who frowned and seemed unimpressed.

"We go up, we go in, we settle everyone, and that's it. We're gone. The concert isn't going to start late because of Digné," the dark suit woman said, and a flash of annoyance crossed Descoteaux's face.

"I wouldn't expect that of course, but given the money that is being donated to the concert, a little consideration of the night before would be

19

appreciated," he said with an obvious dash of tension, and the dark suit woman made a face, before speaking.

"Of course," but the concession couldn't have been more reluctant.

The elevator reached the 92nd floor of Lotte World Tower and the group stepped out, with Ms François leading the way.

"Have I been checked in?" Dana wondered to herself, but she felt Millie squeeze her hand.

"Everything's been taken care of, I guess," the Korean girl assured her, but Dana had to admit she was feeling more flustered than she had been in quite some time. For a moment she wished that the two pop stars had the ability to stay with her, as despite being in a crowd of what now seemed to be more than ten people, Dana couldn't feel more alone. The reassuring physical contact of the G'Star girls was going to disappear and Dana wasn't even sure who she'd be left with.

As they continued down the corridor, Descoteaux seemed to be having an intense conversation with the woman in the dark suit, and both whispered urgently to each other, clearly feeling that their needs weren't being met.

They paused at 9204, and Ms François swiped a card on the door, opening it and standing back to allow everyone entry. Mee entered first, taking Dana and Millie with her. Exactly who followed in what order was lost on the model as she gazed around the room she had entered. The room felt like a traditional Korean room, even down to the padded cushions on the floor around the small wooden table with the simple, white porcelain crockery on it. It was separated from another room by doors that seemed to emulate shoji screens and could be used to shut the adjoining room off. This made sense as it was a bedroom, complete with a large, double bed on one side and a television set up on a row of wooden cupboards on the other.

Floor to ceiling windows gave a stunning view of the Han River and the brightly lit night side of Seoul shone through, though again this vista could be shut out with the upgraded *shoji* screens. Large water colours hung on either side of the bed, and in the other room as well behind the table, and small vases with delightfully non-Australian plants were scattered around on the various wood cupboards.

"The Korean suite," Ms François said as she handed Dana the door card.

"It's so beautiful," Mee gushed. "The bed is amazing. Can I try it out?" Dana paused, unsure of what to say to the request and not quite sure what was meant, but Millie shot a meaningful look at the others in the room and Mee's enthusiasm waned. Dana sighed a little as she realised that this was a work visit and they would have to start listening to what was being said.

The woman in the dark suit said something to Descoteaux in what was presumably Korean, but Dana couldn't pretend to understand it, though both Mee and Millie quickly snapped to attention.

"We have to go," Mee muttered, though again Dana wasn't entirely clear on why she was whispering, feeling as though her visit was going to leave her perpetually confused. "Our manager wants us to be ready for tomorrow's concert and we have a lot of work to do. I can't wait to see you then and introduce you to the other members." She bowed a little and Dana quickly stood up and bowed back, not entirely certain it was the right thing to do, but it seemed to spark a small wave of bowing from the manager and her assistant as well. Millie bowed a little and also gave a little wave, but by then the manager was ushering them out of the suite. At the door Mee turned and brought her thumb and forefinger together in a heart gesture. The door closed, leaving Dana and the Digné company alone.

"You probably want to have some rest," Descoteaux said, smiling, and Dana noticed that the smile rarely reached his eyes. "We'll have everything ready for you to start at two tomorrow, if that suits. Ms François has sorted out your make-up, hair and accessories. I have a collection of things right here," and he handed across his tablet to her, "that you can sort through and choose for what to wear. We're assuming you're going to go casual for the concert." Dana nodded absently as she flicked photos across the tablet, recognising cut out jeans from the likes of Dolce & Gabbana and Roberto Cavalli. She was of a vague mind to wear something a little daring, but was also conscious of what the standards were in Korea. Despite ostensibly being edgy, in truth the country preferred a little more modesty, and that applied even more with their music idols. Attending a concert baring too much would make things awkward for Millie and Digné, and Dana wasn't prepared to do that to the people who were being so kind to her.

Especially not if it was going to make her some solid money.

"I've got the important accessories sorted," grinned Descoteaux, and this time it did reach his eyes. "You and Millie will be a small fortune each, but the publicity of the two of you together will be completely worth it for us, particularly ahead of both of you recording some advertisements." He pronounced the word to emphasize the 'tise'.

Dana smiled, suddenly feeling a little overwhelmed and she handed the tablet back to Descoteaux who shook his head.

"No, no, choose what you want and then get it to us in the morning if you can, and we'll make sure they are ready for you to wear tomorrow afternoon."

"Right, yeah," Dana nodded.

"You are overwhelmed," Descoteaux nodded, and dramatically began to usher his people towards the suite door. "Out, out the poor girl needs some rest!"

Ms François was the first to the door and she opened it, but to everyone's surprise there was a member of the hotel staff standing there, dressed in his uniform dark suit. There was a pause as everyone felt the awkwardness, but the staff member bowed and then handed over what he had been carrying to Ms François.

It was a bunch of white flowers and he said something which Dana only partly caught – *him-nay shay-o*. She had no idea what it meant, or even if she had heard it correctly, but curiously everyone in the room seemed as puzzled as she was, with the exception of one Descoteaux's staff who was Korean. He looked…haunted, almost. Descoteaux laughed a little.

"It looks like you can't escape the gifts," he said, though it seemed a little forced. "Come, come, let's leave Ms Spectra to her night." He bustled everyone through the door, but the last one to exit was the Korean gentleman and he turned to Dana.

"Be careful," he said quietly.

"Err, OK," replied Dana, by now very puzzled.

"The flowers," he added and then walked out. Dana frowned as the door closed and wandered over to the flowers. She took a picture of them and put them into a picture search where it returned nothing particularly interesting except that they were chrysanthemums.

Idly, she did a google search to see if there was any significance of chrysanthemums in Korea, and her immediate result was *a symbol of happiness and pleasure*.

Weird, Dana mused.

And then realised that the full sentence noted the flowers were originally from Korea, and that was what they meant to the Japanese.

She scrolled a little further down, when something caught her eye.

White chrysanthemums symbolise grief.

Usually given at funerals.

Be careful.

Dana got a slight twinge and she looked to her hand luggage which had been deposited on a chair. Inside was the soft case that had been given by Karim Narogin, the man from ASIO, which would hide her golden G48 Glock from airport security. She had been hesitant to bring it and to her own annoyance, her brain chose being very careful – be prepared for anything. The idea that she couldn't go anywhere without stumbling into drama was ridiculous really, but given that she had two recent incidents in her life which had brought her into contact with the spy fraternities of a half a dozen different countries, she was starting to feel a little paranoid. Her therapist had assured her that was to be expected and she needed to work on the idea that they might have been simply isolated incidents and would be unlikely to happen again. But when she had point blank asked her father if ASIO had a continued interest in her, he had looked guilty before assuring her it was unlikely. All of which led to the golden Glock being packed into her hand luggage and kept safely by her side should she need it.

Be careful.

The following morning Dana had set her alarm to ensure she woke early. There was one particular touristy thing she was keen to do before she got ready for the big concert that night, and she wanted to make sure she had enough time for it.

On waking she had picked out what she wanted to wear for the night and emailed her choice through to the address that had been left on the tablet. Ms François appeared to be the hyper efficient type, and she replied in less than a minute to assure Dana that everything would be taken care of.

With that out of the way, Dana made sure to take a quick selfie with her back to the window, taking in the spectacular view of Seoul and the Han River that her room afforded her. It was amazing, and even though the morning had robbed the city of its neon glow, there was a beautiful golden wash over the buildings from the sun that brought everything to life. Seoul was quite spectacular and Dana wondered if she would have much time to explore it after the concert, given the advertising schedule planned.

She sent a few text messages to her sister and family, and made sure her social media was updated with the selfie, before heading out of the room to get some breakfast. Though there were a few nice restaurants in the hotel, her attention had been caught by the pastry salon on the 79th floor, but unfortunately it didn't open until 11. As such she opted for Stay on the 81st floor.

To her surprise she was welcomed on arrival, and ushered inside as a special guest. Although this seemed puzzling, her phone had begun to buzz, and when Dana risked a glance, she saw that her sister had started sending her messages about the news reports on her arrival and meeting with the girls from G'Star. This, it seemed, was quite big news. There were also rumours about what she and Millie would be wearing, with some eerily accurate. Dana shook her head, but at least understood the sudden interest in her, and she pocketed her phone.

As she did, though, something – or more accurately someone – caught her eye. She swung around to get a better view, but what she had thought she saw was no longer there. There was no sign of the curly, black hair and the off-the-shelf suit she thought she had seen.

"Spectra-*ssi*?" the waiter that was attending her said, and Dana turned and bowed her head, muttering sorry. He guided her over to a small table with a bright yellow chair, at which she sat down and gratefully took the menu. For the first time she inhaled the various aromas that were wafting around the room, the smell of fresh fruit and coffee, blending with the hot, sweet pastry and egg. It was sumptuous, and she could feel her mouth-watering, so she quickly summoned her waiter back and ordered (her natural instinct had been to wait, but she had heard that in Korea it was not considered impolite to summon the waiter).

Dana finished her meal of fresh fruit, croissants and sweet Earl Grey tea, and after a brief conversation with the waiter about payment (which, he assured her, would be attached to her suite so was not something to be concerned about), she set off for the elevator once again. This time her destination would be much further up than her personal floor.

She had dressed in a set of V9 performance tights, along with an athletic singlet, both in black and both from Bodyscience. They had been sent complimentary to her at some point in the past week, and she felt she should probably try to get some pics of them on her social media. When Mee had told her what Lotte World Tower was noted for, she knew precisely the best pics to get.

Lotte World Tower stands at 123 floors, the top of the building peaking at almost 555 metres. It is one of the five tallest buildings in the world, and the hotel section occupies floors 76 to 101. Floors 42 to 71 are residences, while 14 to 38 is office space. 105 to 114 are more office space, but floors 117 to 123 are occupied by Seoul Sky, a set of observation decks which is nothing short of astonishing. And Seoul Sky gives access to the Skybridge – a relatively thin bridge open to tourists, linking the top two peaks of the building.

In truth, Dana had first made her way to the lobby to find out what was the best way to get to Seoul Sky as it was clearly not possible to simply jump on a lift at some point and get there. Most lifts started from the very bottom of the building so that the general public had as much access to the decks as anyone else. The clerk had politely (and profusely) apologised that unfortunately there was indeed no easy way to get to Seoul Sky from the hotel. What Dana hadn't noticed the night before on her hurried and flustered arrival was that the building has been designed to have different access points for different facilities. Nonetheless, the clerk did say that she was able to book Dana access to Seoul Sky and also the Skybridge, which she was more than happy to do.

On a whim Dana asked for two tickets to the Skybridge. She had vaguely hoped she might get someone to accompany her, but that now seemed unlikely.

It turned out that aside from having to take a 79-floor journey down to the lobby only to take a 117-floor journey back up again, things were relatively straightforward. The queues were surprisingly short, all things considered, and the journey up was much faster than the journey down, helped in no small part by the elevator being a series of screens which, as it went up, displayed a video which suggested the elevator was moving horizontally. It was a strangely unsettling experience, but those around her let out appreciative oohs and aahs, and Dana felt a little like the Grinch for not being more impressed.

However, as she stepped out of the elevator and was ushered forth, she saw what she thought she had seen earlier – the off-the-shelf suit and the black curly hair. There were a number of people standing around in dark blue uniforms, clearly security or at the very least guides, and Dana marked them all out before making her way from the alcove that housed the elevators out and across to the observation deck.

This deck stood out from the building and had a glass floor which allowed people to not only look out of the windows at the spectacular view of Seoul in the morning, but also the dizzying drop that was directly below them. Dana didn't have a particular fear of heights, but she had to admit that even she felt her stomach lurch when she looked down at the drop below her. She took a little gulp and looked up, noticing that a number of people were less-than-surreptitiously taking photos of her. She gave a little smile and a wave, and they bowed, which made her bow back. A person with short spiky white hair and eyes so dark they seemed black, took a quick photo, but there was no smile on the androgynous face. Dana gave another quick wave, feeling uncomfortably exposed.

This gave her, though, the opportunity to step away from the floor and head to the corridor that led to the other side of the building. On her left were windows allowing her to view the city still, but the right was a wood panelled wall. As she moved around there was a doorway into a disabled toilet and Dana quickly opened it and slipped inside. She kept the door ajar to peer out of. She had drawn enough attention to herself such that she hoped the person who was following her would take the bait.

Sure enough the suit walked passed the door. As the figure walked past, Dana pulled the door open and grabbed the man by the back of his jacket, yanking him into the toilet and closing the door with a foot, even as she shoved him up against the wall, twisting his right hand around and up his back.

Colonel Indigo Spectra had decided that since his daughter had recently had two run-ins with Interpol, it was for the best that she got a little self-defence training. This suited Dana perfectly, as she had decided on her return to Australia that she wanted to be a little more capable in a fight, rather than just attacking like a blunt force object. As such, Karim Narogin whimpered as his arm was pushed further up against his back.

"You're going to fucking break It, Spectra!" he whined.

"Why are you following me, Karim?" Dana hissed in his ear.

"I need to talk to you," the man replied. "Fuck's sake, seriously, Dana, let me go." Dana released him, and he turned to her. He was the same man she remembered, short and scruffy, with wild, black hair and deep brown eyes – a testament to his Indian and Indigenous ancestry.

"I don't work for ASIO," Dana said, and leant back against the sink that was on one side of the room. Karim looked around and then shrugged as he sat down on the toilet.

"You're now what we like to call an asset," he said, rubbing his right shoulder.

"Not for you lot," growled Dana. "Not for anyone."

"Spectra, it doesn't work that way," Karim sighed. "It is what it is. If you're an asset, you're an asset. You don't get to decide whether you are or not. You are now one. Which, yes, it seems we share with Interpol."

27

"You can't tell me what to do, and neither can they."

"Look, you can have your hissy fit later," Karim sighed. "Let's just get over it for the moment and talk about the reason I'm here."

"It will be to take photos for my Instagram," Dana said with a characteristic smirk.

"You do that a lot, you know, that smirk."

"It's my thing. People know me for it," replied Dana, rolling her eyes. "What do you *want*, Karim? ASIO's not even supposed to operate outside Australia, are they?"

"You know which label G'Star is signed to?" Karim asked, ignoring the question.

"Of course," Dana said, before realising that she actually had no idea. "Not one of the big ones," she added lamely.

"It's called Moonlight," Karim supplied. "It's not one of the top five, but it is up there. They've had a fair few acts do well recently. Also they are part of a big move to create supergroups in K-Pop. But not just from their own talent – talent across the companies."

"Ok, so?"

"They've also had five artists die in the last year," intoned Karim, like some grim reaper.

"That's," Dana paused, wondering what to say. "Unlucky."

"Very," agreed the analyst. "In fact, if one were being cynical… unreasonably unlucky."

"Oh my god, why would ASIO possibly be interested in the deaths of K-Pop idols?" Dana sighed, suddenly seeing her fantasy trip taking a turn for the worse.

"Well, obviously nothing," Karim replied pointedly. "Except…"

"Except?"

"Do you know much the K-Pop industry contributes to Korea's economy? It's billions, by the way. You don't have to answer."

"ASIO thinks that some musical groups not even signed up to one of the big five music companies is an attempt to destabilise the Korean economy?" Dana almost laughed with incredulity.

"Well, not all of those deaths were Moonlight talent. Two occurred when Moonlight created their supergroups, so some talent did come from *the big five*. But even then, ASIS wouldn't normally show an interest," he conceded.

"ASIS?" Dana said, incredulously.

"There have been rumours, initially from the CIA but then… others…that an idol may not be what he…or she seems to be." Karim suddenly seemed very awkward, as though he needed to tell someone that their pet cat had just died. Dana frowned slightly as her mind began to put together what she had been told.

"You think a K-Pop idol is a spy?" and the idea seemed almost as incredulous as her previous guess.

"Not every idol is from Korea," Karim reasoned. "Thailand, China, Japan," he began to list, but then paused. "North Korea."

And then suddenly it clicked into place.

"Oh my god, you think one of G'Star is a spy!" she blurted out, and Karim jumped up nervously, gesturing for her to keep her voice down.

"I didn't say that," he said, *sotto voce*. "I'm saying that ASIS think that," and he had the decency to look shamefaced about it.

"You're not seriously asking me to investigate them?" replied Dana, trying to keep the shock out of her voice.

"ASIS asked if they could use our asset," Karim began, and Dana found herself so furious she tugged at the door and stormed out of the toilet. Karim followed, blushing a deep red when a few of the other tourists looked over at him; an elderly Korean woman looking particularly disapproving.

29

Dana made her way back to the main observation deck and went straight over to the escalator that led to the next floor, Karim in tow desperately trying to catch up.

"Dana," he hissed, as she strode straight on from the escalator to the stairway that led up another floor.

"Excuse me," a blue suited Korean man stepped forward to Dana as she entered the SkyCafe on floor 122, "is that man bothering you Miss Spectra?" Dana turned back to Karim, a little satisfied to see him struggling up the stairs, and glowered, but turned back, her face full of joy.

"Oh no, that's just my chauffeur. We're going to the Skybridge. Is this the floor…?"

"Ah, no, you have to go up again," the attendant smiled warmly. "Would you care for a complimentary tour, Miss Spectra?" he asked politely, and Dana immediately smiled before accepting the offer. "If you would care to step this way, Miss Spectra, and, your friend," the attendant continued.

"Thanks," Dana grinned, and the attendant led them to the only elevator on the floor. Dana took a quick look and saw that it was indeed separate to the one that ran from the basement to the 118th floor. This one seemed to go up to the 123rd, where the exclusive 123 Lounge was located (Dana had glanced at the prices online and realised that it was probably not going to be an option for her).

"Wait a minute," Karim spluttered. "What do you think you're doing?"

"*We* are going on the Skybridge," Dana smiled sweetly.

"But, don't you have to book a month in advance or something? You can't go in the morning?"

"The joy of being a celebrity, it seems," replied Dana, and stepped forward into the elevator which had arrived. Their attendant followed, and Dana paused to look at Karim. "Come on," she ordered. With a grimace the analyst stepped forward.

They exited the elevator into a lobby which seemed to have a pine floor with a stylised sand pattern against the wall (though presumably it wasn't sand). Dana could see the 123 Lounge itself, and exclusive VIP restaurant that was currently closed. The attendant led them in the opposite direction and soon the pair found themselves in a less impressive room, with racks of red jumpsuits and black strapping hanging from the wall. Here there was a woman in her thirties, her eyes lined from smiling and her black hair pulled back into a pony tail. She was wearing one of the red jumpsuits.

"*Anyeong!*" she grinned at them. "My name is Dahyun," she bowed as she spoke to them, and both Dana and Karim returned the gesture, "and I'll be your guide for today on this very special trip. Lucky for you I was around," she added with a wink. "The jumpsuits are there if you want them, but you're not obliged to wear them. They provide a bit of protection from the wind, but you'll probably not feel the cold," she added almost laughing. "The good thing about them is that you can attach your phone so if you drop it, it won't fall 541 meters!"

"Can we leave our phones somewhere safe?" Dana asked.

"Of course," Dahyun replied. "I can take them and lock them up safely."

"Oh good, then you can use my phone to take pictures of me," Dana said to Karim, raising her eyebrows.

"Wait, I'm not going up there!"

"You absolutely are," replied Dana. "If you want me to give slightly more than no thought to what you were talking about earlier." She put her hands on her hips, watched by the bemused Hyun. Growling, Karim stormed over to the jumpsuits to find one that fit him. "I'll just wear this," Dana said.

"No problem," Dahyun replied, but it felt forced and Dana sensed she disapproved of the decision. "You'll still need to wear the harness though, that is an absolute must."

"Oh yeah, of course," agreed Dana, and she took the harness that Hyun handed across to her, stepping into it and bringing it up over her shoulders. Hyun got behind her and made some final adjustments, tightening it so that it closed around Dana's body. Karim got the same treatment, looking miserable in a jumpsuit that managed to look like it was oversized.

31

"Right," Dahyun said, "we're going to go up some stairs, and it's a bit of a journey. It's also a bit dark, so your eyes will take a moment to adjust when we get to the Skybridge. There are, however, a few more small points of safety I need to go through with you."

IV

It was about twenty minutes later when Dahyun pushed open the door that led to the platform that the Skybridge stretched away from, making its way to the opposite structure. Dana was mildly regretting not wearing the jumpsuit, as the wind whistled and blew her hair around, biting into her bare arms. Beside her Karim was almost pale.

"I can't believe you're making me do this," he whispered.

"Yeah, well, if you want something from me, you'd better be prepared to earn it," Dana growled back. "You need to take pictures of me as I'm crossing the bridge. Make sure I look great. Get the clothes, and try and get the background."

Dahyun was busy clipping the harness to the safety rope, and both Dana and Karim felt the strong tug as the guide tested to make sure that they were safely attached. With that, Dahyun turned to them.

"We're going to cross the bridge now," she said, the grin still on her face. "Make sure you place your feet carefully so that you don't step on nothing," she added. "I would say you shouldn't look down, but that sort of misses the point!" With that, the Korean woman strode confidently onto the bridge and began to cross. Dana gave Karim a side glance and a wink, and then walked over to the bridge. For the first time she could see how thin the bridge seemed to be, and how flimsy it was. Made of metal, it still looked like the sort of wooden bridge that connected trees in forests; not much wider than two meters and the bridge itself was made of metal slats. When Dana looked at her feet, she noticed that some of the slats were spaced further apart at the beginning of the bridge, meaning she would have to treat them like stepping stones. Cautiously she placed her foot on the first panel and then stepped onto the next one.

The height was dizzying and Dana lost all sense of the cold as her body activated its panic responses. She could feel herself starting to sweat. Strangely, she had made her way across a bridge quite high up a few months back in Switzerland, but at 541 meters above ground, Dana's imagination played overtime as she realised were she to slip through the slats and fall down the tower, she would be nothing more than a rag doll.

"Come on, there's nothing to worry about," Dahyun said and waved at her. Dana took a little gulp and took another cautious step across the next gap, her hands gripping the railing so hard her knuckles were white. She risked a glance behind and was a little surprised to see that Karim was indeed taking pictures, and with her image at risk she straightened her back and took a few more steps until she met up with Dahyun in the middle of the bridge.

By now Karim had put the phone away and grabbed the railings to walk across and join Dana and Dahyun. Dana was impressed at how the little man was coping, though she noticed that he still looked very pale as he reached them.

"What I want you to do now," Dahyun said to them, "is a couple of star jumps! *Hana dul set!*" With that she did a star jump, demonstrating what she wanted. "*Hana dul set!*" she called again, and this time Dana joined in, though she suspected her feet never left the ground. From the grin on Dahyun's face she knew she was right.

"*Hana dul set!*" and the three all jumped. Dana turned to Karim to congratulate him on what he had done, but several things happened at once which were a little bit distracting. The first was a strong gust of wind which pushed them to the side of the bridge, and all three grabbed the rail to support themselves, but Karim dropped the phone in the process which fell, though thanks to the jumpsuit, merely ended up around his knees. At the same time, Dana saw someone close the door on the platform they had come from.

Someone else had been on the platform?

"Is there anyone else up here?" Dana turned to Dahyun.

"No, just you. Special treatment for a star," Dahyun grinned. "Moonlight has a lot of pull. Why don't you sit down on the bridge and dangle your legs over the side?"

"You're not serious?" gulped Karim.

"Everyone does it," came the effusive reply. Dana couldn't help but smile, and she lowered herself carefully.

"I suppose you want photos," grumbled Karim, and he reached for the phone, but as he did, Dana realised that the bridge was more slippery than she had initially thought. Her left foot gave way and she felt Dahyun's hand under her arm.

"Careful," the guide said.

"Right," Dana replied, both hands gripping the rail. She frowned as a strange smell reached her nose, but as she lowered herself again her feet gave way one more time. There was something on the bridge that stopped Dana getting a grip, and she felt her feet slip out from under her and through the gap.

Her bum hit the bridge, her legs straight out in front of her, but she could feel the momentum moving her forward, and whatever it was that had made her feet slip also made her backside slip as well, and she could feel her whole body sliding forward. Desperately she grabbed at the metal rope but her body pulled her down and her hands stung as the rope pushed into them, forcing her to release her grip automatically.

Both Karim and Dahyun were shouting, but Dana couldn't understand them as the wind whipped up around her. Her body continued to fall, and she looked up, grateful for the safety rope, and realised that there had indeed been someone at that exit. The other end of her rope flew untethered along the bridge. Karim must have understood what was happening as he reached out to grab the rope, but only one hand was successful, so he was yanked forward, dragged to the gap that Dana had slid through.

Dahyun's experience kicked in quickly and she too grabbed at the rope, but it sheared through her hands. Dana's stomach lurched as she continued to fall, unable to do anything except watch her potential saviours. She saw Karim slide under the gap, but to her surprise he twisted his body around so when he slid off the bridge, he managed to fall on the other side of the bridge rail, resulting in him becoming a counter balance for Dana, whose fall jerked to a stop. To his credit, Karim had grabbed his side of the rope with both hands and was clinging onto it for her dear life.

34

Much lower than the little spy, Dana paused for a moment, not daring to make a movement in case the rope was somehow cut through by the metal siding. Cautiously she grabbed at it and tested to see if she could pull herself up a little. Karim refused to release his grip on the rope, and Hyun had reached down to start pulling Dana up to safety.

It took a surprisingly short time before Dana could grab hold of Dahyun's hands and between them Dana was hauled back onto the bridge. As soon as she had her knees on the bridge, Dana started pulling the other side of the rope, dragging Karim up, and with Dahyun's help the trio were back on the bridge again.

"We have to get you off," Dahyun said, grabbing hold of Dana's arm, and Karim did the same. Together they returned to the safety platform. Dahyun kept glancing around, and Dana wondered if the tour had been filmed. If it was, that was something she was definitely interested in looking at when she had a free moment.

V

Dana Spectra and Karim Narogin were seated in the 123 Lounge at 11.58 am, both sitting drinking water, though more elaborate and certainly more alcoholic drinks sat in front of them. Through the speakers the moody sounds of (G)I-dle were being piped, and the view from the window in front of them was undeniably spectacular.

However, if you had seen that view hanging from an untethered safety rope, the appeal tended to evaporate. The news was already reporting the incident, a news helicopter having captured some of the action and Christa Adams, along with Mainard Descoteaux had called to ensure that everything was alright. Police were talking with Dahyun, but Karim had managed to make them disappear allowing Dana to get a moment's rest, which she was genuinely appreciative of.

"I don't want to say I told you so," Karim began, finally breaking the silence between them.

"You shouldn't, because it doesn't make any sense," retorted Dana.

"You can't say that was an accident," protested Karim.

"I'm not saying someone didn't try something, but how could they possibly know I was the target?"

"Wasn't it Moonlight representatives that set up the bridge walk? Maybe even a member of G'Star in particular?" Karim put his drink on the table and sat back, his arms crossed with a satisfied argument-winning look on his face.

"It's such a leap, Karim," Dana whined, petulantly. "Surely the Korean secret service…" She paused for a moment. "Wait, does South Korea have a secret service?"

"Err, I think it's pronounced *Daehanminguk Gukgahangbohwon Gukseongwon*," Karim replied. "It's the National Intelligence Service. When it was set up it was the Korean Central Intelligence Agency, of all things. It's one of those organisations that have had their powers restricted a fair bit since democracy was achieved. And, Eastern intelligence services tend to be very protective of their information when it comes to the West," Karim shrugged.

"Out of curiousity, how open is ASIS to the NIS?" Dana asked, sitting forward. Karim opened his mouth to argue, and then shut it again, clearly unwilling to outright lie.

"Yes, alright, they don't exactly play fair either," he grudgingly admitted. "The thing is, maybe the Koreans have looked into this K-Pop star, maybe they haven't, but you have to admit there's something very odd about the deaths."

"I still don't understand why it bothers ASIS so much. Or the CIA for that matter," Dana added. "Why not just get Interpol to work out a communication channel between you guys?"

"I never thought I'd hear you advocating for Interpol," Karim grumbled.

"Look, outside of its crappy operatives, I'm sure the whole idea of it is great," Dana said. Her water had finally run dry and so she grabbed the red drink in front of her. "What is this again?"

"Negroni," Karim said. "Should give you back some of your

energy."

Dana took a sip and pulled a face. "I hate gin," she said. "Just for future reference."

"Of course you do." Karim leaned forward. "Look, can you just keep an eye out or something. Do that thing you do to get into people's," he paused for a moment as Dana shot him a look that could have comfortably melted the glass window behind him. "Heads," he finished, and the relief was almost tangible. "It would be better for us to know if there's a North Korean spy, especially if the Koreans already know and just can't be bothered telling us."

"I don't even know how I'd do it," mumbled Dana, taking another sip and wincing. She looked around and noticed that the room was starting to fill up. There were a number of flashes from photographers and Dana wondered if the press had found her, but she realised that she wasn't the target as she overheard someone saying *Boom*. Bella's lessons had included the name Boom – a K-POP idol of some repute and definitely more interesting than her. She had a little under two hours before her preparation began, and she had to admit she was feeling shattered. She closed her eyes and for a moment didn't want to open them again. The thought of drifting to sleep and not waking up was more enticing than anything else that was on offer at that moment. She let out a deep sigh, not sure if it was at the fact she couldn't sleep or Karim's request.

"Fine," she said, placing the glass back on the table. "I'll see what I can do. But for the record, I think you're wrong about this."

"Cool, prove me wrong," Karim replied, slumping down in his chair. "Oh, here's your phone," he added, realising it was in his jacket pocket. Dana took it and absently flipped through the photos. The ones of her posing on the bridge were quite impressive, she thought. The background was astonishing and the wind made her hair blow like she was a superhero descending from the skies. Plus her ass looked amazing in the leggings. That was definitely going up on the social media sites.

The next along, was a video of her walking across the bridge and doing star jumps. Well, sort of doing them. Her fear must have got the better of her, as she wasn't quite the monument to confident athleticism that she thought she had been, her arms never straying too far from the sides of the bridge.

Then there was another video. It was difficult to make out in many ways, as it started with Dana lowering herself to slide her legs off the bridge, but her fall was captured in all its glory before the picture went crazy, presumably as Karim let go of the phone. The entire incident was captured, though not particularly well; the camera flipping around taking in Dana dangling on the end of her rope, and Karim scrabbling to grab the other end. She pulled the video back a bit and looked again at her feet sliding. There was definitely something there, some sort of clear liquid. Not water…it was thicker than that.

"Did you smell something when we up there?" Dana asked of Karim. "Like," she paused trying to remember the smell.

"Fish?" Karim said.

"Yeah but…fish oil," Dana mused.

"You think someone put fish oil on the bridge?"

"No, but what sort of clear liquid smells like fish oil," wondered Dana.

"No fucking idea," replied Karim, and he grabbed his Negroni, swigging it back quickly. Dana shut down her phone and sat back in her chair. Across from her, the sun continued to rise above Seoul.

Someone really had tried to kill her.

VI

Having announced his need to leave, Karim Narogin took Dana's phone and plugged something into the port which immediately caused it to seemingly die. The little square device he had, however, immediately come to life and displayed a vast array of swift moving icons and moving bars. He turned the little device towards her and she saw her own face reflected, with the word *scanning* below it, and then asked her to press her little finger to the device. He then asked if she used her thumb or forefinger to activate her phone (she drily replied she used her face) and he nodded, asking her to touch her forefinger to the device, which was also duly scanned.

He handed the phone back to her with a small grin.

"Probably should have checked if you had the memory capacity for that, but fortunately you did. I figured you'd be a "only the best phone" kinda girl."

"What did you do to my phone?" Dana asked, glowering a little.

"There's a second phone beneath the first," Karim replied. "When you do your normal thing, you'll see that there's a small red dot in the top corner?" Dana frowned as she failed to see it, but then her eyebrows raised in surprise as the small little dot became evident. "Touch it with your little finger," Karim suggested, and Dana did as she was instructed. Her phone went blank, and then suddenly rebooted with a totally different set of apps. "Lots of little handy things there," Karim explained, "but the most important is that it's effectively a burner phone. If you used it to phone, it would read as a totally different number, and also sends the signal to at least two different towers, which means it can't be readily traced. Put in any numbers that you would only dial as an asset." Dana glowered again at the word, but didn't take the bait. "That way we can get you, you can get us, etc, etc."

"How do you get me if I've got my other phone on?" Dana asked.

"Oh, you'll feel a little vibration and the red light will blink. If you can't answer, we get voicemail. The other thing, if you press the red button with your forefinger...STOP!" Karim grabbed her hand as she was about to do it. "It will delete the background phone completely," Karim added.

"What, so it's easier to delete the phone than it is to use it?" said Dana patronisingly.

"Yes," replied Karim, his patience slightly gone. "So if someone forces you to, you can easily get rid of it in a simple move."

"Oh," Dana replied. "I suppose that makes sense."

"Another gift, courtesy of ASIO," Karim said acidly.

"Given they want me to spy on some girl they think might be a North Korean agent, it's the least they can do." Dana's reply was equally frosty.

"Well, true," conceded Karim.

"So why are you my handler?" Dana suddenly snapped indignantly.

"It turns out that no one was really lining up for the job," came the biting reply. "I was stuck with the job of dealing with you. I did point out I was an ASIO analyst not an ASIS spy, but apparently that wasn't enough to give me an excuse to avoid it."

"Thanks," Dana said, pulling a face. Karim raised an eyebrow.

"Good luck," he added, as he got up and left the restaurant.

Without paying.

Bastard.

Fortunately, when Dana left, she was told that the drinks were entirely complimentary after the incident. They were, naturally, she supposed, rather desperate for her not to sue them.

When she returned to her room, she realised that it was almost closing in on two, and for the first time that day she felt a slight weariness. After everything that had happened, she was ready for a rest, and yet the real action was only just beginning.

She turned on the TV to a shot of her dangling from the Skybridge, and wondered who had taken it, but it was unimportant. The article was clearly about her, and her picture featured prominently, alongside G'Star, which was probably not the publicity that anyone was hoping for.

For a moment she wondered what she should do, thinking to contact either her sister or Adams, but then she made the decision, and posted a set of photos to her social media accounts. For her story, she posted a small segment of the video of her sliding, captioning it: wasn't planning on hanging around, but sometimes you don't get to choose!

The moment she hit post, her account reacted, and there were so many messages that it was going to be impossible to read them all. She looked at the notification count increase, and then sent a text to Bella asking her to log in and do some responding. Bella replied quickly, asking if she

40

was OK, but there was a knock at the door and Dana had little time to send anything other than a thumbs up.

When she opened the door, it was to a group of people, all of whom swept in and began setting up around the room. The dedicated Ms François led the pack, directing people to various positions and clearly indicating the correct order. Dana was sent to have a shower, and exited wearing nothing more than her white lace underwear, but no one in the room batted an eyelid, except for one gentleman who put a dressing gown over her shoulders before taking pictures with the phone he had brought.

For the next few hours, Dana was carefully brought to life. Sasha set to work on her face, while her hair was carefully coiffured into something that was absolutely astonishing. Dana had to admit that with the added extensions, her hair had been curled and styled such that it sat, almost in a seventies style, like a golden mane around her face. It was absolutely beautiful and something she would never have considered for herself, yet it looked amazing.

Her makeup, meanwhile, was just as incredible. With her clothing decision being a set of impressively ripped Roberto Cavalli jeans and a Calvin Klein lounge bodysuit, it was Ms François' choice of a blossom yellow cropped snow mantra parker by Angel Chen that added the colour and determined Sasha's make up direction. Dana's face was brought to life in shades of yellow, with her eyeshadow being a vibrant yellow carefully blended into a burnt orange, while her lipstick and blush was a bronze.

After four hours of work, during which Dana sneakily took photos and posted the various stages – as well as getting the all-important selfie with Sasha, who she was delighted to find she got along with particularly well – Dana was ready to go, and she had to admit she looked incredible. The outfit was chic, and modern and she looked, essentially, *cool*. Not some sort of fashion horse, nor something she'd got from her own wardrobe, but an image that her followers would love. Sexy and stylish. Dana's personal contribution was her Tresor Midnight Rose perfume. She had overruled the other choices and insisted on it, much to Ms François' disappointment.

However, it was the jewellery that the representatives of Digné were most keen to show off. There were five pieces in total, starting with an astonishing set of ear rings that contained a brilliant diamond in each.

On her right ear was a cuff as well, which had been designed to look like a star falling towards the diamond earrings. The star was also a light catching diamond, with more diamonds in the stylised tail of the star. Around her neck was a necklace that looked like it was a set of golden rings attached together in a vaguely Greecian style. This was a slightly more colourful design as the front three rings were a ruby, a sapphire and an emerald with little diamonds surrounding them.

Ms François explained that the entire set was *universal* and the necklace represented a solar system with different planets orbited by their diamond moons. The exact same design, though slightly smaller, was matched on her wrist by the bracelet.

There was another bracelet, a much simpler golden chain, and a similar chain was around her waist. The final additions were the rings on her fingers. On her left she had a complex set of rings that included a full finger ring on the fourth finger, a larger ring on the middle finger that had a matching counterpart just under her nail, and a smaller ring on the forefinger, all of which were connected to the simple golden bracelet, and another piece that rested on the back of her hand. The diamonds glittered off this, and Dana had a flash of nerves as she realised how much money was on her right hand. On her left, she was given two much simpler rings and she again had to ask Ms François what they represented.

"That's a promise ring, to Digné," Ms François said, a slight smile cracking her serious demeanour for the first time. "It's a little tacky, sorry, but we thought it might be fun if you could flash it a bit." For the first time, Dana noticed the distinctive "D" logo of Digné on the ring and she grinned back.

"That works for me," she smiled. "What about the other one?" On the same ring finger of her right hand was another ring that seemed to be made of two parts with a gap between them and a complex design above it in which sat a diamond.

"That's a…" Ms François paused for a moment as she tried to choose her words. "A friendship ring," she decided upon. "It has a sister – Millie will be wearing it. It would be great if at some point you could get a picture of the two rings together. The design is complete then."

"A friendship ring?" Dana said, raising her eyebrow and giving a smirk.

42

"Of course. All friends with Digné," Ms François said lamely, but Dana just laughed.

"Excuse me, Miss Spectra, we have to leave," said a tall Korean man in a dark suit. "We have to get you to the concert," he explained.

"Oh yeah, of course. Oh gosh, we have to hurry," Dana said, seeing the time.

"It's fine," Ms François said. "We're running to schedule. But we leave now."

"Right," Dana agreed. To her surprise she saw the Korean man hold out his arm and Dana looked confused for a moment, wondering if she should link arms, but Ms François rescued her by taking her right hand and placing it on the man's arm.

"Dam Hoon will look after you," Ms François assured her. And Dam led her to the exit.

VII

Dana Spectra discovered why no one was particularly concerned about the trip to G'Star's concert. Their performance was in the Olympic Hall, a concert hall in Olympic Park which was a quick drive. In fact it took about ten minutes to get to Bangi-dong, one of the neighbourhoods in Songpa-gu, the largest district in Seoul, and also home to Sincheon-dong, the neighbourhood in which Lotte World Tower stood. As such, Dam Hoon, a man who Dana had come to think of as a human brick, had essentially become her minder and drove her to their destination quickly and without a lot of conversation. Dana was able to discover that the man was 42, and the father of two small children. He also admitted that his step-daughter, a girl in her mid-teens, was actually a huge fan of Dana. At this, when the traffic flow came to a halt, Dana had taken his phone and snapped a selfie of the pair to send to Dam's daughter.

Olympic Park had been built in 1988 for the Seoul Summer Olympics, in the largest and most populous district of the city. There are two subway stations that give good access, though the most impressive entry point is the World Peace Gate, designed by Kim Chung-up and built in the two years leading up to the opening of the Park. The gate consists of four pillars supporting two wings which have a stunning mural entitled *The Painting of Four Spirits*. An eternal flame sits at the centre of the pillars, calling for peace and harmony to the world. Sadly, Dana only saw this as Dam drove past on Wiryseong-daero. Given the four lanes on the highway going in the opposite direction, she was barely able to see the entrance, let alone the flame.

Having turned left into Yangjae-daero, traffic started to become a little more obstinate, and Dam was patient with the drivers around him, though Dana watched as those around them changed lanes without indicating (though, rather strangely, they would sometimes indicate an apology). Dam himself seemed to have no problem switching lanes on the journey without giving a proper indication and the speed limit seemed to be very much a guide. Actually entering the park though East Gate 2 left Dana slightly breathless, as Dam seemed to override the traffic rules in order to do so, and got a couple of severe honks from those around him. Nonetheless, no one seemed seriously put out and certainly the police didn't seem particularly interested in interfering.

Once inside, Dam made another left turn, and then another, driving the car past a large open-air venue that Dam informed Dana was for tennis. Moments later, he was pulling the car to the side, where people were milling around and several white merchandising stores had been erected. When Dam came around and opened the door for her, Dana stepped out into a series of bright flashes.

They were directly in front of the hall itself, a massive white building with a sloping roof, and over the glass entry way was a giant banner heralding G'Star – the four faces of the members painted in gold and staring out like goddesses watching over their subjects. Security guards had come forward to clear a path for Dana, and those standing around took out their phones to snap their own pictures. Dana made sure to raise her left hand to her neck, making the Digné pieces obvious in all the photos and she paused to smile and wave. To her surprise, people were thrusting pictures towards her with sharpies, and Dana realised they wanted her autograph.

Not for the first time in her life, Dana was struck with imposter syndrome, knowing full well she was simply copying those she had seen on tv and in paparazzi photos. As she made her way through the crowd toward the entrance, pausing to sign and take selfies, she kept her hand on Dam's arm as she had done the previous night with the other minder. She felt her stomach lurch slightly as the nerves struck her. This was unlike anything she had ever been through before in her life. Being photographed was simple, even signing autographs at little events was fairly straightforward. But this...this was something completely different. She had no idea if they were interested in her, rescuing a cat, falling from a tower, suddenly friends with an up-and-coming pop sensation, or simply because she was wearing hundreds of thousands of dollars' worth of jewellery. Whatever it was, the press was keen, and that made the bystanders equally as keen.

Once inside, Dana was ushered through the lobby, with Dam handing paper over to the security guards, who then passed it on to a person who was clearly some sort of usher, and from there, they were led straight into the hall.

Olympic Hall itself is an ovular shape, with one end housing the stage, and the rest of the room holding seating. There seemed to be three sets of seating – an "upper" section that ran around the room, a "lower" section that sat in front of it, and a "middle" section erected on the blue portion of the floor. The building wasn't as big as some places she had seen, and Dana was briefly taken back to Théâtre d'Apollo where the Miss Green Earth pageant had been held. It seemed to be about the same size, but not the same shape.

Dam Hoon led Dana down the aisle on the blue section, taking her towards the stage where, in the front row, were two empty seats. She was obviously a little way back from the stage, but to be that close to any stage was utterly incredible. As she sat down, the man beside her turned and gave a small bow of his head, which Dana mirrored, and this seemed to domino down the line a little. Dam leant forward and whispered: "More of our - of Digné's staff." Dana nodded, suddenly understanding that this section must have been bought by Digné even before she had been unexpectedly added to the roster. Millie's appearance was all important, and was going to bring Digné a lot of new business.

A slight tap on her shoulder caused Dana to turn, and behind her was a man in his late twenties, with dyed blue hair fashionably sculptured into a flowing mane, and dark brown eyes. His appearance sparked a memory and Dana realised this was the man who had drawn the attention at Lotte Tower earlier that day.

"Dana?" he asked in perfect English. "Dana Spectra?"

"Yes?" she nodded.

"I'm Boom," he said with a smile.

"Oh, of course, yes," Dana nodded, full of understanding thanks to Bella's K-Pop briefing.

"I'm a huge fan. Did you get my flowers?" Boom gushed, and Dana felt her cheeks go warm. "You're a fascinating person. And so beautiful. You and Millie are great choices," he continued and for a moment Dana wondered what he meant.

"Oh thanks," she replied, and brought her hand up to display the jewellery, though even to her it seemed an odd thing to do.

"I hope we can talk later?"

"That would be amazing," Dana replied, but the conversation was cut off as the lights dimmed. Dana smiled apologetically and turned back, noticing Dan was scowling. She briefly wondered why but then the stage seemed to sparkle and lights in different shades of yellow and orange flicked over it, while on giant screens at the back of the stage, the glitter seemed to be forming into faces – the four faces of G'Star.

Around her, the strains of the music started to float and strange, discordant harmonies reached across the rooms, silencing everyone. As the lights dimmed, four explosions seemed to take place on stage, and when they cleared, the four members of G'Star stood. To the left was Amy, dressed in a golden coat with black shorts and a black crop top, her hair a golden bob. Beside her, Mee, with her long blonde hair, was dressed in tight little gold dress with long black boots. Then was Millie, her short black hair now spiky and golden tipped, was in golden hot pants and a short, midriff coat with long tails. Finally, on the far end, her long, dark hair blowing in the wind of some fan that must have been off-stage, was Soojin. Her soft features were framed by a golden tiara, while a long, flowing gold top swirled around her, looking a little like a mini-dress.

When the music started up again, Amy's rap belted out and *Epic* began.

Throughout the performance Dana took some footage with her phone and snapped photos, sending them back to Bella, gushing over the show. G'Star's music flowed through her, sending her mind to a variety of places, thanks to Mee's light girly voice, Soojin's husky tones, Amy's growling rap and Millie's whispering vocals in both rap and melody. They were a unique ensemble, and their music was enthralling. At one point Dam passed her a box in which was a black stick with a clear top that lit up gold when she pressed the button on the side. All around her in the Hall, fans were carrying similar light sticks and in the dark the dots of white and gold created a glittery effect that complimented the lighting on stage.

As ridiculous as it seemed, between the magnetic sounds and mesmerising lights, Dana felt like she was falling in love with the group. All thoughts of what had happened earlier in the day were completely gone. She was genuinely Glitter.

VIII

Immediately after the encore and people started to flood out of the Hall, Dam Hoon proffered his arm and Dana took it, but not before bowing to the other Digné staff that were to her left. Boom had already disappeared, to Dana's surprise. Guided by Dam Hoon to one of the side doors near the stage, the security guards there opened the door to give them access to backstage. They were taken down the side corridors where backstage crew hustled back and forth on their way to check equipment and ensure that everything was shut down. The staff of the Olympic Hall had their fill for the night and were keen to get out and go home. Very few people paid any attention to Dana as she was escorted by Dam down the corridors.

When they came to the green room, Dana was not entirely surprised to see that Ms François was already there, looking a little edgy. She said something in French which Dana didn't quite catch, but as she glanced at her watch, Dana suspected that they were waiting for the rest of G'Star to make an appearance – or perhaps more accurately, just Millie.

As Soojin stepped out of the doorway that led to the dressing room, Ms François leapt into action and grabbed Dana by the elbow to lead her to an opposite door. Dana looked a little puzzled, but was curiously reassured to see Dam Hoon right behind her, and as she was led out of the door she found herself in the outside world, though clearly Digné had prepared this for *the* moment.

Photographers were already there and Ms François gave Dana a little nod – go do your thing, girl. With her left hand back against her throat, Dana stepped forward to allow herself to be photographed. Out of the corner of her eye she saw a girl in a short black dress carrying a tray of drinks, and Dana wondered if it would be inappropriate to grab one as quickly as possible.

This inclination was certainly not swayed by the bombardment of questions that were being fired at her, which ranged from the simple ("Did you enjoy the concert?") to the obvious ("Do you feel becoming an ambassador for Digné is a highlight of your career?") to the awkward ("Is it too soon for you to be out after someone tried to murder you this morning?") Most of the questions were in English, but Dam whispered to her when they came in Korean and even Ms François supplied a translation when someone snapped out something in French.

Dana looked around to see if she could see Boom, but he was nowhere in sight. However, Dana thought she saw someone familiar in the crowd – an androgynous face with short, white blonde hair.

"Hi there. Mason Lemon, nice to meet you." Dana turned to see who was talking to her, but when she looked back, white-blonde had disappeared. Puzzled, Dana turned back to talk to the American who had introduced himself.

The conversations with journalists seemed to take an eternity, but in fact later Dana realised that Ms François' planning was impressively well timed as Soojin's appearance in the green room obviously heralded the arrival of the rest of G'Star, and sure enough the group stepped out of the exit, stealing away some of Dana's publicity.

Millie had walked up to Dana, and for the first time Dana realised that the girl was about the same height as she was. Both in heels now, Millie was wearing stockings with a Cettire sleeveless tartan dress in white. Millie's silver jewellery gave the impression that she was the moon and Dana was the sun, which caused Dana to genuinely smile at the skill of Mainard Descoteaux and his launch. Millie slid her arm around Dana's waist and the model reciprocated causing a swell of flashes. Millie's usually serious face had become more playful, almost flirty. Dana suddenly remembered that

Bella had described G'Star as one of the Girl Crush K-Pop bands – groups that embraced the power of being women and were aspirational. Dana slid her hand into Millie's, who gripped it, and the two stood in what Dana hoped would make them look a little like superheroes. This had the desired effect of generating more photos and questions were again shouted at the two girls.

At some point the rest of G'Star joined the two, and Dana realised she had lost all track of time, not sure how long she had been answering questions or posing for, but for the first time she was actually enjoying the entire process. Amy and Soojin introduced themselves, the former having as much energy as Mee, bouncing over and bowing before Dana embraced her, and Soojin bowed far more officially before offering her hand and smiling. Mee whispered in her ear that Soojin didn't have particularly good English and as such was more reserved about conversing with Dana, who had no Korean at all.

Nonetheless at some point the woman in the dark suit from the night before, with the iPad wielding assistant, again stepped forward to start issuing instructions to her staff and to inform Ms François of what G'Star was about to do. The French woman didn't seem remotely concerned, and when she flashed a smile for the first time at Dana, Dana realised that the evening had played out the way she had planned. The media attention was exactly what Digné wanted and at that point everything was satisfactory.

The woman in the dark suit signalled to the G'Star's staff, and they started to move the girls off towards a waiting car. Soojin suddenly said something and spoke quickly to the other members of G'Star. Millie stepped away from the group, heading over to Dana and took her hand.

"Do you want to come back to our place and celebrate tonight?" she asked, her face having resumed its neutral expression.

"Oh, you guys probably want to do stuff…" Dana said, but Millie shook her head.

"We want you to come. Even Soojin. She wants to get to know you. We have tomorrow off, and we can't go out because of the rules."

"The rules?"

"Our company has strict rules, remember. No nightclubs. But we can celebrate. You should come with us." Dana paused, feeling the other girl's hand in hers, and suddenly she was back in the concert, the music and the movements filling her head.

"Of course," she whispered. Millie took her hand and drew her back into G'Star's world.

IX

The journey from Olympic Hall took place via the spacious Genesis GV80 that G'Star had travelled to. Dana had no idea where they were going, or really even how long the journey was – all she noticed was that they crossed the river Han twice. In truth the atmosphere inside the car was far more exciting, as all four members of G'Star were still hyped about their performance, and with the omnipresent cameras no longer on them, they were allowed to cut loose, turning the music in the car up (not their own, but rather other groups like (G)I-dle, Blackpink and Itzy), singing along and laughing at their own jokes. Even the typically dour Millie was far more relaxed. At one point Amy had turned to one of their managers and asked if they could stop off for alcohol, but he gave her a severe look, and she stuck her tongue at him, before bursting into laughter and falling back onto the chair, almost in Mee's lap.

Dana noticed that away from the cameras, the four girls relationships were subtly different. Their friendship was obvious and shone through to the world of the stage, but behind closed doors there was a chemistry between Mee and Amy that suggested something far more intimate, as they barely let each other go. Dana wondered if she was reading too much into it, but Soojin and Millie seemed indulgent, which suggested there was something to indulge. She guessed that the managers were aware but chose to do nothing about it. As long as it didn't go public, Dana suspected that Moonlight would be happy. Though striving for more equality for the LGBTQ community, South Korea still wasn't at a point where they would be happy for their idols to reveal anything scandalous.

The car slowed, and Dana leaned forward to get a better look at their destination – three massive towers linked by a walkway around the middle of the smallest tower. The car jerked and Dana fell forward into

Millie's arms who giggled and both Amy and Mee pulled her back, though Millie grabbed at Dana's arms and pulled her forward, causing another eruption of laughter at the human tug-of-war.

Dana finally slumped back between the two younger girls, breaking them apart.

"Where are we?" she asked.

"Raemian Caelitus," Soojin answered, surprising Dana a little. Soojin had barely spoken much to Dana, and though she seemed distant, Dana guessed it might be because the older girl didn't have a strong grasp on English. "We live there," she grinned.

"It's very private," Amy said into her ear.

The driver had come off Gangbyeonbuk-ro and driven around Ichon-ro, before turning down the street that gave access to Raemian Caelitus and its carpark, which the Genesis easily turned into without stopping, the boom gate opening, presumably in response to a signal from something in the car.

Once the car had been parked, the women all piled out of the car and G'Star headed straight to a set of elevators, dragging Dana behind them. The smell of concrete and diesel brought Dana back to Earth, as all the excitement of earlier, with the myriad of scents from the smells of Olympic Park, the fragrances that everyone had been wearing and the aroma of the food that was being offered, was swept away by the mundanity of everyday living. It may have been for a very expensive apartment block, but a carpark was a carpark regardless of who you were with.

The elevator doors opened and the girls entered, with their managers and Dam Hoon keeping up behind them.

"They aren't coming with, are they?" Dana giggled a little, and all four popstars laughed with her.

"No, just to see us into our rooms so we aren't disturbed and then they'll go home and leave us be," Mee grinned. "They're very protective. It's so nice."

"But so unnecessary here," Millie pointed out.

The men remained solemn-faced, and Dana realised that she hadn't even taken time out to see who they were. They had just become faceless bodyguards. She felt slightly ashamed of herself for being that way, and she touched Dam on the arm and said thank you. He smiled at her, though his fellows remained unmoved.

G'Star's apartment was in tower two on the 31st floor, and was comfortably one of the most luxurious apartments Dana had ever seen. Large and spacious, the most noticeable thing about it was the floor-to-ceiling windows that looked over the Han River, though from the other side of where Dana would have been viewing at the Signiel. The floors were all wood panelled, with elegant lighting set into recesses in the ceiling. The kitchen was a little more cramped that Dana would have expected, but with the open plan of the majority of the apartment, it still seemed large. Soojin had immediately turned on the big black television that hung from the wall and slumped down onto a couch opposite that was large and pink and not only looked a little like a mouth, but threatened to swallow the K-Pop star up. Millie had gone to the fridge and opened it to reveal that alcohol had not been necessary. With music now pumping out of the television, Millie supplied the other option, pressing a beer bottle into her hand which had a distinctive blue and white label. Millie tossed one over to Soojin who caught it with practiced ease and flipped off the top to start drinking. Millie glanced around the room, and Dana followed her eyes to see that Amy and Mee were too busy giggling and holding hands.

"Hey! Beer, you two!" Millie called out, and the two turned and let loose another burst of giggles, before coming over. "Take your coat off and get comfortable," Millie continued, talking to Dana. Dana nodded and shrugged off the Angel Chen jacket. She looked around and Millie pointed to the dining table, where Dana deposited the jacket and also took the phone out of her bum pocket and slid it into the yellow material. The jacket caught on her hand as she took it off, and so she also popped her bag on the table and took off the ear rings, rings, necklace, bracelet and hand piece from Digné, and slid them into the bag.

"Good idea," enthused Millie, removing her pieces and dumping them into Dana's bag as well. "You can give that back to them from me," she grinned. "Saves me the trip."

"You're very talkative all of a sudden," Dana teased, poking the Korean girl in the side.

"Very excited from the concert. I'm...what's the word?" Millie paused, grasping for a word that was clearly lost in the multilingual vocabulary bank in her head.

"Hyped?"

"Yeah, hyped," grinned Millie.

"How many languages do you guys actually speak?" Dana wondered aloud, suddenly realising that finding the correct words in any one language would be a frequent problem.

"Korean fluently. Pretty good English and Japanese," answered Millie.

"Amazing Japanese!" called out Amy from the couch where she and Mee had fallen on, beside Soojin.

"Chinese," added Soojin.

"But no English," Mee giggled, turning to Soojin, who glared at her and smacked her hand. The energy of the four was extraordinary, Dana mused, and wondered what on Earth they were going to be like when they were drunk as well.

X

Any concerns Dana had were tossed out the door as she got as sloshed as the idols. The music belted out, and they danced and sang and behaved like fools simply because they could. At one point when the music took on a seductive and sexy tone, Dana pushed Mee onto the couch and pushed her legs apart, as though to start of a strip tease. The Asian girls all burst into laughter, and gave a loud "ooo!" as Dana sat on Mee's lap. When the doorbell rang, however, the mood immediately changed and all four idols suddenly looked at each other guiltily.

The hierarchy took control, though, and Soojin immediately leapt up, mumbling an apology as she bumped into Dana and raced to the door.

There was a modern doorbell on it, and Soojin pressed a button bringing the little screen to life to show who was outside the door. To Dana's surprise she immediately recognised Boom, and she was even more surprised when Soojin appeared to breathe a sigh of relief and opened the door. Standing with his traditional swagger, Boom remained framed in the doorway until Soojin pulled him in and closed the door. Before she could go any further, Boom grabbed her and pushed her up against the wall to kiss her. Dana's mouth dropped, but she had little time to think as Millie had pulled the model onto the chair beside her.

"Don't worry," whispered Millie. "He and Soojin have been an item ever since he joined Moonlight. She got him in, actually."

"Really?"

"Yeah, it was a bit wild. The first non-Korean guy in Moonlight."

"He's not Korean?" Dana asked, curiously.

"Boom is short for Boon-mee. Boon-mee Sirisopa. There's not a lot of non-Koreans at all, really. Just a Thai and a Japanese girl," she added with a wink.

"Oh, and a North Korean," Amy rejoined playfully. Dana couldn't quite place the series of reactions, but she knew that Amy's comment made it clear that Millie was North Korean, and after Karim's discussion, she definitely reacted. Millie's response was even more intense, but whether it was to Amy's comment or Dana's reaction, Dana wasn't sure. Either way, Millie managed to get up, forcing Dana to fall to one side of the couch, and left the room, her arms wrapped around herself.

Soojin had noticed and walked up to the younger girls, speaking quickly to them in Korean. Boom said something as well, but Soojin replied and waved her hand at the same time, while the younger girls sat chastened, but saying nothing. Soojin said something again, and then looked at Dana and in her stilted English said, "I so sorry." With that she turned and grabbed Boom, leading him into one of the doors around the lounge.

Totally confused, Dana turned to the younger girls, and they both got up and came and sat on either side of Dana.

"I shouldn't have said that," Amy said softly, her head low. "Please don't tell anyone that Millie is a defector."

"She's a refugee?"

"She and her father escaped North Korea ages ago. They ended up in China and then came to Seoul," Mee explained. "No one knows that Millie is North Korean outside of us and maybe some of the Moonlight executives. Definitely no Glitter. It can't get out. Even Boom doesn't know, and Soojin is going to make sure he heard nothing." She took Dana's hands. "Please." To her surprise, Amy took her hands as well.

"I've been a terrible person," whispered Amy. "I know we barely know you, and we just got carried away and we've all been stupid. Normally we do this when it's just us so it doesn't matter. It's so wrong to ask this of you…"

"It's fine," Dana said, squeezing both sets of hands. "Honestly I promise. I won't tell anyone. It's got nothing to do with me. And it's not an issue for me. I promise you." She squeezed their hands again, and the two members look relieved.

"I'll go talk to Millie," Mee said.

"No, I will," Dana reassured her. "You guys go back to being you. I'll make sure Millie knows I'm not going to destroy her life." The two singers looked uncertain, but when Dana squeezed their hands again they gave a visible sigh of relief. The model hopped up and set off after Millie. Halfway across the room, she turned back to see the girls looking at her, cautiously. "Get back to it," she grinned, and Mee smiled in understanding, grabbing her friend's hands.

Millie had gone down a corridor past the kitchen, so Dana wasn't entirely certain which room she had gone into, but she could hear something from one of the rooms, and she pushed open the door to catch Millie in nothing but her g-string.

"Oh, god, I'm so sorry," Dana said, backing out.

"It's OK," replied Millie, her hand across her chest. "You can come in." She paused for a moment, and then turned and grabbed a t-shirt which she pulled on, though it just covered her boobs.

"I just wanted to tell you I'm not going to tell anyone your secret," Dana started. "I promise. It has nothing to do with me. But I don't know why you're worried." Millie's face remained blank, but there was a slight twist of her mouth when Dana finished.

"You're not Korean," Millie said. "If you were, you'd have something to say about where I come from. Trust me, they all do."

"Surely not all," replied Dana, but then shut her mouth, realising she had no experience of what the other girl had been through, and really had no right to say anything. To her surprise, however, Millie sat down beside her.

"No," she agreed, "not all. Those girls out there have never judged me or hated me. They treat me like a sister. They're my family and I love them so much. When they found out they just embraced me, and I hoped and prayed that when Moonlight formed a girl group I would be with them. But others…" She paused and shook her head, remembering. "People have been so cruel. My father…" She was unable to continue, and Dana reached across and took her hand, which Millie accepted. "So many people hate us because we are North Korean. We didn't have a choice. We didn't want to be there ever. It was horrible. Getting away from there…I don't remember much because I was really young, but I know my father didn't limp before we left. And I know I had a mother before we did."

"I'm so sorry," Dana whispered, appalled.

"I'm not evil. I was just born in the wrong place." There was silence, and Dana felt ashamed of herself for even buying into Karim's suspicions. On a whim she reached out and took her fellow Ambassador's hand and they sat in silence, with just the moon gazing upon them.

XI

Dana glanced blearily at the clock that shone brightly, the back of her mind somewhere taking in the fact that it read 3.14. In the morning, she guessed, noting that she was in darkness. Her arm was across a body and as she turned her head, she smiled a little seeing the face of Millie beside her, her short hair spiky from sleep, and drool coming from her mouth. Dana removed her arm carefully, and as her eyes accustomed to the dark she took in the details of the room she was in. They had sat in silence, and then laid back and talked. Somewhere in that, Dana realised she was fading in and out, and there was a point when she thought Millie had fallen asleep, but she assumed she had followed, because she couldn't remember anything much beyond that.

Dana stood up and padded softly to the door, sliding it open and stepping into the corridor. She needed water and she realised that she had woken because she needed to pee. The water shouldn't have been particularly difficult to find, but the toilet, that was another thing. She hadn't actually bothered to look beyond the communal area when she had entered the spacious apartment.

She walked to the doorway opposite and slid it back, but realised she had made a mistake. Two naked bodies, glistening with sweat, were sprawled out on the bed in front of her. Dana shook her head slightly and wondered how often concerts around the world ended up in this state. Probably quite a few, she reflected. Music seemed to cover all the common ground.

She made her way into the communal area, grabbing a clean cup from the neatly ordered stack on the shelf above the sink, and poured water into it from the cold water dispenser on the fridge. Then she set off down the opposite corridor, sipping at her beverage.

Another door revealed another bedroom, unused, while the next door was another naked G'Star member – this time the perfect Soojin, in much the same state as the other girls; vulnerably just herself.

Where the fuck was the toilet?

There was another door at the end of the corridor, but when Dana opened that it was just an empty room with musical instruments laying about. Surely this girls must use the toilet at some point, she thought, a little annoyed. As she headed back, she realised she hadn't shut Soojin's door properly, but then she noticed the sliver of light near the back of the room, and with a little astonishment at her own stupidity, Dana realised that each room would have its own en suite.

Feeling utterly stupid, she pondered about heading back to the corridor to use Millie's or ducking into the empty room, which became her path of choice. Having relieved herself, she headed back to Millie's room to finish her sleep, but as she did, she passed the dining room table and her Angel Chen yellow coat, which prompted her to get her mobile.

As she did, the jacket slid, and Dana tried to catch her handbag from falling off.

Except it didn't.

It wasn't there.

Almost like a switch, Dana became alert, and she scanned the table, grabbing her phone at the same time so she could use the torch to give a better view. The bag, however, was assuredly not there.

"Fuck," murmured Dana, as she flashed the torch around, scanning the room. However, there was obstinately no sign of the bag. Dana could feel herself getting physically sick as the implications of what might have happened began to sink in. She began pulling the cushions off the couch to make sure there was no sign of the bag. "Oh fuck," she said, a little louder this time.

"Hey, you'll get cold," came a voice behind her, and Dana spun to see Millie, wrapped in a robe, but Dana shook her head and turned back to the table. "What have I done?"

"The bag has gone," Dana hissed.

"I don't understand," Millie said, confused.

"The bag," repeated Dana. "The one with the Digné jewellery in. It's gone!" Whether it was the urgency in her voice, or simply the same implications that had hit Dana earlier, Millie's face immediately changed, and she quickly went over and activated the huge overhead lights, illuminating the communal area. Despite covering the same ground, she joined Dana's search, but they soon returned the same results.

At this point, however, they had attracted the attention of the other girls who had woken up and staggered out. Like Millie, they were all wearing dressing gowns, whether a practical, woollen gown like Millie's, or a skimpy, modesty protector like Mee's.

"What's up?" Mee asked, the same bleariness that Dana had earlier in her voice. Millie replied in Korean and alarm crossed the faces of the other three girls.

"You should cover in case Boom sees you," Soojin said to Dana, taking her arm, but as she did, Dana snapped around to look at her.

"Boom?"

"My boyfriend," she replied in stilted English.

"I know who he is," Dana growled. "Where is he?" Soojin looked puzzled and then realised what Dana had also worked out — Boom hadn't been in her room. Without waiting for a response, Dana turned and stormed down to Millie's room, grabbing any of her garments that had been lost earlier in the night. By the time Millie followed, Dana had already got her clothes on.

"What are you doing?" she asked.

"He's taken the jewellery," Dana snarled, and strode from the room to the communal area to get her jeans.

"No," protested Millie following. "He wouldn't."

"Why?" Dana said, turning so fast Millie almost walked into her.

"He's…Soojin's boyfriend," Millie replied meekly.

"He's not here," Amy said, and Dana turned to see the other three were in the room as well.

"When did he leave?" Dana asked, turning on Soojin.

"Hey," Amy said, grabbing her arm. "Don't be mean." Dana turned to her, ready to fight, but instead drew a deep breath. She bowed her head to Amy and then to Soojin.

"I'm very sorry," she said, "but I'm terrified. If I've lost the jewellery…"

"We," Millie said, touching her on the shoulder. "We lost it. You don't have to do this alone."

"We'll help in any way we can," Mee assured her. Dana paused, and thought she was going to burst into tears, but Mee did it for her instead, and to Dana's surprise the others gathered around her, embracing her. Even more surprising, Soojin grabbed her and pulled her in. The truth of Millie's earlier words about them being a close-knit family hit home and Dana let the tears flow a little.

"I didn't know he had left," Soojin said, as she held the embrace, and Dana again took a deep breath and got back control. This was no time to cry.

"Do you know where he lives?" Dana asked.

"Just downstairs," Amy replied.

"I show you," said Soojin, her English becoming more stilted in proportion to her stress, and she dashed back to her room. Her change was quick, and she was at the door with Dana even as the group hug ended. Soojin pulled the front door open and she and Dana stepped out, but as they did, Dana looked up and down the corridor.

"Where's Dam?" she asked.

"He must have gone home," Soojin said. Dana narrowed her eyes, unconvinced, but Soojin was already heading towards the lifts.

They headed down to the next level, and Dana continued to follow Soojin, who led her to a room and then typed in a code on the side of the door. Once they were inside the apartment – which was smaller than the one G'Star owned, but given that it only serviced one person instead of four, was arguably much more grandiose – Dana knew she should have been surprised to see Dam Hoon lying on the floor, blood pooling around his body, but a part of her knew that she would find the man like this. There was clearly a bullet hole in his chest, which meant that Boom had lived up to his name and was already armed. Dana pulled the man's coat open and saw a taser tucked into a holster on the belt, which she removed, as well as a set of car keys. Rather more depressingly she found his wallet, inside which was a picture of his two young children.

Soojin was rooted to the spot, her hand to her mouth. Dana looked around the room, and quickly went down the corridor, mentally noting that the layout of the apartment was not dissimilar to the one upstairs, though with only one corridor, and therefore half the rooms. There was no sign of Boom, who had clearly left the building, taking his earnings with him. Yet he had come back here, because Dam had followed him, obviously suspicious about what he was taking. Once inside the room, Boom had access to his firearm which gave him the upper hand.

She crossed over to the kitchen where there was a plastic container of brake fluid. When she approached it, the smell of fish oil became more obvious and as she sniffed at the top of the container it was even more apparent.

"Son of a bitch," she murmured, remembering the smell from the SkyBridge.

The only problem now was, what was she going to do? She had no idea where Boom might have gone, and he had left no obvious trail that she could tell. All she had was her taser and phone, and neither of those were going to give her Boom's location.

Or could they?

She took out her phone and placed her little finger on the small red dot in the top corner, and as demonstrated earlier, her phone went black before rebooting with a new interface. Dana looked at the apps that were available to her and to her delight she saw one marked "Phone Trace".

"Soojin, do you know Boom's number?" The Korean girl looked at her confused, and Dana held up her phone. "His telephone number?"

"Oh, yes, yes! 011 4820 2791," she read from her phone, and Dana tapped the app and typed the number in. To her surprise the phone started to ring, and the girls stood transfixed as they wondered what was going to happen.

"*Nuguseyo*?" came Boom's voice, and Soojin gasped, but Dana clapped her hand over the other girl's mouth. "Hello?"

Dana's heart pounded in her chest, but she kept her hand over

Soojin's mouth and watched the screen of her phone. A map had appeared and a large circle appeared over what was clearly Seoul. The circle got smaller and smaller as Boom said "Ahh!"

Terrified that he was about to hang up, Dana coughed and it was enough to catch Boom's attention. "*Nuguseyo??*" he demanded again, but the circle had now gotten as small as it was going to, changing from the shadowy black it had been to a pointed red. Dana disconnected the phone and found a specific longitude and latitude had been given on the map. Dana copied it, and closed the app, finding a map app that allowed her to plug her copied information into, and within seconds there was a neat red line leading from Raemian Caelitus to where Boom was currently hiding.

"What are you going to do?" Soojin asked, touching Dana on the arm.

"I'm going after him. He's taken the jewellery, and we need it back."

"But," though before Soojin could continue, Dana pointed to the corpse of Dam Hoon.

"This has gone way too far, Soojin," Dana said softly, not without compassion. A sudden gasp made her look up and she saw Amy was standing in the doorway, clearly shocked about the dead bodyguard.

"Amy, take Soojin back to your apartment," Dana instructed. She guided Soojin out of the room, and Amy linked her arm with the older girl's. "You lot stay here. I'm going to get the jewellery back," Dana explained.

"You can't do it alone," whispered Amy. "Call the police. They will help."

"I think it's better if we handle this in house," Dana said with a slight grimace. As they approached the elevator, Dana saw that both Millie and Mee were standing there, and like Amy they were all dressed casually. "Look after each other," instructed Dana. "I promise I won't be too long."

"You'll need your coat," said Millie, and Dana suddenly realised that Millie had been wearing it.

"Thanks," Dana grinned. She leaned forward and embraced Millie, before doing the same to the other three girls. "It's going to be fine," she promised. "Trust me."

"How do you know," Mee began, but Dana put her finger to her lips.

"You really don't want to know."

The elevator arrived, but it was heading down, so Dana stepped inside it. "Look after each other," she repeated, and the let the doors slide shut.

XII

Dana drove the Genesis SUV through the streets of Korea, with a fierce intensity until several things began to hit her. Firstly, the traffic was very limited, which was probably not surprising for the time of morning, but it might mean that she would be a target for the Korean police, if she was doing the wrong thing. And that would be a problem because she suddenly realised she probably wasn't allowed to drive in Korea. She certainly didn't have a Korean licence, and the less said about her blood-alcohol level, the better.

She was already a little worried, given that when she had started the car, there had been a curious bump, and Dana briefly panicked, thinking she had reversed into another car. It was, however, a moot point. She had to find Boom – that was her main priority. She could deal with the other details later.

Dana couldn't help but give a wry smile as her map displayed a number of names that were immediately familiar to her. She was heading into the Gangnam district, and her map picked out a number of buildings that exploring the K-pop world had exposed her to. SM Entertainment and JYP Entertainment both had their headquarters near to where she was driving. Gangnam was an affluent district of Seoul, and even as she crossed Yeongdong Bridge, she could see that the traffic was starting to build up a little.

Her phone was sending her along Yeongdong-Daero, a street filled with the traditional buildings most big cities were made from, glass and concrete separated only from the rest of the world by the Hangeul on them. Having passed a Tesla storefront and two hospitals, Dana pulled to a quick stop when she realised her phone was indicating she had reached her destination. Her aberrant driving didn't attract any undue attention and deciding to risk something that might get her into trouble, she pulled into the nearest carpark which was out the front of a hospital, recognisable only by the red cross on the front.

As she stepped out of the car, her phone map zoomed in on the area she was supposed to be, and gave her a more precise path to walk – in fact right next door where a three story glass building stood, utterly empty. Utterly empty except for the man with the sullen features and the dark suit standing at the front. He stared impassively ahead of him, guarding the doorway behind him, which was odd given the building seemed to have nothing in it.

Who puts a guard on an empty building?

It wasn't unheard of, Dana supposed, but she had a weird sense that something was wrong.

She glanced around, taking in her surroundings properly for the first time. Most of Seoul tended to light up like a Christmas tree at night, but Yeongdeong-Daero was sleepy, though Dana wasn't sure whether that just happened to be the time of night or not. The air was cold, something which hit Dana for the first time since her arrival. It was winter in Korea and at 3 in the morning it was freezing. No longer pumping adrenaline, Dana felt the cold starting to bite, particularly around her exposed legs. She was suddenly very grateful that Millie had given her the jacket, not least because it also gave her a place to hide her taser.

Dana Spectra pondered on her options, whilst her phone resolutely pointed towards the glass building. Chewing her bottom lip, she guessed that she could maybe try to find an alternative entry point, but that could be difficult, and who knows how much time she had – after all she had no idea what Boom was doing in the building. Screwing up her courage, she decided to go for the front door approach.

She strolled casually up to the security guard who initially didn't give her a second glance, but when she was standing right beside him, he turned to regard her with a fair degree of dispassion.

"Hi," Dana smiled. "Uhm, I was wondering what was going on in there." She pointed to the revolving door behind him, but the guard just raised an eyebrow and turned to face the front again. Dana took a step toward the door, but the guard's hand was in front of her, making it clear she was not to go in. He even deigned to look at her again, this time shaking his head slowly.

Dana nodded, and felt the taser in her pocket.

"Sorry," she said. "I just...oh what's that?" She pointed up the street, and was genuinely astonished when the guard turned to look at what she was pretending to point at. Quickly she whipped out the taser and jabbed it in the guard's neck, activating it. Ozone sizzled and the man literally shook in front of her, before collapsing to the ground. Dana quickly searched the guard, looking around to see if anyone had seen anything, but the darkness seemed to have kept her actions hidden from view. She paused for a moment when she thought she saw someone, but when she blinked, she realised she was alone.

Needing a weapon to give her an edge (given that it was clear Boom was also packing), she searched the guard and gave a slight smirk when she found a gun – a shining grey Colt M1911, with a bright red grip. The guard started to groan, recovering from the electricity that had coursed through his body, so Dana swiftly headed to the revolving door and pushed her way into the building. She slid the gun into her waistband in the small of her back, feeling it tug down on her jeans sitting there a little uncomfortably, but she didn't let it bother her. Unless they were about to fall off, she could live with the awkwardness.

Inside, the building was large and empty, and Dana wondered if it had perhaps been a car showroom at some point. There didn't seem to be any activity coming from the floors above, so she moved forward into the darkness, trying to find something that might lead below. When she passed a door, she felt a hum of activity behind it, a faint vibration of sound or electricity. She turned the handle and it easily opened into a set of stairs that did indeed lead down to another doorway, light streaming behind it and a bass line thumping.

Dana headed down the stairs and opened the door to enter, but more movement in the corner of her eye made her go through and close the door behind her. The guard had clearly followed her and was looking for her, so she banked on the fact that there was a crowd she could lose herself in.

To her surprise she had entered what appeared to be an underground casino, populated mostly by Korean nationals. She made her way around the outskirts of the casino, noting it was busy with tables and cards, well dressed croupiers flicking out cards and scantily clad barmaids bringing drinks to those that required them.

There were a few foreigners, mostly women, dressed in a variety of ways and looking ultra-cool on the arms of their Korean partners, who were dressed equally fantastically in clean suits with thin lapels, and collarless shirts. As such, Dana blended in rather nicely, and no one gave her a second look (well, they let their first look turn into a lascivious gaze, but beyond imagining her naked, they didn't cast a second glance).

As she made her way around the room, she found exactly what she was looking for – a table that was playing Texas Hold 'em, with four Korean gentleman seated, dressed in a variety of styles. One had a pale blue suit, blue hair swept to the side and a model's good looks – Boom. Cards were being laid down, and as the croupier flipped them over, Boom's smile grew.

Until the heavy-set gentleman beside him turned over his two cards. The croupier leant forward and rearranged the cards in the centre of the table, and it was clear that whether Boom had a good poker face or not, the cards had not gone his way. The heavy-set gentleman gave a belly laugh, obviously knowing that Boom's cards were ordinary, and sure enough when he flipped them over, Boom slumped back in his seat accepting defeat.

And then someone else appeared, and for a moment, Dana couldn't quite believe her eyes. Approaching the table in a svelte deep purple velvet bodysuit with high neck, no sleeves and ruffled shorts, as well as a cool black leather biker jacket was Millie. Dana's heart sunk.

Up to this point things seemed pretty obvious – Boom had stolen the jewellery and was the one who tried to kill her on the Skybridge. Karim's agitator was probably him, surely? There was certainly no reason to automatically suspect the North Korean refugee. Except they were both with Moonlight and so both had access to the people who had been killed in the past. But why was Millie here now? How did she even get here before Dana?

Unless she knew where to go…

No reason to suspect the North Korean refugee, sure, if you discounted the fact she shouldn't have been here.

Millie rested her butt against the table, her long legs – made even longer by the short shorts – attracting the attention of everyone, including Boom. She placed her hand on Boom's shoulder and then made a gesture to take in the whole table. Standing in the crowd to remain unseen, Dana had no idea what they were saying, but whatever it was, it appealed to everyone except Boom, who looked annoyed, and then resigned. He shrugged his shoulders and stood up, bowing his head at the other players and then took Millie's hand in his and led her away from the table.

Quickly Dana followed, her left hand reaching to the small of her back to rest on the Colt there. Boom had got to a door, which he opened and gallantly let Millie enter. Dana sped up to get to the door before it closed shut after Boom had entered, and when she burst through, she had the gun out, ready to shoot.

Inside the room was a stack of lockers, and both Millie and Boom turned around in surprise, Boom at one of the lockers. Seeing Dana, he pulled a gun from the locker and grabbed Millie, holding the gun to her head.

"Well, well, look who is here, cobber," drawled Boom, a grin on his perfect features. "You wanna toss a shrimp on the barbie?" Millie's face had gone pale and Dana frowned a little uncertain about what exactly was going on. There was still one fact she was certain of, and that, she decided, was what she would run with.

"Where's the jewellery?" she snapped.

"In the locker," came the surprisingly honest response. "Why are you so bothered? Who gives a shit? They are insured. Digné will not mind."

"I mind," Dana replied.

"Me too," whimpered Millie.

"Let her go," demanded Dana.

"Oh, I don't think so," Boom sneered. "Whacha gonna do? You can't shoot me. You might hit her. That wouldn't look good."

Dana squeezed the trigger and the sound of the Colt going off sounded strangely loud to everyone in the room, though the shock on Boom's face made it clear he had definitely not expected her to do what she did. When he realised he hadn't been shot, however, a look of relief flooded his face.

"You missed," he grinned.

"Did I?" Dana asked innocently. Boom's puzzled features turned slightly and he saw that Dana's bullet had gone through a calendar that was on the wall behind him – directly through the centre of the 14th. When he turned back, he looked a whole lot less certain than he had before.

"It's not the 14th," he said, trying to regain some confidence.

"I'm superstitious," Dana smirked.

"I could still kill her," Boom said, but there was a little less certainty in his voice now.

Colonel Indigo Spectra had once told his daughter, when they were wandering through a rainforest looking for the rest of their family, that everyone often faced a moment where a decision needed to be taken and the heart and head would fight over what to do. If the head won, then it was as it should be. If the heart won, then that was a moment you needed to listen to yourself, because the compass of morality had been defined. When she had asked her father what that meant he had laughed and told her of the time he had been desperate to take her mother on a date. Unfortunately, his car had broken down, which meant there was no way to get to her. But, he announced with all the passion of an old school preacher, he was working for a pizza delivery company at the time and he had the opportunity to, well not steal as such, but *borrow* the company car to meet up with his girlfriend.

His head had emphatically tried to stop this from happening. There were so many reasons why this was a bad idea, not least because no matter how often he used the word *borrow* it didn't change the fact it was nothing more than a fairly obvious pseudonym for steal. But his heart was in the driving seat and so the car was *borrowed*. That, he realised, was when the compass of his morality had been decided. One woman was more important to him than stealing a car, and so he knew he had found the love of his life.

Some months earlier, Dana had come to the very solid conclusion she wasn't a killer. She had killed, but she wasn't a killer, and she had no desire to cause the death of anyone. But she had made the decision, the choice between her heart and her head, the choice that decided *who* she was. She was many things – a sister, a daughter, a model, an animal activist, someone who drank too much on occasion, and someone who had a tendency to leap into bed with people a little too quickly. But none of those were *who* she was. She rescued Dine, the cat because it was the right thing to do, and that was the person she had decided she was. She would do the right thing, and she had to be pragmatic under those circumstances. The right thing was laid out before her. But she didn't have to take a life to do it – in fact she would actively avoid it.

But she would be pragmatic and she would do the right thing.

And she needed to have confidence in herself and her abilities.

So when she squeezed the triggor a second time, it was with the confidence she had absolutely aimed for the 14th on the calendar. It was with the confidence she would hit her target.

The bullet hit Boom in the right shoulder, causing him to immediately drop the gun as he was spun back, and setting Millie free.

"Mother fucker," he exclaimed, grabbing his shoulder and falling to his knees.

"Get the jewellery," Dana ordered Millie, and it wasn't lost on the Korean girl that the Australian had not dropped the gun. But she kept it on Boom, and when Millie stepped up with the stash safely in her hands, Dana reached into her jean pocket and gave her a small card. "Signiel," she said, and Millie nodded. "We have to talk," Dana added, her words weighty, but Millie simply nodded a second time and left the room. As she did, Dana could feel the butterflies in her belly and she desperately hoped her gut instinct was the right one.

What she didn't notice was the arrival of someone else – her guard friend from the front door. In fact, she didn't notice until she realised

Boom was looking at him in some relief and when Dana turned the guard gave her the same sardonic look as before.

"Can I have my gun back?" he asked, politely, but without a smile. Dana looked at Boom and the guard and then turned and handed it over.

"Sure," she said with the sweetest smile she could muster, and to her surprise the guard smiled back.

"You are one crazy bitch," the guard said as he gave the gun a quick look over. "I've never been assaulted and had my gun stolen before. I might be in love."

"Oh, I try," she said, still uncertain as to the guard's intentions. Boom had started to get up, but the guard trained the Colt on him.

"I'm Jihoon," he smiled, before turning to Boom. "Don't move *byung shin*. There are some gentlemen out there who are not happy with you. You've drawn undue attention to our little operation."

"I don't understand," Dana asked.

"Gambling is illegal in Korea. For nationals, anyway. These little joints are pop ups but we can't afford to have the police looking into them. So, no unnecessary attention. And certainly no *bin dae sae ggi*."

"They stole my credit," Boom protested.

"Oh please, you stole from us," Dana pouted. "And you tried to kill me. *And you tried to kill me!* What the hell was that about?" Boom looked at her and Jihoon.

"Someone has a little problem. And not enough money to cover the problem," Jihoon said, supplying the answer.

"I got a call. Said if I dealt with you permanently all my money problems would go away. And I don't have a problem dealing with some talentless Australian," sneered Boom.

"Who?"

"These people don't give names," Boom replied, and Dana felt her stomach lurch.

"You're lucky I don't have the gun anymore," Dana growled. "What are you going to do with him?" she asked Jihoon.

"Oh, we won't kill him. That will make things more complicated. But I don't think Boom's little boy band is going to be a complete unit for the next few months." The look of panic on Boom's face gave Dana a small glow of satisfaction, and she turned to the door. "Hey," Jihoon called to her. "Can I get your number?"

Dana paused for a moment, and then turned back with a smile. "Got a pen?" she asked sweetly. Jihoon tapped his pockets with his free hand.

"No," he said, disappointment etched all over his face.

"So close," she grinned, and gave him a kiss on the cheek. "Maybe next time?"

And with that she stepped out of the room. Jihoon turned back to Boom.

"Maybe I really am in love, huh?" he said with a smile. The gun now trained on Boom didn't look quite so happy.

XIII

Boom was hauled out of the building, looking far more miserable than Dana would have thought someone could look, though in all honesty, given the delicate and expensive jewellery he had stolen, and the fact he had tried to murder her, she found she didn't have a lot of sympathy for him. She suspected he was going to get quite the beating, but the truth was, Boom was a money maker, and presumably a useful asset, so he would be going on an unexpected hiatus for a few months before he returned to business.

"Hey," she said, and Jihoon turned, gripping Boom. "Maybe you didn't get a name, but who were they working for?" There was a pause, and Jihoon shook Boom.

"Answer the *yeoja*," he said. Boom seemed uncertain, and then

71

opened his mouth. To Dana's astonishment, a neat little hole suddenly opened up in Boom's head, before a second opened on the opposite side, and blood started to dribble down his face. Boom's stressed look relaxed as he lost control of his muscles and then Jihoon dropped him, bringing his gun up to point at Dana.

But Dana was already looking for where the shot had actually come from. She saw movement from across the road, but as she took a step forward, her peripheral vision caught something to her right – a small figure in a suit, with white-blonde hair.

Dana dashed after the figure, but to her surprise, the person didn't run or hide. They simply turned and waited for Dana to catch up to them. This made Dana slightly wary, and she slowed as she approached the person, stopping so she didn't get too close.

She recognised the person immediately, remembering them from the Skybridge incident, the concert, maybe even when she had arrived earlier. Whenever she had seen the person before, she had felt uneasy, the germ of an idea that her killer might be the suited figure growing in her subconscious. But she had been wrong; they had been targeting Boom the entire time.

Dana paused and wondered what to say.

The person opposite her was Korean, wearing a black suit, with a black shirt and black necktie. The white, blonde hair was short and framed a face that was impish and cute, with thin lips and eyeshadow that created a strong cat-eye effect around the hazel eyes.

Dana opened her mouth to say something, but to her surprise, the person raised a finger to their lips.

"It's better this way," they said, their voice neither high nor low, but accented all the same. Then they smiled and brought out a key fob, which they activated. The bleep shocked Dana, and she turned to see she had totally missed the Lamborghini parked right beside them. Sleek and black with two cut-outs in the bonnet revealing the red underneath, like two fangs below the windscreen, the sports car had blended into the night perfectly. Now it lit up as the fob beeped. The person smiled again, and Dana was struck by how beautiful it was. Then they got into the car, and the doors were pulled shut behind them.

"Holy shit," Dana heard from behind her, a low whistle accompanying the comment. "You know that's a Sesto Elemento? You know how much that costs?" Dana turned to Jihoon who had followed her, but shook her head. Dana wanted to know so much more, but quietly and without fanfare, the car slid out of its park and into the night. The answers would not be coming in a hurry, and a shiver ran through her as she wondered who had authorised the justice she had just witnessed. Was someone tired of being cheated, or was something else involved – something she had encountered before? Or, worse, had the government decided to settle the score?

The truth was, she reflected, there was always a bigger fish out there waiting.

XIV

When Dana Spectra pushed the door to her room open, she saw, sitting on the floor looking very much like the shell of a human being, Millie. The room was warm, though outside it was still dark and cloudy, and it looked very much as though snow was about to disrupt Seoul's new day.

Dana shrugged her Angel Chen off, pulled her phone out from her back pocket and placed it on the closest flat surface near her (a small table that was to the side of the door) and sat down beside Millie. The girl was clutching Dana's bag to her chest, and she looked very shaken. Given everything that had happened, Dana supposed that wasn't an entirely unrealistic reaction. With all that, however, there was still one very important question unanswered.

"What were you doing there?" Dana asked, trying to keep her tone as free from judgement as she could. Millie looked at her, her eyes wide, before replying. Dana remembered reading somewhere that eye enhancement surgery was very popular in South Korea, as wide eyes and pale skin were the traditional markers of beauty in the country. Every country has its idiosyncrasies, Dana supposed.

"I thought you might need some help," Millie replied. "I know you told me to stay put, but I was worried about you. I didn't want anything to happen to you."

"How did you even know where to go?" Dana rejoined, and this time the doubt was clear in her voice.

"I didn't," the singer replied. "I just got in the back of the SUV and watched where you went after you got out. I have a key."

"Oh," Dana said, her voice small. The person she thought following her in the display building wasn't the guard at all. And the bump in the car hadn't been a bump at all, it had been Millie getting in the car, which was why the reverse sensors hadn't beeped. "That makes so much sense," Dana added. "You can sure get changed quickly."

"It's part of the job, right? I followed you and found the gambling den but I lost you. Then I found Boom and told him I wanted the jewellery."

"He took you inside to pretend to get it…he could have killed you, Millie!" Dana blurted out.

"I thought he'd just give the stuff up when he was caught. And there were so many people around they might have decided to kill some foreign girl. It's not like you're a crazy action girl spy or something."

"No," agreed Dana, crossing her fingers behind her back.

"Although the way you handled that gun," Millie added. "I mean, you were incredible."

"You can thank my dad," grinned Dana. "He was very keen I should be a good marksman." Dana reached forward and took the bag from Millie, not entirely surprised to feel her shaking. "You're an idiot," she whispered, and gave her a gentle push.

"What now?" Millie wondered. Indeed, Dana thought. What now?

Boom's death would come out, but Dana suspected it would be conveniently recontextualised, and Soojin…well, she would get over him. G'Star would be shaken, but the truth was they were part of a system, and there wouldn't be a lot of time to grieve. Rehearsal, promotions, recording, performing and advertising would ensure there would be virtually no time for Soojin to mope about the loss of her lover. Or the betrayal, which was probably more important in the long run.

But then there was Karim's problem of the agitator within Moonlight Entertainment. Having discovered Boom had stolen the jewellery and tried to kill her on the Skybridge, Dana had been convinced that she had found who Karim was looking for. The fact he wasn't Korean added to that cause as well. Except on the drive back, a clearer mind pointed out that he never admitted, or even suggested that he had killed anyone else. But he had been paid by…well, whoever he was about to reveal, so he probably could be easily bought. If Millie had killed those others…well, then she was an extraordinary actress. A simple night where a gun had been pointed at her head reduced the girl to a bundle of nerves (*was that really the definition of a simple night now?*). If she had killed people before, then the easiest way to find out if she was the killer would be to check her work-related activities the following day and see what state she was in, most of which could be found on YouTube. That's assuming she had time to pop out for a quick assassination between trips to the local convenience store. Truthfully, she had really got Karim his answer.

Ultimately ASIS' concerns seemed to stem from CIA worries, and the vague possibility that a North Korean was part of a K-Pop group that was becoming more and more successful. Maybe, just maybe, the earlier deaths were nothing but unfortunate accidents. It wasn't Karim's problem, it wasn't ASIO's problem, it wasn't ASIS' problem and it certainly wasn't her problem. And now, thanks to the well-dressed assassin, it wasn't even the CIA's problem.

"Fuck it," Dana decided. "I've got four more days here. Tell me I'm not going to be spending them alone," she added. She could still feel Millie shivering, and that alone convinced her she was making the right decision. If the CIA was right and someone was trying to shake confidence in the K-Pop industry, she wasn't a superhero. She reached out and grabbed the older girl's hand, feeling Millie squeeze back appreciatively.

The two stared out of the hotel windows and Millie rested her head on Dana's shoulder, as they watched the moonlight reflect on the Han.

BOOK TWO

JUSTICE

LAP ONE

"Well damn, girl, don't you look mighty fine?"

"Damn, right, I do," says I, with a knowing wink. Because, fuck do I look fine. String bikini with a black and white leopard print, cut off denim shorts that hug tight, and are high enough to give enough cheek at the back, a sleeveless denim shirt – open of course to ensure the girls are displayed in their bikini-clad glory, and a big ass, mother fucking hat. Oh, and don't forget the boots. I mean…there are fuck me boots and there are *fuck me!* boots. Ever since I wandered over to the fenced off gully, every single cowboy has been checking out my (let's be honest, here) mighty fine ass.

"See now, a girl with an attitude like that is the kinda girl that people here wanna take home to meet their mothers," slimes Grease Monkey. He's sort of hot. Nice bod, deceptively gentle face, but with an absolutely shit moustache that makes his brown eyes browner. What he doesn't know is that while he's desperately trying to find out who I am and what my deets are, I already know who this fuck is. In fact, I can hear it being whispered in my ear as I turn and walk towards him.

"Errr, that's Ted Hawley, chief mechanic for Gold. Aged 33, been working there for, uh, 7 years now. Probably a good start point."

Noted.

"I'll tell you what," I say with a wry smile. "If I guess your name, you gotta give me the *special* tour of this place."

"Well, if you can guess my name, girl, you can have a special tour of any goddamn where you like," he shoots back, full of confidence.

"Ted," I say, and for a moment he frowns.

"Now, how the hell…" He pauses, frowns a bit more and then laughs. "OK, so someone set you up for this. Who was it? Mitch? Prick. Well, you won fair and square. Knocked me down a peg or two. I'm man enough to admit I'm wrong."

I smile, concerned that I may actually be starting to like this guy. Maybe the "deceptive" part of the gentle face was unfair. As I head over to the fence to look into the gully, I can feel his eyes on my ass, and decide I'm probably not too far off the mark. This is the place for it, after all.

"So, what's your name, girl?" Ted asks, and the girl bit is starting to wear a bit thin.

"Kelly Court," I lie in return.

"You a model?" As come on lines it's not the best, but given past circumstances…

"As a matter of fact, I am," I grin back. "What about yourself? You a model?" To my surprise he actually blushes.

"Err, no, no, ma'am," and I won't lie, the sudden display of respect actually earned him bonus points with me. "But thanks for the compliment." He joins me on the side of the gully, hands over the fence like me, and this time his eyes are glued to my boobs. Fair enough, that was the point. "You like the cars then?" he asks, a little hesitantly.

"Oh, yeah," I say, as casually as I can. While he takes

80

in my cleavage, I give the area a good look round. It's all a bit primitive here, what with the orange rock stretching out for miles, the mountain sides carefully carved away into their different layers. It all looks like one of those really old cartoons, where you could expect a bird to be chased by a coyote, massive rocks precariously balanced atop a pile of much smaller ones. Not like that's the case here. The rocks are definitely not that ridiculous.

Then there's the gully below us, which presumably the fence is to stop idiots from sliding down and reenacting *The Lion King*. I can hear the sound of the cars echoing through the chasm, but I can't see where they are, and I'm not entirely sure if I've just missed the start of the race, or am in time to catch the ending.

"You're not a con or something, are ya?" Ted suddenly asks. "We don't like that sort of thing here. No matter how pretty the face." He moves and I'm not sure whether its intentional that he shows me the Smith & Wesson M&P Shield he's carrying. It doesn't bother me. Before he could even get it out of the holster, I'd have had him disarmed and eating the barrel. These guys are all the same, regardless of how competent they think they are. And they'd be guessing a woman would be unlikely to be able to stop them.

For a brief moment I feel like putting it to the test, but Ted and I aren't the only ones out here. The others have lost interest a bit, but every so often my ass brings their attention back to me, so if I were to make the point, there's the slightest chance that one of these guys would have less interest in saving Ted's life than they would in ending mine. Ah, well. Looks like Ted is lucky today.

"What kinda cars we talking?" I ask, innocently and doe-eyed, blinking a little in the light. He loves it and I can see his dick getting hard, though whether it's over me or whether it's over the cars is hard to tell.

"Oh, we're talking standard F1 cars, today," he says, finally noticing my face. "I dunno know what you know about cars, exactly, but basically these are your standard open cockpit cars which have been engine stacked behind the driver and front and rear wings. That sound you hear is 1.6 L V6 configuration engines with an MGU-K system. Obviously, we ain't using them for racing at the moment, but you never know what's just around the corner. Most of my job isn't too stressful, a bit of plug and play with the parts, and some tinkering here and there, but nothing too outta line. Though, like I said, these ain't anything we're racing with."

Still cagey because he doesn't entirely trust me. Clever boy. That said, I don't give a shit about the cars, to be honest. They aren't the reason I'm here. I turn back and lean against the fence, pushing my crotch forward a little so that I strike the right effect.

"You, err," and he stumbles as though he's not sure what he wants to offer. I'm vaguely intrigued. "You wanna try one out?" Have to admit, I wasn't expecting that. Also have to admit, as much as I have other reasons for being here, I can't lie: driving an F1 car has always been a dream. That said, I'm guessing I'm not getting in one of those. Maybe something a little slower – F3 or F4 perhaps, but still. It's an opportunity I'm not likely to ever get again.

"That's a no go from here."

I shouldn't ignore that.

"Seriously, he's going to be pissed if you do this."

"I mean, how can I say no to an offer like that?" I smarm.

"For f…"

Ted takes me over to a nearby building, which looks a little like a boring shed (but then, truth be told, they all do), but when we step inside, I'm surprised to see an elevator. We take it down, and I'm not surprised when we step out and see the track I was just watching. The cars are pulling in, riders getting out and people with clipboards engaging them animatedly. I can't see the main AutoGold driver, Sandy Hamilton, but I suppose he probably wouldn't waste his time with the little people. Who knows who these nobodies are, but if they keep up, they just might become a somebody and it will all be worth it.

On the condition nothing terrible happens in a race and they die. Most things in life are a gamble, but the truth is here, sometimes you're playing with stakes that are much higher than a couple of grand. You gotta respect that kind of madness. It's YOLO to the extreme. I don't know if I could do that.

Except I'm clearly about to, so perhaps I'm judging myself harshly.

Ted offers me a coverall, and I pull it on, taking my shoes off to do so.

"You're gonna need different shoes," he adds, and then I realise that there's a virtual wardrobe along the backwall. Coveralls, helmets, shoes; everything a person needs if they're going to go for a spin. Initially I'm not sure why they'd bother, but then it dawns on me that those newbies talking with the clipboards are probably angling for a job. They wouldn't have the gear, so there's stuff ready to go. It's a smooth operation.

"I'm gonna let you go out in one of those," Ted continues, pointing at the cars as I pull on the shoes I've been given. I love car racing, but I wouldn't claim to be an absolute expert, and so I'm not sure what he's pointing at exactly. One thing I do notice, though, is they aren't the standard Formula 1 car that AutoGold races with. These are slightly different, the chassis clearly built by an outside company. Not Formula 1 and these are drivers looking for a job, so maybe Formula 3? Formula 4?

Ted isn't giving me much in the way of answers, and as he strolls out of the building we're in, helmet in hand, and into the pits. When we get to the cars, however, I realise I'm wrong. He has plenty to say. He just likes props to speak with.

"Formula 3," he announces. "No turbocharging, 3.4 L V6 engine. It's pretty much the same as Formula 2 cars, but we use theses ones for 3. Once you're on the track, you won't be able to get much faster than 180 mph. Maybe 185, but that would be tops." I notice that we've gained a degree of attention from some of the clipboards, and a few other engineers around. I'm a little surprised at how nervous I am.

He hands me what looks like a white balaclava, and I pull it over my head while he continues to talk. "You're gonna do a sighting lap, kick off from the starting point. You'll see it as you head out. Take it slow on the first lap. You're just having fun. Once you feel confident, hit it with a bit more rev and build up speed. You need to trust the car. There are times when your instincts are gonna wanna pull the car back, particularly when you go into a corner. Don't. Fight against that and trust the design. And you're gonna feel some g-force as well. It's all good, don't panic." Ted pauses and looks at me. "You still game?" and he's got a smile on his face which, to his credit, isn't entirely smug. It almost looks as though he's hoping I'll say yes, but I get the feeling he's ready to hit me with a comment if I say no. My entire body is tingling, but I'm definitely not backing out.

"I'm ready," I say, and give him a challenging look, but he just grins savagely.

"Phone," he says, holding out his free hand, and I pause for a moment, before realising I'm gonna have to give it up. This requires a brief unzipping of the racing suit, and I pull the phone out of my pocket and hand it to him. As I zip it up, he hands me gloves, and I wonder how the fuck he was able to carry so much.

Oh, in the helmet, of course.

"Fairly certain I have the right size," he says, and he holds up the helmet, to which I nod. The car which we're standing beside is white. There's a sallow faced man standing on the other side, and he wanders around the car, examining it, before he looks up and gives Ted a nod. "Looks like you're good to go," Ted grins. The sallow faced man gives me thumbs up and I nod back.

Then I get in the car.

LAP TWO

He wasn't wrong about the g-forces. My sighting lap wasn't too bad; as I made my way through the rocky canyons around the course to bring me back to the starting position (which wasn't too far away from the pit I had come out of) I didn't really get the car too much over 100 mph, and I had found myself driving at those speeds more than enough in the past. So when I start proper, and comfortably push the car forwards to around 120 – 130 mph, I feel the force push back.

When I take a corner at 150, it hits home with a bang.

There are times when I pay attention to what I'm told and, on this occasion, I'm kinda glad I did. Sure enough when I take that first left corner, my gut immediately wants to pull back and slow down. I have plenty of distance to my right, but the speed at which the canyon is approaching makes me scream to slow down and brake, but aside from the fact that I have no pedals (the brakes are on the steering wheel, which is a blessing when your foot is stamping on the floor) there's another part of me that is heeding the advice I was given.

I'm the last person who wants to throw their life away, but I decide to trust in the fact that Ted knows what he's talking about and so I rely on the car, and it doesn't let me down. When I get around the first corner successfully, my adrenaline is pumping and I'm feeling confident that I understand a little better what I'm doing.

Then there's the power pumping through the car, the sound of the engine closer than it's ever been before. My whole body is tingling as the vibrations pass through me, and I'm beginning to understand why people think they can marry a car. Or at least fuck one. If my body wasn't on edge from the fear of losing control, I'd definitely need a little one-on-one time with my hand. I may still need it, truth be told.

When I hit a long stretch, I risk pushing the car to 170 and it's an experience. Perhaps what surprises me the most is how quickly I adapt to the speed. My brain takes in the twists and turns of the track and on lap three, I'm pushing the car almost on automatic.

After lap five I slow the beast down and return to the pit. Not that I'm not enjoying myself, but going around and around a track loses its appeal after a while, regardless of how exciting the actual car is. It would definitely be different in a race, with the competition pushing the desire.

"Not bad, girl," Ted says as he pulls my helmet off. I get out of the car ignoring the girl bit and take a few steps. My legs are a little more unsteady than I thought they'd be, but I don't let Ted see that. Instead, I pull the hood off, and then unzip the suit, releasing it so that my upper body is totally exposed, covered only by the bikini top.

It's my own little power move, and with the sweat on my body creating a sheen, it has the desire effect of everyone pausing to take me in. I've gone back to being another sweaty, hot body they can dream about. Anyone thinking too deeply about my drive will be forgetting about it now, concentrating instead on the bimbo.

Everyone except one person, which is surprising.

What's more surprising is that it's a she and she's black.

"Who's that?" I ask, trying not to sound too suspicious,

but Ted doesn't give a shit.

"Oh, don't worry about her. We're stuck with her. A bit of a know it all. She doesn't come from round here. Not our sort of person." I wonder what he means precisely by that. The fact he was a racist wouldn't have surprised me, but was it more than that? She has an unusual confidence.

She intrigues me, but I can't go wandering over to her just yet without drawing undue attention. Also, I notice that no one in my ear is giving me any particular help on this topic, which is annoying. Or maybe I'm still in trouble for taking the test drive.

"Hey, uh, no offence, but are you deaf?" I flick my head to him sharply, and Ted looks apologetic. He taps his ear, and I realise he's seen the bud there. Fuck, he's much sharper than I gave him credit for. I smile meekly.

"Well, you know what it's like growing up around loud noises. Sometimes it takes a toll."

"Oh, yeah, sure," he nods, and it's gone. I think I even hear a sigh of relief in my ear, but I'm probably just imagining it.

"So, you work on all these cars?"

"Oh not all, ma'am," he shrugs. Three drivers are coming out of the building and along the tarmac to the pit. Ted takes my arm and leads me back inside, and I watch as the drivers get into the cars. The sallow faced man from earlier examines my car again, but this time he shakes his head and points to another car. The one I just drove is taken away. When I look at Ted, I notice that he's started to grin slightly. We watch as they take their sighting lap, and then they're off. Ted's grin gets broader as the smell of rubber burning and the engines screaming becomes stronger. When they come past it's like a storm. "Holy shit!" I hear Ted say. He points I follow his finger to see a display board light up. There are times on it, but I realise he's grinning at the speed of the cars, which are all over 200 mph. I mean, that is fucking fast.

There are three cars, bright red, bright blue and jet black, each with gold stripes running from the nose to the wings at the back, spreading out like a wave.

"We recently made some changes to the engines, and they are amazing," Ted says to me, his smile so large I think he could wank to what's going on. "I gotta tell ya, it's working out a treat. Did you hear that?" I smile, his enthusiasm infectious, and I have to admit I sort of feel the thrill in my loins as well. There's no denying that the throb of the engines and the squealing of the tyres on the asphalt have a certain evocative effect. I risk a look and sure enough his dick is hard as.

"You know what, soldier, I'mma let you go do your thing," I give him a hefty slap on the arm and he takes it well. Give him his due, he loves what he does. Didn't get to find out if he loves his boss, and that's really the entire point of having tried to meet him.

LAP THREE

"Jürgen von Golde," Broadsword says as he slides a piece of paper across the table to me and then leans back in his chair. I get the vague feeling he's losing weight, as his white, linen suit sits a little more loosely around the shoulders than it used to. I wonder if he's been dieting or working out. Either way, I'm not keen. Broadsword has an image which I'm used to and I don't like change all that much. "Heard of him?"

"Err, no, I don't think so," I shrug, as I glance at the picture. He's a sallow faced individual with grey eyes and thinning, sandy hair. There's quite a sizable scar down the left-hand side of his face which looks like it probably hurt to receive.

"He wears a mask," Broadsword says, reading my mind. Somehow, he had an unerring habit of being able to do that, and it rankled. "They call him the Phantom," he adds, and I wonder if he's being serious.

"Von?"

"Oh, that's an affectation. The Germans think he was born Jűrgen Goldstein, but changed his name to Golde, and then von Golde to make it sound like he came from nobility. He was von Golde when he opened AutoGold."

"Oh," I exclaim, a little loudly. "That's where I've heard of him. AutoGold."

"Exactly, makers of high-quality engine parts and other auto accessories."

"So why do we care?" I wonder. "Doesn't he live in the US?"

"He does, decided to move there a few years back when Merkel was Chancellor because he was very unimpressed with her in the position, but more, the idea that she was becoming a respected figure in global politics turned his stomach." Broadsword leaned forward and clasped his hands, his eyebrows rising as though he was a fisherman who had just hooked something unknown, yet definitely worthy of the challenge.

"We don't like von Golde?"

"He thinks he's related to Hitler," Broadsword's eyebrows raised again, but there's no smile. Broadsword isn't famous for his sense of humour.

"Fuck off," I reply, forgetting where I am. Fortunately, Broadsword is one of my bosses who I can get away with saying that to. I've been pretty lucky to have him looking over my shoulder, because if I were to be honest, I was probably not what anyone would think of as a golden child. Part of the reason I had been relegated to desk duty of late.

"Genuinely," Broadsword said, leaning back again, as though enjoying a particularly good tale. "He bought a hair on eBay which belonged to Hitler, apparently, and had both the hair's DNA and his tested, and they were a match."

"That's got to be a con," I say, my jaw dropping.

"I couldn't possibly comment," Broadsword replied, but this time without doubt there was a trace of amusement with what had happened. "The thing is, he is, shall we say, a touch fascist."

"Ah, one of those," I nod sagely.

"One of those indeed. And given that Germany is busy turning its back on the past and forging a future where it is very much an essential and welcome member of Europe, von Golde decided to pack his bags and move to a country where he could be much happier." I sighed, because I knew what was coming.

"You're going to say America," I scowl and flop back in my chair.

"There are a lot of groups who quite like the ideas that Herr Hitler once espoused," Broadsword said, and I want to slap him for saying *espoused*. It's his subtle way of telling people that their countrymen are dickheads. It's worse when he's right.

"So, he feels more at home in America," I muse and Broadsword's steely grey eyes lock onto me.

"Possibly more than that. They've welcomed him with open arms. AutoGold brought with it job opportunities in Nevada and around the other states nearby where he has opened up his factories. Then, of course, he started his own Formula 1 team," and he pauses to look at me. I wish I had the poker face with him to remain calm, but my eyes light up because I *adore* Formula 1 racing.

I once knew someone who suggested that I could possibly get off just by the noise of the engines and the throbbing through my body. He was more accurate than I would ever admit to. And that was where I really knew him from. I was well aware of AutoGold as a company that ran cars in the F1, but while I knew all about their racers and cars, I didn't really know that Júrgen von Golde was the CEO. Or maybe I did hear that at some point in the past. Whatever, the point was it only just resurfaced in my brain today.

"So, I guess that still makes me wonder what all this has to do with me. Us," I quickly correct myself, though in fairness he summoned me, so I assume it must have something to do with me in the long run.

"Our friends in the US have been keeping an eye on Mr von Golde for a little while now. The CIA were concerned about him when he was a Firestarter in Germany, but when he moved to America, the other law enforcement divisions there took an interest as well. The CIA, of course, took a step back as it was outside the scope of their control. But that being said," and with that, Broadsword sat back in his chair, presumably for dramatic effect. "With that being said, they're very concerned that he might have decided to pursue his dreams of empire there."

"And?"

"Drink?" Broadsword suddenly said, and I frowned a little. He was a good boss, but he was prone to the dramatic, though when it happened it was usually because he was concerned about something. He strolled away from the vista behind his desk and headed to a cabinet at one side of the room, giving me the complete view. Broadsword's office is in Singapore, which is a country he's tremendously fond of. It's in the middle of Orchard St, at the top of one of the high rises that many wonder what actually takes place there. There are large windows behind his desk, allowing a view of the city and in particularly the Marina Bay hotel and Singapore Bay, but often, like today, the view is obscured by rain.

At the cabinet he retrieved two bottles of Icelandic Glacial water. He didn't particularly indulge in alcohol, and to make up for this, he had ridiculously expensive water sitting in his faux drinks' cabinet. It did suit the rest of the office, which was modern, pine and white. He came over to me and handed me a bottle, which I opened and drank from immediately – just because I prefer something with a bit more kick doesn't mean I'm stupid enough not to accept expensive gifts. And water is never something you should turn your back on.

"The US have tried to reach out to Germany to get some help with their intelligence but as you may be aware, recently they haven't exactly made a lot of friends with their behaviours. As such there was a polite, but negative response. We then got contacted for help, and were able to do so. Our resources suggest that von Golde has a desire to indeed raise something of a fascist army. The psychologists and analysts think it's the sort of thing a man like him would do." Broadsword opened his water and took a slug, before heading back to behind his desk. I was still a little curious about what was going on, but by now I had the impression that it was something a little more interesting than I first guessed. The question was, though, how did that affect me? After all, I still hadn't been totally forgiven for the McCabe killing, and while I knew I was one of Broadsword's favourites, I was also acutely aware he had taken a shine to Dana Spectra, and given that Dana had feelings for McCabe, and given she was very upset that I had put a bullet between McCabe's eyes, I sometimes wondered if my punishment was also from Dana.

And I mean, I get it. If I'm really honest, now I'm not sure exactly why I killed her. In my report I made it clear that I thought McCabe was working for her gun running father and was a clear and present danger, but the truth is, looking back, I'm not sure that was the case anymore.

But it definitely wasn't out of jealousy. I'd fucked Dana by that point. I didn't give a shit that she was fucking McCabe.

When I vocalised the idea it might have been a personality clash, the psych assigned to debrief me looked at me with the kind of look that said "I'm not judging you, but I'm well aware you're a psychopath."

Fuck, it annoyed me that the incident rankled with me. I'd killed a few people before in my life. I was certain of what I had done then, and it shat me that I was uncertain now.

Broadsword had begun speaking again and I cursed myself a little that I'd let myself get lost in my thoughts. I went to take another sip but was surprised to find I'd already finished.

"I thought it was something we could achieve," Broadsword was saying, and he had the smile on his face that suggested I wouldn't like what he wanted me to do.

"Sorry?" I asked, hoping he would just repeat himself.

"You wouldn't mind running the operation, would you? I thought it was something we could achieve."

"Oh, uh, well, yeah," I shrugged.

"Did you just ignore me?"

"No, not as..." I grimaced slightly. "Sorry, I got distracted. The rain," I lied pointing out the window and Broadsword turned to see that – thank god – the rain had increased.

"Oh, I think it's going to be like that all week. Anyway, I'll repeat myself, for those that found the inclement weather more interesting than my dulcet tones." Big words again, chosen to highlight his annoyance. I waved my hand, and gave him a look. "The CIA are keen to prevent him from assembling any of the fascist-slash-neo-Nazi groups that are popping up all over the place in your country into some sort of force. But they think that's exactly what's going to happen, so we've been asked to pop in and take a look around."

"Us?"

"Downplay intelligence service rivalry, allow the CIA to know what's going on with something outside their jurisdiction, and keep Germany in the loop without looking as though they are trying to." Broadsword shrugged. "I understand. Would be much easier if they could just agree to talk to each other, but it's like a group of teens who aren't talking and keep asking someone to pass on a message." I could relate to that.

"So, you want me to run it?"

"Exactly." He beamed at me.

"And what, send Jazmin or someone into the wild, wild west to dig around," but at this he shook his head.

"No, no," he continued shaking. "No, it would be better if we send in an American, definitely. The information supplied to us about his company suggest that everyone that works there is American, so it definitely has to be one of the gang."

"Wait, so I get to go in?" I felt my heart leap a little. I had assumed that the plan was I would be running Ops from the control centre with the analysts, but suddenly it seemed like I was being asked to actually go back into the game. Had I been forgiven?

"Well, let's just say you're got your wheels back but you're still on a leash," grinned Broadsword, and I realised I had accidentally spoken my thoughts out loud.

"I can live with that," I said, and I think I was grinning back at my boss. The thought of going back into field was too good to be true. I hadn't realised how much I hated being cooped up at a desk, and when a recent operation had let me get out to make use of my skills, it was like I'd gone vegetarian and briefly been asked to have a steak. The flavour and taste came back so easily that it was hard to go back to doing the right thing.

Now it looked as though the diet was off.

LAP FOUR

My transfer to Interpol came after working as an FBI agent for a time. It was standard work, nothing too taxing, but I was effective and efficient and though I wasn't looking at becoming Assistant Director any time soon, Special Agent-in-Charge was the position I held before Interpol had come a-knocking. Initially it was just a quick job, working together, "would you mind being our contact over there?" sort of thing, but I impressed someone within Interpol and was invited to join them on a more permanent basis. The man that approached me was codenamed Katana (I have no idea where they came up with their codenames, but for some reason they revolved around weapons) and when I asked what exactly they wanted me to do, he said it was a slightly more exciting and interesting job opportunity than what I was presently doing.

Funnily enough it had been a guy that convinced me to make the change – my husband, no less. Dating an FBI Agent had been a fun ride, and marrying one was just as good. But when I became the SAC, suddenly our marriage got a little tougher as I didn't have the time to be the good wife all the time. We mostly had things working, but when he was diagnosed with terminal cancer, things got more complicated. I actually made more time to be with him, but he got angrier and nastier and then walked out of our marriage. I didn't know what to do from there, because ultimately everyone we had been friends with stopped calling me. Despite everything he had done (and by "he had done" I mean "he had become a total and utter prick") the terminal cancer card was an easy one to play.

One night I came home and found him on my couch, passed out from drink. I don't know how he got in or why he had decided to come back to our marital home, but when I walked in and started to remove my gear, including my Glock G17M, for a moment I held that piece in my hand and wondered whether it would be worth putting a bullet into the head of my worthless husband, who was sadly not quite my ex-husband. It would save money, it would save time, and it would put him out of his misery as well, because he was a very unhappy man.

I didn't kill him, but the following day during the joint Interpol operation, I decided to join my team, and it was surprisingly easy to put down the bad guy that day. I felt no remorse, and in fact was slightly annoyed with myself that I hadn't decided to pull the trigger a few minutes earlier and saved us all a lot of time. Getting home the following night, hubby was back on the couch, this time awake, drunk and abusive. It was the first time he ever slapped me, and I held back because I couldn't bring myself to hit someone who was dying.

When Katana made the offer, I accepted immediately. He was in the middle of telling me that I would have to leave the US, but I didn't care. I just wanted to leave my house, my home, my country and my fucked-up life. When Katana explained that I would actually be acting as a Special Response Operative, which was slightly more complicated than the standard Interpol agent, again I blithely said yes. I didn't care. When he said it might require killing in cold blood, my "no problem" was as cool as ice. I wasn't sure if I had lost respect for human life, but I had certainly lost a degree of interest in it.

My patriotism didn't ever actually wane, though. I still think the US is the greatest country on the planet. I know that we have had some shit-house Presidents, but no country can say they've had a perfect run of world leaders. Sure, we've made some questionable choices in regards to looking after the country and its people, and we have a fairly segregated view of foreigners and even women. The latter I was always opposed to, but I was perhaps a little shocked to discover that I had a streak of racism running through me. Six months working around the world with various foreigners can cure you of that very quickly. I stopped making jokes about black people the night after I fucked an Englishman named Joe, whose smile lit up the dark when we shagged. It felt strange and uncomfortable, and I realised that I didn't want to be that person. My conservative views were challenged even more when I had to fuck a Russian woman I met to get information out of her. I wouldn't say I was a card-carrying rainbow warrior, but I certainly wouldn't be welcomed at family reunions if I admitted that Anya had made me feel something that my ex-husband certainly never did. I wish the more hard-line part of the US conservative movement could budge on those particular scores, and maybe open their eyes to what is going on around them, because at the moment they weren't being constructive in trying to defend the constitution. And we need people to defend it.

Connections being everything, when I arrived in the US, I quickly called some old friends in the Bureau to ask them a few questions about where might be a good place to start in my investigations. Turns out, the agent in charge of the AutoGold investigation was an old friend, Steven Miller. Steven was incredibly keen to help me, and I guessed pretty quickly that he had been caught in the middle of a turf war with the CIA and NSA over who exactly should be investigating AutoGold.

"You know me, Jus," he drawled in his Kentucky accent. "I don't give a shit who gets the gold star, I just want to put the bad guys away. So, you wanna go in and do some cleaning, by all fucking means go. If it keeps the others off my back, you're my hero."

"Cool," I drawled back, and he laughed as he always did when I gave my weak impression of his voice. "But where do I start,

Steve?"

"Nevada," he replied, very promptly. "You ever been?"

"Only to Vegas," I shrugged.

"That's where you're going. There's an AutoGold factory out there, making people very happy."

"Oh yeah, my boss mentioned it."

"Thing is, von Golde also has his own F1 track built. It's a massive stretch of land, but he's laid a track down and that's where his cars practice."

"Well, now, that's all you had to say," I replied, happy at the success of my main contact.

"I'll have a package sent down to you with a bit of tech that can help, and if you like we can be your support," Steve offered, but I shook my head (even though he couldn't possibly have seen me do it).

"Nah, it's not necessary, Steve. I have contact with my Interpol Ops, but I'll make sure we link you in so we can all communicate together, yeah?"

"Is that just to shut me up?"

"No," I reassured him. "Promise. You'll definitely be in on every step of the operation. I'm not going to throw you under the bus."

"I appreciate it," Steve replied, and I could hear the genuine relief in his voice. "This is an important one, Jus. We need to make sure this guy doesn't do what he wants to. You know how we normally deal with other agencies. Well, this time the AD said we could give the CIA exactly what they wanted, just as long as the job was done. If that doesn't convince you of how important what is going on is, well…" He let the sentence hang in the air, and that was fine. I got the point he was making perfectly. When the FBI and CIA are in bed together, you know the bad guy's really bad.

A quick trip to Nevada, and it was time to find out a little more about AutoGold.

Cue my brief meeting with the wolfish Ted Hawley, but I was curious about the black chick that had been less than welcome by the rest of her team. Strolling across the grounds to where she was, I could feel the eyes on my ass, but that was fine. I had learnt a long time ago that when people are looking at your tits and ass, they ain't looking at where your hands are, so disabling your opponents – or just shooting them in the head – became a whole lot easier in a bikini.

Speaking of bikinis, as I walk into the workshop, I notice, hanging on the wall, a poster of a certain Australian model decked out in a white bikini, her familiar smirk looking at me as if to say "caught ya!" I feel a little unsettled as I always do when Dana Spectra is concerned, and wonder if her poster was deliberately there to get on my tits. I'm clearly lingering on the poster for too long because a little voice in my ear says: *not that you're obsessed.*

"Shut the fuck up," I mutter under my breath and there is more than one laugh in the background. Say that your support team are a bunch of pricks without saying they're a bunch of pricks.

I look around the room, and take in the black girl. She's in her mid-twenties, I guess, with long dark hair and a permanent scowl on her face. I wonder briefly if that is her resting face, or if she has something to scowl at, but it's hard to tell.

"Well?"

"Errr…no?"

"What the fuck does that mean?"

"Nothing. She's not coming up on any facial recognition, she's

99

not…we're drawing a total blank on her."

"Steve?"

++ We've never been able to work out who she is exactly. We think she might be a specialist brought in from somewhere, but there's no record of her entering the country, but at the same time we can't find a match for her in any system. ++

"That doesn't make sense."

++ Agreed. She should turn up on a database somewhere, but we can't even find a school record of her. ++

Interesting. A second phantom at AutoGold. Definitely someone worth investigating, though, and as I take a step forward, a man blocks my way.

"Are you alright? Can I help you?" His accent is curiously more Brooklyn than Nevada. He has one of those voices that you just know would bellow out "Hey, I'm walkin' here!" if given half a chance. This time he just stays his ground.

He isn't particularly huge, either, just a slight sort of guy, and he has a pair of rimless glasses on, which, combined with the several-day old growth, gives him a slightly unkempt appearance (which is not particularly hard given that he is dressed, like everyone else around here, in blue overalls with a gold streak running through them).

"I was just," I don't finish and instead point at the woman across the room. He turns around and squints before turning back to me.

"Why are you here to see Ariel?"

++Ariel?++

"Ariel?"

"Old friends," I shrug. "From uni," I add, trying to make a leap that would be believable.

"You and her?" the mechanic says incredulously.

"Yeah, why's that so fucking hard to believe?" I retort, and bite my tongue. Honestly, I can do tactful, I can.

Please don't let Broadsword be listening in.

"Oh, you obviously are then," he raises his eyebrows exasperated, and throws his hands in the air, clearly unable to deal with life. Genuinely I have no idea what has changed his mind, but it doesn't matter.

I make my way across the garage, the smell of the oil getting a little stronger as I do, and I notice that there are more and more stains on the floor as well. Clearly this part of the complex is in frequent use, and I suddenly realise that each of AutoGold's cars possibly have their own garage and set of mechanics.

"Hey," I say amiably, and Ariel turns to me, her eyebrows narrowing as she does.

"Who the fuck are you?" she barks, and I realise *that* was what had caused the mechanic to think we were associated. Both rude as fuck, clearly.

"Kelly," I smile, relaxed. I wasn't inviting, because that wouldn't work on this bitch. She was already cautious, her body like a big cat that had heard the sounds of hunters nearby. She was careful but worried that someone was out to get her.

Which might very well have been true.

"I'm just taking a wander around."

"You have friends in high places, Kelly?" Ariel says, almost spitting the words out.

"Well, I have an uncle that works in head office," I respond, and Ariel looks at me like I am poison.

"What do you want from me?" she barks, and I shrug again.

"Just looking for a bit of girl talk," I say. "There're a lot of guys around here who are very nice, but it would be nice to talk to someone who wasn't always looking at my cleavage."

"You're not exactly making it easy to miss, are you?" Ariel says pointedly, but I notice that her demeanour had softened a little.

"Oh, come on," I laugh, and it was probably the most genuine laugh I had all day. "You don't want to wear this all the time in this weather?" There was certainly a lot of truth to that statement. Las Vegas in August was abominably hot, and wearing the bikini did actually make me feel a hell of a lot cooler than if I had been wearing the blue overalls that all these worker bees were wearing. Ariel looks at me, and I can see I was breaking down the barrier, especially with this new topic. She reaches up and unzips her overalls, pulling it down to her crotch, whereupon she pulls it apart to reveal the bright yellow bikini underneath.

"I feel ya, girl," she says and this time it's accompanied by a grin. "So go on," she continues as she zips the suit up again. "What brings you to Vegas?"

"The cars," I answer truthfully. "I'm curious about them. I love F1 racing, always have. So, I thought, since my uncle has friends in high places, maybe he might be able to arrange for me to see the other side of the field."

"I get that," Ariel nods. She sticks her hand out, then pauses and wipes it on her overalls before thrusting it forward again. "Ariel Lang."

"I'm still not getting an Ariel Lang."

++ *I'm running it through all the databases I can, but we're not getting anything back here either. She can't possibly be working for AutoGold and not have a licence can she?* ++

"She can't possibly have not gone to school, can she?"

I click my tongue in annoyance at this conversation going on while I shake hands with Ariel, and both Steve and Niamh, the primary Interpol Ops voice, go silent.

"Kelly Court," I say. "What do you do around here?"

"Not a lot," Lang replies. "I don't really fit in."

"It's a bit of a boy's club," I nod, but she raises an eyebrow.

"Oh, you'll fit in perfectly, babe. Whitey don't like the darkness down here," she says, and the scowl returns. For a moment, my mind wonders if she has been working here and getting harassed from the day she started. I never knew quite how bad racism could be, usually because I wasn't ever going to be on the receiving end, but when I had been digging through social media sites, I had once stumbled on a white supremacist message board which had sent shivers down my spine. The pure hatred made me wonder how they managed to make it through the day.

How their targets made it through the day.

I want to ask her how bad it has been, or even simply what she's going through, but again there's that distrust. She doesn't trust me because she sees me as privileged, and I guiltily realise I probably am compared to her. I'm not going to make any headway here, so this is a pointless exercise.

"I'mma go," I say, and Lang looks at me with a flash of guilt. "I didn't mean..." I trail off, because I genuinely don't know how to approach her. I will have to talk to the analysts and see if they can suggest a way in, hoping that I haven't blown it.

"Hey, look," she suddenly says. "I'm sorry. I...You seem cool."

"Thanks," I say. "If you ever want to chat about cars, I'm keen," I add. "But you're busy and all."

"You're staying at a hotel? In Vegas?" Ariel asks.

"Yeah," I nod. "The Excalibur."

"Oh, that's cool. Look, There's a thing tonight, you might be interested in going to. I wasn't planning on going, but maybe if I had someone to talk to, it might be worthwhile. You want me to come get you and have dinner, then we can head to the thing?"

"What's a thing?"

++ I'm not entirely sure what the thing is, but there's always plenty of stuff going on in Vegas. I'm guessing a party of some sorts. ++

"Cool," I grin. "I like the idea of a thing." She laughs and it's a strange sort of bark, which is so funny it actually makes me chuckle.

"Cool. I'll meet you in the lobby around five?"

"I'll be there." I turn to walk away, but then turn back again. "What should I wear? Or is this enough?" This gives me the opportunity to flash my flesh, and manages to get the scowl off Ariel's face.

"Ah, no, you might wanna try something a little more elegant-party."

"A lot more elegant-party," a voice behind me snaps, and I turn to see the unkempt man.

"Say hello to Fabio," Lang drawls and for a moment the juxtaposition is so ridiculous I laugh, which does not impress Fabio at all.

"Sorry, it's just…Fabio?" I ask, and the incredulity in my voice is blindingly obvious.

"Oh, sorry," Fabio snaps, "Sorry my family name doesn't suit your misconception of the world around you. Sorry that you think it's easier to laugh at the little people that work for you and rich bitch friends."

Get outta the way! I'm walkin' here!

His diatribe is making Ariel laugh, but I manage to bring a semblance of control back to myself and I even look a little chastened, though I'm clearly not feeling that way at all.

"Sorry," I mumble, and then quickly exit.

It's not helped by the laughter coming through my earbuds either.

LAP FIVE

The Excalibur is pretty nice, to be honest. It's a hotel that looks like it has an old-fashioned castle built in the middle of it, the white towers topped by red, blue and yellow peaks that light up at night. That part of the hotel is actually the casino, while the four towers that rise to the sky around it is the hotel section. There are two royal towers and two resort towers. Rather thoughtfully I've been booked a Royal Superior King Room, which, aside from coming with a very large and very comfortable King-sized bed, more importantly comes with a deep soak tub, and that is pretty much the reason I never want to leave the room.

After the trip to AutoGold's little complex in the middle of nowhere, I returned to my room and went straight to my tub, stripping off everything I own to get into the tub and just enjoy the soak. You can't see the tv, or even out the window, which is sort of annoying, but as I lean back and close my eyes I don't really care too much.

Steven, on the other hand, cares a great deal, and he's in my chair, which he's dragged across the room, so he can talk to me. I'm not remotely bothered that I'm totally naked in the tub. I've known Steven for a very long time, and though once I would happily have fucked him, after attending his wedding it became a lot harder to destroy his relationship.

I mean, that and the fact his partner's name is Michael. Which, if I'm honest, means it's not totally my good conscience that stopped us fucking.

"Here's the thing," Steve says, and I hear him, even though my brain is telling me in no uncertain terms that a sleep would be really nice about now. "The whole formula one thing makes a lot of sense, right? Because of Vegas, right?"

"Because Vegas is racing now," I say.

"Exactly. Exactly." He stuffs his hands in his pockets as he gets up, but then sits down again and runs them through his thinning hair. He has a luscious beard, but after being apart for some time, I've noticed that the hair on top is not as thick as it used to be. It's going grey as well, and he looks a little more stressed. This, I might add, proves my point about not becoming an Assistant Director at the FBI. It will destroy your looks.

"But how does that tie in with what the CIA are worried about?"

It's a good question, and I'm not sure yet how to answer it. Because, obviously, maybe it doesn't. In fact, that small fact has been nagging at me slightly.

"You were the one who suggested I start here," I point

out, without moving any part of my body whatsoever. I'm quite enjoying the feel of the water against my body. It's cathartic. Helps me think. I need to do this more often, I decide.

"Because do you know how many people work at AutoGold and are active on the white supremacy websites?"

"I can take a guess," I reply, remembering how people looked at Ariel Lang. "If you were going to build a racist, fascist army, this would supply a fair amount of talent."

"Exactly. Exactly!" I forgot he had a habit of doing that. It's slightly annoying and I hope he doesn't do it again. That would make me very aggressive.

"Look," I say very calmly, because I am *so* calm at this point not even a joint would have made me more mellow. "Perhaps this *thing* tonight that Lang wants to take me to is going to be somewhat useful."

"I'm worried about the thing," Steve mutters, but I go out of my way to wave my hand and send the worry on its way.

"It's nothing to worry about," I reply. "Let's be honest, they aren't going to indulge a black woman in their little neo-Nazi party, are they? Whatever is going on tonight will be very straightforward, and I shall look amazing, and then...well, something will happen."

I don't have to open my eyes to know what Steven is doing. Even when we worked together, the pose with his head tilted and his hands on his hips was practiced. He was doing it now; I could sense it. The thing was, it was his super concerned pose.

"Do you want to know what worries me, Jus?" he asks, and I sigh a little and open my eyes for him. He's standing as I predicted, but the concern is clear.

"Shoot."

"One," he ticks off a finger, "we don't know what Ariel Lang does at AutoGold. She was annoyingly vague, so we have no idea exactly what her job is there. In fact, two." Another finger. "We don't even know who this woman is. No one, not us, not you, not the CIA, the NSA, the fucking cops…no one has a record of this woman. So, either she has completely changed her identity, and god knows why she would do that, but it's definitely not for a good cause, *or* she's not American. She's been smuggled in from some country, totally under the radar, and why would that happen? Why would someone be brought into the US in such a way? She's not a fucking refugee jumping the border." He looks at me, and the truth is, he's right. Before I can even credit him that, he's off again, checking off another finger. "Also, does it not bother you that the CIA are being strangely cooperative? But at the same time, remarkably useless?"

"If they've got someone on the inside, that someone will know who I am," I reply.

"Jus, I know you have a cavalier attitude towards life and death, and fine, you know. That's cool, that's you. But I can't do that. I can't send you somewhere that I know will result in a bullet in your head. I just can't do that. I want to know what we're going into."

"Well, my friend, you may want that, but it ain't happening." I shrug, and stand up, the water cascading down my absolutely fine figure, but sadly totally wasted on a man who won't take his eyes off my face. "We have to play the cards we've been dealt, and this time we've been dealt a doozy. If we're going to get to Jurgen von Golde and find out what's going on, Ariel Lang is our best entry point, and she's making it easy. I agree about the unknowns, but what do we do? Pull out and sit around waiting to see what happens?"

"Do you think von Golde will be at the *thing*?" Steven looks at me, as though maybe he can see a vague lifeline.

"Well, is he in Vegas?"

"We're not certain," he admits. "He's not always easy to keep track of, and our resources don't extend to keeping a full-time physical check on every person we need to know about. Unfortunately, the Phantom tends not to use social media too much, so there's no obvious sign here either."

"We don't know where he is?"

"No." Steve's head shaking is one of the saddest things I've seen and I can't help but giggle a little at how forlorn he looks. He looks a little offended, but I grin at him, as I wrap the towel around me.

"It'll be fine. You'll be in close contact; everything will be OK. Have a little faith, babe. Now, if you're not going to take advantage of the fucking amazing bitch standing before you, get out of my room. I have a hot date," I wink at him and he smiles, shaking his head.

We have an understanding.

LAP SIX

Because I work for Interpol, I'm pretty poor really. I mean, I have a nice wage, and I enjoy my life because there's no one else left to please, but after my little foray into the world of high-class modelling, I realised there are a ton of things out there that women like me will never be able to afford. I had noticed recently that Dana Spectra had suddenly become a viral sensation over a cat, but that meant she was wearing more and more expensive clothing, while I, on the other hand, no longer being paid to be an undercover fashion model, had to go back to wearing fairly basic items. As such, while I made sure to put on my Dolls Kill "Spoiled but not rotten" lace Ted (it's extremely cute, and should I need to rely on being cute at some point this will definitely save me), the dress I put on was a no-name solid cowl neck slit midi dress in teal, which doesn't quite match the Ted, but I can pull it off.

I have to admit that my shoes – Steve Madden vala pumps – and my Margot Elene "Awaken Within" perfume are my extravagant spends. The dress sits nicely, but the slit allows my legs to be seen, and that means the dress is secondary to me. My older sister, Cassie, once said to me that women are looking at your shoes, and men are easily distracted by perfume and flesh. That's where you need to spend your money, Jus. I took that to heart, and as I strolled out of the elevator and into the hotel lobby, I noticed the attention I was receiving, which suited me just fine.

The Excalibur is designed to look a little like a castle, with the various trappings of faux turrets and their crenelations, but the gold and amber lighting somewhat take away from the conceit. I'm never quite sure how I feel about Las Vegas. On the one hand it really is the city of sin. With its neon-soaked buildings and ridiculously over the top architecture, it's got to be a place built solely for tourists.

Except, there are actual people here, and while the tourists come and spend their money on overpriced concert tickets to see artists who have found the genuinely best way of getting a good pay packet, or going on rides that can be found everywhere, there are a group of people addicted to gambling, traipsing in every day like zombies in the desperate hope they might win the fortune that will get them out Vegas. The irony being, of course, they could probably take the money, get a Greyhound, and get the fuck out of dodge.

I'm not sure I have the time for idiots who have no self-respect, and there's a part of me that would like to take a few of them out and give them a good slap. But that's not what I'm paid for. No doubt God will sort that out for them at some later point.

110

The lobby is part of an open plan in the Excalibur that is inherently designed to get tourists to waste their money as quickly as possible. Come down to the left to check in. To the right, why not get a drink and play some poker machines?

I have to admit to being a little surprised to find my date waiting for me. She's prompt and she's in the lobby which is actually where to be if you haven't bothered to exchange numbers. She's looking rather stunning in a gold high neck mini dress. Her shoes are a very sweet silver strappy heels pair, and that gives her calves some impressive definition. It's not my intention to fuck her, but I have to admit I won't be hugely devastated if I'm required to.

"Hey," she waves and I stroll on over, my clutch swinging freely from my shoulder. "You look great," she adds.

"Thanks," I say. "I wasn't sure what to wear given that I didn't know where we'd be going, so…"

"I know, I know," she smiles pleasantly. "You'll not be disappointed, I promise." We pause for a moment and there's the awkwardness of two people who don't really know each other, and are about to spend time together. That blind first date thing, which truthfully, I can't stand. It grates and I have to break the ice as quickly as possible before I get more and more uncomfortable and blurt out something which will either be immensely embarrassing, or worse, break my cover. "Did you want to get something to eat before we head to our *thing*? It won't be a proper dinner, so I'm not sure what the food will be. It might be better to eat before we get there."

Thank God she spoke, I reflect.

"Sure," and I look around the Excalibur. There are a few restaurants here, all themed with the King Arthur vibe, but I notice Ariel Lang is looking a little awkward. "We don't have to stay here," I add.

"Oh, it's just," she pauses and looks more uncomfortable than she did before. "See, I'm not super rich," and I stifle a giggle, suddenly realising what the problem is.

"That's cool, we don't have to eat here. Shit, I'm happy for a burger and fries to be honest," and she genuinely smiles at this.

"Well, in that case, I know exactly where we can go!"

Strolling around Las Vegas can be either ridiculously easy, or quite complicated. Wanna stroll down the strip at night? Pick a side and start walking. Couldn't be simpler. There're escalators that can take you over roads, or links between casinos, huge sidewalks. Genuinely simple as. However, if you want to cross over Tropicana Ave, or worse, the Las Vegas Freeway, well…good luck. We weren't that far from an In-N-Out Burger's, but it would require us to cross both the aforementioned roads, and that was not going to be easy. As such, we take a stroll from the Excalibur, along Excalibur Way, until we get to Frank Sinatra Drive, and from there, we hail a taxi. It's a short journey, but the driver knows how to get there and that relives both our stresses.

If I'm honest, In-n-Out Burger isn't a place I usually frequent. It's pretty much just McDonald's – not that either of them is particularly bad or good. They are just burger joints, performing a service, getting food to customers and then moving onto the next customer. It doesn't matter where in the world you are, that's how they function, and there's something reassuring about that. In-n-Out is just that simple and when we get there, I order a cheeseburger combo. Ariel does the same and we are able to find a table, which works nicely. I'm conscious of the fact that I'm actually dressed up nicely and took the opportunity to do my makeup, so I'm careful not to squeeze mayo onto my dress. What a fucking waste of time that would be.

"So, what do you do?" I ask, between a mouthful of burger. "You seemed to be spending a bit more time on the computer than most of the mechanics, but obviously you're in the garage, so what's the go?"

"Research and development," she replies, also between bites. "I don't know if you know much about F1 cars, but for the most part we're to abide by fairly strict rules. There isn't a lot of change you can make, but there are some components we're allowed to replace, and AutoGold is looking at power at the moment. My job is to see if I can…" she pauses and then smiles. "Basically, to see if I can make the car go faster. I won't bore you with the specifics. I mean, unless you're desperately keen to know."

"Nah," I shake my head. "I'm good. You make the vroom vroom go faster. Got it," I give her a thumbs up and she laughs. The funny thing is, as she's talking, and without the anger, her voice has become more unique to her, and while I thought her accent was fairly straight forward, now I'm thinking there's something else to it. It's like she's affecting an American accent. Or even that she's been affecting one for so long, she has developed it. But there's a word, every so often, that just doesn't seem quite right. I'm almost convinced she's definitely not American. Not originally anyway. Smuggled into the country, or she entered the country and then… changed her face? I mean, it's not hard. Plastic surgery is easy enough to get done. I can't see any obvious signs, but that doesn't necessarily mean anything.

It's annoying that I can't work her out. More so because it means I definitely can't trust her. Nice and friendly she may seem, but she's not who she says she is and people only lie when they don't want you to know the truth.

"So, does Fabio work in the same area?"

"Yeah, he's technically my boss. Sort of. But you met him. You can't really take him seriously. So, he does his thing, I do mine, and we just report to Ted and that's the end of it." She takes another bite of her burger and reacts quickly when something squirts out, avoiding getting it on her dress.

"That was close," I chuckle, and she laughs as well. "So come on, where are we going next?"

"I'll call a cab," she says, getting out her phone and again I'm wondering what we're doing and where we're going. I'm not feeling unsafe, but I'm the kind of girl who likes to walk into a room and know exactly where she's going to walk out. This lack of control doesn't do well for me, but I don't have much of a choice. For some reason Lang thinks that she's doing me a favour, so I suppose I'll have to make the most of that.

LAP SEVEN

Happily, there's only so many secrets you can hide before you pull up in front of a giant hotel in Las Vegas that has a massive sign at the top screaming out "Mandalay Bay" to everyone in the city. At the south end of the Las Vegas strip (not too far from the Excalibur as it happens), the 43 story Mandalay Bay is a resort and casino (what a surprise), which is fucking expensive, of course. There's a Four Seasons hotel, a House of Blues club, Shark Reef aquatic attraction, and perhaps most famously it's where a guy killed 60 people at a music festival with no less than 24 guns and 1000 rounds of ammo. He killed himself, but that was small compensation for having already done that much damage. I mean, I'm a huge fan of the second amendment, but fuck me if something like that doesn't suggest we keep a closer eye on people with guns.

The Bay has a sort of south seas motif. Instead of the gold, deep reds and battlements of the Excalibur, there's gold, deep reds and palm trees. Not that I'm cynical but sometimes even the shine of Las Vegas can wear thin. The people are the same, split into the gullible tourists seeking entertainment, and the desperate locals trying to escape. I have to wonder why I'm so down on Vegas, or (I wonder, briefly perturbed by this surprising new insight into myself) am I down on the US? Jazmin Roan, one of my colleagues, recently implied that my loyalty wasn't to Interpol but to America, and while I might have secretly agreed that was the case, I'm beginning to wonder if I'm going native.

"Not here," Ariel says, and leads me away from the casino area towards the shopping complex. In fairness, the Mandalay is massive, and our taxi dropped us off at the rank, which meant we had to go past the Orchid Lounge, past the EyeCandy nightclub and then towards the "Shoppes at Mandalay Place". Whereas we had started in the gold and reds, by the time we got to the shops, things had become a more sedate white, the south sea vibe virtually non-existent (and I'm not counting the sea bird art above the escalator we had to go up).

As we ascend the escalator, on the right is the Minus 5 Degrees Ice Experience, which looks interesting. Massive furry coats and hoodies are on display near the counter, and the floor is littered with animal paw prints and snowflakes. The fact that Ariel continues to stride without even glancing at it makes me realise that we are definitely not going there, and I can't help but feel a little disappointed. The idea of going to an ice bar has always seemed a little appealing, and I'm rather desperate for a drink if I'm honest. As it turns out, though, Lang is not going to disappoint me.

She stops at the next entrance, which is much smaller on the outside, but bears the words 1923 Prohibition Bar, and I'm feeling a lot happier. I should have realised this was where we were heading, as there are a lot of people milling about trying to get in. The bouncers at the door – large bricks of men with no hair and a similar style in humour – inform most of them that they need to leave. It's a private function, I overhear one of them say and he looks as though he wants to put his fist through the face of the man demanding that he's on the guest list.

Ariel pushes past and squeezes between the lout and the thug.

"Lang," she says. "Ariel Lang. And guest," she adds, reaching back to grab my arm and drag me forward. The bouncer looks down at the iPad, and raises an eyebrow, before nodding and jabbing a thumb in the direction of the door behind him. There are two red velvet curtains pulled back on either side of the door, and we enter the room beyond, which is…well, it's exquisite.

When we enter, I have to admit I'm pretty impressed. The wall paper is just grey with red lines, but the floor is polished wood, and there are ornate mirrors hanging to the left, while to the right is the desk that presumably is usually reception. Tonight, there's no need, as the guests entering are able to use the entire space, it seems. There is a small sign on the reception desk which reads "AutoGold Celebration" and the final mystery is revealed.

"Everyone's going to be here tonight," Lang whispers to me, her gold dress looking more at home in the faux 1930's environs than my teal one. I, of course, don't recognise a single person, and unfortunately, I don't have my usual connection to my analysts to provide any information. If I'm going to find anything out, it looks as though I'll need to actually rely on my own personal skills.

Directly in front of us after we entered, is the State Room, which seems to be a room with a lot of couches and a pool table in the middle. There are a lot of men all smiling and laughing, and a lot of women who are considerably younger than the smiling, laughing men. Something tells me that this is not really a "bring your wife" do. Which does make me think that the women who are here fall into either one of two categories: paid escorts or extremely uncomfortable. The paid escorts are definitely doing the right thing, laughing appropriately, drinking a lot and politely moving hands away from their asses. I notice that one of the people playing pool is my old friend Ted Hawley. To his credit he is playing pool rather than sleazing onto the blonde beside him who is definitely lucky if she's out of her teens.

Lang clearly has no interest in going to the State Room as she has headed off to the right, a corridor which takes us down into what is definitely the bar. I am absolutely in agreement with this; Lang has considerably more taste than I gave her credit for.

The bar seems small, but I suspect that's because there are a lot of people standing around drinking, and also because the bar itself is a massive square wood panelled affair in the centre of the room. There are television screens hanging from the ceilings showing old black and white movies, while some sit on the walls at lower heights displaying fireplaces, and there are chairs clustered around so that the men can sit and smoke (literally sit and smoke; I'm almost bitter I don't anymore). I notice that a few people have glanced in my direction, which is nice to know because there are still a couple of paid ladies trying to earn their wages.

Perhaps what is most surprising is that the atmosphere is very jovial, to the extent that I overhear someone turn to Lang and offer to buy her a drink. Racism in the workplace, but we can be friends behind closed doors? Strange system.

I can't see Jűrgen von Golde anywhere, which is frustrating, and though I figure I'll probably have some nice liquor tonight, I get the feeling that this is possibly going to be a waste of time. Steven will be able to crow about this for a while.

"Can I buy you a drink?" someone says to me in a drawl that is definitely not southern. I turn and see a tall man with a very square jaw and the kind of eyes you want to get lost in.

"Hello," I purr, and I realise I've done this before I've even thought about it.

"You're not like the other girls here tonight," he says, gesturing around, and I can't work out if he's fishing or genuinely making conversation.

"In that I'm not twelve?" I reply sweetly and he laughs, a little embarrassed. Points for that.

"Well, I wasn't suggesting," he stammers a little, but I laugh.

"Drinks are good," I say, and he takes the hint, guiding me up to the bar. Curiously I notice that the people step aside from him and I wonder who he might be.

"Gatsby's Gin Fiz?" he asks, and I shake my head.

"Not a gin drinker," I reply. "I'll let you pick but steer clear of gin, if you please."

"Right, then Al Capone's Mule Kick," he smiles. "Two, please," he says to the bartender, and as he puts the money on the table, I notice that he turns away, satisfied that he's not interested in the change. It's a power move, but one that I have to admit works on me. There's something vaguely hot about a guy who doesn't give a shit about money. Though, in fairness, those guys usually have so much it genuinely doesn't affect them one way or the other, or they have nothing and are going into debt to impress.

"What's your name?"

"Kelly," I say, wondering if the conversation is going to get awkward. "And you?"

"Noel McNabb," he says, though he has a strange look on his face, as though he's surprised I didn't know. Which makes me wonder if I should have known. I got a little bit of a chance to peruse some important things to know about AutoGold before I went in, but I'd decided to rely on my own personal knowledge. Now I realised that while I could happily list off names and dates for companies like Red Bull and McLaren, AutoGold wasn't actually at the top of my fan list and I knew less about it than I thought.

Time for plan C then.

"Noel McNabb?" I reply innocently. "And what do you do at this little company?" He looks at me quizzically, but I think the word little has the desire effect and he smiles a broad grin.

"Oh, you're..." He pauses, shakes his head and raises an eyebrow. "You're too cool for school," he finishes, and the drinks arrive allowing him to get them and hand them out as he contemplates his strategy to finish this conversation. "Well, I'm just a simple rev head driver," he smiles, and I have to admit it's quite a smile. The truth is, his name and face are vaguely familiar, and I'm sure I've seen them somewhere before. Simple driver, though, suggest he's anything but, and I wonder if maybe this guy happens to be the big time.

"Have you won anything?" I ask innocently, my smile as coy as I can make it and this elicits a genuine laugh from him.

"Ah man, you are something else," he grins. "Well, a couple of things. I may have won a little something called the Formula One. Have you heard of that?"

"Oh, that sounds important," I say, and purse my lips, now on more solid ground. The bell is rung. Noel McNabb is one of the two drivers for AutoGold. In point of fact, McNabb has won an F1 before, but the team's other driver, Sandy Hamilton, is actually the more famous of the drivers for AutoGold, having raced many times and won three times, much to the surprise of the punters.

"Well, I like to think it is important," he says, continuing to smile, though it's a slightly smug smile, and I'm tempted to knock him off his perch, because I'm a bitch like that. As it transpires, however, I don't have to, because Sandy Hamilton himself strolls on over.

This guy, I can recognise on sight, and he has the vague air of an older brother to McNabb, who clearly shrinks before Hamilton. Hamilton is like McNabb, though dialled up slightly, and as such just a little wrong. His smile isn't smug, it's supercilious, and while he might be a bit buffer and a bit taller, there's also no denying the hair isn't quite as thick, and when he smiles, the crow's feet are pretty obvious. There's nothing on the forehead, which suggests the Botox is doing its job.

I like McNabb a bit, and if I was going to fuck someone, he would be the choice, but Hamilton is the one that will get me closer to von Golde. Looks like it's time for the little boys to go to bed.

"Well, well, well Nabbs, what do we have here?" Hamilton claps McNabb roughly on the shoulder, and it's clearly a little too rough as it makes the younger man stagger.

"I was just chatting to this young filly here," and even if I was tempted to call him out on the use of the word *filly*, I don't have a chance, because Hamilton is straight in.

"Well, now, does this young thing have a name?"

"Kelly Court," I lie sweetly, and when he grips my outstretched hand, the grip is like iron.

"Sorry," Hamilton smarms. "Big hands," he adds with a wink, and I want to vomit.

The question is, where do I go from here? The night has just started, and already I have two useful targets in my sight, but neither of them is the one I actually want. In addition to that I seem to have lost Ariel. I definitely need a plan.

"Would you both excuse me," I simper. "I need to go to the little girl's room."

"Oh sure," they both say, nodding enthusiastically. I briefly wonder what they think I'm doing, but I don't dwell. Men aren't worth that. As such I quickly meld into the crowd, looking for either Ariel or the toilet.

LAP EIGHT

I find the toilet first, and sneak inside to discover I'm not the only woman who's using it as an escape room. There are at least six girls already inside, two sitting on the bench, three of them on their phones texting, while one is looking in the mirror doing her makeup. All six look at me when I enter and their faces are nothing but guilt. I just shake my head.

"All good, I don't work for them. Just a guest," I say, and there's a slight look of relief on their faces, though they are still cautious. Clearly it's a them or us situation, and while I have taken the first steps, I'm not quite "us" yet.

"Hey, any of you girls got gum? Or mints? My breath stinks," I say, and all six of them smile quickly, digging through their purses. Nothing bonds like sisterhood, and after I take one of the mints shoved in my face, I lean against the wall and look at them.

"So, what's the go? You guys just here to get groped, or you gotta do more?" I ask, keeping my voice interested but definitely not judgey. It rings true.

"Maybe more," one of the girls says, glumly. She's quite stunning, a pale redhead with dark eyebrows that arch perfectly. "I didn't think it was going to be that kind of crowd, to be honest, but there's at least five guys out there who know exactly how thin my thong is."

"Be like me," says a voice, and out of one of the cubicles comes someone who is tiny, but undeniably perfect. She's short, slim, almost boyish, but her face is alive, her dark eyes sparkle and her red lipstick contrasts with her pale skin and jet-black hair. I suspect if she wasn't Asian, she would have been the first choice for most of those out there. "Oh, you can't," she continues, confirming

121

what I thought. "You too Yankee," she grins, and the girls playfully push her.

"Stick with me," the redhead says. "Come on, say that we're a team, and they can't have one without the other." The little Asian girl looks thoughtful and seems to almost consider it, but then sticks her tongue out. "Bitch," the redhead says without malice, but her eyes make it clear she's disappointed.

"Can I ask," I drawl, leaning up against the door, effectively stopping anyone from coming in, "are any of you in line to be with the big boss?" The all look at me blankly, clearly having no idea who the big boss is. That shouldn't surprise me, I suppose. They weren't experts in the car manufacturing business.

"How do we know?" the Asian girl asks, and it's a genuine question. I turn and lock the door to the toilets. The room is big enough to hold conference, with the wood panelled cubicles to the right and the sinks that the girls were congregating around on the left. I turn back and take them in.

"Here's the deal," I say, an idea starting to form in my head. "I need your help. I need to meet the big boss." They look at me puzzled, and perhaps a little distrustful. I'm definitely losing them. "The thing is," I say, and I lower my voice, conspiratorially, which gets the attention of all seven girls, who unconsciously lean in a little. "My uncle works on the board. And he's about to be kicked off. I don't know if you know this, but there's a slight racist element out there."

"I mean, yeah," one of the girls says – a brunette with two nose piercings. "It's not like Emma is getting much attention, and they specifically said no blacks. Those guys are not into anything that doesn't come vanilla."

"I don't care," Emma – the Asian girl – says, "but we know. This crowd is not nice."

"I think they only let her stay because they thought she might be underage," the redhead says, and my stomach turns slightly at that thought. I hope it's not true, but it's not something I have time to muse on for the moment.

"Well, this is the thing," I press forward with my advantage, "my uncle is pushing for diversity quotas in the business, but they're all totes against him. They want him fired. So, I figure I could maybe find the guy that runs this place, and maybe, do a bit of the old blackmail on him."

"You think he's married?" a blonde says, blinking large lashes at me with confusion on her face.

"Yes," I gush, at this point lacking the will to bring any honesty into this.

"So, you're going to fuck him?" asks the redhead.

"While a helpful friend who comes with me films the whole thing," I say with a smile. At this point, all seven faces light up.

"Well, obviously I'm in," Emma says. "But I don't think he'll show much interest in me."

"The thing is," I say, "he doesn't have to. You just need to find him, tell him you have a girl who is fascinated to meet him, and then drag me over."

We're interrupted by a banging on the door, and I realise we've been chatting for way too long, and the bathroom has been off limits for that entire time. I give the girls a pleading look, and the redhead speaks for them.

"We're on it, babe." She holds up a hand, and I'm obligated to deliver several high fives before I open the door, only to find Ariel Lang standing there.

"Where the fuck have you been?"

LAP NINE

Ariel is gushing about something but I can't pretend to be that interested. My mind is genuinely working overtime at this point, and I'm not sure if I've put something into operation that I can't control. Tracking down von Golde is becoming more difficult than I thought, and truthfully when we walked into the Prohibition Bar, I honestly thought I had struck gold...Golde...

Ignore that.

Ariel is looking at me expectantly and I turn to look at her and say "What?" hoping that she will just think that the general atmosphere has caused me not to hear what she's been saying.

"I think," she says, "that there might be a chance you and I could have some fun tonight!" I frown at this, not quite sure what she means. "You ran into Sandy and Noel, didn't you?" and I nod, faking an interested look. "I think they might be up for a bit of the good stuff. The thing is, I've sort of got a thing for Noel and I've been trying to impress him for a bit. Sandy doesn't bother me. I mean, he's not likely to touch me, is he?"

I don't think I want that elaborated on, because it's probably going to be something annoying, so I shrug and nod my agreement. Though I pause then, because I suddenly realise what I may have just done, and if I've accidentally hinted I will fuck dear old Sandy, then we have a serious problem. Ariel has led me around the bar to one of the monitors set against a wall that is showing a cosy fireplace. There are antique chairs scattered around, and Sandy and Noel are on either side, with a variety of people surrounding them, listening attentively. I can hear piano music for the first time, and guess that the entertainment has begun, but I can't make out exactly where the pianist. Sandy, however, doesn't care, and emits an enormous walrus bellow of a laugh which may have included him spraying his drink over the people nearest him.

I mean, I have, haven't I? I've unwittingly said that I'll help Ariel fuck Noel, by fucking Sandy. What a fucking disaster. There's no way I'm letting that guy near me.

I bet his back is as hairy as a fucking porcupine.

"Hey, hey! Come here," Sandy is bellowing, and I know it's at me because I really don't want it to be. "Come on, put on a smile," he continues. "You look really pretty when you do." For the first time I feel the Ruger SR9c that is holstered on the inside of my thigh. Normally I can't feel it, it just sits there barely making its presence known, but now, as I feel the urge to put a bullet in someone's head, I feel the holster wrapped around my upper thigh. I take a deep breath, however, and refrain from killing. The Ruger was essential for operations like this, small and light, it could tuck in without being obvious. My Nightwing Agent 2, on the other hand, would have been far too noticeable.

It did mean that I would have to be careful when people started getting grabby around me. If they were going to go for something, it would have to be the ass. Most guys preferred that anyway, and only the real assholes tried going between the legs. That said, Sandy was clearly a real asshole.

"I want to sit down," I say, waving at the lack of space around, and Sandy turns to the girl tucked in beside him and tells her to go and get some drinks.

"Something with some rum!" he shouts, and there's a holler of support. I suddenly wish I hadn't just walked away from my drink earlier. Speaking of which, I notice Noel is looking a little disappointed, but I'm not sure if that's because I've been forced to sit next to his superior. Ariel is hovering around behind Noel, but he doesn't seem to notice. I wonder how often the two come into contact and if Ariel's desire to get him into bed is just a pipe dream.

"So, I was thinking," Sandy says in a voice that I'm fairly certain he thinks is a seductive whisper, but is clearly heard by everyone around, despite the chatter and background music. "Maybe you and I should go and get a room. I mean, we are in a hotel after all. You ever stayed in the Mandalay?"

"Is your place not free?" I ask sweetly, and he looks at me blankly, before I put two and two together.

"I don't think that would be appropriate," he says, and even as he does, he's dropped his left arm down the side of the chair, because I realise now how obvious the wedding ring probably is.

"The thing is," I murmur, and he has to lean in to hear me, because the noise is growing steadily as cheering has broken out for reasons that I'm not entirely sure why, "I was hoping to meet with Mr von Golde." I leave the sentence hanging in the air, and he looks at me, his expression unreadable.

"Oh, he won't fuck you," Hamilton says. "He's not interested in that sort of thing. He might like to watch you and me do it, though. How's about that. He might even want to, ah...have a touch at some point."

"What?" because I genuinely can't quite believe my ears.

"Oh, come on darlin'," he grins and the smell of his breath is quite revolting. "Don't pretend we need to be all woke. You want to suck some dick, I got a dick that needs sucking, and we could easily put everything together."

"Would you like a drink?" I ask sweetly and he looks at me blankly for a moment. I notice he briefly looks around as well, presumably for the girl he sent to get drinks, but she obviously had the sense to be somewhere else.

"Well, yeah, actually," he says, and his eyes glint. I suddenly realise what makes him a good driver – a ridiculous amount of confidence. One girl has already disappeared never to return with his drinks, but he's absolutely confident it won't happen a second time. In fact, he may even think the first girl will return, and that's what gets him in that seat, ready for a brilliant drive; an absolute certainty he is going to win. I'm not sure whether I'm impressed or not.

"I'll get you something," I say, touching his leg. "With rum." He licks his lips and leans forward to whisper, "Maybe I should drink it off you when you get back." I smile, though I'm fairly certain it doesn't reach my eyes, and set off for the bar.

I make sure I make my way to the opposite side of the room tucked in the little space between the bar and the red curtains that hang against the wall. Truth to tell, I'm pretty over it. I'm not going to meet von Golde, that I'm pretty certain of, and more than that, I'm not getting anything useful out of the night. At this point I may as well just retire back to the Excalibur and go to bed.

"Oh, it's you," I hear someone say, as I rest my elbows on the bar. To my surprise, his hair a little tamer, Fabio is at the bar.

"Hey," I say, a little surprised at how I'm not entirely unhappy to see him.

"I see you over there trying to get into Hamilton's pants," Fabio says, and he looks disgusted.

"Not that it's your business," I reply tartly, "but he was trying to get into mine."

"Whatever," Fabio dismisses me, and taps at the bar. "Water please," he calls out.

"Don't go crazy," I say with a grin.

"Unlike you," he replies, "I have to work tomorrow. I have

things to do. Important things. We don't have an awful lot of time left, and I certainly can't afford to waste a day. If I didn't have to be here, I wouldn't."

"Time left?" I wonder.

"Before Washington," he says, and turns to me as though I'm an idiot.

"I know there's a race coming up in Washington," I say, raising an eyebrow that would normally kill. "But what has that got to do with you? You're not driving."

"Who do you think is coming up with the new power system?" he asks, fixing me in his sights like he's an eagle having just found a small rodent. "Lang? Some newcomer turns up and thinks that she can develop something better than what I did? I will be the one to come up with the advancements, thank you very much. I'm the one who will improve on the earlier design, which was done by me. Not some rando from out of the country."

A rando from out of the country? I wonder what makes him describe Lang like that. I mean, presumably he knows that she is, but how, why? The mystery of Ariel Lang continues to get deeper and deeper.

However, the fact that they have a deadline...the fact that it needs to be done before Washington is also interesting. Washington's acquiring of a street race is relatively new, but it's been known about for long enough to have done the work on the cars. Why leave it so late?

"I could sort her out for good, you know," Fabio says, and I wonder if maybe he changed his mind and had something stronger that water earlier on.

"What are you talking about?"

"Lang. I could have her disposed of, and no one would

care you know. You know who controls our security? I mean, they have a proper name and all that, but you know who it really is, don't you?"

"Please tell me," I mutter, deciding it's definitely time to go home.

"The Blades," he whispers, and I pause for a moment because I'm not sure I heard him correctly. To the best of my knowledge, the Blades are a little-known nationalist pride organisation from the UK, so it's unlikely to be that group. And yet...

"The Blades?" I ask, puzzled.

"Yeah, the Blades. You know, the skinheads. The..." he drops his voice and I think he's trying to say Nazis, but I'm not sure.

"I have to go," I say, and I turn to walk away, though I hear him muttering about something. I see that Ariel is now in Noel McNabb's lap, so it no longer matters about me. I need to get back to Steven and Niamh, and try to get some information. If the Blades have a branch in the US and are working with von Golde, then that suggests the move to assemble a fascist army might actually be true.

I head for the door, and as I come into the foyer, I cross over to the exit, only to be stopped by a voice. It's not loud, but it's commanding, and I find myself doing what I'm told.

"Excuse me. Please come here." I turn, and look straight into the State Room. There is no one playing pool anymore, though there are several people on the sofas around the room, drinking and enjoying themselves. "Come here, please," and the speaker is obvious to me. He is wearing a tailored suit, one that Dana would no doubt be able to identify immediately. I can't, though I can smell the expensive coming off him. I can also smell the Roja Brittania coming off him, and that might as well be the smell of expensive. His suit is grey, neat, and the shirt is black. The tie, however, is a vivid red and white. Against the black of the shirt, the symbolism isn't lost.

His hair is slicked back, but his face is sallow and pale. His eyes are almost jaundiced, though I can't imagine why. He gives off the impression of being utterly sickly, and it's not helped by the black mask that covers the left-hand side of his face.

"My name is Jürgen von Golde. I very much would like to talk with you."

LAP TEN

I walk into the State Room, because I have no choice really. The moment he spoke was the moment I noticed that there were several people in the State Room who were all carrying. They were trying to hide it, but they weren't that good at it. They didn't need to be really, they were security, and they weren't hiding anything. The Blades, I presumed, and I realised that they were all skinheads, tattoos poking out their sleeves and collars. All men, all white, all looking like someone had told them to put the suits on so they could at least look decent for the day.

There were four, one at each corner of the room. Interesting. I wondered if they were just not good at their jobs, or if they had been told there was no real need to stand outside the room. I gave them little nicknames – Ape, Gorilla, Orangutang and Monkey. Monkey was the smallest, in the far left corner, scratching his neck constantly. Gorilla was in the other far corner, much bigger, much bulkier and not moving an inch. He had sunglasses on so I couldn't make out what he was looking at, but I was betting he was probably scanning the room constantly. He struck me as the most professional.

Von Golde – the Phantom – tapped the couch to the left of

him, but he didn't seem inviting or offering. It was an instruction. The girl that had been sitting there had got up immediately and I realise it's the redhead from the toilets. She can't meet my eyes, so obviously feels guilty about something, but I don't know what. I did tell her to invite me in.

The entire room is surrounded by couches, and I notice that there are beautifully framed portraits all over the walls, but they don't always seem to match the Prohibition theme. Perhaps they weren't necessarily meant to. While the bar area was very much a world of red, the State Room is greener in hue.

When I sit down, I look back to the entrance at Ape and Orangutang. Orangutang is ridiculously overweight. I have no idea how anyone thinks he can do his job, but it's almost embarrassing. His gun is stuffed into his belt to his right side, which makes him more a liability than anything else. Gorilla clearly has his holstered under his left armpit, while Monkey's is holstered on the belt. This leaves Ape, another muscular thug, but he seems bored, looking around constantly, waiting to be let off his leash. He has a swastika tattooed on his forehead, which is a little on the nose even for these guys. This is the one guy whose gun I can't see, until he turns, and I realise it's tucked into his back.

Which meant, broadly speaking, that if I was to go on the offensive, Gorilla would definitely have to be my first target. He was the one that could actually cause me some pain. While that would give time for the other three to arm themselves, I had a pretty strong suspicion that Gorilla's professionalism would count for more than the other three's guns.

I'm pretty good at assessing so I swing around to the Phantom almost as soon as I sit down, having taken in everything I needed to.

"Hi," I say sweetly, but I can tell that my charm will have no effect. I'm not wrong.

"I didn't catch your name," he says, and his fingers stray across his mask. It seems automatic and I wonder if maybe the skin below is irritated.

"Kelly Court," I reply, though I'm trying to be careful here. I need to be able to work out what makes this guy tick, and so far, I'm not getting through. My body is clearly not enough – there are plenty of girls around here who can give him that. But I suspect he isn't particularly interested in women for their intelligence.

Von Golde has never married, and though we suspect there might be a few children floating around, he has no interest or need for women. They are useful only if they can be thrown away. Which, I suppose, is not great news for Ariel Lang, though she may not have reached that conclusion yet.

"You've had an interesting day, Miss Court," von Golde continues. It's strange – he's trying to hide his German accent by affecting an American one, resulting in something which is neither one nor the other. Every so often his consonants sound Germanic, but then he will slip into American. He's been in the country long enough to pick up the accent, but it's not totally perfect.

"Yeah, it's been exciting," I say.

"You were at my factory?"

"Yeah." Don't give too much away. I need to know what he wants. Probably best not to babble. Though at the same time, probably don't come across as obstructive. "It's really interesting." He doesn't care what I think of his factory, but there's a slight softening of his face at me speaking more.

"May I ask why?"

"I love Formula 1 racing. It's amazing. When I said I was coming down here, my uncle suggested I should check out the factory and the track."

"Oh yes, your uncle," the Phantom says, and it's so off the cuff it scares me a little. "What's his name again?"

"Do you know your board?" I say, and when he looks at me, I realise it was the wrong thing to say. There's hostility in his eyes, and I'm not sure whether it's because I've questioned him, or whether the suggestion he doesn't know his board is offensive. "Just wondering…" I add, though it doesn't help much.

"I know every person on my board," he spits.

"My uncle is Chip Burgess," I reply meekly.

"Ah," he says and I realise he doesn't know his board at all. He likes to pretend to be in control, but he doesn't care about the little things. Chip Burgess was definitely on the board, and Steven was banking on the fact that von Golde wouldn't know his members because he was so arrogant. It was a gamble, but it seems to be paying off. "Good old Chip," he adds, and that confirms what I was thinking. He has no fucking idea who I'm talking about. "And, tell me, did you enjoy what you saw?"

"Well, I saw the cars racing for a bit, which was wild. And then I wandered into one of the garages and met a couple of your guys. It all seemed pretty interesting, though honestly, I have no idea what it's about." I pause for a moment because there's something I'm tempted to try. It's risky, but I think I might give it a shot. "I'm a bit surprised at who you had working for you."

"What do you mean?"

"Well, you had a…" I leave the sentence hanging, wondering if he'll pick up what I'm putting down.

"Oh, Lang," he mutters.

Yup. Hard core racist.

"She's useful at the moment," he says. "You don't like

133

her?"

"Oh, she seems fine. But you know…she's…taking a job we could have." I don't feel guilty but I have to admit it's not pleasant to say. Von Golde's nod of agreement makes it worthwhile.

"True. I like the way you think Miss Court," the Phantom says, and weirdly he puts his hand on my leg. It's not sleazy or seductive, it just is. His fingertips rest on my inner thigh, and I remain motionless, my heart in my mouth. What if he touches the holster?

"Careful," I whisper, deciding to go for gold. "I don't want you to shoot me." I spread my legs, and the dress slit allows me to show the holster straps on my right thigh. His look of surprised impression is pretty much what I guessed his response would be. If you're carrying, you're one of us. He even squeezes my thigh in appreciation, before taking his hand away.

"I like you Miss Court," he says, and I think he's genuinely trying to be charming, though it sounds more like dried leaves being stepped on. "How long are you in Vegas?"

"I'm leaving tomorrow," I reply, because I most definitely am now.

"So sad. If you like the racing you should come to the Washington race. I think you'll really enjoy it. Leave your details at the hotel and I'll make sure you have passes that let you go where you like."

"Thank you, Mr von Golde. That's very kind of you," I simper.

"Not at all, Miss Court. Thank you for indulging me." It's definitely the end of the conversation, which is weird, but he switches off without any interest whatsoever. As such, I get up and head towards the exit, and out of 1923.

LAP ELEVEN

I decide to walk back to the Excalibur because it's not quite midnight, and Las Vegas is one of those cities that apparently never sleeps. There's a lot of truth to this statement. It's sort of the right time of year to be wandering the streets, in that the temperature is fairly reasonable at night, coming down to the early twenties, as opposed to the sweltering heat during the day. The casinos are still active, and they pulse with light and energy as I walk past them.

I'm not totally sure how, but I find myself strolling down Luxor Drive, which takes me past the impressive Luxor Hotel, a dark pyramid that shines a beacon into the night from the top. It looks impressive, but I suspect I'm on the wrong side of the building to enjoy the complete spectacle. Instead, there's just a dull brick wall to my right, while on the left is the slightly duller car park. Nonetheless, even as I continue my walk, the red and gold spires of the Excalibur are obvious in the distance, and really, I just want to get home, because frankly I'm a little tired.

However, something is becoming clearly obvious. I'm fairly certain Monkey is following me. When I casually look back over my shoulder, I don't see anyone, but as my phone is out to help me navigate, I take the opportunity to switch to camera and I can see the little runt behind me. He's scratching at his collar, as though he has some sort of dermatitis there. I don't think he plans to attack me, which means he just wants to follow me back to the hotel. Which means he wants to search my room, in all probability.

I toy with the idea of taking care of him there and then, but people are milling about the carparks, and there are a few people going into the Luxor through the entrance I've just passed. That makes disposing of Mr Monkey a little more awkward than I thought. But there's no chance he's searching my room, so if I can't deal with him before I get back to Excalibur, I suppose I'm going to have to deal with him then.

Which means it might be time to just put a bullet through someone's head and let the FBI clean up the mess. Not ideal, but that's life.

By the time I get to West Reno Ave, Monkey is less conspicuous, which suggest he's just really bad at his job. I'm not entirely surprised by this. The Blades as a group aren't known for their subtlety. They tend to be thugs, deployed by other groups who just want a blunt force object to throw at their enemy. The Blades themselves don't care much about who they fight, as long as it furthers their neo-Nazi agenda, which makes them very useful foot soldiers for more insidious fascist groups.

I head into the roundabout at the front of the Excalibur, and make my way to the main entrance. Once inside, I have a slight advantage, and as soon as I enter, I quickly move straight to the lifts and summon one to take me to my floor. There are people everywhere, and conversation fills the room, while the scent of stale breath and alcohol is fought by perfume and the cleaners doing their best to keep the carpets beautiful.

I slip into the elevator and the door slides shut, but I catch a glimpse of Monkey as it does. I'm fairly certain he didn't see me, which is a plus for the night.

As I get to the twentieth floor and my elevator doors *pings* open, I notice that there is no sign on the door to my room. My *Do Not Disturb* sign has been taken away, which means that something has happened to my room while I was away.

I ponder my options, and then decide to go for the obvious route, and pull out my Ruger, feeling it slip easily into my right hand. I reach into my clutch to get the door card our, but I change my mind and instead knock on the door. I make sure I'm standing to one side of the fisheye lens, but the door opens freely and as it unlatches, I shove it hard.

136

I hear the *oof* and a stagger as whoever was behind the door falls back, but my gun is in the man's face and Noel McNabb is desperately getting his hands in the air.

"What the fuck do you think you're doing?" I demand, furious that he is in my room.

"I'm sorry, I'm sorry," he protests. "Honestly, Kelly, I'm sorry, I didn't mean…" he pauses. "Were you gonna shoot me?"

"You're in my room! What did you think I would do?" I demand. Other places might suggest my actions were over the top, but in Vegas, it's an acceptable answer. Even Noel can see that. However, as Noel is indicating to me whether he can lower his hands, my brain is kicking in and the implications of what has happened are becoming clearer. I race back and close the door, locking it.

"Were you followed here?" though I don't really pay attention to his answer. Even if he was, it's unlikely they would have let themselves be known, and Noel wasn't savvy enough to pick up on someone keeping an eye on him.

If Monkey followed me, then one of the others probably followed Noel, and if Noel found my room that means so did his shadow. And if that's the case, then Monkey probably has a friend.

"Shit," I mutter.

"Is there a problem? I thought we might get a drink and get to…" but I don't have time for inane wittering, so instead I spin around and stick my gun into his chest.

"How the fuck did you find my room?"

"I knew you were at the Excalibur and there's a receptionist who's a fan and owes me."

"People who can't do their fucking jobs," I mutter, but my

brain is working overtime and I formulate my new plan. I grab Noel and shove my gun in his back. "Get out there," I say and push him towards my door.

"Jesus, girl, I just wanted to…", but again his yapping isn't helping.

"Go," I hiss, and shove him forward. He does as he's told and as he pulls the door open, I shove him into the corridor. Then I peek around and see that there's no sign of any of the simians that followed us. Quickly I propel McNabb down the corridor, heading towards the massive stair case that will take us back downstairs. But even as we come into the space where the emergency exit is, I see Monkey and Ape.

Shit.

Without a thought I shove McNabb forward and take a shot at Ape, hoping I might get him. Unfortunately, it goes wide. I'm a dab hand with a sniper rifle, but my general shooting has never been as good as I want it to be, and certainly not as good as Dana Spectra who has an unerringly accurate aim.

Noel stumbling into Monkey, as Ape spins to avoid getting hit does help though, and in the confusion I'm able to quickly push forward and enter the emergency exit.

It's exactly what you would expect. A dull, featureless vertical tunnel with stairs winding up and down on either side. I pause, however, and push myself up against the wall. I'm fairly convinced that Monkey and Ape will follow, with Ape going first as he's the boss. Sure enough, the door opens and Ape steps through, so I take the opportunity to shove him as hard as I can and force him to stumble and fall down the stairs.

Monkey grabs me, of course, but I twist around, his lack of familiarity with expensive clothes making it difficult for him to know where to quite grab. As he goes in to grab me again, I move to the side (rather elegantly I might add), and grab him by the arms to swing him around. In my peripheral vision I see Ape picking himself up, with the intention of coming back up to attack. I have options, neither of which are totally ideal, though.

Annoyed, I swing Monkey and force him to the guardrail. When he hits it, he is shocked and drops his weapon, but while he fumbles, I duck down and grab at his ankles, pulling them up. He panics, suddenly aware of what I'm doing, but I'm quicker and better prepared and so he finds himself off his feet, his back on the guardrail like a seesaw fulcrum. As he tips, he grabs out, trying to stabilise himself, but the best he can do is grab one hand onto the rail. It's largely irrelevant as I swing him over and he falls, his grip on the rail now the only thing to stop him from falling down the slim hole between either side of the stair well.

Ape is far more single minded, and doesn't give two hoots about his partner. Even after he punches me solidly in the face, he doesn't turn to help Monkey. My face hurts like you wouldn't fucking believe. So much so that I drop to the floor, but truthfully, I'm angry at myself for not keeping track of Ape. It's a rookie mistake, and I sort of deserve the face punch. I know that he's going to kick me next, so I roll away to avoid it, but on the landing there's not an awful lot of space to roll. Which means that I decide to do something which is, possibly, insane.

I roll off the landing edge.

Sure enough Ape kicks out, but my roll means that he connects with Monkey, and fortunately the force has dissipated, because Ape was expecting to connect much earlier. Monkey is a little bitch, however, and squeals, letting go with one arm. This is a problem for me because when I rolled off the landing, I grabbed him. I'm hanging from Monkey's waist, and now both our weights are dependent on him holding on with one hand. And being honest, that is not going to work out well for anyone.

I'd always been struck by that story about the guy who jumped out of a high-rise window when the room he was in was on fire. Solve one problem at a time – get out of that burning room. If the only way possible is to jump out the window, do it. Once you've solved the problem of burning to death, solve the problem of crashing onto the sidewalk.

Having avoided getting a broken rib, I now had to find a way to avoid falling to my death down a stairwell shaft. I opt for the only thing that really leaps out: I decide to slide down Monkey, and then swing into the stairwell below. There's no real time to build up momentum either, but once I let go, I will need to grab Monkey's feet to swing in, and when I do that, he's definitely going to let go of the rail in shock. But if he falls back, that can add to my swing's momentum.

Ape is coming forward, ready to find a way to deal with me, so I take my opportunity. Sure enough when I grab Monkey's feet, the jolt goes straight through him, and the little bitch squeals again and let's go. By then, I'm already swinging forward. As he falls back, I let go, and I swing through the gap between the concrete stairs and the railing, clipping my foot which immediately shoots pain up my leg and is definitely going to swell, but at least I'm not fucking dead. Yet.

Monkey on the other hand, based on the sound of something heavy hitting metal, and then something heavy hitting concrete, probably is. I'm not remotely sorry.

Besides I have more important things to do. I know that Ape will be on his way down the stairs to finish the job, so I race up the stairs, guessing he won't be expecting it. Or maybe he will? The truth is, I'm not entirely sure I know why they are trying to attack me. It's something to dwell on later.

I ignore the pain in my foot, and I see Ape heading towards me. He's much bigger than me, obviously, so he's lumbering down the stairs, rather than running. I, on the other hand, despite the pain in my foot, am sprinting up the stairs. So, while he looks in surprise at my approach, I dive into him, crashing into his legs and knocking him back.

I didn't hear the crack, but I can certainly see the blood leaking out the back of Ape's head. Clearly his impact on the stairs was much stronger than I anticipated. As I pick myself up, he groans, so I take the opportunity to raise his head and then smash it back down. This time I hear the crunch, and the look on his face tells me it's definitely over.

Good. Fuck him.

I quickly search through his pockets to see what I can find. He has a wallet, with money and various cards, most of them with the name Rob Derek on them. Weird. I wouldn't have picked him for a Rob. There's also a SIG Sauer P220. Unusual. Looks like a 1990's model, so probably an old favourite. I pocket both gun and wallet.

The real question, I muse as I head up the stairs, is why Ape was trying to kill me. What was the point of that? Did it mean that von Golde hadn't trusted me? Presumably he hadn't because he sent Monkey to follow me, but what the hell was Ape doing? I would definitely have noticed if Ape was following me, and if they knew I was at the Excalibur, Monkey could have been waiting for me here as well. Although, maybe von Golde wanted to know if I met anyone on the way.

Or was Ape following McNabb for another reason?

That was a more interesting possibility. Lang talked about wanting to get McNabb into bed. Had that already happened at some point? Was he considered to be tainted? Was von Golde suspicious of his number two driver and thought maybe he was going to meet up with Lang. There were a lot of possibilities, but it did suggest that I might be able to add McNabb to my list of potential allies.

A list which currently had one name on it.

And that was a name I couldn't totally verify.

As I walk into my room, I notice that McNabb is already there, and it suddenly strikes me that he did fuck all when I was getting my ass kicked.

"Thanks for the help," I grumble, as I grab my mobile phone from the floor. Can't actually remember how it got there, but it's still working.

"Sorry, I called the cops," he says and I roll my eyes. I've already dialled the number and it barely rings before it's answered.

"I've delayed the cops," Steve says, and I sigh. "We were monitoring police calls in case something came through from the Excalibur. Two thugs fighting a girl on the stairs rang a bell pretty quickly. I've already sent in a team. What are we looking at?"

"Two bodies in the fire stairwell, Royal Tower far north, I think. One dead from a very big fall, the other dead from a nasty accident when he smashed his head on a concrete stair."

"North?"

"I dunno. You know my room number. It's the fire exit nearest that."

"OK. You OK? You need medical help?"

"No, I'm fine. I'm going to have a very big drink, then soak and then fuck some guy I barely know."

"Right, well that's excellent news. I hope it all goes well. I'll contact you tomorrow unless there are further problems."

"It is tomorrow," I sigh, and hang up. McNabb is looking at me, his eyes alight.

"Were you," he pauses and points at the phone. "Were you serious?"

"Yes," I reply deadpan, and slide out of my dress. From the look on his face, I realise I may have already started to bruise. "Grab that champagne, get out of those clothes, and get in that tub." As I unhook my bra and let my breasts free, Noel McNabb smiles a broad grin.

"Yes ma'am!"

LAP TWELVE

Let's not go into the sex. I mean, I seem to recall thinking it was pretty good, but waking up, I feel like shit in so many different ways, and that makes me think that maybe I wasn't that great the previous night. Certainly, the lack of Noel McNabb in my head might help sell that idea. There's a card with his number on it, telling me he has an early start at the track, but I can call him if I want.

I don't want.

The thing about sex, for me anyway, is that it's a bit disposable. I've fucked a lot of people, and often just before or after killing someone. Sometimes that very person that you're currently enjoying the penetration from. It has a strange effect on your romantic life and an equally strange effect on your sex life. It's difficult to engage, I suppose, knowing that there's a chance you might end up killing them later, and I definitely don't want to hesitate over killing someone.

Although, admittedly that attitude has recently bit me in the ass, but let's move on.

I pack my bag, not particularly quickly, but I have no desire to stay anymore. At some point there may be repercussions to the deaths of Ape and Monkey and I don't really want to have to deal with that. McNabb didn't attempt to go through my things, which means he definitely only came for the screw.

I ring for a porter to take my luggage down, and then head for the door. I might perhaps get breakfast before I go. If I'm honest, I'm not sure this trip has been a huge success. Aside from the less than subtle hints about Washington, and the presence of the Blades, I'm not sure I've actually achieved anything concrete. All in all, it's been a bit of a pointless exercise, and I'm not sure Broadsword will be happy about that.

I stop at the Casino Level to check out and to my surprise I see Steve Miller lounging in reception. As I head over to him, I pause because I see someone else. Ariel Lang. This puts me in a quandary. For a moment I muse on what to do, and then head to Steve.

"Excuse me," I say, waving an arm. "Excuse me!" He looks at me a little puzzled, but I push on. "My bags are on the way down. Can you make sure that they are sent straight to the airport, please? Also, here's my door pass, just check me out. Thanks." I go to the trouble of handing him a $50 as well, and I can see he is struggling not to laugh, but it doesn't matter. I don't bother looking back and head straight towards Ariel.

"I don't even work here," I hear Steve say, but I don't even know how to, and Ariel is genuinely laughing.

"Oh my god, girl," she says, heaving in a breath. "You have some attitude."

"Oh, well, I'm hungry," I reply, grabbing her arm. "Want to head to the food court and grab something to eat?"

"Oh, sure," she grins at me, and we both head to the

144

escalators that will take us to the Castle Walk level. I risk a quick glance back, and Steve sees me and gives me a thumbs up.

Luggage taken care of? Check.

Avoid drawing unnecessary suspicion by meeting my FBI contact in the foyer? Check.

Breakfast? Check.

The Castle Walk level is even more touristy than the Casino level. There are retail stores, a food court, and I see signs pointing to the "Thunder Down Under" and "Australian BeeGees" shows. I shake my head a little, surprised at how difficult it is to escape memory prompts to my favourite Australian model.

Fortunately, I have no desire to head towards the shows anyway. I was genuine in my desire to go to the food court. The Buffet is large and varied, but it doesn't have the best of reviews with most people generously describing it as "average". The Camelot Steakhouse tucked in front of The Buffet is closed at this time of day, and I'm ruling out the Italian restaurant for much the same reason, which leaves the food court. Aside from the fact that at the very least I can get a coffee from Starbucks, Cinnabon is my real target. I'm desperate for a cinnamon roll. I tell Ariel what I want and she offers to get me my White Chocolate Mocha while I get my classic roll.

Oooo, and also a cheesy basil pesto minibon. I'm hungrier than I thought.

With my food in hand, I head towards the table that Ariel is already seated at. I'm a little surprised at how busy it already is, but I guess it's around 9 so perhaps I shouldn't be.

"How was your night? Did you get your end away?" Ariel asks, leaning forward intently. It's an odd turn of phrase, and works against the idea that she's American. The more I think about it, the more I'm convinced she wasn't born in the US.

"Oh, yeah, absolutely," I say, a little dismissively. "What about you?"

"Oh, Noel disappeared." I bite into my minibon in the hope I'm not asked any questions about having seen him. Bad enough I fucked him, worse to have to admit it to Ariel the following morning. "I ended up going home."

"He was shit anyway," I say, before realising what I said. Ariel has picked up on it and looked at me. I'm good at defence though. "Well, sorry, that's just how he came across. Maybe he's better outside his group of friends and away from that other fuckwit driver, but at 1923, he was shit."

Ariel's eyes are understanding, and she relaxes, though she's still defensive.

"Sandy Hamilton is not an indication of Noel McNabb's personality," she says, with a pout. "Honestly when he's by himself he's so nice. That's when I see him. I work in his garage."

"So, Fabio works in Hamilton's?" I ask, curious.

"Oh yeah. We hardly ever interact. You just happened to get a day when he wanted to talk to me about something. Von Golde prefers it if we behave as two competing teams. The winner is the one who gets to lead the next race."

"The one in Washington," I say casually, sipping my mocha.

"Yeah. Though it'll be us. I've definitely got the edge this time round."

"Von Golde invited me to Washington. Said something exciting was going to happen there. That I would really like it." Ariel looks at me sharply, and she is clearly trying to work out what to say. Which definitely confirms she knows something more than she's been letting on.

"Well, there'll be a race," she finally says.

"Which you'll win," I reply with a smile, and Ariel smiles as well, though I can see she's still a little tense.

"Yeah," she says.

"And von Golde wins accordingly," I continue, grabbing my classic roll for another bite. She keeps looking at me, desperate to say something, but clearly uncertain how to. Finally, she can hold it back no longer.

"Do you," she pauses, trying to decide on the right wording, I guess, "share von Golde's approach to life?" Now I'm as tense as her and I don't know quite where to go.

"Do you?" I reply, carefully.

"I have to," she says. "I work for him."

"I guess I do for most things. But for other things," I pretend to look around nervously, hoping to set her slightly at ease. "Well, I wouldn't want anything to happen to you," I finish.

"Thank you," she says, and grabs my hand, squeezing it.

I suppose that's positive. If it's a choice between von Golde and herself, Ariel will survive. Something to remember for the future. More importantly, von Golde's ideals are definitely what's being tested in Washington, and Ariel is part of his plans. Maybe this wasn't a total waste of a trip after all.

LAP THIRTEEN

I once read someone describe Washington DC as unique but wholly unremarkable, which is an odd way of putting it, but there's a strong element of truth to it. It's quite nice, and quite diverse and full of quite interesting monuments and buildings, not least including the large white one that the President spends most of his time in. But replace that with the word "monarch" and you could probably describe a lot of different cities. Sure, the temperature is different – at the moment it's a comfortable 22°C, though last night it dropped to 17°C, which I would prefer at this time of year. Additionally, the chances of rain are quite high, and this is a not unusual time for that to happen. But, for all that, Washington DC doesn't really stand out. Trip Advisor's top ten things to do in Washington are nearly exclusively visiting monuments and museums. And I'm not sure the Library of Congress doesn't fit into either of those two either.

Of course, for some, Washington holds something of particular interest at 935 Pennsylvania Avenue – the J. Edgar Hoover building, headquarters of the Federal Bureau of Investigation; an ugly concrete block of a building that looks as though it's been carved out by a sculptor who got bored with the project and just decided to carve an awful lot of windows. It is here that I'm meeting with Assistant Director Steven Miller, along with a number of other FBI Agents. On the wall is a large map of Washington with a very specific path marked out. Curiously enough, it's two days before the actual race, which makes me wonder if someone wasn't particularly interested in getting out input beforehand.

When the idea of a street circuit in Washington DC was mooted, there was a great deal of resistance from most of the security agencies for all the obvious reasons. However, there was a great deal of support, not only from the local community, but from a large number of congressmen and women who thought that this would help the country heal in a fashion – either to demonstrate that they weren't afraid of what might happen if they did, or to trust enough to allow it to happen. Both sides of the aisle were, surprisingly, in agreement, and with the support of the Mayor, the plan was pushed into action. Law enforcement blanched, but that wasn't enough to change people's minds, especially as Liberty Media saw it as yet another win.

The track that had been marked out on the map was a four-mile track, which would have suggested to me that it needed about 47 and a bit laps to meet the course requirement (190 miles in total). However, to my surprise it was only 40 laps. The exception for this was a compromise for everyone involved, and had a degree of precedent – the Monaco Grand Prix being only 160 miles as well, because it is a slow course. The same requirement was being made here, though whether it was due to the course being slow, or whether there was a request to end it in a slightly shorter time, was not entirely clear. Either way, the agreement had been made.

The route started on Constitution Ave at the 17th St intersection. From there, the drivers would head east along Constitution before turning right onto 15th St where they would head down and around the Washington Monument and then turn left onto Independence Ave. They would then drive west along this, following it until it turned into Ohio Dr (and cruising around the Lincoln Memorial in the process), and then they would swing left before twisting right onto Rock Creek and Potomac Parkway. Heading north along this, past the Watergate Hotel, then would turn right onto Virginia Ave and then drive all the way along to 19th St, where they would turn right again, and then left back onto Constitution Ave and to their starting point.

It would be quite spectacular, to be honest, and taking in so many monuments in the process, would certainly stamp the official feel of the US on this particular track. It took me less than thirty seconds to realise that virtually no one in the room wanted it to happen, with the exception of the Deputy Mayor, who was clearly beside himself with excitement.

"I think," an FBI Assistant Director is saying, "that the files you all have should make all security arrangements very clear, and also make each department's responsibilities equally clear. This has been worked on by a large number of people and organisations, so we aren't playing any games here." This last line seems to be directed to the Deputy Mayor, who is flicking through his manila folder with all the casualness of a tourist whose travel agent has just given him his itinerary, though I can't help but feel it is partially directed at us. "With that being said," the Assistant Director continues, "I would like to offer the floor to Assistant Director Miller, who has further information that we would like to share."

"For the past few months, we have been working with Interpol," and at that he indicates me, so I nod gracefully. "We now believe that there is a credible threat to security that is being posed by someone out of the AutoGold team." The tension rachets up a degree, as several people sit forward, the deputy mayor not being one of them. Though he is paying a little more attention now.

"What sort of threat?" someone asks, and I see that the little plaque in front of him reads WPD. Miller turns, not to me, but to a stern, grey haired lady in her sixties beside me. She's short but clearly fiery. Her plaque reads CIA.

"My name is Mansfield. I'm the Deputy Director Transnational Issues. We've had our eye on AutoGold for some time before Jürgen von Golde migrated to the US, whereupon it fell outside our jurisdiction, though we have continued to monitor his operations in other countries. We have also been working with the FBI and Interpol in an effort to determine what sort of a threat AutoGold might pose. Our understanding is that some form of terrorist attack will take place during the race." There is not a collective gasp, but there might as well be. The Deputy Mayor has finally decided to take part in the conversation, I note.

"What sort of terrorist attack?" he asks, and both Miller and Mansfield look to me. I stand, rather reluctantly.

"Kennedy. Interpol. We're not certain of the details, though our intelligence clearly indicates it will be at the race." I look suitably grim.

"To what end?" asks the NSA representative. This time I look to Miller, who looks to Mansfield.

"We know that von Golde has been secretly funding a number of white nationalist groups," Mansfield says. Then she nods at me.

"We have a suspicion it's a rallying call to far-right groups to unite. So, it will be an attack on something they hold dear."

"Based on the circuit, there are probably three options," Miller says. "The Capitol, the White House or the Lincoln Memorial."

"There wouldn't be any particular need to damage any of them," Mansfield states. "As long as it's clear what the target is, the call would be clear."

"But let's face it," I say, because suddenly things are starting to make a little sense to me. "It's going to be the Lincoln Memorial, isn't it? The Capitol and the White House are too far away to cause proper damage, and if a car tries to veer off course it would be stopped by cops before it got to its destination. But the Memorial will be 100 metres away from a turning. Ridiculously..." And then I stop, because it's obvious to me now why Ariel Lang has been employed at AutoGold. "It's McNabb's car," I mutter, and everyone turns to me.

"Sorry," the Deputy Mayor speaks up. "Just to be clear, what evidence did you say you have of this?" There's an uncomfortable murmur, though I have to admit I'm lost in my own thoughts.

"We have no actual confirmation of anything," Miller says, "though we have…" But he's cut off before he can continue.

"So, no evidence, no confirmation, just some possibilities from the CIA about the *evil* far right about to cause damage to the Capitol yet again." I would say I'm surprised at this, but it wouldn't be the first time a Democratic lawmaker had seemed to be more supportive of their opponents. It's certainly not helping our cause, as there are a lot of people at the table muttering. I'm not sure whether they are actually on board with this guy, or if they simply don't fancy an additional set of problems to everything that's already on their plate. Either way, I'm beginning to see why we've been invited to the party late. "If I may, we have security. You three seem to think there's a problem, so I'm assuming you're dealing with it. It's not something the rest of us have to worry about, I assume, and presumably you'll have it in hand so, there's no real problem. If there's even a real problem now. Which you can't say there is anyway."

I am furious, of course, but Mansfield and Miller have sat down. I notice the other FBI Assistant Director is looking uncomfortable, but they all seem to accept that this is the end of the conversation.

"Good, well with that in mind, let's look forward to a fantastic race!"

"Sorry, are you a fuckwit?" I say, and I hear Miller's head hit the table, but I don't care. "We came to you with a serious threat. A credible threat. And you've gone all Amity Island Mayor on us, because it's too difficult. Are you seriously not going to do anything about the situation?"

"I've made a decision. It has the mayor's backing. And we don't need Interpol any longer. That's also a decision that has the mayor's backing. Thanks heaps, Agent Kennedy, but why don't

152

you fly back to wherever you came from and let us take care of the proper US business." He looks at the two men by the door, and when I turn to them, Mansfield stays eyes front, while Steve looks apologetic. With little option I head to the door.

"You should contact Mr von Golde," I say to the Deputy Mayor, before I walk out. "I'm sure he'll be very appreciative of how easy you've made this for him. He might even donate."

LAP FOURTEEN

Obviously, I sulked in my hotel room for the rest of the night, refusing to take Steve Miller's call, even though I know he's not to blame. I just didn't want to talk to him, because watching so many people roll over at the urging of some political bigwig annoyed me. And yet, I also know why they did. I've been told often enough to learn to pick my battles, but I have never found that a particularly easy thing to do. What I really wanted to do was go out and punch somebody, so that night I went to a pub and got blind drunk. I'm not sure if I did punch somebody or not, but when I wake up the next morning, I'm on the bed in my underwear, and my knuckles hurt like shit. I feel really awful, and when I look at my phone, I see there are a ton of messages. Steve mostly, though I see that Niamh has been trying to get in touch with me. Awkward.

I pause for a minute as I hold the phone in my hand, and then reluctantly tap the message and flick it to speaker.

"Archambault Services, how may I help?"

"I'm returning a missed call," I reply, a little guiltily.

"Do you have an extension or name that the call may have come from?" comes the polite reply, but I know how this works. At this precise moment in time, the person (and the voice is so androgynous I couldn't even begin to guess at a gender) who is taking the call has summoned a supervisor. The line is very specific, requesting a code for the day. My head hurts so much, but I blearily take in the day and date, and then look at the time. My mind quickly attempts to work out the code and happily it doesn't take too long.

"Sumlet, 581. I'm calling from Washington DC, USA."

"And your number please," comes back the polite voice. It's not the phone number they want, but instead I give them my code, the first three digits coming from the mobile I'm using.

"One moment please," the polite voice says and the line goes to hold music. It's fucking killing me. It's light and frothy and doesn't help my head one little bit.

"Kennedy?" I hear Niamh's voice and that makes me wince a little more.

"Hey Niamh," I say, closing my eyes.

"What's the situation? We haven't heard from you in a while. Broadsword was going to send in the cavalry."

"We've been dismissed from the case. It's being handled in house, apparently." I try not to sound bitter, but even I can hear the petulance in my voice.

"I understand. We'll be expecting you soon, then," Niamh replies.

"Yeah," I mumble. Except, it doesn't sit well with me. In spy stories this is where the agent goes rogue and does crazy shit. I guess the truth is, I'm about to go rogue and do crazy shit, because fuck that stupid mayor and fuck that security strategy. I had almost forgotten because I was so angry, but it makes sense now. Blowing up a car near a monument or in a monument, or whatever isn't going to be that strong a rallying call. But when they discover the bomb maker is black, that will stir up the racial hatred. Von Golde's rhetoric, his speeches at his events talking about national pride, will hit home. The threat isn't vague, it's very specific. That's why Ariel Lang was employed. She's going to be his scapegoat. But why do so willingly, that's the one thing that doesn't make sense. Unless she doesn't even realise she is. She's designing a new power cell that will explode?

I need to get in and see what is going on.

"I might take a couple of days," I say, and even I can tell that my voice is different, more assertive, and less hung over. Niamh's not an idiot. I've worked with her before, and met her on occasion. An albino woman with pink eyes, startlingly sharp features and a very sexy Irish accent. It's easy to meet someone like that and file them under "unique looking", but Niamh didn't have her job because of her appearance.

"Kennedy," she says, and I can hear the warning tone in her voice.

"Niamh, I'm just going to watch the race," I protest, but I know I've been rumbled.

"Broadsword says you are allowed to watch the race," Niamh replies, and I wonder exactly where she is. I had assumed she would be in the Operations Centre, but now I'm beginning to think she might be in an office with rather spectacular views of Marina Bay. "He says he hopes the race goes well and you enjoy it. He also says he's not particularly interested in pouring oil on troubled waters."

"Right," I reply. It's tacit permission, but if this fucks up, I'm in big trouble. Last warning? Maybe. But hopefully all will be fine. "Thank you."

"Good luck."

LAP FIFTEEN

One thing I have always learned from my time as an intelligence agent is to dress how you want people to perceive you. You rock up in a suit, people will immediately assume you are law enforcement and their guards will be up. Sometimes you don't have a choice, but in my current role, my outfits were usually my own choosing, and so I approach the AutoGold pit wearing a white body suit. It has long sleeves, but a deep v on the front which emphasizes my cleavage (though truthfully my cleavage is not tremendously impressive, but that doesn't mean much). I have big white sneakers on, and a G-string that is clearly red and shows through the white suit. No one notices my face as I walk up to the pit area, though everyone is appreciating my body. It's not subtle, but it gets the job done.

When I get to the barrier, there are people nodding appreciatively, but happily Ted Hawley is strolling about and when he sees me, it brings a broad grin to his face.

"Well as I live and breathe," he says, wandering over. "The boss said he invited you. I wasn't sure you'd actually show. You want in?" He opens up the gate in the barrier and I walk through as security stops others trying to do the same thing. Briefly I wonder if it's a Blade, but it's not the time to find out. Ted is already walking, expecting me to follow. "So, you want to watch the race from the trenches?" he is saying and I nod, smiling like an adoring fan. "Well, you'll get it down here. We've just finished the second qualifier. Sandy and Noel are both in the front ten, which is good news." It was also old news. I had been following the qualifying races, so I was aware of how AutoGold had done. I was intrigued that both racers had done so well, but I wondered if it was the result of the drivers coming to terms with a new track.

"Where did you want to sit?" Ted turns to me and looks

expectant, but I have no idea what he's thinking.

"I didn't realise I had options," I reply with a smile.

"Oh, there's always options," he says with a wink, but I'm getting the vibe that Ted just likes a good flirt. I'm on board with that. It makes life a lot easier if you aren't really invested. He points towards the makeshift stands above and behind us. "This is all AutoGold. There's a box in the middle, air conditioned, all the rest. You're welcome to go there, that's where the boss is. You're welcome to sit in the stands. It's better seating than, well, standing. But if you want to hang around here, and not get in the way, you're welcome to do that as well. I can't guarantee you'll see much of the race, but it's certainly a lot of fun."

"Is Ariel around?" I ask, innocently. "I thought I might have a bit of girls' time." Ted shakes his head, and I can see that the mention of her name certainly hasn't won me any fans.

"She's back there," he says, pointing towards the makeshift garage that has been prepared for the event. The nature of street racing pitstops is different to the ones on the tracks, where a pit lane exists for the drivers to head down to the garages and make the change. On the streets it's a street off to the side where the team will leap out and make the change, having to make sure everything is ready for them. The decision in Washington was to give the teams a degree of help by allowing them to create makeshift garages under the seating stands that have been erected.

Ted is already sorting out his team, making sure that everything is being lined up and ordered for the race as it's required. The twenty-one men in their helmets and coveralls look like automatons, cloned for a single purpose, be it to remove a tyre, or to jack the car up from the front. Each one has a very specific job, with the overall idea being that the actual tyre change of a car will be around two seconds. Anything longer and it might cost the driver the race. The team has to service both cars, so Ted's job is to make sure that the team is not only ready to go with the right tyres, but also the right tyres for the right car. It's a tough job, and I have to admit, I admire him and his team.

I head over to the little garage, which is, honestly, nothing more than a storage room. There are tyres in sets of fours ready to be wheeled out in a moment's notice. Tools are set aside should anything require a very quick adjustment. There are also a couple of laptops set up, with Fabio hovering over one of them, deep in contemplation of what is on the screen.

"Hey Fabio," I call out, and he glances back at me, pauses to put his glasses on, and then sneers. Delightful. "You don't know where," I start, but he has turned his back on me.

"I don't have time for this," he calls back. "I have a lot of work to do."

"The race is starting imminently," I point out, a little bored with being treated like a second-class citizen. "It's a bit late to be making changes now."

"It's not making changes," he turns and almost spits the words at me. "It's about monitoring. What I've done is a subtle, but fundamental change to the nature of the car, which will deliver a far more explosive surprise than anything yet seen."

I suddenly remember something that he said back at the Prohibition Club. Quickly I make my way up to his computer and, to his astonishment, I take a look at what he's got on the screen. Most of it is way beyond my comprehension, which I think he's actually saying to me while I look, but what I can understand is very simple – this isn't for Hamilton's car. Not that I know the vital statistics of either car, but at the top of the screen is McNabb's name.

"Why are you monitoring McNabb's car?" I demand, but I don't need an answer. I know why. Explosive surprise isn't even subtle. Whatever Fabio was working on is clearly some form of bomb, and Ariel is the fall guy because she was the researcher on McNabb's car. Someone builds an explosive device in the power cells, which goes off, destroying an American monument, and it turns out that the bomber is a black woman. Cue Jürgen von Golde just in time to make another speech about how the fundamentals of our society are being destroyed by the blacks, and every organisation with a line to AutoGold, from the Blades to the Ku Klux Klan suddenly have a leader and a cause to stand behind.

"It's not what you think," Fabio is protesting, but I don't care.

"How do I stop it?" I demand, turning to him. My Nightwing is in my bag, and I'm about to pull it out, because it might be my only advantage.

"Stop it? You can't stop it. It is what…" but I cut him off.

"I know what it's going to do. But I'm not letting you blow up a car and a national monument!" I shout.

"What?" Fabio says, and he looks genuinely surprised. Ironically, it's a suitable look for his death, which follows as the back of his head is opened by a bullet. I, on the other hand, swear, as Fabio drops to his knees and then falls forward.

Behind him, standing with a literal smoking gun, is Ariel Lang. She's dressed in her coveralls, and she looks ready for anything. Truthfully, I'm slightly shocked. I mean, I understand the urge, but unless she knows how to stop what's happening, this hasn't helped at all.

"I hope," I start, but she interrupts me. And I realise she hasn't lowered the gun.

"I don't know who you are, but you aren't the niece of an AutoGold board member, are you? Mr von Golde did a bit of digging. Chip Burgess had no idea who you were. But I'm guessing it's FBI?"

"No," I reply, slowly.

"Doesn't matter," Lang says. "All that matters is you definitely aren't stopping my cars!"

LAP SIXTEEN

Surprise, surprise, I was tied to a chair with those annoying zip ties that everyone thinks is cool to secure people with these days, thanks to the American police. Not, I might add, before I was told to haul Fabio's body into the corner of the room, away from what was going on. Part of me thought this was genuinely insane, but at one point, four men raced in wearing coveralls, and then they wheeled out some new tyres and didn't at any point notice I was sitting there, or that there was a dead body in the corner, all of which was pretty obvious to me. Not so much to them.

It also struck me, as I was dragging that corpse across the room, that I had no idea what Fabio's last name was. I didn't know anything about him, except he was a bit weird, and I was fairly certain that he had been building a faux-bomb to destroy a national monument. The last bit was definitely not true, so maybe the first bit wasn't either. Talk about karma.

"When is the bomb going off?" I ask casually, and Ariel turns to look at me for the first time in what seems like ages.

"Still think the FBI can stop this?" she quizzes and I weigh up my options on replying.

"I'm not with the FBI," I say calmly. She doesn't seem phased.

"CIA, then. Or NSA, whatever."

"Neither of those either," and this time she actually seems caught off guard.

"You're not NCIS," she says laughing, and I actually do.

"What, are you just basing everything off what you see on tv?" I say, unable to control the laugh. "Ask me if I'm part of a crime lab, next. Or maybe a novelist assisting the police." Turns out she doesn't have much of a sense of humour, as her gun is right in my face, pressing against my cheek, and she is clearly on the edge. You can see it in her eyes. She even has a bit of a tic in her right eye, the wink definitely uncontrollable. "I'm just a model who is interested in Formula 1. Apparently, that's a crime now." That doesn't seem to sink in at all.

"We knew you were watching us overseas. We knew we had registered on the international level, because we are a genuine. Fucking. Threat!" The last word is screamed, and I suddenly realise something I hadn't seen before. She's a convert. Von Golde has actually turned her into an acolyte. She believes everything he's selling, including the fact that her skin colour makes her less a human being than others. I genuinely don't understand it. I can't wrap my head around how she could possibly believe it, but then, I also couldn't understand why women would vote for someone who molested women and seemed proud of it. Broadsword had voiced the idea that people latched onto something that they would believe in, and that was of more import than their own personal self. It was like the very religious. It didn't matter whether there was hypocrisy in the readings, or if it had a negative impact on them and their families. All that mattered was that belief. Some of us watch too many movies, some of us drink too much alcohol, and some of us find something that is so strongly ingrained into their personalities they believe it no matter what.

Maybe it was something to be admired.

"We're going to save the world," Ariel is saying, and I pull myself back to the now.

"Who are you?" I ask, and she looks at me coldly. "I mean, you're not Ariel Lang. So, who the fuck are you?"

"Oh please," she replies, and I'm a bit surprised at her sass. "Who the fuck are you? Kelly Court? I looked into you. This model (and she has the audacity to use air quotes, the bitch) that enters a single big competition but never competes again. Bit convenient, don't you think? So, what are you, model by day, spy by night?"

If she knew the history behind the Green Earth operation, she might be entertained by how close to the truth that statement is for some. Not me though.

"Not really," I reply smoothly – I'm well prepared for this – "it's surprisingly easy to get tainted when you enter a competition that has to end because the owner dies on his sunken yacht!" She looks a little taken aback at the logic, realising that it makes sense. "Meanwhile, here's Ariel Lang, someone who AutoGold knows has a fabricated history. Yeah, my uncle looked into it."

"Do you know how easy it is to come into this country, have plastic surgery and then disappear, reborn as someone else?"

"I do actually," I reply, a little bitterly. Because of course it is. You come into this country legally, and then you go to a doctor and suddenly it's a different face. Money can buy you that, and it can buy you the documents you need to create your new identity. I have no idea how old Ariel is, but I'm guessing now that she's older than I first thought.

"And you want to know what the original story is?" she continues, and I do.

"See," I say, conversationally, "it's like this. I can see the picture. I've got enough of the jigsaw pieces in place to work out what the picture is supposed to be. But I kinda like the detail. I like noticing the little things, and one of the jigsaw pieces missing at the moment is who you are. I see the picture, but I don't see that detail. And it's a little annoying." She looks at me, and I think she's weighing something in her mind.

"Deal with it," she replies, and turns to head back to the entrance. Fucking bitch.

The good thing about being secured by zip ties is that you have a degree of control over how it happens, particularly if you're dealing with an amateur. Ariel wasn't used to carrying a gun, she wasn't used to holding people at bay, and she certainly wasn't used to killing people. All that meant she was pretty keen to have me tied up as quickly as possible. So, when she sat me down and told me to put my hands together, I did exactly as she asked, and she secured me. But putting my two fists together gave me the leverage I needed.

So, as she stood at the door, listening to the sound of the cars racing by (and can I say, the mere *throb* of that as it came across the street had my hormones racing. What with that and the adrenalin from the gun, if I didn't murder Ariel, I was definitely going to fuck the bitch), I extended my fingers and put my palms flat together, feeling the zip tie go loose a little. It was enough. It wasn't immediate, but after a little wiggling, my left hand slid out of the tie and it fell off my right. I caught it before it hit the floor.

With that, I stood very softly and padded forward, trying to be as quiet as possible. Fucking oil, however, ruined that and my foot slid on the floor. It wasn't loud but it was enough and Ariel spun around and saw me, but she had no chance. I disarmed her ridiculously quickly, pushing her arm up, squeezing her wrist in just the right place so the gun was released, and then turning her weight against her so she spun and fell to the floor.

She looked at me confused, like a dog that had been taken out for a last run, not quite sure what was going on.

And similarly, I put a bullet in her head.

LAP SEVENTEEN

I strip Ariel down and grab her AutoGold coveralls to put on. We are – were, I guess – roughly the same size, so I slide it over my catsuit without any problems. I leave her gun with her – it's a Ruger Max-9, which isn't a bad gun, but I prefer the Nightwing Agent 2 in my handbag, which I get. I also grab a helmet, because there's a couple lying around. Not sure why exactly – perhaps they are spares for the pit crew, or perhaps Fabio and Ariel had their own. It's hard to say.

Before I go out, however, I take a look at the computer Fabio was looking at. Had he worked out what was going on? To be honest, the readings make no sense to me and it's hard to tell exactly what I'm looking at. It's all too much for a basic bitch like me, so at this point I could do with the help of an engineer. When I turn to leave and find myself staring down the barrel of a Walther PDP, I realise that my engineer has arrived.

"What the fuck is going on here?" Ted demands and I give a little smile.

"You probably wouldn't believe it if I told you," I admit, but he doesn't see the humour in my statement. I'm not entirely surprised.

"You killed Ariel?" he says, though his voice is more incredulous than shocked.

"In my defence, she killed Fabio," I reply, pointing to the corner. Ted does exactly what I thought he would, and as he turns to look, I disarm him with the same efficiency I did Ariel. Because I am fucking good at my job.

"Who are you?" he asks, and he almost sounds shell shocked.

"Ted, we don't have time for this," I say, and I flick the safety on the Walther and throw it into the tyres. Then I shove him towards the computer. "Do you understand this? What's going on?" He looks at me, fear in his eyes, so I forcibly turn his face to the computer. He skims it, and I'm pleasantly surprised to find he's good at this job too.

"There's something odd about Noel's power," he says. "It's," he looks at the graph that is being shown on screen in real time, and then taps on the keyboard doing something which might as well be magic to me. "The new power unit. It's…." Again, he taps the keyboard. "If he keeps this up, he's going to explode it," he finally says.

"Ted, Ariel was aiming to destroy the Lincoln Memorial," I say.

"She couldn't," he starts, but then looks at the computer screen and takes a short breath. "She has the ability to remotely overcharge the unit." More tapping and the computer brings up a map, which looks to me like the track of the race and a small yellow blip is moving along it. "Fucking hell," he utters.

"She can't do it anymore?" I ask, maybe sounding a little too relieved.

"No, I mean," he shrugs and points to her corpse, but obviously it's not enough. "The thing is, it'll still overheat before the end of the race. The car will definitely explode. I don't know where, but…it'll kill…"

"I have to stop him," I say.

"You can't. That's the thing. That's why I came here. We've lost contact with Noel, we can't raise him, we can't…" He shrugs again, but I can see he is genuinely terrified.

"Then I have to get on the track to catch him," I say.

"That's insane, Kel," Ted breathes. "I mean, we don't have a car for a start. And you've only driven the once…" He lets the sentence trail off, because the meaning is obvious.

"I need to get into Hamilton's car."

"So, we lose the race?" and AutoGold's chief mechanic is back with me.

"For fuck's sake, Ted," I grab his hair and twist his head back to the computer. "How many lives is that fucking prize worth? That's assuming they even announce a winner once it goes off." There's a brief moment of uncertainty, but he nods and then the nodding becomes a little more determined.

"OK, OK," he agrees. "We won't have time to explain everything. The pitstop is less than two seconds, so you're going to have to do something. I won't stop you. Once you're in the car, I'll do what I can."

"Fine," I agree.

"Well, we'd better fucking hurry. He's about to arrive."

"What the…? Why didn't…" There's no time to dig deeper, but my brain is making connections. If Hamilton was about to enter the pit, then it makes sense they would need to contact McNabb. But I'm running out the garage already, and I can hear Ted is close behind. He grabs my arm and hands me a helmet, which I don, and then puts one on himself.

As we approach the pitstop, the team are standing by, ready to go. Four are already kneeling, their tools in hand, anticipating the arrival. The lollipop man has his sign in hand, and the front two jackers are ready as well. Four men have tyres by their sides, another four hovering to take tyres away. Two more men with jacks stand ready for the rear, while the side steadiers are in the middle.

It's a ridiculously precise operation that will see the car brake at precisely the right spot, thanks to the lollipop man. As soon as the car has stopped, the nuts are removed, the wheel is pulled off and rushed away, but even as the wheels come off, the replacements will go straight on, and the nuts are put back in place. If all goes to plan, the process takes around two seconds, and everyone is out of the way for the driver to set off again.

It won't go to plan today, hopefully. The start of which is Ted grabbing one of the side steadiers and pulling him away. No one in the pit notices or cares – they are too focussed on their own jobs. I have no idea how it's being reported to the real world, but it's probably being questioned. I move in and take the missing person's position, my hand on my gun, stuck into the pocket of the coveralls.

The sound of Sandy Hamilton's car builds steadily, and soon it is screaming into position, the lollipop man making his signal, and Hamilton arrives at precisely the right position. The bolts are already removed by the time I pull out my gun and grab Hamilton. The new wheels are on and everybody has stepped back, but Hamilton has turned and the gun is in his face.

There's a tension in the air, and when somebody takes a step forward, I shove the gun firmly into Hamilton's visor, and they retreat, getting the message. What they don't know is that the safety is still on. I have no idea where I'll put the gun once I've done what I need to do, and I have no desire to throw it aside, only for it to go off and kill someone. Or worse, me. Hamilton raises his hands, but I give him a pull and he realises I want him out of the car, which he does. It's quite quick, and I wonder if he's still thinking about the best way he can win this race, which is sweet on some level, I guess.

I push Hamilton back and take his place in the car, my gun still trained on him. Everyone around me has no idea of what is going on, and even less as to why. But it doesn't matter. Once I'm seated, I finally put the gun down, flick the two panels on the wheel that work the clutch and slam my foot on the throttle.

LAP EIGHTEEN

Important things to remember as I hit Constitution Av, number 1: it's a clockwise circuit. When I risk a glance to the left, I just see the White House, but mostly I see lots of people lined up watching the race. It sorts of hammers home the fact that if that car explodes it's going to kill a lot of people, not just possibly a monument. A small part of my mind is wondering if Noel is in on the idea and was going to physically drive the car into the monument, or if the plan was to remote control it somehow. Thinking about it, that doesn't make a lot of sense.

In fact, I realise that I'm not entirely sure where Noel is, so I hit the little blue button on the wheel to communicate with the team. Well, with Ted, hopefully.

"Kel, is that you?" I get, and I'm grateful Ted is actually on the ball. Actually, I'm slightly more grateful he's helping out. It means that not everyone in AutoGold is committed to von Golde's insanity, so on the plus side at least it won't be an absolute disaster. "Some guy called Steve contacted us. Apparently, they wanted to know what's going on with you taking over. It was on tv. He says he's FBI or something?"

"He's fine. Tell him everything, it's all good." I won't lie, that sort of makes me feel a bit better as well. Now the entire situation can be helped a little bit. I mean, on the track fuck knows how that will happen, but you never know. I might get lucky.

"OK, you know you're about to turn right?" Ted says, and with a shock I realise I need to swing right to head down 15th Street.

Everything is flying by, and the Washington Monument, the great stone tower with its pyramidal peak, is getting closer and closer. Part of me realises I didn't even notice the National Museum of African American History and Culture to my left.

Another thing that would fuel von Golde's incendiary speeches. *Look how they destroy the monument to our greatest President, but their own culture remains untouched!*

"Where the fuck is McNabb?" I shout.

"Err, we're having trouble reading him," I hear Ted say. Great. I suppose it makes sense though. If they've lost communication with him, the GPS might have difficulty relaying. Oh, of course. The interference from the power build up. I'm no mechanic, but that make sense. "Looks like he's about half a lap ahead of you," Ted suddenly interrupts. "I think he's going a lot fast than you. He's doing about 225. You're only at 175."

"I'm doing my best," I hit back. The numbers on my wheel have been showing 175 pretty solidly, and when I was on the track in Vegas, I was pretty proud of myself for keeping that speed up. Now, though, I can't help but admit my gut is churning. I'm swinging right again to get onto Independence Avenue, but doing this course for the first time is keeping me from increasing the speed.

Ted seems to be able to read my mind, because before I can ask the question "How long til I turn again," I hear him say: "You've got a bit of a straight run before you have to make another turn. The road curves a bit, but it's clear running. You have to move, because if you don't, he'll lap you," Ted says.

"Right," I nod, even though Ted can't see it. I take the opportunity to increase pressure on the throttle, and the car picks up speed, heading towards 200. I'm not sure if I want to risk that speed, but as the car speeds up, the people beside me become more of a blur, and that gives me more incentive to try to catch up.

Except then it hits me. I'm going about this the wrong way.

"Ted, where in the pack is McNabb?" I bark, hitting the communication button.

"Uh, he's about fourth from where we last saw him," comes the reply.

"Try and get the other cars to go to their pits," I say.

"Oh, Steven's doing that already. The ones in front of McNabb refuse to come in," Ted replies.

"*Fuck*!" I scream, but I don't have the communication button on, so no one hears my frustration. I realise I'm coming up to the winding part of the track that will take me closest to the Lincoln Memorial, and I make my decision. As I ease into Ohio Drive, I take my foot off the throttle. It's clear now exactly why I haven't seen any other cars, which is good, but it also means there are four cars that are going to catch up to me shortly.

With the last bit of momentum, I turn the car, effectively blocking off Ohio Drive. It's a decision that's borderline insane, but hopefully it won't be a total disaster. Working it out in my head, I'm guessing that those other four cars will be on me in about a minute, which means I don't have much time at all.

"Get those front runners off the track, Ted!" I scream as I hit the comm button. "Tell them there's going to be a fucking pile up!"

I don't wait for the response. Instead, I jump out of the car as best I can, and run towards the crowds on the sides of the road, pulling my helmet off.

"Get back!" I scream. "Get back, away from the track!" Initially there's confusion, among the crowd, but as I run toward them, I see they're getting the idea and some have already worked out there's going to be a disaster on a huge scale. I'm desperately hoping that having angled the car to the left, when McNabb hits it, he'll be thrown into the river. Fuck knows what's going to happen to McNabb himself, but I have a grim feeling he's not going to make it out alive.

I know I should flee as well, but the feeling in my gut is that I need to stay, just in case there's something I can do. It's fucking insane, but I have to make sure that car enters the river.

I hear the roar of a motor, and to my delight I realise it's just the one car. I don't know what's happened to the other three leaders, but for whatever reason they've pulled back. I risk a glimpse back and am also a little delighted to see that the Arlington Memorial Bridge has been cleared as well.

It takes less than ten seconds before McNabb's car hits mine. My car is thrown back, and I watch it pass me, almost like its slow motion, crashing through the makeshift barrier and ultimately being stopped by the trees which refuse to give way. McNabb's car has rolled, and it goes to plan, tumbling the opposite direction into the Potomac River.

There's no immediate explosion, but there's also no immediate sign of McNabb.

I'm not sure how long I linger trying to make a decision, but however long it is, my conscience gets the better of me. I don't know whether it's because I fucked him or whether it's because I'm not sure he's part of von Golde's insane little group, but I can't convince myself he's a bad guy. And it may be fucked up, but while I'm happy to ignore the life of the bad guy, if it's shades of grey, I can't totally commit.

Fuck you, Dana.

I pull off my jumpsuit, running towards the Potomac, and when I get to the edge, I dive in. The bodysuit is like a swimsuit, which makes it easy to swim down to the car and as I race in, I realise that the car has gone out a little further than I thought. Initially the river isn't so deep, but it takes a sudden dip, which means the car is totally underwater, but relatively easy to get to.

The problem is that it's clearly upside down, and as I get a little closer, I realise why McNabb didn't come up; his head is twisted at an angle that is clearly not right. I feel my breath running out and I know there's no point in staying, but even as I start edging away from the car and back to the bank, I can't take my eyes off Noel McNabb.

Unfortunately, I sort of forgot why I was there, because then the car explodes.

LAP NINETEEN

The doctors let me out of hospital after a couple of days, which was nice because it was fucking boring as in there. The sum total of my communication was with Broadsword who let me know that while he wasn't happy about what I had *done*, he was happy about *what* I had done. In fact, I was almost forgiven. The only obstacle was that he had specifically told me he wasn't interested in oil on troubled waters, so I may have to do some apologising. That's fine, I can handle that.

As it turns out, I'm not that badly damaged. A trifle burnt, but it looks like a moderate sunburn which, again, is OK. Oh, and a lot of bruising which is probably worth mentioning, because when I looked at myself naked in the mirror, I was genuinely surprised at the places that had been busted up. Unbelievable.

Getting out of hospital also meant it was definitely time to go. It had been nice to come home (and by home, I mean America, not Washington. Though I had lived here for a bit, I don't think I'd ever consider it home. Particularly not now that the smell of weed has become a little omnipresent. I'm not one to judge, but fucking hell, it seems everywhere now!) but there was a reason I left.

Dulles International Airport was my next stop and I was delighted to see that Steven Miller was waiting for me at the front of the hospital. I wasn't really in the mood to flag a cab, so knowing I had a lift was uplifting.

"Hey, wanna go to Dulles?" he calls out.

"Sure," I grin, and limp over to him. He chuckles at this, and I remember this isn't the first time we've been like this. There was an incident once, way back when, and that resulted in my falling down a flight of stairs and breaking my leg. I was deskbound for two months, during which time Steve would mimic my uncomfortable walk when he went to get me coffee. Smug dick.

It's a fair old drive to Dulles, but Steven has a ton of updates for me, and when he starts, he barely has time to finish. At various points I'm tuning in, but my head is still throbbing a little so it's hard to take everything in.

"I believe, and this will shock you, that Chip Burgess has taken over as CEO of AutoGold," Steven is saying, and I turn at this.

"My uncle?" I say, a little incredulously.

"Your uncle," he laughs. "He was going to kick up a bit of a stink about someone claiming to be his niece, but when he found out that von Golde was planning on destroying a national monument, and also that the company had been secretly funding radical groups around the country, he took a back seat."

"He probably just wants to save the company," I muse.

"I think you're probably right," Steven agrees. "After all, I'm not sure that the other teams are going to be impressed with the fact they were trying to blow up a national monument. Also, I think that's the end of Formula one in Washington."

"You almost sound like you regret that," I say.

"Well, it was an event, wasn't it?" he responds. There's silence for a bit and then finally he says what I'm guessing he was trying to avoid saying for quite some time. "Von Golde's disappeared. Sandy Hamilton knew a lot more than we thought and what with the deaths of Ariel, Fabio and Noel, he pretty much told us everything we wanted to know. Once we had that, it was nothing to get search warrants and clean the place out. Von Golde probably saw the writing on the wall and decided it wasn't worth the effort." He looks at me sideways and I shrug.

I think I am too worn out to do anything else. Von Golde would turn up somewhere else and there'd be issues. We'd be called in to try and sort out an arrest and extradition to…well, who knows. Broadsword mentioned that Germany was now seeking him for questioning in regards to AutoGold operations over there. The fact is, the world is a small place when it turns against you, and von Golde is going to learn that the hard way.

By the time we arrive at the Main Terminal at Dulles International, it is getting dark. At night, it's quite pretty, as the dull concrete in the daylight takes on a paler tone in the moonlight, and the massive glass windows that hold the uniquely curved roof give off a greeny-blue light – not quite aqua, not quite teal.

Steven risks getting out and giving me a hug goodbye.

"You call me if you need, me, OK?" he says, and I smile.

"OK, Dad." With that he shakes his head. "I miss you, kid," he adds as he gets in the car, and I wave at him. I miss him too, but I've never been able to say that. It's almost as if I do, I'm admitting that leaving the FBI was the wrong thing to do. One day I need to work on reconciling my inner demons and thinking about things in shades of grey. Logically I know you can miss someone without missing the organisation, but being paranoid that people are always judging me has often helped me in my job.

I stroll on in through the glass doors and heads towards the central check in counters, all of which are lined up almost as soon as you walk in. It's easy enough to find my flight and easy enough to check in, though as is typical of Dulles you have to wait a considerable time to actually get anywhere. I'm flying Korean Air, so ticket counter two gets a brief visit and I'm in and out without so much a raised eyebrow.

Except, as I walk away, I see someone who I'm sure I shouldn't be seeing. I'm sure that, walking into Forbes News near ticket counter 1 is Jŭrgen von Golde.

If I was being brutal, I would say that Dulles by name, Dulles by nature. On a scale of International Airports, if Changi in Singapore is near or at the top, Dulles has got to be close to the bottom. It's functional to the nth degree. There are few attractions as such – some newsstands, a couple of restaurants, and most of them are in the Arrivals section. Departures is simply boring. Based on that it is hardly surprising that von Golde is doing the only thing you could do, and that's go to the news stand.

In fairness, news stand is being harsh – it's the typical airport bookshop, and this one has two entrances, backing into the check-in as it does. I make my way through the nearest one, and von Golde is there, flicking through a magazine. I'm trying to wrap my head around this slightly, because I would have thought he would want to be away, rather than hanging around an international airport there was no way he was going to leave because the police will track him down.

And so when someone points a gun in my back, I sigh because…well, rookie error.

"Hey girlie," I hear, and I'm not totally surprised to hear Sandy Hamilton's voice. "Wanna go for a ride?"

"You know how easy it is to get attention, right?" I ask.

"Yeah, but I will kill you stone dead, and I won't give a shit. I'm already in deep, so adding your murder isn't going to make much difference to me." Sandy Hamilton is one of those people who has nothing to lose and it shows. I should have expected that too. Given that he gave his boss up, it surprises me that he's still working for von Golde.

Speaking of, von Golde has turned to smile at me. He has his mask on, and I wonder if anybody is doing their job at this airport. How hard can it be to find a fucking masked Phantom?

Ten minutes later, we're outside in a car, driving away from the airport. I can't help but admit I'm fucking pissed. It's a nice big SUV, however, and Sandy is sitting beside me with a gun pointed at me, while the Phantom sits opposite, doing the same.

"Kelly Court," von Golde finally says. "You are a big thorn in my side."

"Thanks," I reply glibly, though I don't entirely feel it.

"One single race and you get me thrown out of the empire I had built from scratch."

"Well, that's the problem when you go all in. Didn't you learn anything from being in Vegas?" I'm rather proud of that one.

"Yes," he sits back and smiles. His fingers go straight to his mask.

"I'm surprised you're happy that old Sandy here sold you out so quickly," I add. I am genuinely curious to know why von Golde has forgiven the driver.

"We reached an understanding," Sandy said. "He knows I had to do what I had to do."

"I do," the Phantom agrees. "But so do I," he adds, and

176

with that shoots Sandy in the head. I don't know how to react to that, but automatically I slide my hand forward to see if I can grab Sandy's gun, though von Golde is all over this. "No, no, no, Miss Court," he says, and the gun is back on me. "Let's not play silly games. You can see I'm not in the mood. The only reason he went first is so that you can be terrified when I shoot you as well."

And that's my cue. Von Golde isn't going to let me live, and now I have nothing to lose, so I take a chance.

"You know an FBI car is following us," I say, and he gives a small smile.

"Please," he says.

"My friend, Assistant Director Miller dropped me off at Dulles. Didn't Sandy tell you? I'm sure they met when he spilled his guts." I point out the window and von Golde is caught off guard. I don't know if it's me mentioning the name Miller, but I see von Golde's eyes flicker to look to where I'm pointing. It's a fraction of a second, but it's enough.

I kick out as savagely as I can, and knock the gun from his hand. I don't know who is driving the vehicle, but they are like monks, never looking back and never taking an interest. I did notice there wasn't a single bump when Sandy was shot dead, so this driver is taking discretion to a new level.

Von Golde isn't sure whether to protect himself or go for the gun, but I leap across to him, and despite the fact my elbow is bruised, I smash it into his face, knocking the black mask off. He automatically tries to cover the scarred face, but in truth, I've seen worse. I mean, it's a horrific scar and clearly the plastic surgery hasn't been effective, but it's not as bad as someone who's been burnt. Von Golde's vanity is more obvious than ever.

I knee him in the balls, and he coughs like any other guy, but he gets the chance to punch out at my chest, and I'm not quite prepared, so he knocks the wind out of me. I fall to the floor, covering myself with my left arm as he descends on me, trying to hit me, but incredibly he's grabbing his dick with his left hand. I'm not sure if he's ever been kicked in the nuts before, but he's reacting like a child.

I curl up a little trying to get my breath back, and he senses defeat, but what he doesn't realise is that I've landed on his gun. With my right hand I grab it, and wait for the pause in the beating he's trying to give me. I won't lie, every time he hits a bruise – and there are a few – he's causing a great deal of pain, but what he doesn't know is that I'm still on pain killers and as such, all I'm getting is a throb.

When he pulls back for another punch, I spin around and club him with the gun, straight onto the wretched side of his face. He recoils and I kick out with my feet, shoving him against the door. He scrabbles for Sandy's gun which is close, but now I'm on my feet it's child's play to snatch the gun. I kick him in the nuts again, more for my own satisfaction than anything else.

As he screams in pain, I throw one of the guns back to the chairs, and reach forward to open the car door. Then I reach down and grab him by his tie, hoisting him forward.

His eyes fill with terror as his head is shoved out of the car, my foot now on his throat, pushing down.

"Please, Kelly," he begs.

"That's not my name," I reply. I push forward with my foot as he desperately tries to grab my leg. With the gun pointing at his head, I have one last thing to say to him.

"I'm Justice."

BOOK THREE

MANHUNT

I

Mason Lemon's funeral was a typically sombre affair, notable only for the fact it was being held in his parents' back yard. It was an unusual decision, but it was where Mason had hoped to be buried, so the powers that be allowed it. There was no reason to complain and the burial took place accordingly.

Everyone there remained quiet and respectful, dressed in their dark suits (there were a lot of suits – even some of the women were dressed the same way) or their black dresses, and everyone faced forward, a look of contemplation on their faces as they remembered Mason and everything he had meant to them.

As the crowd settled in their places, Nathan Coulter felt he should possibly be closer to the memorial and tomb of his old friend. He was aware that he was perhaps not being sombre enough. Already his charcoal grey suit and pale blue shirt weren't, perhaps, satisfactorily dark. Maybe the necktie's yellow stripes were too loud. Nathan didn't want to draw attention from anyone, but he was certain that he had. It rankled, and so he paused, which meant that he stood awkwardly to the side of the crowd, not quite in front of them, but also not a proper part of the assembly. Also, he was standing while everyone else was still seated.

Yes, he was definitely drawing attention.

For a moment he tried to pretend he could sit down, but there was no chair and when he lowered himself, he remembered where he was and cautiously stood up again, because it would look stupid to sit on nothing, and even more stupid to fall.

"Mason's favourite Biblical quote," the priest at the front was saying – and if anyone was surprised to find that Mason Lemon had a favourite Biblical quote, they certainly weren't showing it – "was John, chapter 16, verse 33. *I have said these things to you, that in me you may have peace. In the world you will have tribulation. But take heart. I have overcome the world.*"

This prompted a flood of tears from a number of people, including a very beautiful lady in her twenties with long blonde hair and a very short skirt. Nathan Coulter thought she didn't fit in, but then, neither did the Biblical verse, so perhaps he really didn't know Mason as well as he thought he did.

Which wouldn't have been all that surprising, to be honest.

"At this point, perhaps it might be nice if we were to come up and take a moment to reflect on Mason's life and remember what he meant to us." This was the cue for a variety of people to stand up and start to make their way to the front and Nathan hesitated, thinking he really should go to the front and say his goodbyes. Conversely, though, it was also a good opportunity to leave, and there was something very tempting about that.

He deliberated for only a tiny moment longer, before turning and bumping straight into someone. The man was taller than Nathan, wearing a dark suit, but also had a pale blue shirt, which Nathan wanted to believe was validation for his own wardrobe choice. However, the man who stood with a gaunt face, lined with years of expressing displeasure, clearly wasn't there to tell Nathan he had made the right choices in life. In fact, Nathan knew full well that the man in front of him would most likely say quite the opposite.

"Deputy Director," Nathan said weakly in greeting.

"Nathan," the Deputy Director said cheerfully, though his face didn't reflect this in any way. "It's nice to see you here. We haven't seen you around the office for some time. People were starting to worry. They thought you might have had an accident." The cheerfulness never left the Deputy Director's voice, but Nathan thought he might as well have threatened to shoot him there and then.

"I'm aware what people think of me, Deputy Director," Nathan replied, trying to keep the quaver out of his voice, and also not lose control of his bladder. There was, in truth, nothing but fear in him, and he was not totally convinced he would walk away from the funeral in a state that was better than Mason Lemon was presently. He could also smell the Deputy Director's aftershave, and the tart smell reminded Nathan that he himself hadn't shaved that morning. He had other things on his mind, after all.

"Then you can probably imagine why people are surprised that you're at Mason Lemon's funeral," the Deputy Director continued. "A lot of people think that you're responsible for Mason's death."

"I had," Nathan began, but he was interrupted by the Deputy Director, who clearly wasn't listening to a word that Nathan was saying.

"I don't, of course," the Deputy Director continued. "No, when the Associate Deputy Director came to me and said that he thought you might be stealing files here and there, I said that was unlikely. Very unlikely, I said. And then when the Director called me into his office and said that Mason had been killed on assignment, an assignment that your team was responsible for the analytics of, and that the Associate Deputy Director had indicated several files had gone missing and potentially got into the hands of, shall we say, the enemy, because it's terribly over theatrical, don't you think? When the Director said that to me, and then asked if I thought the Associate Deputy Director was right and that you might be responsible for that, I said, it's very unlikely, Director. Very unlikely." For the first time he paused and even though he hadn't taken his eyes off Nathan for his diatribe, for the first time Nathan got the impression the Deputy Director was actually looking at him. "It *is* very unlikely, isn't it, Nathan?"

"I'm sure if anyone had any evidence that I'd done anything like that," Nathan began, but he was interrupted again.

"Treason, is the word you're looking for, Nathan," the Deputy Director pronounced, and he seemed to have developed shadows even with the sun in his face.

"I'm sure I'd have been arrested by now," Nathan managed to spit out, and he could feel his bladder threatening to betray him, but he was proud of himself for standing up to the Deputy Director.

"I'm sure you're right," the Deputy Director agreed. "In fact, I'm sure it's a lot of hoo-haa over nothing, wouldn't you say?" The Deputy Director's Bronx accent made the word "hoo-haa" seem inappropriate, but Nathan couldn't find that funny. "I'll possibly catch you around the next time you're in the office. Maybe you should drop in and say hello. Let the Associate Deputy

Director know that you're all right." His eyes suddenly bore into Nathan's, as though they were searching his brain for what he was looking for. But then, just as suddenly, the Deputy Director turned and walked away, going straight over to the blonde lady in the short skirt. Nathan wondered why he found the woman vaguely familiar, now that he could see her face. However, it was something for a later time.

No one else at the funeral had moved, but Nathan was certain that he was being closed in on. Taking a deep breath, he slipped away from the funeral and headed straight to his car.

II

The Deputy Director grimaced slightly, and wondered if he was still actually in Virginia. His driver had pulled off Live Oak Dr and headed down the Potomac Heritage Trail, moving through the forest until he drove under the Capital Beltway Bridge, and the Trail came to an end. It wasn't quite where the Deputy Director had wanted to be, and so he set out on foot, heading for the riverside itself, making his way through the tall, spindly trees that, at this time of year had brown leaves gripping to the skeletal structures, as though they were clinging to life. Given the amount of foliage he was walking through, the Deputy Director guessed that was exactly what the leaves were doing. For a brief moment he envisioned them all as people hanging off the edge of a cliff, with Winter some sort of maniacal killer that was going to push them off.

"We are all but autumnal leaves, gripping to the skeletal branches of winter," he said aloud. He would have to continue that at some later point, he decided. There was something satisfying in his soul about that line.

By the time he came to the Potomac, he wasn't far enough away from the bridge. The thunder of the cars and the lights seemed like a distant storm, and the Deputy Director wondered if there wasn't some sort of message in that. Not that he particularly cared. He needed to deal with a problem, and unfortunately, he personally couldn't.

Well, he probably could, but it would require a lot of discussion and negotiation and the Director wasn't the sort of person who enjoyed discussion and negotiation. He was the sort of person who liked his Deputies to walk and say, "Don't worry about that, it's all taken care of."

The Deputy Director wasn't really a down-the-line sort of person, but he was something of a people pleaser, which had helped him get as far as he had with his job. The other trait that helped him get as far as he had was a ruthless pragmatism. Mason Lemon's death was a big problem. There was no reason that he should have been discovered doing what he was doing, unless someone knew something they shouldn't have. And the only way someone would have known something they shouldn't have was if another someone had passed that information on. Possibly to a third someone.

Fortunately, Nathan Coulter wasn't that bright, at least not in the opinion of the Associate Deputy Director. In a time when information was digital, removing it without leaving a trace was a little easier than it used to be. After all, copying data didn't take the original data away. And unless you had a reason to go looking, copied data didn't immediately leap to the eye.

Physical data, on the other hand, should never be taken. The Associate Deputy Director had posited that maybe Nathan Coulter had assumed no one would look at it, and that by taking it, he would be making less of a deal about it, because no one would notice a missing folder. And even if they did, that sort of thing went missing all the time. Perhaps, the ADD had added, he was quite intelligent because copying data would have possibly alerted another analyst.

This conversation had annoyed the Deputy Director, who demanded to know if Coulter wasn't bright, as they had first suspected, or was indeed quite clever after all. The Associate Deputy Director shrugged, indifferently, and suggested it wasn't particularly important. After all, they knew that Coulter had taken the files. The information had got into the wrong hands, and that led directly to Mason Lemon's death.

The pragmatic side of the Deputy Director was forced to agree.

When the Director found out, he agreed they could arrest Coulter and then question him. But in doing so, they would probably need to get another agency involved, and that was awkward because it might lead to publicity and in this day and age, with certain politicians looking down their own metaphorical gunbarrel, the Director had no desire for the CIA to have to admit they had a leak. Classified documents turning up in the wrong place was beginning to look like part of the government job description.

So the Director suggested that maybe the best approach would be to simply suggest to Coulter that he pack his bags and move to Puerto Rico, and that would be the end of it. Except, the Associate Deputy Director had said languidly as he reclined his chair, they didn't totally know everything that Coulter had taken. This had the effect of causing the Director to noticeably scowl, and that brought the people pleaser side of the Deputy Director into light.

"I'll take care of it, Director," he said, with firm confidence, and the Director grinned, happy that the problem was going to go away. He trusted this Deputy, and secretly hoped that he would succeed the Director when the time came. The problem would be sorted.

All of which passed through the Deputy Director's mind as he shut out the sounds from the bridge, and watched the moon's reflection on the Potomac in a cloudless sky. There were certainly worse ways to live.

The Deputy Director took a moment to glance at his watch to see what the time was, and decided that he was getting close to wrapping things up. It was past midnight and his patience was finally at an end, no small achievement. Putting his hands into his jacket pockets as the night air took a sudden chilly twist, biting at whatever flesh was visible, the Deputy Director turned to head back to the car.

However, before he could, a woman stumbled across his path out of the forest, and for a dread moment, the Deputy Director wondered if he was going to be caught up in a tawdry criminal occurrence. She had a beanie, a bedraggled scarf around a threadbare green jumper, and beneath that a blue dress that had definitely seen better days. Normally his brain would have been happy with this, and written it off as a homeless lady, probably looking for her fridge box under the bridge nearby.

Except, the Deputy Director wasn't someone who had been promoted to his position out of convenience. He had earned his title, and been regarded as a damn good field agent in the day. As such, as his eyes took in every detail about the woman, when she looked at him, through the grime and dirt on her face, she opened her mouth a little and the Deputy Director saw her teeth, all of which were fine. They weren't the bright white of a Hollywood superstar, but they were clean – whoever this person was they had the ability to maintain their dental care, and homeless people were rarely in that position.

She looked at him and simply said: "Yes?"

The Deputy Director nodded. "Immediately," he replied. He reached into his jacket and pulled out an envelope, handing it over to the "homeless" woman. "I take it you are the courier?"

The homeless woman didn't respond, instead she just took the envelope and stuffed it down the front of her jumper. Then she lifted her dress up ignominiously, revealing greying leggings beneath, and from a pocket she pulled out a small card, which she then handed over.

"Half now," she whispered, her voice sounding forcibly aged. "And I mean now."

With that she turned out and started to shuffle off, though the Deputy Director wondered who the performance was for. It didn't matter. Things were in play and the problem would be sorted soon.

"A woman shambled across the path, approaching with all the speed of Pinter. She said, We are all but autumnal leaves, gripping to the skeletal branches of winter." Yes, he decided, sheer poetry.

III

In Maryland off Route 28, there is a small town called Dickerson. It's part of Montgomery County and is unincorporated, but with a population under 2,000 that's not really an issue that anyone in the little town has. It is, surprisingly, home to a nuclear facility called Neutron Products Inc, has its own recreation centre and even has a train station. The houses are few and far between, but they are big, which is one of the advantages of living in a small place near a nuclear facility.

The disadvantage, of course, is that should you be living within a one-kilometre radius of the facility, there's a very good chance you will have radioactive contamination. It's one of those things that people have talked about for decades, but strangely nothing ever seems to get done.

Eric Coulter wasn't particularly bothered by this. He had worked out that his house was at least 1.2 km away from the Facility and therefore was not contaminated. He was absolutely fine. He wasn't a farmer, but his house was on Mouth of Monocacy Rd, which was certainly populated by people with barns and fields. Eric Coulter didn't know them very well, despite having lived in Dickerson for a considerable period of his life. He had friends once, but once his son started working at the CIA, those friends disappeared. In fairness to the friends, it was Eric who had shut them out. He wanted nothing to do with them, and those friends came to the conclusion that clearly all that talk about CIA agents being nuts was probably true.

Eric therefore tended to stay to himself. Where necessary he would travel to Dickerson Store, and sometimes he would even make the journey to Dickerson Market. Most of the time, however, he sat at home and binge watched episodes of crime dramas, wondering if his son's life was anything like that. He hoped it was, because that would suggest he was doing a lot of good, and a lot of bad guys were being locked away thanks to his boy.

Eric had to give up work sometime earlier after a stroke had got him at the tender age of 46. Smoking and drinking had not helped his lifestyle and when it happened, he had got very lucky. He hadn't been paralysed as a lot of people were, as the stroke had been in his Cerebellum, but he had lost his coordination, and standing up for any period of time led to him having nausea. His boss at the paper mill had shrugged slightly and apologised, but ultimately pointed out that it wasn't really going to be practical to keep him on. Also, they had an illegal migrant worker who was willing to step in for a much-decreased pay. It was time for Eric to move on.

And so, Dickerson was his next port of call. The house was only one story – a brick affair with a red roof and large chimney, it sat on a sizable property which was not particularly useful to anyone, as there were far too many trees scattered around. Eric didn't care. He liked the greenery outside his window, and enjoyed watching it grow between visits from the man he paid to keep his lawn.

The status quo for Eric Coulter was very rarely altered.

As such, when there was a knock at the door at 7.28 pm, Eric Coulter was a little surprised. He made his way to the front door and swung it open, not caring to see who was outside first. No one was going to cause any problems, so it was safe not to check.

Rather curiously there was a person standing on his veranda.

An Asian person.

She (or maybe he? It was hard to tell) was probably no taller than 5'1", and he (she?) was wearing a black suit that seemed to be tailored. The shirt fit perfectly, and the tie sat on the chest without a single crease (oh, had to be a he…).

But the man's (actually…maybe it was a woman…) hair was pure white and was styled in a strange spiky, swooping fashion that seemed modern and cool, but also a little sci-fi. More disturbingly though were her (his?) eyes. They were jet black, and even with the light shining directly on their face, Eric couldn't separate the iris from the pupil.

"Can I help you?" Eric asked, trying to put as much confidence in his portly face as he could. There was something distinctly unnerving about the person standing on the veranda, and strangely it was making him feel quite inadequate. He was suddenly acutely aware of his tubby belly and jowly jaw; almost as though he knew if he had to run, he wouldn't be getting very far.

"I was hoping I could help you," the Asian replied, the voice largely neutral, though Eric guessed that English wasn't their first language. "I'm a friend of Nathan's," they added, and Eric narrowed his eyes at this.

He loved his son dearly, but there was definitely something going on, and over the past couple of days, he was absolutely certain that he was being followed. In Dickerson you knew everyone, so the car that was occasionally on the streets stood out like a sore thumb. No one had a black car, and certainly no one had a Toyota Yaris Sedan that was definitely straight off the rack. A 2019 car in Dickerson? No, that was not the case. And he knew it was a 2019 Toyota Yaris Sedan, because he heard Crazy Ralph and Old Luke talking, and though Eric didn't talk to anyone really, he knew Old Luke was a huge fan of cars. Knew everything about them.

So now there was a peculiarly well-dressed Asian of indeterminate gender standing on his veranda while a 2019 Toyota Yaris Sedan had been following him the last few days.

"I don't know what you're talking about," Eric opted for, as politely as he could. "I don't mean to be rude, but I have some things I need to be getting on with. I don't know where Nathan is, but I'm sure you'd best be calling him rather than coming to me. Much better state of affairs."

Eric stepped back to close the door, but the Asian put their hand up and rested it on the door. Eric couldn't close the door without pushing the hand back, and for some reason he was nervous about doing that. He gulped slightly, and muttered, "Excuse me."

"I don't work for the same company that Nathan does," the Asian said, their dark eyes boring into Eric's. "I also know he needs help. We agreed to meet here if that help was ever needed." The Asian removed their hand and stood back. It was a simple gesture, but it oddly filled Eric with relief. "Do you see up your driveway," the Asian asked, without looking back. Eric did as he was told, and his blood chilled when he saw the Toyota Yaris parked across the road from his drive. Before his brain could connect the Asian to the car, they were speaking. "They do come from the same company as your son. I would very much like to know they don't think I'm causing a scene."

Somewhat to Eric's own surprise, he stepped back and inclined his head, inviting the Asian into his house, which they took advantage of. He gave a last lingering look at the Toyota and then closed the door.

"What do they want?" he asked, following the Asian down the hallway, though he had no idea where they were going or what they thought they were doing.

"What do you think?" the Asian replied, softly.

"Are you here to take them away?" asked Eric, because the relief he had briefly felt was starting to linger. He hadn't particularly wanted to be his son's personal filing cabinet, but when Nathan had explained the situation, he understood why it was necessary. Despite that, having the documents in his house had made him nervous, and Eric was keen to get rid of them as quickly as possible.

"Nathan can't come here," the Asian replied. "But I can take them to him so we can get Nathan in a better situation."

"Oh good, good," Eric gushed. "Come this way," he beckoned, and turned just before they got to the kitchen. As they headed to the left, towards the only door that stood at the end of the corridor, Eric noticed how creaky the floors were, hearing the footsteps more precisely than ever. He couldn't work out why that made him nervous, until he got to the door and reached up above the door frame to get the key. The floorboards creaked as his weight shifted, but he realised that the Asian hadn't caused the boards to move at all. It was like there was a ghost following him.

He unlocked the door and flicked the light switch just to the right side, bathing the stairs leading to the basement in light. He turned and gave a small smile before starting to head down.

"I know that Nathan probably wasn't supposed to have these, but he gave me all the reasons, and, I know I don't understand much, because I'm certainly not as smart as he is, but I took him at his word. Because he knows things. He knows the law and he knows justice. He's a smart guy. I knew he would make sure they'd never catch him if things fell apart." He was babbling really, as he got to the bottom of the stairs, but he couldn't help himself. He didn't stop as he made his way to the safe that was situated in the corner. It was a classic. Big, green, sturdy and unbreakable. They didn't make them like that anymore. "I mean, I thought some of them seemed a little beyond his pay grade, but he's probably very high up, and can't tell me the truth. So I wasn't that put out."

"Sorry," he heard the Asian say as he bent down to turn the dials. "Sometimes my English is not so good. Did you say that you looked at the documents?" Eric heard the lock click into place once, twice, three times, as he spun the dials left and right, entering the sequence that would remain locked in his mind forever – his wife's birthday.

"Oh yeah, just the couple at the top. You know. I mean I didn't go beyond that, but I'm not totally stupid." He heard the lock clunk a fourth time.

"That's unfortunate," the Asian said. Eric frowned, and then stood up and turned to the Asian.

"Sorry?" he started to say, but he was cut off by two things. Firstly, he realised the Asian was pointing a gun at him – a slim thing with a tube on the end that he knew was a silencer. The second thing that cut him off was the Asian using it.

IV

In October, it doesn't tend to rain an awful lot in Maryland. On average, in fact, of the 31 days, only 8 of them have rain, and that only produces about three inches. As such, Nathan Coulter was slightly disappointed to see it bucketing down as he edged his car around Dickerson.

His car was a yellow 1980 AC 3000 ME, which, given he was comfortably in his forties, he had a lot of trouble explaining on his last blind date. He couldn't remember the name of the woman for the life of him, because the date had been astonishingly boring, and in truth even the thought of sex had floated away half way through the night when her nasally voice reached a point that was driving him insane. Having forgotten her name, he was about to end the date, when he was a little surprised by her asking him if he could drop her home. She had come by Uber; would that be too much of a problem?

If Nathan had any backbone he would have said no, but he really didn't. He had worked his way up the ladder at Langley by being a "good boy" and doing the right thing. He didn't rock the boat, and so by 43 was a senior analyst. Mason Lemon, who he often provided backup for, was in his thirties, and was a field agent. A senior field agent at that. Mason Lemon had not played by the book, and was not a "good boy", and yet the Deputy Director seemed to think the sun shone out of his ass, so suddenly premium assignments were given to Mason. An Iranian oil tanker had disappeared off the coast of India – let's give that investigation to Mason Lemon. A Japanese diplomat disappears and the Japanese government remain strangely uncommunicative about it – let's give that investigation to Mason Lemon. An Australian model meets up with an ASIO agent in Seoul – let's give that investigation to Mason Lemon. Premium assignments, because they were trips that didn't require a lot of work by Mason himself. Nathan and the rest of his team were doing most of the work. Mason was simply gathering up information on the ground.

Nathan said yes to the woman, and took her to his AC 3000 ME, and she laughed for a good minute when she saw it.

"I mean, it's cool, in a retro kind of way, right? Do you like retro shit?" Nathan had opened his mouth but then closed it. It didn't matter because she had seen his Trump sticker on the back window. "Oh, you don't do you?" she asked and he knew what was coming.

He was wrong, as it turned out. She hadn't given him a long-winded lesson on the evils of Trumpism. Instead, she just held out her hand (which he automatically shook) and then said she would find her own way home.

"Have a nice life," she said, in a way that managed to rhyme with "go fuck yourself". Somewhere, Nathan decided, his life had definitely gone wrong.

The rain pelted down as he eased his car along Dickerson Rd, his subconscious doing the driving as it sought out Mouth of Monocacy Rd, the light from the AC 3000 ME struggling to make a dint in the pouring rain. Nathan remembered the laughter at his car and it stung him, in the same way he had felt when as a 13-year-old he had asked a girl out and she had scoffed, suggesting that there was literally no chance that would ever happen. There were times throughout his life he wished he could turn to his sister, but he had burned that bridge spectacularly many years ago.

His brain turned the car into Mouth of Monocacy Rd, and immediately he paused, thankful for the rain. He shifted the gear stick into fourth gear from second, and the car immediately stalled – a quirk of this particular vehicle he had discovered ages ago (go through the gears, Eric had said repeatedly).

There was a car on the street, in the dark, its lights extinguished, but there were clearly shadowy forms in it. It was a black Toyota sedan, though beyond that Nathan couldn't quite place it. It didn't matter – no one in Dickerson was driving that sort of car. He turned his own lights out as he started his car, and then pulled back onto Dickerson Rd, turning the lights on again when he had gone a little distance.

The Deputy Director was clearly already making good on his word, and they had guessed he would make his way to his father's home. Logic dictated that he go straight to his home, but the fact was he really needed to get into that house. If not to make sure that his father was OK, to get what he needed from the house.

It was complicated, however, by a number of factors. The front way was clearly out, and if he headed any further down Mouth of Monocacy Rd, the men in the black Toyota would no doubt intercept him and ask him to go somewhere deeply unpleasant. They were unlikely to be CIA, but that didn't matter. He didn't fancy being taken anyway by either the NSA or the FBI. And ultimately it made no difference; on this particular occasion the Deputy Director would be his final port of call.

In addition to that, the further he went along Dickerson Rd, the further away from his father's house he was heading. The land was well spaced out, and the roads were few and far between. In truth, he needed to pull over quickly to ensure he didn't have to spend too much time making his way through the back fields, if not for the distance, for the fact that the rain was definitely not easing up.

Sighing, he pulled the car over, but then paused to see if there was any better cover around. There was a chance that whoever was in the Toyota had seen him and would try to catch up with him. To his right there was nothing but a long, well mowed field. To his left, however, the grain was tall, and so impulsively he turned off the road at the nearest break in the grain fields and drove into them, looking for a place to turn again and keep his car out of sight off the road. For once the low AC 2000 ME would help him out, and the rain would also add to the cover.

It didn't take too long before Nathan had turned the car off and was sitting in the dark, in the rain, in the middle of a field with tall grass on either side of him. Rather ironically, it was the safest he had felt in the last couple of days.

Taking a deep breath, he opened the car door and stepped out in the dark. He knew roughly where he was, but it had been a while since he had visited his father and it wasn't a case of going back to a family house, he had grown up in. But he still had a better idea of the area than the people in the black Toyota, and so he set off in the direction that he knew would take him roughly to the back of his father's land.

It took him less than five minutes to get to where he was going, but Nathan was thoroughly soaked by the time he was at the fence that marked the boundary of his father's land. He jumped over it in a style he thought was very smooth, but the back of his mind was saying that getting his foot caught in the metal netting of the fence was less Mason Lemon and more Three Stooges.

He also landed awkwardly and lay on the ground in the mud bemoaning his life for what seemed like a good hour.

Fortunately, it was significantly less time than that, and he made his way to the back of his father's house, reaching into his pocket to get out the key that he kept on his key ring at all time. He mentally berated himself for not spending enough time with his father. There came a point in everyone's lives where you get lazy about staying in touch with people, and take your family and friends for granted.

Nathan realised, as he slid the key into the lock of the back door, that he had definitely been guilty of that. He had been on several dates recently, but couldn't honestly remember the last time he had actually gone out with friends to enjoy a drink – and not just work mates after a long Friday, proper friends that he enjoyed spending time with and playing games with, or simply just talking shit with. He had grown up with Chris Long, a boy that he had met in his very first year of schooling, where the two had bonded after Chris had hit him with a wooden block. They were young at the time and it was the opening to a beautiful friendship that lasted a considerable period. Even now, Nathan would confidently say that Chris was his best friend, but when forced to address when the last time he had seen his friend, he could also confidently say that it wasn't in the decade past. He had let his friendship slip, and he hadn't even noticed it.

Now, he would think about calling Chris, asking to catch up, see if he wanted to have a drink, but every time he reached for the phone, his brain wondered if there was a reason they hadn't been in touch after all this time. Maybe Chris didn't want to talk to him. Maybe that was the real reason the two had become estranged.

Nathan decided, there and then as he slid the door open, that he wasn't very good at "adulting". Adulting required maturity and proper thought, but the truth was, Nathan didn't like to give too much thought to anything, and while he did like to think he was mature about things, ultimately, he probably wasn't doing great on that score either.

Which is why, when he found his father on the floor, a single gunshot wound in his forehead, he simply sat down and cried.

195

V

Dusty Springwood (named after the singer, because her parent's had genuinely thought it was Springwood; they were devastated when someone pointed out that the name was so close to Springfield) looked at her reflection and decided she wasn't really keen on what was looking back at her. There were times – mostly when she was stone cold sober – that she hated her job. She could see every single imperfection on her face and heard that voice tally them up. Eyes are looking puffy – you could do with more sleep. Pimple breakout, but then you do wear a lot of makeup, don't you? Those fake eyelashes are completely overdone, but let's be honest, it's better than the rubbish eyelashes you actually have. Looks like that little red blotch on your nose is coming up again; another symptom of too little sleep.

You can't polish a turd, Dusty.

She could hear someone in the toilet cubicle, breathing heavily, but they were probably not fucking someone else. Rather they were probably trying to calm down from the effects of whatever drug was being taken. Dusty put her face in her hands and sighed, before catching sight of the bruise on her upper arm.

Fuck me, bitch, what the hell's wrong with you? You need to see a doctor, the amount you bruise.

Her hair looked brittle as well. She needed to go to a proper hairdresser the next time she decided to peroxide it. But that cost money, and she needed to pay for school costs next week for Braiden. Everything had gotten so much more difficult since Mason's death.

"Oi," bellowed a voice from the door. "There's no one on stage. It's been almost fifteen minutes. One of you bitches needs to get up there." He didn't wait for a response, rather he felt slamming the door made his point.

"Fuck you," mumbled Jewel, as she sucked on her vape. Dusty envied her slightly – even in the club, Jewel managed to look like she was going out for a proper evening. Everything about her seemed perfect, from the shapely legs to the perfect waist and the amazing tits.

Oh, I'd pay a shit ton for tits like that, Dusty sighed inwardly. Jewel had them from simple biology. Some bitches had all the luck.

"You want me to go?" Jewel asked, and Dusty was annoyed at how Jewel not only looked perfect, but was always so friendly and agreeable. Nothing was too much effort for her, and she seemed determined to prove it.

"No," Dusty sighed – realising it was probably the fourth time in as many minutes she had done so. "I need the cash."

"Shit for the kid?" Jewel asked, not unkindly. Dusty envied Jewel that as well. No kids, the freedom to what she liked and make as much money as she wanted to. Jewel didn't need this club, but they sure as hell needed her. There was no way Rattlesnake was going to give Jewel any shit.

But Lexie, as Dusty had christened herself since starting at this club, wasn't going to fight back, so Rattlesnake would give her all the shit he wanted to.

"Bitch if you keep sighing like that, you gonna fold in on yo'self," Ginger said from the far corner, and Dusty couldn't not giggle at her friend's comment.

"I'm not feeling it today," she confessed.

"She's lost her regular," Jewel supplied, and again it wasn't a nasty comment.

"What, the spy man?" Ginger said, raising an eyebrow.

"He probably wasn't a spy man," Dusty said, feeling she should probably steer the conversation away from that ill-chosen word from conversations past.

"He gave off spy vibes," Jewel said with authority, as though she had encountered many such spies in her time.

"What's a spy vibe?" Ginger asked, curiously.

"Didn't you see the way he was always looking around, whenever he walked in. Subtle, like, but as soon as he walked in, he would lean at that bar and take a look around. He used to check us out for precisely five seconds. Like that guy that used to come in and look us up and down, but would always end up booking Lolita."

197

Dusty's eyebrows shot up, and she looked at Jewel.

"You thought Mason was a pedo?" she asked genuinely surprised.

"No, you twit," grinned Jewel. "I'm not saying that at all. After all he never booked Lolita, did he?" Lolita was comfortably twenty-two, but her waifish frame, small tits and boyish body made sure she was the pick of any man who preferred his girls younger. "I'm saying that when he checked us out, Mason seemed to be doing it for show. Just like the pedo. He would suss us all out, to pretend he was genuinely looking at everyone. But he wanted Lolita, and that's who he was going to book. Spy man was always going to book you, babe. But he was checking out the room every time he came in. He'd pause at that bar and drink the room in, but he made sure to give each of us five seconds, so that anyone looking thought he was checking out the dancers."

"You know everything," Dusty marvelled, and even Ginger appeared to be in awe. Jewel turned to them with a big grin.

"I'm fucking good at my job, bitches. How else do you think a lesbian can get straight men to book me?"

"I said," bellowed Rattlesnake, swinging the door open with such force, Dusty was sure the wall shook slightly, "will someone get on that fucking stage. *Please?*"

"Fuck's sake, 'Snake," Jewel groaned. "Lexie's going out now. Give her a chance to get there."

"Oh right, sorry your highness," Rattlesnake hissed.

"My lady," Jewel responded, loftily. "I'm a lady. That's how you address us." Rattlesnake paused, uncertain what to say. There had been a rumour sometime back that Jewel actually was a titled lady, and her cool English accent helped that rumour spread. Dusty wasn't certain whether it was true or not, but she was tempted to believe it.

With a weak smile at the other two girls, Dusty stood up and headed towards the door, being held open in a very sarcastic manner by Rattlesnake, though he still seemed to be struggling with how to respond to Jewel.

The club wasn't bad, to be honest, and there were a few options in Washington DC if you were interested in that sort of thing. From the outside, the club was not ostentatious; in many ways just another building sitting between a bar and, of all things, a wedding dressmaker (someone presumably had a sense of humour, though it was unlikely to be the owner of The Asylum Gentleman's Club). Clients had to ascend a short flight of stairs to get to the doorway, where they were greeted by a large man, wedged behind a tiny desk and dressed in an ill-fitting suit, who would take money, confirm age appropriateness, and then wave people through, unless, of course, one of those previous things didn't meet his approval, whereupon he would point them back from whence they came.

Once inside the club, there was a certain uniqueness to The Asylum. The stages had faux cages around them, bars stretching up to give the illusion the dancers were prisoners. Jewel said this lent to the idea that the dancers were prisoners for the men, which she confidently informed them that most men quite like the idea of. Dusty – now Lexie – was inclined to agree, as she entered the centre stage and tried to get the feel of the music.

There was a depressing lack of originality to that as well, with a rapper belting out a song that made some insinuation about women taking their clothes off for money, and said rapper throwing money at his bitches. Lexie didn't particularly want stirring power ballads, but it would have been nice, maybe, to just have some straight rock or even pop.

The other two stages were off to the side of the room, which occupied most of the bottom floor of the building. There was a bar at the back wall, but all the stock for it was in the basement below. The only other room was the women's changing area, with it's boring white walls and cheap red lockers. The money was being spent on the actual bar itself, but Lexie wondered if had been worth it. As the purple, pink and blue lights ensured that things seemed murky and mysterious, most of the effort that had gone into the velvet chairs and occasional tables was lost.

Not that anyone coming into the room was there for the décor.

Lexie gyrated, her mind on autopilot as she pondered other aspects of her life. As soon as she heard the change in music, she automatically unclipped the gold bra she had on and let it floor to the floor, her breasts gaining a degree of *whooping* from a couple of the men watching. They were easily pleased, Lexie reflected.

She had chosen, for the night, a genie style outfit, which was a bra, matching panties and sheer, flowing trousers that secured at the feet, all in sparkling gold. She loved the outfit, to be honest, and as the trousers were more white than gold, and the bra gave her boobs a pleasant lift, Lexie felt very comfortable with what she had chosen. Her spirits lifted slightly as a few of the clients pushed money through the bars of the stage.

She was slightly surprised, as she glanced at the money, to see that someone had pushed a $100 note through. Lexie was good enough at her job to know that she had to give whoever that person was a degree of personal attention, and so she slid to the floor and crawled over to the patron, collecting the money as she went and tucking it into the belt of her pants. As she got to the bar, she arched up, spreading her legs and grabbing the bars, pushing herself against them.

To her surprise, however, she saw someone she recognised. She wasn't sure of his name exactly – she thought it was something like Nate – but definitely knew he was a friend of Mason's. In fact, she even recalled seeing him loitering at the funeral. She wasn't sure exactly how close he and Mason had been, but she remembered Mason bringing Nate in several times, though usually Nate would have two drinks and then need to catch an Uber home. He was no Mason, and Lexie hoped he wasn't going to try to take Mason's place.

That would make things very awkward.

"I need to talk to you," he whispered, urgently, and Dusty (Lexie had disappeared thanks to this distraction) looked around a little nervously, wondering who was watching.

"Book me after this," she said, Lexie resurfacing a little.

"I mean," he started, but she put her finger to his lips and gave a sweet smile. Rattlesnake was prowling around, and had started to pay attention. She got up, suddenly aware the music had changed, and she turned to drop her silky pants to the floor, unclipping the anklets so she could step out of them (and also making sure her precious tips were tucked away as well).

Standing in nothing but her g-string, she began working the poll, Lexie having taken over once again, and all thoughts of other things pushed from her mind.

VI

Nathan Coulter had decided on his first visit to the Asylum Gentleman's Club, that he didn't particularly like it. He wasn't a nightclub sort of guy, if he were honest, and even though he loved the sight of a naked woman, he objected to having to pay for it. He could get nudity online in an instant, without having to resort to throwing money at people. It was an outrage, and as Mason wandered in like he owned the place, a wide smile on his face while he tipped everyone from the bouncer to the bar staff, Nathan resented everything about it.

Especially the floor. His shoes stuck to the floor with every step he took, and he could hear it as the spilled liquor turned the place into one of those mouse traps, where the mouse gets its feet stuck to the ground and can't escape. Perhaps there was no single better metaphor for a strip club than the floor he peeled himself off in order to follow Mason Lemon.

Now, having handed over a couple of hundred dollars, it wasn't just the sticky floor that irritated him. He could smell sweat from the dancers as they gyrated under the lights, and the vanilla perfume that they used to try to conceal it. Testosterone oozed through the room from the men, their dicks hard as they fought the desire to touch the naked flesh in front of them. He could hear them asking for the girls' phone numbers or their real names, and some of them played along, lying and giving them a fake real name.

Nathan hated it all. His last dance at the club had been with some woman named Jewel, who was haughty and English and stripped for him seductively, before asking him if there was any chance Mason was going to book another dancer tonight. She had ruined his evening with a single question and made everything about Mason once again.

Everything was always about Mason. He wasn't jealous, he just would have liked someone to be more interested in him than the charming Mason Lemon. Mason, of course, had overheard the conversation and said he was more than happy to book both Lexie and Jewel for both him and Nathan. That had been the first indication that Mason was happy to swing both ways. As the girls danced in front of them, their naked bodies tantalising both of them, Nathan could see how turned-on Mason was, and was angry that he was just as obvious.

But worse, Mason had sat there with his hand on Nathan's thigh, squeezing it every time the girls lent forward to reveal the possibilities of what was to come. His hand had been so close to Nathan's crotch, to this day Nathan couldn't get it out of his mind.

It wasn't a night he cared to remember.

"You know the rules?" Lexie said, gently pushing him down into the comfy chair.

"Yes, I remember," retorted Nathan, realising how angry he suddenly sounded.

"So, did you actually want me to strip?" Lexie asked, and Nathan hesitated for a moment.

"I mean, you'd better, otherwise they might suspect something," he answered finally.

"They?"

"Just take your clothes off," Nathan growled.

"What exactly do you want?" Lexie asked, her eyebrows knitting in confusion. Her bra came off and Nathan briefly glanced at the boobs before deciding they weren't really for him anyway.

"You spent time with Mason outside the club," replied Nathan, and Lexie's eyes widened for a moment.

"I don't know what you're talking about," she said, though it was a weak lie, given they had both been at the funeral.

"I know what went on," Nathan said. "You have to tell me if he told you about the documents." Lexie paused and the two looked at each other, their eyes refusing to back down from the contact.

"Look, you've got the wrong idea," she finally said, and she grabbed her bra, sliding it back on. "It's probably a good idea to end this."

"I haven't," Nathan said, grabbing her arm. She looked at his hand and he quickly recoiled, remembering where he was and what was going on. "Look, it's really important I find out what happened to the documents. I thought I knew where they were, but someone took them, and it's become

202

a real thing."

"I don't know what you're talking about," repeated Lexie. "You need to leave. You're scaring me."

"Listen you stupid, little girl," hissed Nathan, "if you think this is scary, wait til there's a black Toyota out the front of your house and two MiBs knocking on your door. You'll be wishing you bothered to tell me what I needed to know as they weigh up whether to put a bullet in your head or not!" Lexie looked at him and Nathan was glad to see that her eyes started to accept the situation he was in.

"I'm not the person you need to be talking to," Lexie said, her voice so soft that Nathan wasn't certain he had heard her correctly above the noise of the club.

"Then who is?" he retorted, trying to contain his anger.

"You need to talk to Mason's wife," she said, and Nathan had to ask her to repeat what she said, because he couldn't believe what she was saying. "She's the one that knows where the documents are. Go to her, ask her, you'll get what you want. But promise me that you won't drag me into this!"

Nathan's mouth opened to say something, but then he closed it again because his brain wouldn't function to supply him with any sort of sentence. When the club lights changed from green and gold to red and blue, his heart skipped a beat, and he could feel his blood pressure rise.

"OK," was all he was finally able to get out, and he stood up, almost knocking Lexie over, and headed straight out of the dance room. He didn't bother to look back, didn't see the lack of curiosity on the face of the controller, or the relief that swam across Lexie's face. He just went straight through the club, heading down the stairs to the main club level and the door outside.

On autopilot, he walked to his car, got into it and turned the key, his brain focussed on only one question: Mason had a wife?

VII

The Deputy Director of the CIA (or, more accurately, one of), sat at a table in The Hill Café, a delightful little café on the corner of 15th St NE and A St NE (there was, he felt, a real laziness to not bothering to name a street beyond letters. Numbers were bad enough, but simply calling a street "A" showed new depths to city planners' disinterest). The table was positioned nicely, so that he could see the door, but also, he was able to turn his chair a little such that he could take in the counter and most of the back of the café without making it look too obvious he was turning around.

His coffee was absolutely perfect – ideally, he would prefer a Ca Phe Da, but the wonderful owners of The Hill were happy to meet him halfway, and used condensed milk with his coffee, giving him almost the exact taste he needed; a taste he had acquired while spending time in Vietnam on assignment – and the grilled ham, cheese and egg sandwich that went with it was a breakfast of the gods. There were times – rare times – when he felt a little bad about being at work as much as he was, but if there was one upside to that, it was breakfasts like these.

He was mildly disturbed about the crash that was still being reported on the news from a few days earlier. Some rally car event had occurred in Washington for the first time, and given the terrible accident that had taken place, it would probably be the last. It stirred something in his head about a particular report that had briefly crossed his desk, but ultimately it wasn't his department so he hadn't spent much time dwelling on it. One learned very quickly to be able to compartmentalise when working in the CIA.

Sipping his coffee, he was a little surprised to see a young woman standing before him, her blonde hair pulled back in a ponytail, and her shirt and jeans just that little too tight. She had a great figure which was distracting, but the Deputy Director assessed her eyes, nose and mouth, catching a glimpse of her hands for any noticeable jewellery or marks. There was something familiar about her, but the context seemed wrong. If he had seen this woman before she was definitely not a blonde.

"Would you like anything else?" she asked, a little smile playing across her lips.

"No, everything is fine," he said, wondering if his innate paranoia was getting out of control.

"We aim to please, Deputy Director," she said, a little bit of a simper in her tone, but the Deputy guessed it was judged.

"I assume you're who I'm here to meet?" he asked, not bothering to play games. The use of his title was enough to make it clear who she was.

"You wanted the meeting, sir," she said, and the Deputy realised he couldn't quite make out her age. She seemed in her early twenties, but when she smiled, her face crinkled in a slightly older way.

"Would it be unfair to say that I'm worried that my job is taking too long, given the money that I paid for it?" The Deputy Director raised an eyebrow to underscore his feelings.

"I feel, if you simply wanted someone dead, you could have gone to the Fat Man," the girl replied. "I mean, he's expensive but he's terribly effective. My understanding is that you wanted a mess cleaned up, and you wanted it done absolutely properly. Man Garam is very, very good at that."

"I have a dead man I have to deal with," the Deputy growled.

"A dead man who had seen all of the things you didn't want anyone to see. You can't wipe people's memories. You just simply," she paused, tapping her pen on the ring on her lip. "Delete them," she finished, a little anticlimactically. The Deputy Director was annoyed, but he had to admit that the job was being done the way that he wanted it done. "The thing is," the girl continued, "you have to let Garam work at their own pace. Even now, by all accounts, they know where the documents are and they are going to retrieve them. Once it's done, you'll have what you need. In total. Job done. And hopefully paid for." The last line sounded a bit like a threat, but the Deputy Director decided it was just her way of putting things and pushed it aside.

"It is paid for," he decided to say, just to clarify the situation. "Man should already know that."

"I'm not Man," the girl said sweetly.

"No," he grumbled, his mind suddenly locking into place and working out where he had seen the eyes and lips before. The hobo under the bridge who had been Man Garam's other contact. Or, more accurately, their only contact. Or perhaps just the only one he had encountered. Either way, there was a temptation to have this woman tracked and the ghost known as Man Garam located, but in truth, the Deputy Director was sure someone else had already tried that (probably unsuccessfully) and it wouldn't achieve much. It might even result in the girl's – the woman's death. "I suppose," he decided, "you have me over something of a barrel. You should probably let your employer know that we've been forced to make a report and the NSA have been informed of some of the situation. We've formally terminated Coulter's employment and issued a burn notice. The NSA are in the process of attempting to retrieve Coulter. Surprisingly he's being slightly more effective than I would have thought he'd be." He mused for a moment, wondering if he regretted Coulter's actions, but then decided he didn't really care. He certainly never liked Nathan Coulter, so he wasn't going to start giving a shit now.

"I'll let Garam know," the girl said. "Is there anything else I can get you?"

"You don't work here," the Deputy Director snapped irritably.

"Actually, I do today. The ladies are lovely and offered me a job. This is a test run, but you never know. I might like it here." She grinned, flashing a tongue piercing in the process, and turned to go back into the kitchen.

Inwardly, the Deputy Director groaned. Honestly, the people in this job.

VIII

Somewhat ironically, the Deputy Director wasn't the only person meeting a woman in regards to the situation in Washington DC. Nathan Coulter, tapping his foot nervously, was seated at a table just on the sidewalk out the front of Bread Furst bakery, situated at 4434 Connecticut Ave, oddly tucked between a delightful six story building of units, and a carwash. It had once been a realtors, but now, with its windowed front, annexed front door, grey stone roof, and blue and white striped sun shade, it was a relaxed slice of heaven, with the gorgeous aroma of freshly baked goods wafting down the street to do battle with the Burger King sitting across the road from the carwash.

Nathan had his back to the glass wall so he could see the street in front of him. Washington felt like it was on high alert since the Formula One accident. There were hushed talks that suggested maybe a terrorist situation had taken place, but Coulter no longer had access to his usual information channels and was unable to pursue the truth.

It was, in point of fact, his lack of such access that led him to Bread Furst. Having cried for a significant time on discovering his father's corpse, he was initially going to blame himself for the death, but then came to the conclusion it was probably the person who had put a bullet between his father's eyes. He couldn't take responsibility for the situation, regardless of what his father was looking after in the basement safe. No one had to kill to prove a point, and the Deputy Director was definitely to blame for what had happened.

His first thought was to get in touch with his sister, but after all this time it would look highly suspicious and so that wasn't going to be worth his time. In addition to that, there was probably a very good chance that his phone was being monitored, and so whoever was in the black Toyota (the FBI, maybe?) would be all over his call. More often than not, Intelligence agencies aren't keen on sharing information (after all, the idea is to gather information, not disseminate it), but needs must when the devil drives, and Satan was definitely at the wheel today, so the Deputy Director would have called anyone who'd listen to learn about Nathan Coulter.

With his sister ruled out, and all his contacts at the CIA off the list as well, that left very little option, but he had to find out what was going on, and so he decided to take a risk. He had once been given a name at Interpol to contact in case of emergencies, and at the time he had suspected that it was just a case of someone being polite. No one really expected him to call, but with Satan doing doughnuts in hell, Nathan made the call and requested to talk to Broadsword. The call lasted less than ten seconds.

"Yes?"

"I'm Nathan Coulter…"

"Location?"

"Washington DC. I work for…"

"Thank you."

And that was it. The link had been cut off. When Nathan dialled it again, the conversation was very different.

"Good morning, Harreveld, Titman & Swindells Support, how can we help you?"

Nathan hung up immediately, and dialled the number again, convinced he'd got it wrong.

"Good morning, Harreveld, Titman & Swindells Support, how can we help you?"

"Uh, I was wondering if I could speak with Broadsword," he said cautiously.

"I'm sorry, sir, we don't have a Mr Broadsword on staff. Is there anyone else I can put you in contact with. What sort of support were you looking for?" The voice sounded almost the same as the one who had asked for his location earlier but in truth, he couldn't be certain.

"I was," he began, but changed his mind. "I think I have the wrong number," he finished lamely.

"No problem," the cheery voice said, and then hung up.

Ouch.

The quickly reached conclusion was that he had been totally led astray and that there wasn't anyone named Broadsword who was remotely interested in his situation, let alone what he had to say. This would mean he had to track down Mason Lemon's wife by himself, and that was going to be particularly difficult. He had worked with the man for the past few years, and yet there was nothing said at any point about a wife. It wasn't even on his personal record, and Nathan knew he would have known because he had a copy of said file.

And then his phone gave a soft "ping". There was a new message and Nathan tapped the phone to read it.

Abandoning his car (he was in Washington now, so he didn't really need it to get around in, and black Toyota would have definitely known who was driving it by now), he called for an Uber and gave the directions. Consequently, he sat in front of the bakery, sipping on a very black tea and wishing he had ordered something to eat.

When the striking woman with the long, dark hair sat down in front of him, he wondered for a moment if she had got the wrong table. However, her face rang a bell and from the depths of his brain, he remembered a woman, formerly CIA, now Interpol, with the unlikely name of Justice Kennedy. She did look as though she had recently been beaten, but he decided not to question that. He knew her line of work, after all.

"What did you order me?" she asked, with a savage grin, and Nathan immediately felt outside of his comfort zone. Looking back on his life, he reflected he was never very good with women, particularly those that were "in your face" (which, if he were honest, was a description he gave away with gay abandon). He had nothing against women, not at all. He was all for women who were important and got positions above him, and became Assistant Directors.

They just scared him a little.

All this went through his mind, and he opened his mouth only to be met with a "Don't worry, already taken care of." So he shut his mouth again and tried to think of a good question.

"Are you Broadsword?" which sounded lame, even to his ears.

"No. Definitely not. I wouldn't want to be," she drawled. "Rumour has it, Nate (can I call you Nate?) you've been burnt."

"Oh," said Nate quietly. Well, it made sense, and honest to goodness, he was expecting it.

"Rumour also has it, Nate, that you're responsible for Mason Lemon's death." Justice sat back in her chair and raised an eyebrow, which made Nate feel very uncomfortable. She was supposed to be on his side, that was the idea behind summoning Broadsword (or Broadsword's pal, if Broadsword was a person and not some weird kind of codeword that they used in Interpol). Now it seemed like he was justifying his existence.

"I had nothing to do with it," he protested. "I'm just the senior analyst assigned to him. I can't do anything more than give him information. You should know that!" Justice's eyebrow seemed to raise a little more but it cut.

"Didn't he die in South Korea?" she pondered.

"He was there keeping an eye on some Australian woman," came the mumbled response. "There were concerns about one of the…things. That music thing. What's it called?"

"The music thing?" asked a bemused Justice.

"Yeah, you know. In Korea, the thing about the music. They're all groups or, whatever. But it's got a name."

"I literally don't know what you're talking about."

"K-Pop!" Nate actually smiled, happy that his memory had not let him down. "There's a music label where a lot of the artists were dying. It seemed a little too convenient, and Mason went over there to do a bit of digging. He thought that it might be connected to one of the groups, and we needed an in. Then this Australian model turns up, all pally with them, and it turns out…"

"Yeah, I know the rest of the story," Justice scowled. "That girl is in the wrong place at the right time so often it's scary."

"Well, we contacted ASIS, they said they would take care of it, and so I let Mason know."

"The question is, Nathan," Justice lent forward, her hazel eyes burrowing into Nathan's own blue ones. "Why did Mason die?"

"I don't know," Nathan shrugged. "He just turned up dead." Justice sat back in her chair, never taking her eyes off Nathan, which did not help his comfort levels, but finally moved when a waiter brought her a coffee.

"You're lucky, you know. I'm supposed to be in hospital," she said, after taking a sip.

"Oh sorry. Nice coffee?" he simpered.

"No," she said, closing the small talk. "What do you want, exactly?"

"I need to know who Mason Lemon's wife was. I don't have access to my old resources, and I was wondering if Interpol would be able to help."

"Interpol?" Justice narrowed her eyes.

"I have very few options," snapped Nathan. "It's not exactly like I could contact ASIS or MI6 and ask for help, can I? And you've just pointed out that I've been burnt, so no one in the US is going to talk to me. This was the only card I had to play." He stopped, aware of how heavy his breathing had become, and he wondered for a brief moment if his blood pressure was going to kill him before anyone else did.

"I'll see what I can do," Justice said, and Nathan widened his eyes in surprise. He realised he had genuinely thought she would hang him out to dry. "We don't exactly keep files on people," she started, though Nathan immediately thought that was a lie. Perhaps it was the nature of the job, but he was deeply suspicious of anything that came out of the mouths of intelligence agents. "But," she continued, "there are a few files we have as a result of sharing information between agencies. One might be about Mason Lemon."

"I thought you only shared police files," Nathan asked, unable to stop himself prodding the sleeping bear.

"We do," Justice grinned. "But you'd be surprised at how informed the police are. And sometimes we get help from others." She stood up, and stretched, her t-shirt riding up, showing off the definition of her stomach. She was quite attractive really, and Nathan felt his confidence ebb away, as he took in the shapely legs, her gym pants clinging to the curves. "I should probably let you know," she said, and he quickly looked up to her face, his own going red, "that word on the street is Man Garam is gunning for you."

And just like that, all lustful thoughts of Justice Kennedy's perfect bum and gorgeous abdomen, were gone, as his blood went cold.

"Man Garam isn't even real," he murmured, but he didn't believe it, and Justice knew he didn't.

"Well, in that case, you won't feel the bullet when it hits you," she said, but there was no grin. She turned and walked away, the legs and ass in fine definition. But it was wasted on Nathan Coulter.

Man Garam.

If Justice Kennedy was right, he was a dead man.

IX

Although he wasn't a field agent, Nathan had spent enough time metaphorically looking over Mason Lemon's shoulder to have a few basics about "the game". He made his way on foot, ducking into alleys to come out on other streets where possible, to the nearest phone shop he could find. There he bought a new phone which he transferred the number that had sent him the message from Kennedy onto, and handed his old phone over to be deleted and sold.

With that done, his next goal was to find a place to lay low until Kennedy got him the information he needed. He knew he was taking a big risk, but he was gambling on the fact Kennedy might be annoyed enough with the CIA that she wouldn't want to do them any favours. Many always suspected her loyalty, though there were a large number that were convinced her allegiance was first and foremost to the US. Nathan was banking that the first lot were correct, and that she would put her job before her patriotism. Personally, he despised that, but given his own situation, even he had to acknowledge the hypocrisy in that thought.

Once again, he was tempted to send a message to his sister and see if he could get her help, but with the sale of his old phone, there was no way he was going to do that. That was definitely a number that he hadn't committed to memory. There was no point in going to friends because they would definitely be on a watch list. And, of course, he didn't really have any friends.

There were options, however, but they required him to use his phone, of course, and he bitterly regretted not thinking his actions through from the outset. The burner phone he had was limited, a simple Nokia 225, and so he had no real access to browse the web, and internet cafes were few and far between.

Mason Lemon would have thought it through. He would have

used the phone to find an AirBnB that was currently available and hole up there. The only thing that he had kept on him was a gun that he had taken from his father's house – a Beretta Pico, the thinnest pistol currently on the market. Which meant he would have to do something he wasn't going to be particularly proud of.

Live in the forest.

He was actually quite near Soapstone Valley Park, and it occurred to him that he could probably bunker down there until he got the message from Kennedy. Hopefully that would happen soon, because it was unlikely he could survive, homeless, for any great length of time, and also the police would probably be itching to arrest him as soon as they found him. But for the moment it would suffice.

His walk brought him down Windom Pl, and as he headed down the road, seeing the park not too far ahead, he also saw the apartment block on his right. It was an ugly looking building, dull brown bricks, with metal grates positioned on the walls, and a heavy metal door that required you to walk up a set of iron steps to get to. The railings on the third floor had been covered with cardboard, and on the whole the place looked like a mess.

But going up the steps (and the more he thought about it, the more Nathan suspected he was looking at the back entrance), was a young man, probably in his late teens.

He could stay in the park as a homeless person…

…or he could just force his way into the young man's house and stay there until he got the message. That would give him access to considerably more resources.

Turning on his heel, he made his way over to the steps, calling out "Can you hold the door for me?"

The young man did as he was asked, puzzled, because there didn't seem to be any reason for Nathan to need that sort of help. Nathan said a polite thanks, closing the door behind him, and affecting an air of disinterest around the young man.

The young man walked away, down the corridor and as he slid his key into a dull, off-white door and pushed it open, Nathan made his move. He had lingered in the corridor, delighted that his target hadn't needed to go to another floor, and when the door open, Nathan pulled out the Beretta and quickly strode up to the door, pushing the man through the door, and followed, pulling it shut behind him and levelling the gun.

"Get your clothes off," Nathan shouted, trying to sound like Mason. Mason had once told him that forcing someone naked was the quickest way to get that person vulnerable. Naked people were unlikely to make a move, and would sometimes be more concerned about trying to protect their dignity than actually making an attempt to fight back or escape. "Quickly!" Nathan snapped, and turned to make sure the door was locked.

When he turned back the young man had removed his jeans and t-shirt, and was in the process of removing his bra…

Oh.

Nathan's jaw dropped slightly as the young woman stood before him completely naked, one arm across her breast, and the opposite hand between her legs.

"Please don't rape me," she whimpered, tears welling in her eyes, and Nathan couldn't have felt shittier if he tried.

"Get over there," he said, waving the gun, though it occurred to him that maybe it was time to actually look at where he was and what he was doing.

The apartment he was in wasn't great. The dull, off-white colour of the door was the same colour of the interior walls. There was a kitchen table to his left, in a space that had cupboards and an oven, while to the right there was another door, and Nathan quickly pulled it open to see the bathroom beyond.

The woman had retreated to the space he had pointed to, which was the living room, a slightly larger space with bean bags and a television set. She stood in the room looking wretched, and Nathan took her in for the first time. She had a little scar at the top of her forehead that disappeared into the short, spiky hair. She was thin, almost waifish, but there was a Elfen quality to her.

Noticeably, however, there were dark bags under her eyes, and her eyes were slightly bloodshot. Nathan suspected she was a user, and he immediately felt better. Junkies weren't worth the hassle.

214

"Right," he said, confidence returning, "here's what's going to happen. I'll be staying until I get an important message. Once that's done, I'll be gone. You can do one of two things. Either you can wait with me and live, or I can shoot you dead. I don't think anyone will miss you. Will anyone miss you?" He sneered as he delivered the last line, and she looked back, her eyes wide with fear.

"My girlfriend might," she replied, and he wanted to scream *why can't this just be easy?????*

"Does she live here?" he asked, and she nodded. "Is she coming back tonight?" and the girl shrugged. "Fuck!"

Nathan realised that he had automatically started pacing, which was annoying. He liked to think he was in control of his actions and that he was calm, reassured and didn't lose his mind when pressure was applied, but it was becoming clearer and clearer that wasn't the case.

What would Mason do?

"What's your name?" he snapped, hoping that it might inspire him.

"Kim," she replied through sniffles.

"Well, *Kim*, what are you taking at the moment? Is it going to be a problem if you don't get it in a hurry?" She looked at him incomprehensibly and his eyes widened. "Huh?" he growled, miming injecting himself in the arm.

"I don't do drugs," she said.

"Then what's all this?" he waved at her, and the tears in her eyes dribbled down her face. He could see the sheer terror and wondered for a moment what the hell he was doing. What had he been turned into?

"I don't understand," she blubbed.

"You're so skinny, and the bloodshot eyes," he said, but even to his own ears he sounded ridiculous.

"I'm a dancer," she said, "and I haven't slept in a day because we've been practicing for a performance." This was enough for her to actually cry, and she sacrificed her dignity to put her hands to her eyes, falling to her knees in the process. "Please don't rape me," she said again.

215

"I'm not going to rape you," Nathan said angrily, but he could feel the guilt stab in his heart. Frustrated he sat down in one of the bean bags, thinking how ridiculous he must be looking. The situation had gone from bad to worse, and he bitterly regretted the decision not to hide out in the park. Now he had to deal with a crying, naked girl.

Dancer? As he looked over at the fridge, he saw photographs, and in a few there was the girl, dancing. Beside one that had two girls and "Never forget you Lil" scrawled on it, there was even a shot of the girl in a tutu, her hair in a bun, twirling. How could he have missed something so obvious?

There was a bang at the door, and Nathan surprised himself with how quickly he jumped up and trained his gun on the door.

"Is everything alright in there?" came a male voice. Nathan's eyebrows furrowed and he turned to Kim, who looked up at him.

"Who is it?" he mouthed.

"The next-door neighbour," she whispered.

"Get rid of him!" Tentatively she stood up and made her way to the door, her hands once again protecting her nudity.

"Everything's cool, Joe," she said, leaning against the door.

"You sure, Kim? I thought I heard a shout or something?"

"Everything's fine, seriously. I was about to have a shower and I fell. I'm OK, just slipped over and hurt my knee a little. But I'm OK. I just need to rest it."

"Well, you protect that knee. You're gonna need it soon." Nathan pursed his lips, a little concerned at how close this neighbour seemed to be to Kim. If he suspected anything there would be a big problem, but the girl had thought on her feet and come up with a good story.

"No, it's all good. I got kicked out. I'll tell you about it when Lily gets back."

Got kicked out. That explained the bloodshot eyes.

"Lily?" the neighbour said, and Nathan's ears pricked up.

216

"Yeah. Lily's back." There was a pause, and Nathan put his finger on the trigger of the Colt, aiming it at the door.

"OK, wow. Unexpected," Joe finally said. "Alright, good luck."

"Thanks. I'm just going to have a rest."

"Cool. Bye!" Nathan heard Joe's footsteps retreating and Kim turned back to see the gun pointed at her. Nathan beckoned for her to come back to the room and pointed to the corner, where she stood.

"Good," Nathan finally said. "You can sit down. We'll wait. As soon as I get the message, this will all be over."

"Do you need a drink, or something?" Nathan was about to give her a sharp negative, but he paused and realised that he actually really needed a glass of water. He watched her go get it, after replying, and realised he hadn't really paid attention to the girl at all. Her back, bum, legs and arms were well muscled, and her petite frame made it more obvious she was a dancer.

"Why did you get kicked out? I thought you had a performance," he asked. She brought back the glass, but had grabbed a tea towel to cover herself. Annoyed slightly he snatched it away from her as he took the glass, and she quickly tried to cover up.

"Why do you want me naked?" Kim asked. "Is it just to see what I look like?" Suddenly she dropped her hands and stood before him, completely nude. She was lithe, with her muscles clearly defined. Her breasts were relatively small, but there was a beauty to her that he hadn't previously noticed.

"Put your clothes back on," Nathan said, unable to continue looking.

"Why?"

"Naked people are less inclined to run away. No one wants to walk into the streets naked." To his surprise, Kim laughed.

"Oh, no," she said, giggling. She strolled over to one of the beanbags and grabbed a bathrobe, which she then slid on. "I'm pretty comfortable with my body. I've been nude in performance art before. It

217

doesn't really bother me." As if to prove her point, she tossed the robe back onto the bean bag, and turned to Nathan, not bothering to cover. "What message are you waiting for?"

Nathan found himself unable to look at her directly now she seemed to be embracing her nudity, and he wondered if she had decided to turn his ploy back on him.

"It's nothing to do with you," he replied.

"Maybe I can help?" Nathan actually laughed at this, and she looked a little annoyed. "I'm not useless. And you haven't been a runaway success, have you?" He opened his mouth to say something and then shut it again, surprisingly hurt by what she had said. It was no secret he was never considered Top Floor material at the Agency, but to have someone, some random person point this out was brutal. Outside of his sister, no one had ever spoken like that to his face.

However, something was nagging at the back of his mind. The change in Kim's character, her confidence...no, it was more than that. What was it?

His train of thought was interrupted by another knock at the door. This time, there was no question of how he felt. Nathan's senses went to high alert. This was probably Lily returning, which meant...

And then his brain connected two points. There was a photo on the fridge that had said "Never forget you Lil". Nathan turned to Kim, and drew his gun on her. He could see the terror in her eyes, but there was something else – defiance. The bitch had sold him out. Quickly he dashed to the back window and looked out, seeing three police cars and the black Holden all parked.

"Police, open up please," came the firm voice from the front door, but Nathan had moved on, desperately searching for another way out that wasn't the window. His options were limited, and a brief check of the very few rooms there were in the apartment made it clear that it was the window or no way at all.

Making a decision, Nathan opened the window and he turned to Kim, keeping the gun on her.

"Get out," he said, indicating the window.

"No," she replied, a wobble in her voice.

"Get out, or I kill you," Nathan said, keeping his voice low.

"You won't," Kim said.

"I need you as a distraction. You can do it by being alive and climbing out the window, or by being a corpse on the floor here. Your choice." It was enough. Kim swallowed deeply, but went over to the white-framed window and started to climb through. Nathan followed, keeping the gun on her, and was surprised to see a ladder bolted to the wall beside the window. Cautiously she started to go down, and at least one police officer had noticed the movement.

Nathan followed her, but once on the ladder he began climbing up, leaving the police officer to stay and help Kim. He wished he could have shot the neighbour who must have contacted the police, but there was no time for petty retribution. Also, he'd never actually fired a gun in his life before, so he was unlikely to start now.

By the time he reached the roof, he had come to the conclusion that it wasn't his best move, as he really had no way to escape without being seen by the police below, and presumably the two NSA agents on his trail. But even as he had been climbing, he had seen the police officer who had noticed Kim race over to her, and he was likely to have been joined by the others. If the two NSA agents were still inside the building, he did have a small chance. There was probably a matching fire ladder on the other side of the building, and if he was fast enough...

To his disappointment, he almost was. His plan had worked perfectly, but he wasn't quite at the bottom when the NSA agents peered over the top and spied him. They shouted, but he couldn't make out what they were saying – not that it was particularly important. He knew exactly what they wanted.

When he got to the bottom, he ran. The police were already after him, but he quickly ducked into the nearest gap with the neighbouring buildings, seeking to get out the other side where there was a crowd, he could lose himself in. As he ran, he shrugged his jacket off and threw the gun away, both into a nearby garden.

He was at the everything or nothing stage. Now all he had on him was his wallet and burner phone. The crowd on the street he had emerged onto (he had no idea where he was and didn't have time to check anymore) wasn't thick enough to disappear completely into, but he moved swiftly, trying not to attract attention. Occasionally he glanced back, and thought he could see pursuers, but he wasn't entirely sure. Again, it didn't matter. He needed to keep running.

X

The house was largely undistinguished. It was a single-story affair, with large bay windows at the front and a short staircase leading to the doorway, but the colour was a boring not-quite-white, and the roof a boring not-quite-red, resulting in it fading away into the houses around it. If it weren't for the upturned kiddie's trike, there would be nothing really remarkable about it at all. When the smooth black Lamborghini Sesto Elemento pulled up in front of the house, it became the centre of attention. This was perhaps unsurprising, as it was very rare to see a sports car in suburbia, let alone one that cost in excess of two million in the currency of your choice.

It certainly attracted the attention of two teenage boys, who immediately dropped their bikes to come over and check out the car, having been distracted by the growl it made on its arrival. Their attention was redirected when the door opened and two shapely legs swung out, high heeled red pumps the same colour as the Sesto Elemento's upholstery touching the ground. When the young woman got out of the car, she smoothed down the red mini-dress, letting it cling to her perfect figure, and didn't really stop the boys from ogling. They didn't notice that, without the heels, she would probably be about the same height as they were, because they were far more interested in the legs and the butt. Her beautiful Asian features, made up to look even more exotic were topped by short, white hair.

"You need to be more discrete when you are checking women out," she said playfully, but not nastily to the boys. They had the decency to look shamefaced.

"We love your car, Miss," one of them managed to say, and for a moment the woman looked as though she were about to say something, but then thought better of it.

"It's called a Sesto Elemento," she purred, not unlike her ride had. "Do you know what that means? It's Italian."

"The Sixth Element," one of the boys said, and his friend looked a little surprised. "Dad," he said and that seemed to explain everything to his friend.

"Aren't you clever?" the woman smiled. She turned and walked away from the car, leaving the boys to look at her adoringly. However, as she started to make her way up the drive, one of them called out to her.

"Hey, Miss, are you buying the house?" She paused and turned back to them, her eyes obscured by the sunglasses she had put on, making them unreadable.

"Why do you ask?"

"Well, it would be sick to have someone like you in the neighbourhood. But that house is haunted," he said, with all the confidence of a fifteen-year-old who knew everything. The woman turned and walked back to the boys, getting to the car and leaning against it like she was in the middle of a photoshoot.

"What do you mean, haunted?" she asked.

"Well, it's a ghost house," the first boy said. He had long, shaggy dark hair, and it was now obvious that after time the hair resettled in an awkward manner, so that he had to wipe it away from his face and back into the position that he wanted it to remain in, even if the hair refused to comply. "There was a family there, but they were all murdered."

"Really?"

"Yeah, it was brutal," the second boy said, warming to his friend's theme. "Someone came in late at night and slit the throats of all of them!"

"No," shaggy hair said, pushing his friend. "They were shot to death. Like, someone walked in and shot them all. I reckon they were part of a cult!"

"They weren't," his friend said, dismissing the claim. "They were rich. They were attacked like that guy in that movie did. You know, the movie where the guy goes to the house and kills all those actors or something. It's great. It has Harley in it."

"Dude, she's fit," shaggy grinned.

"Dude!" agreed his friend. The Asian woman couldn't help but smile at this, though even with her bright red lipstick, she seemed more like a cat indulging her prey.

"So, we don't know why or how they were murdered, or even if they were murdered, but we definitely know that they are all dead," she summed up.

"Well, yeah I guess," agreed shaggy. Friend nodded sagely, and the two tried to give off the air of wizards who had just foretold the future; or more accurately seen into the past.

"Well, I suppose I'm glad that you told me," the Asian woman said. "After all, I don't want to be killed by ghosts."

"Well, we're good at protecting people from ghosts," Friend said, and Shaggy nodded enthusiastically.

"What does that mean?" Catwoman asked, suppressing a smile.

"Well, we could go in and see if the ghosts are there," Shaggy announced, and Friend looked a little concerned, though the look Shaggy gave him made it clear that this was not something that was up for debate. *She might be grateful!* his eyebrows said, though clearly how she would demonstrate this gratitude was not something he considered.

"I guess we could," agreed Friend, with much less enthusiasm.

"Oh, well if you want to," Catwoman said. She reached into the clutch that was hanging over her shoulder. "Here's the key," she proffered. Shaggy took the key, though both boys were surprised when they looked at it. It seemed much *busier* than most keys they had seen. "I'll follow when you have all the ghosts out," she added.

For the first time Shaggy seemed a little uncertain about his decision, but he bravely headed towards the front door, followed by Friend, whose own uncertainty was magnifying. Catwoman watched them go, looking for all the world like a scientist watching two rats in a maze – a cold, emotionless observation.

Cautiously, Shaggy reached the top of the stairs and reached out with the key.

"Kez," Friend said, grabbing Shaggy's arm. "Dude, there might be ghosts. I mean for real."

"There's no such thing as ghosts, dude. But there is a hot babe with a mint car back there and we need to look cool, not losers afraid of nothing." Kez put the key into the lock, managing to strut somewhat in the process, and the lock easily unclicked. Turning the handle, Kez pushed the door open and he stepped in, somewhat more cautiously than his attitude suggested.

Friend followed, definitely as cautiously as his attitude suggested, and the pair moved slowly into the hallway.

"I wish we'd bought a hockey stick or something," muttered Friend, and Kez nodded in agreement. The house was empty. Literally room after room of nothing, giving the impression that it was much bigger on the inside than the outside suggested.

"Do you know which room they were killed in?" Friend whispered, unable to bring himself to raise his voice. He was delighted when Kez did the same.

"Maybe we'll know when we see the blood," Kez replied.

"What blood?" came a much clearer voice, and the two screamed, grabbing each other and dancing on the spot. Catwoman looked at them with a degree of humour, but also disappointment.

"Shit!" Kez finally got out. "Shit, shit, shit, shit, shit. Don't sneak up on us!" Catwoman extended her hand, and Kez looked puzzled, before remembering, and handing the key back to her.

"Thank you for getting the ghosts out. I feel much safer now," Catwoman said, her mocking smile just a little hurtful.

"Well, you'll be grateful, because you'll never know what would have happened if we hadn't come in," Friend blustered.

"That is true," Catwoman agreed. She held out her hand, and they each shook it. "Maybe we'll see each other later," she said, though it was clearly an invitation to leave. The boys nodded, their eyes a little hopeful, and they both shuffled off towards the front door, whispering to each other and shoving playfully. Catwoman actually had to admit she was growing quite fond of the pair. She was glad she wouldn't have to kill them.

Alone in the house, Catwoman moved from room to room, standing still before turning ever so slightly, taking in every detail of the room that she was in. She would even get on the floor, looking straight up to the ceiling and drink that view in as well. Whatever it was she was looking for, she clearly was not able to find it.

Until she got to one specific room. This time she performed the same ritual, standing at the centre, examining one wall intently, before turning to do the same to another. But when she got to the third wall, she spent a little bit longer.

And then she broke the ritual and walked over to the wall. There was something not quite right about it.

She ran her fingers over a part of the wall, and then took her sunglasses off to look more closely. There was a square on the wall that was just not quite the same shade of white as the rest of the wall. It had been repainted using the same colour as the original, but it was newer. At a casual glance, it wasn't noticeable, but if you were looking, it became more obvious. Running her fingers around the square, she could feel the slight bump where the wall had been repaired.

She straightened up and mused for a moment about what she was going to do. The room faced the back yard, so there were no curious onlookers trying to see what was going on. That suited her purpose well. Grabbing her clutch, she opened it, and pulled out a small switch blade, which she expertly flicked open. She touched the wall one more time, then decided exactly where she was aiming for and forced the knife into the wall. There was a little resistance as it slid through the putty, but her accuracy had been exact. She slid the knife along the wall until she reached a point which required her to turn 90 degrees, and she did the same again. Soon she had come back to her starting point, and after applying a degree of pressure, the panel fell out, revealing the safe behind it.

A safe that had bloody handprints on it.

Well, Catwoman reflected, there was certainly some truth to the rumours. On a whim, she reached into her clutch again and pulled out a small, stoppered vial. With the knife, she then took some of the blood and popped it into the vial. You never know, she mused.

With the vial safely back in place, Catwoman pulled out her phone and selected an app which she then held up to the safe. The safe had a handle to one side, and in the centre, there was a number panel on it. She began to press certain buttons, and on the screen a little bar moved forward slowly, every so often changing colour. She continued the process, and there was a click. Nodding satisfied, Catwoman turned the handle on the safe and pulled it open.

There was nothing inside. Catwoman pursed her lips and stood up. Her expression was unreadable, but she turned and exited the house, not bothering to pull the door shut behind her. From the sidewalk, Kez and Friend watched as Catwoman slid back into the Sesto Elemento, and activated the engine, before slipping away up the street.

Though Kez and Friend would tell the story with much elaboration later on, they did end it with the absolute truth. Both boys knew there was no chance they would ever see the woman in the Lamborghini ever again.

XI

It seemed like forever, but it was, in point of fact, less than twenty-four hours since Nathan Coulter had gone on the run from, well from whoever the Toyota belonged to, and forced a girl to strip naked so he could have some kind of hostage situation. In the scheme of things that were ridiculously stupid, he had chalked up quite a few. Which made his ability to stay off the radar and free from arrest even more impressive, in his personal opinion.

However, twenty-four hours without food or shower facilities and hunkering down either in overpasses or alleys was starting to wear on him, and Nathan began to wonder if he shouldn't just hand himself over to the authorities. In all likelihood he would probably end up in jail, but that was better than what he was currently doing and certainly better than being swept away by Man Garam (if Man Garam was actually after him, if Man Garam even existed, all of which were two very big ifs, if you were to ask him personally, which no one was likely to do given the circumstances).

Therefore, at six twenty-three in the evening, when the sun was beginning to set and Nathan's phone pinged, it was his his first bit of good news in a considerable time.

New York. 4ᵗʰ St.

For a moment, Nathan wondered what it meant, and then he remembered the message he was supposed to be getting. Mason's wife, the mysterious Mrs Lemon, was in New York. Which meant all he had to do was get to New York and find 4ᵗʰ St. And then find where the house was on 4ᵗʰ St. Which would be tricky, because he didn't really know New York, and so he had no idea how long 4ᵗʰ St was.

But it was a start. The next thing he had to do was actually get to New York, which would definitely be absolutely simple because there was, of course, no chance the men in the Toyota Yaris were going to be watching for him.

Bus stations and Ronald Reagan Airport were both out of the question – it was far too difficult to get past security without any significant help from the outside world, which he didn't have. Which really only left one option – hitch hiking. The drive to New York wouldn't take too long; it was about four hours which meant that he could possibly get to New York by the following morning if he got started now.

Serendipitously, his drifting through Washington had brought to Arboretum, which meant getting to New York Ave wasn't going to be particularly difficult at all. The difficult part would be trying to get someone to pick him up, and the part of NY Ave he was near didn't particularly lend itself to slowing down and picking up hitch hikers.

It wasn't impossible, of course, but he would have to weigh up the odds of being picked up before he attracted the attention of the police. The road itself was largely fenced off from the areas around it, but he was able to get near an off ramp, and it was there that he started trying to get the attention of the cars heading north, presumably to New York. He wasn't entirely surprised that the majority of his appeals were met with no interest whatsoever, and a few people even paused to give him the middle finger, angry that he was daring to hitch hike in the first place. Nathan couldn't work out why that made them angry, but as his own temper was not exactly the best (and the last few days had certainly proven that), he probably wasn't in any position to judge.

He was, therefore, slightly surprised when a dark red car indicated it was about to pull aside to let him in. Astonished at his good luck (and perhaps the fact that the traffic had eased up to allow the driver to make the decision to pull over) he quickly ran to the car (take note: Mazda 3, possibly mid 2000's, dark red, Washington DC plates with the *Taxation without Representation* banner, six numbers no letters) and jumped in the front. The driver immediately pulled back into traffic and got onto New York Ave before any conversation started up. There was no time for talking in the evening traffic.

"Thanks," Nathan muttered, turning to the driver. It was a woman…

"Oh god," Dusty Springwood said as she turned to see who her passenger was.

"You," they both exclaimed at the same time, though Dusty followed it with a simple "Shit."

"This can't be a coincidence," Nathan said, now hyper alert.

"You smell disgusting," Dusty replied, which Nathan felt like a slap in the face.

"I've been on the run," he said.

"If my son smelled that bad, I'd force him into the shower until he didn't come out."

"Why did you pick me up," Nathan interrupted the attack on his personal hygiene.

"I thought I'd give someone a break. If I'd known it was you, I definitely wouldn't have bothered."

"Thanks a lot," he replied, muttering again.

"What do you want? A medal? It's like I've picked up a fucking hobo," Dusty barked. "I thought you were going to New York days ago!"

"Yeah, well, I got caught up," Nathan said. "Also, what the fuck? You knew the wife was in New York?"

"I thought you knew it was New York," Dusty retorted. "I've been trying to work out what the clue was supposed to mean. It took me a bit, but now I know, I'm going."

"What clue?" Nathan asked, feeling like the entire world was in on a joke he wasn't getting.

"At the funeral?"

"There was a clue at the funeral?" and Nathan had to admit he was ashamed at just how stupid he sounded.

"You didn't think the Biblical quote was a bit odd?" Nathan sighed deeply and realised he just really wanted to sleep. He didn't need some stripper making him feel stupid. He had enough people in his life to do that already, he certainly didn't need someone else's voice in the chorus.

"I'm going to sleep, if that's OK with you. I'm genuinely shattered. I don't think I've slept since I spoke to you." Lexie had the decency to look surprised at this, but she didn't say anything, instead fixing her eyes on the road. Nathan closed his own, and sleep swept over him, as quickly as someone closing the coffin lid at a funeral.

He was gone before he even had time to muse on the morbidity of the comparison.

XII

As much as he hated New York (and quite frankly, he did), Nathan had to admit that there was a vibe to the city that was radically different to Washington. It felt metropolitan, and he could see that Lexie was enthralled by the idea of walking down the street and seeing so many different backgrounds in the one area. Nathan preferred walking down the streets seeing a bunch of Americans (and he wasn't racist, but you had to admit that there were problems with black communities and quite frankly you could see how it affected New York in all the ways it didn't affect Washington).

"Why are you in a funk?" Lexie asked, wide awake and smelling great. He couldn't help but feel a little resentful at the fact she looked amazing, while he felt like a two-week-old kebab.

"Isn't there somewhere I could shower, or something?"

"I don't have a place in New York, you know, right? I'm visiting in the same way you are." He grunted in annoyance and stuck his head against the window to see where they were, and was a little disappointed to find that it looked like they were driving through a bathroom. "There're two 4th streets," Lexie announced, and Nathan grumbled, reminded again that this woman had worked out where to go before his sources could get him the information.

"So where are we going then?"

"Brooklyn," she replied.

"Oh." He suddenly realised that his instinctive dislike of New York had been a little premature; they must be in the Holland Tunnel, crossing states from Jersey City to New York. The dull yellow light and white tiled walls made much more sense now. He was surprised that the traffic wasn't particularly crushing and as they exited the tunnel into the dull morning, the imposing grey brick of the walls on either side ensured that his mood remained the same colour.

It felt cold.

"Maybe we can find you a place to actually get cleaned up a little and have some breakfast," Lexie offered and even though he didn't want to, he was grateful for the suggestion.

"Sure," he murmured, though he wondered if it meant he'd end up in a McDonald's somewhere. As he looked up at one of the buildings on his right, the various shades of grey that made up the bricks were hidden by a large advertisement that featured an Asian skyline with four beautiful women dressed in gold, covered in gold dust, sipping from elegant flutes.

Towards a dream, the advertisement announced. Not really likely, Nathan thought sourly.

229

There wasn't any place that they could actually pull over, and Nathan watched the large green signs counting down the exits before the turn to Brooklyn. The sun started to become brighter in the sky as it crawled across the blue to be seen over the rooftops, and Nathan winced as the light hit his eyes.

An hour later he was still hungry and feeling sorry for himself. Lexie's offer seemed contingent on getting to 4th Street, and so before long they had gone through Tribeca and were heading to Two Bridges, where they used the Brooklyn Bridge to cross. Nathan found himself sinking into a pit of depression every time they passed a café, despite the fact that they weren't open. He suddenly realised he had no idea what time of day it was, and he took out the phone to discover that it was twenty past five in the morning.

That explained the small amount of traffic, he supposed.

Finally, Lexie eased the car into a car park that she spotted on the side of the road, and once parked, got out, not waiting to see what Nathan was going to do, and stretched. Nathan also got out, and the realisation of how long he had sat in the car hit him as the stretch felt like one of the best things he had ever done with his life. He needed to stretch like that more often.

They had found 4th St, and he had to admit it looked pretty good, all things told. It was picture postcard New York, with Brownstones on either side, and trees precisely placed on the side walk, reaching up and across to their partners on the other side. The weather had turned and so the green was giving way to brown, but it looked picture perfect all the same.

Of course, this was where Mason Lemon lived, Nathan reflected, surprised at how much bitterness he felt. The man's life had been perfect, but the hidden side of him was even more so. Talk about landing on your feet. That was all Mason ever seemed to do.

Well, until he was killed, of course.

Lexie had her phone out and was dialling a number, which immediately sparked Nathan's paranoia.

"What are you doing?"

"I'm calling my son, if that's OK with you," she retorted, and for a moment he was going to go and snatch the phone off her, but he quelled the anger. While she wandered off, whispering into her phone and occasionally glancing at him, which didn't help the paranoia one little bit, Nathan saw that Bagel World, just ahead on the corner, was starting to open, and so he headed towards it. There didn't seem to be anywhere he could shower, which was probably to be expected. Maybe he could use a shower at Mason's house.

He pushed the door to the Bagel World open, but the employee on the inside shook his head and waved at him. Nathan pulled a face, not understanding what the point of the gesture was, but as he pushed the door, the employee again waved, but it was clearly a shooing gesture. He turned as if listening to someone else speak, and then he reached under the counter, before coming to the door.

"Hey, guy, here," he thrust a wrapped bagel into Nathan's hand after opening the door. "Don't bother coming in, right? Just take that and go down to the park and eat. Off ya go." Nathan stared slack jawed for a moment, before realising that he just wanted food. As such he turned and started to head down the street, though given how the employee had gesticulated, it was presumably not in the direction of the park.

"Hey," Lexie said, giving a little wave as he approached. She was vaping by the side of the car, her phone in her hand.

"What?"

"Nice bagel. Did you get one for me?"

"I was given this and told to fuck off."

"Right," Lexie pursed her lips. "You remember how I said there were two 4th Streets?" she asked, and Nathan was suddenly struck by how normal she looked. In the club she was mysterious and alluring, full of promise, but now she just looked tired. She needed more sleep, and her hair was brittle. She wasn't unattractive, quite the opposite, but she just looked a little like the last choice in the club as the sun started to rise.

"Yeah."

"Well, this isn't his. His is in Queens," she said with a pout.

"Of course it is," Nathan said, expressionless. He took another bite of the bagel and closed his eyes in silent pain. When he opened them again, to make a comment about how painful he was beginning to find this whole exercise, and, you know, in truth, fuck Mason Lemon and his stupid documents because he deserved to die and he was a pain in the fucking arse, even after fucking death, and what the fuck was he doing being married anyway without that information being on the actual records at the CIA? I mean, how did that even happen? It just made Nathan look even more incompetent, and he didn't need any help with that at the moment. But it was opening his eyes to expel this diatribe that he suddenly paused and saw a matte black Toyota Yaris at the top of the street.

Was...

I mean...

How the fuck?

"We have to get out of here," Nathan whispered as urgently as he could, not quite certain as to why he was whispering, particularly urgently as it was clear that Lexie had no idea what he was saying, but he did so all the same.

"Sorry?"

"Lexie, don't fucking argue, let's just go!"

"My name's not Lexie, you know that right?" Nathan wanted the gun back so he could shoot the stupid woman and get in the car and escape from whoever the fuck was in the Toyota Yaris, but instead he had to grit his teeth.

"What is your name?" he asked, as politely as his current mood allowed.

"Dusty," she said. "Why do you suddenly care?"

"Dusty," he responded in very measured tones, "there is a car up there that has been following me since Washington. They have guns and we need to get out of here as quickly as possible." She turned to see what he was saying, but the car had gone.

"I think you're being paranoid, Nate," she replied.

"OK, so for the sake of argument, let's assume I'm not, and go,
232

just in case it's true." She looked at him in the same way someone looks at a child who has difficulty in understanding what's being said to them, and opened her mouth to say something, but ultimately changed her mind.

"OK, let's go," she shrugged, and took her keys out.

"Also, bearing in mind this is for the sake of argument," he continued, "if we see a black Toyota Yaris, can we make sure we avoid it at all costs. I could drive..." but he got not further.

"You're not driving my car. I'll accept your lunacy, but you're not touching my wheel, do you understand?" For a moment he couldn't work out if it was a euphemism or a genuine comment, but decided it was the latter, and reluctantly slunk around to the passenger's side.

The red Mazda 3 pulled away from the parking space (which was quickly filled by someone who was happy to get the find), and Dusty pulled out of 4th and began the journey towards Queens. She had her phone open and was being guided by it, which meant that Nathan was able to see they were heading to Astoria, which sounded impressive, and made more sense to him. After all, if they were going to take a step up from the delightful houses in Brooklyn's 4th, then Astoria would be logical.

They pulled out onto 5th Ave, joining the yellow school buses that were beginning their daily runs, easing through the busy Brooklyn street, as the crowds began to grow on either side, and the city became more alive. Looking at the map, Nathan was slightly disturbed to see that they seemed to be heading away from Queens, which he opened his mouth to point out, but almost before he could say anything, Lexie...Dusty spoke out.

"I'm going to get on the Expressway. It should be quicker to get to Queens, and if you are being pursued by Feds and they are back there trawling the streets, then this should be a better route, right? Right?" The look she gave bored into his head and he bit his tongue.

Getting back onto the expressway proved slightly more difficult than getting off it, but Dusty proved to be surprisingly adept at driving in Brooklyn, and even though it seemed to take forever, before long they were on the Prospect Expressway, and from there it was no time at all when they were on the Gowanus Expressway. Once they turned onto the Brooklyn-Queens Expressway, they were committed. They were walled in on either side by red and brown bricks, blocking off all view of what was going on in the world outside them. Occasionally the wall on the left would drop, and suddenly they would see the traffic heading in the opposite direction, but outside of the ubiquitous green exit signs and the graffiti on the walls, for a long time nothing changed.

Soon the walls gave way to wire fences, which gave way to a concrete wall, before the views cleared and they could see across the city below them, now that the Expressway had climbed above the general roads.

The sun continued to rise in the sky, making the blue even lighter and causing a degree of irritation to Dusty. Soon the view on either side was obscured by greenery and Nathan wondered if perhaps they hadn't crossed into Queens. The build-up in traffic increased this, although as they were well and truly into peak hour, that perhaps was unsurprising. Every so often Nathan glanced around to see if there was any sign of the black Toyota, but there wasn't. The greenery continued, though the walls returned and the trees started to thin out, now only popping up every so often.

Before long the Kosciuszko Bridge was behind them, along with Newton Creek, and then the Long Island Expressway passed beneath them. Finally, they saw a turn off for Astoria Boulevarde, and Nathan felt confident enough to declare they were in Queens, without looking like an idiot.

"Queens," he said, for no one's benefit.

"What?" Dusty asked, the irritation on her face obvious.

"Oh, erm, nothing," he shrugged.

Astoria Blvd spectacularly failed to impress Nathan, and he still wasn't impressed when the car eased into 27th Ave. There were nice houses, but if anything, it looked a little like a step down from 4th in Brooklyn. As they continued, trees become more abundant, and Nathan started to feel a little more confident they were on the right path.

And then the trees gave way to rubbish and construction.

When Dusty pulled the car to the right, Nathan's heart sank. A Goodwill building was on their right, while the left was boarded for whatever was going on behind the wooden green barrier. A brick warehouse of sorts followed, and then a solitary white, low set house which had definitely seen better days, and some sort of black car parked beside it.

"You can't be serious," Nathan murmured.

And then Dusty pulled the car over.

"16 4th St," she said. She pointed to a building that had scaffolding around the outside, though there was an entrance. "We want apartment 33. John's the fourth book of the Bible," she added by way of explanation, but Nathan no longer cared how smart she was to have worked out the secret message.

There was no way that Mason Lemon and his secret wife lived in this shithole.

No way.

XIII

They entered through the construction walls that had created a path to the dingy, mouldy looking glass front door. Dusty pushed it open with a quiet confidence, which rattled Nathan who was wary about any building that didn't require people to be buzzed in, let alone didn't actually need a key to get into the foyer. Once inside, the smell of...lettuce? Old lettuce? He couldn't quite place it...the smell immediately assaulted his nostrils and made him want beat a hasty retreat back through the stained door. Dusty had no care, and continued towards the stairwell.

There wasn't a lift, of course, which meant he was probably going to have to hike up a flight of stairs. Heaving a sigh, he followed the stripper, reluctantly, into what was becoming ever more like the bowels of hell.

They climbed seven flights of stairs, until Dusty pushed at a door and made her way through. The door wasn't any cleaner than the front door – indeed, it might have actually been worse – but Nathan braved following her, until finally she stopped at a door, gave a slight peripheral glance to Nathan, before reaching up and knocking.

There was no reply.

The light overhead was flickering, casting occasional shadows around them, and every so often plunging the corridor into darkness. Even when it was on, it lent nothing more than a sodium glare, changing the walls to a mustard yellow, regardless of what colour they had been originally. It was tremendously dramatic, and despite the fact it was one of the single most disgusting places he had ever been, Nathan was revising his opinion on whether Mason owned the place or not. He had a strong flair for the dramatic, and Nathan could see him luring people to this death trap before possibly springing the…springing the trap.

Some sort of black car. It had been a sports car, surely? An expensive one, way too expensive for this neighbourhood.

Dusty had walked into the apartment. Nathan followed, his brain screaming at him to stop, and yet they were committed to the path.

She had opened the door. No one invited her in, no one opened the door. Dusty opened it. What was the number on the door? Had there been one? What was the number on the building? He hadn't checked. Had no idea if it was 16, or if this was apartment 33.

There was a soft click, and Nathan knew what it was.

They had walked down a short corridor and entered a small bedroom. Dusty was already making herself at home, but Nathan knew it wasn't going to be an option for him.

She had said Mason had a wife. Had Justice Kennedy been in on it?

He turned, slowly, and saw someone standing before him. They were Asian, wearing ripped denim jeans and a t-shirt. The eyes were so dark they were almost black. They were waifish, and strangely androgynous, but the body was possibly shapely, though he couldn't be certain.

Well, he couldn't be certain of the gender. He could definitely be certain about one thing.

"Man Garam," he whispered.

"*Anyeong*," they replied. "Nice to meet you, Mr Coulter."

"Is it?" he asked, hollowly.

"I can see why you needed these," they said, holding up a familiar folder.

"I don't know what you're talking about," he replied, though even he could hear the note of defeat in his voice.

"Lots of official documents. The ones from your safe, I'll return them to where they belong. All the time you were keeping some of Lemon's side hustles from the CIA. But then there were the documents that pointed to Mason's exact location in Seoul. What made you turn on him? Did you know about the documents in his safe? They do not paint you in a very good light."

"Mason asked for those documents..." Nathan's mouth started working before his brain did, but he knew it was a waste of time. Mason's field assessments, his ongoing reports, detailing every step of his mission. Nathan remembered copying them, emailing them to a man named Boom, and then sending them to his father.

"What?" Dusty asked, reminding the room of her presence.

"It's easy to use someone who has a problem," Man said, and their mouth twitched a little, almost smiling. "Someone in the CIA tried to cover it up, but something like that can't stay hidden, not really. Someone is bound to find out, and then suddenly you have a way in. Maybe Mason Lemon was protecting you, but I think you thought he was using you."

Protecting. It was an interesting word. No one had ever found out about what really happened with his sister and her family, and yet as they had lain in the bed, Mason revealed the truth as he gently rubbed his still hard dick. Nathan had misunderstood and did something he thought he'd never do. When he swallowed the result, Mason had grinned and said he had no idea why Nathan had performed so. In fact, he said, he wasn't going to tell anyone. Why would he? If he was going to blackmail him for sex, he'd have brought it up before he fucked Nathan.

And he meant it too. He had no interest whatsoever in hurting Nathan. The sex was experimental, Mason revealed. Something had happened at the strippers' which led to what they had done, but he didn't want to do anything nasty. He trusted Nathan completely. After all, Nathan knew all about the little money-making schemes Mason had on the side. The odd jobs for the criminal underground who paid in cash.

"I don't think Mason gave you the share you were expecting," Man

237

said softly. Nathan wasn't really paying attention. He was already putting together the other information he had.

"You're the wife?" Nathan asked Dusty, softly.

"Mason told me about this place, but I'd forgotten the details until the funeral. He said if he ever died, I should come here. He said it was in his wife's name, but…"

"But there is no wife. It's your name." Nathan carefully sat on the end of the bed. It was a double bed, but not King size, and the spread over the top was knitted with white cats on a deep red background. Of course, it was a trap. The walls had pictures, but they were all of vague scenes that could have been from anywhere. The desk had a picture of a woman on it, but it wasn't Dusty, and was so non-descript that Mason could have claimed it was anyone from a youthful picture of his mother to his wife to his sister.

No, not *his* sister. With a shock, Nathan realised it was his own sister. A final parting gift from Mason.

And then the final piece of the puzzle fell into place. In this drab room, with its drab beige walls and drab, meaningless paintings, the old brown cupboard that was open, full of clothes that Nathan knew Mason had never worn, clearly housed a safe that was now open. The documents inside were gone, but it wasn't the classified CIA files he had stolen. They had never left his father's possession.

"You killed my father and took the documents," Nathan said, his voice devoid of emotion.

"Yes," affirmed Man, and they almost sounded sad about it.

"She knows…" Nathan vaguely waved at Dusty, but Man's response was what he expected.

"The bait in the trap. Why do you think she picked you up?"

"I got a text message," Dusty started, but Nathan waved her into silence. She didn't have to go on.

The smell of old lettuce was present again, and Nathan briefly wondered what it was. In truth he suspected he would never find out. The dull orange light was constant in the room, and Nathan wondered how many people had sat under it, pondering what their future was.

"Why?" Dusty asked.

"What?"

"I'm right about Mason, I know. But why your sister?"

Good question, Nathan mused. They had moved in idiotic circles, that was true. They shared the same opinions on America, but his sister had taken it too far, and become obsessed with one of those cult leaders you read about online. Nathan had argued for her to simply reign it in. There was a limit to what they could do, nowadays, and no one in the family needed someone on the watch list, particularly not him in his job.

But she and her stupid husband who worked for that idiotic car firm just couldn't help themselves. Posting about some black guy they'd hit in their car and simply driven away from. The fight was enormous. Nathan didn't need their insanity when he had his own problems. It was just fucking thoughtless. Everything about his stupid fucking sister and her stupid fucking husband and that fucking, ridiculous kid who was apparently autistic or some shit but who just needed a good fucking back hander when he was getting out of line...

Even now he remembered his anger, his rage. And yet he didn't remember stabbing any of them. Part of him wished he did. He just remembered the anger, and then the next thing, he needed to clean up the fucking mess.

Even in death they had been thoughtless.

Had he said that out loud?

Man Garam had handed the documents they had over to Dusty who was reading them, her face getting paler and paler. When she looked up, and then over at Nathan, it was a look he had seen before, when his father had found out the truth.

Mason had kept the evidence here. Good old Mason.

He didn't even hear Man Garam shoot Dusty. When she fell onto the bed, the hole in her head dribbling blood, Nathan was going to mention Dusty's son. But why bother? It was too late now.

239

What a place to die, he mused. A squalid little bedroom in the backstreets of Queens. Humiliating. Man Garam was good. Super good. They'd probably somehow make it look like Nathan himself had killed Dusty. He desperately hoped it wasn't spun as some sort of lover's tiff, or jealousy over who of them was fucking Mason. You can have a hundred hetero flings, but you fuck one guy…

And then, Nathan thought no more.

XIV

"Well, I can't say I'm totally surprised," the Deputy Director said, his sallow face deep in shadows. Beside him, wearing very short shorts, a bikini top, and making herself as comfortable as she could in the back of the CIA car, was the woman he had met twice before under different circumstances. This time, the old woman guise and the waitress persona had been dropped for what he could only describe as a beach bum. The tattoos and piercings had gone, and the hair was a cropped, dusty blonde, and despite an impressive set of boobs, she was giving off the vibe of an eighteen-year-old looking forward to Spring Break. The Deputy Director secretly wanted to employ her, but he had the suspicion that the CIA probably didn't pay as well as Man Garam did. "I am delighted that he killed a stripper before killing himself though. That makes things a lot easier."

Bikini girl didn't really respond, busy as she was playing on her phone. She gave a vague grunt of agreement, but said no more.

The Deputy Director continued to peruse the files that he had been given, and wondered if it was worth handing them over to the police to resolve the murder of Erin Coulter and her husband and child, but decided he didn't really care enough about the situation to do so. Instead, he slid them back into the manila folder, which he then slid into his suitcase, resolving to destroy them as soon as he got to the office. Erin Coulter's death would remain a mystery til the end of time, allowing podcasters to talk about it incessantly with their ridiculous paranoid conspiracy theories. Dusty Springwood's murder was resolved by the home invasion of a man who was fucking her husband. After shooting himself, everything worked out nicely.

"Well done Man Garam," the Deputy Director said, more to himself than anyone else.

"I'll pass that on," Bikini Girl said, finally stirring from her phone and raising a bored eyebrow. "I'm obligated to ask about payment." She left the sentence alone, but the Deputy Director waved it away.

"The final transfer has been done. Your boss should have all their money by now."

"Oh, good. Well, catch ya round, I guess. Don't hesitate to call the next time you have a mess." She grinned and opened the door, showing under-bum as she got out of the car and then sauntered off, looking for a lift, presumably. Good look, the Deputy Director reflected. There was a reason he had chosen the location. He tapped on the window to his driver, and then sat back and dialled a number.

"Kennedy," came the quick response.

"Ah, Justice. Just wanted to thank you for your help. Appreciate you setting up dear old Nathan," the Deputy Director said, sitting back as the car set off.

"Oh, no problem. I quite liked Mason. He was one of the good guys. Certainly, didn't deserve to be shafted, especially not by that prick."

"He was a prick," the Deputy Director agreed. "But he's a dead prick now, so it's the end of story."

"No problem. Glad to help when I can."

"Your patriotism is appreciated," the Deputy Director replied, and ended the conversation. He should probably inform the NSA that they could step down, but he would do that when he got back to Langley. There was no hurry. They would probably enjoy the overtime.

The car passed the Bikini Girl, who gave a jaunty wave, and it continued on its journey. The Deputy Director was mildly surprised to see a black Lamborghini coming in the opposite direction. Just goes to show you can never predict how discrete a meeting place is.

Although, he reflected as his mind went back to the files Man

Garam had passed on, it turns out you can't predict people either. Nathan Coulter had been quite the pest, and Man Garam had been worth every cent. Murdered his own sister and got a top agent killed. Justice had been meted out, pardon the pun. It almost deserved a poetic epithet.

Would there be a point in turning back the wheel of time to atone for past sins? For given another chance, would we choose differently, or simply make the same choices over and over again?

Yes, you would, you prick. Forget the poetry. Fuck you, Nathan Coulter.

BOOK FOUR

THE DOVES
TARGET: DANA SPECTRA

ONE

People were leaving Olympic Hall relatively quickly, though a number of fans were stilling hanging around in the hopes of seeing G'Star, and various industry names were schmoozing each other and the celebrities that were also there. In amongst the crowd there was also a potential killer, but Mason Lemon decided there wasn't an awful lot of insight to be gained from hanging around.

He had taken a lot of photos, got a lot of names, and come to the conclusion that hopefully someone would die soon and that would point him in the direction of who the killer might be. Yes, there were those that would argue it would be better to find the killer and prevent the next death, but Lemon was pragmatic. There were no further leads to be gained from the night and so it would be better to simply go home and start afresh in the morning, if everyone was safe and sound.

Besides, it was pretty clear that the Australians had come through for them, and their asset was now in play. In truth, he could probably go home, go to bed, and leave everything to her. Not that he was lazy, but a cushy assignment was a cushy assignment. Not everything had to be done the hard way.

He was staying at the Fairfield by Mariet Marriot Seoul, and contemplated simply walking back to the hotel. It was a nice night and while it would be a bit of a stroll, it wasn't too challenging and could be quite pleasant. Plus he was enjoying Seoul as a city. It had a nice vibe. In some ways it felt like its own country, what with each district having a degree of autonomy, such that in some ways Seoul seemed like a city made up of a lot of little cities. You could get immune to metropolises, but once you started to actively seek out the quirks each one had, then they established their individuality.

When he found himself on the middle of a darkened street, which was definitely not a main street, Mason Lemon decided he had taken a wrong turn and the walk home was a bad idea. He had no idea how long he had been walking but it was clearly the wrong direction, and it was very, very late. His phone, rather unhelpfully, told him he was on Garak-ro 7-gil, which didn't make a lot of sense to him. All he knew was that on one side was a park (sort of? There was a lot of concrete for park), and on the other were a lot of red-brown brick buildings that didn't look new, but certainly looked lived in. This was definitely not where he needed to be.

With a little shrug to himself he turned to head back out of the street and find the nearest main road and transport home.

And that's when he saw the woman with the long, red hair standing in front of him. She was wearing a cute little black dress with white collar and cuffs, making her look a little like a ginger Wednesday Addams. She had black stockings, some beautiful bling and high heels. She was also gorgeous, and quite familiar. Mason was convinced he had seen her earlier that evening but couldn't immediately place why.

"Hello?" he said, hesitantly.

"Mason?" She had an accent but he couldn't place it. Not American was what he was going to go for.

"Yeah, that's right." He smiled an affable smile and wondered what his chances were with this particular hottie. She smiled back. Before Mason got the chance to open his mouth he felt a pain in his gut. He looked down to see blood spreading across his shirt, and looked up to see the woman holding a gun. Another shot rang out but this time he didn't hear it. A small mushroom of blood had opened on Mason's forehead. He was dead before he hit the ground.

The red-head looked at the body of Mason Lemon for a few moments, and then retrieved his phone and quickly patted him down, taking his wallet as well. She paused for a moment, and then slipped out Lemon's US driver license, and put it into her coat pocket.

With that done, she casually strolled away.

TWO

Michael Chen suppressed a yawn, and stepped through the door and onto the footpath. It was a pleasant day, and he had decided he wasn't going to work. He didn't really need the money, and so Chen was in the fortunate position of being able to say yes or no to supply teaching days as he saw fit. There was certainly enough work around to be picky, and today he definitely felt picky.

He exited onto Kenny St, and then took a left down Ardlie St, heading down the hill to Fawkner St, his final goal being the small little shopping complex there where he hoped to get something to eat. He wasn't sure what he wanted yet, but he was hoping that he would know when he got there. That was the problem with food. It was so subjective.

He was at the roundabout that connected Ardlie and Fawkner when his phone pinged, and after smoothing his goatee, he opened the phone to see what the message was.

Need help? Why not call us? We do anything, anywhere, anytime.

Chen regarded the message for a moment, and smoothed his goatee again.

Pocketing the phone he continued on his path, crossing the

little bridge and coming to his destination. On his right was where he had intended to go – Mayflower, Miss Flora, Claudio's IGA. There were other food places in the complex, but instead he turned left. Here was another set of shops, happily stacked together. The Milk Bar, the Tattoo Parlour, Salon West and Fish & Chips. Rather than going to any of them, however, he made his way down the left side of the Milk Bar, not following the path, but instead, clinging to the green brick wall, until he came to a small door at the end of the building, where upon he pressed his thumb to a discrete black panel and the door slid back.

Stepping inside what was little more than a booth, Chen looked into what seemed to be a little lens which scanned his eye print and then another door slid open. This time the room was every-so-slightly bigger, with a comfortable chair, computer monitors on the wall, and a keyboard on a small bench.

He tapped slightly on the keyboard and then said: "Michael Chen". The darkened screens came to life, and there was a pause before he heard a slight click.

"Good morning, Michael," came the disembodied voice from the hidden speakers. It was impossible to tell who the voice was or even really what gender the voice was, as it was clearly computer generated and sounded more like some strange Tik-Tok voice over than an actual person.

"Good morning," Chen replied politely. One of the screens' displays changed into the image of a person. He was a good-looking man, with wavy brown hair and an affable smile. He had what Chen would have described as a "good ole boy" vibe about him. Michael didn't like to judge, but the guy was definitely American.

"This is Mason Lemon, a member of the Central Intelligence Agency." Chen allowed himself a smug smile of immodesty. "Four days ago, Mr Lemon was executed in Seoul. He was investigating a series of murders that were occurring in the Moonlight Entertainment company. The CIA believed that there was a foreign agitator attempting to destabilise the Korean popular music businesses, which could have had a consequence on the Korean economy. It's not in the best interests of America for that to occur."

"With the greatest respect," Chen said, "how do you know all this?"

"A number of documents became available to a variety of intelligence agencies, some nefarious. These appeared to be leaked by a man named Nathan Coulter, a senior analyst at the CIA who was working with Lemon. Coulter was found dead yesterday." Another screen's display changed, this time showing a tall, gangly man with a somewhat idiotic face, lying on the ground in a pool of blood. He had a bullet in his head and gut. Chen mused on that for a moment. It was an unusual assassination. Usually two shots to the head was the norm, but this seemed to indicate either this wasn't a professional hit, or the professional had been instructed to deliver pain, followed by retribution.

Ouch.

"Do you have any idea who might have killed them?" Chen wondered.

"A woman was involved in both shootings. Nathan Coulter was at his sister's house, which had also been visited by a woman that day. Two children were questioned about this, but aside from describing her as very beautiful in a stunning red dress, and having an impressive black sports car, they weren't much help. Whoever killed Coulter also killed his father. I should say, in the interests of openness, that there is every chance Coulter killed his sister and her family. There are things about him that remain difficult to pin down, but he isn't the topic of this assignment. Lemon is."

The screen with Coulter's corpse blacked out, to be replaced by Lemon, who had been dealt with in a similar fashion – a bullet hole in the head, and a large red strain around the stomach.

"We have a little more information about Lemon's killer." The picture of the smiling Lemon was replaced by a new picture that had low resolution, but it wasn't difficult to see that it was a red-headed woman in a little black dress. Chen guessed she had a nice figure based on the image, but if he were honest, he'd have to admit the blurriness made it difficult to confirm. "Lemon was a friend of mine," the voice continued. "Normally I don't like to use this organisation for personal reasons, but Lemon was a good agent. He should be avenged." Chen kept his face neutral, but he was surprised by this admission. It was certainly not the norm. "I would like you to track down his killer and deal with her. Your team has already been selected, but as team leader the mission details are your responsibility. You have free reign to pursue this mission as you see fit, but your goal is absolute.

Find and kill Dana Spectra."

THREE

The weather was a cool 8 degrees Celsius in Paris, and though it was warmer in Charles de Gaulle airport, Charlie Maxwell had definitely dressed for what would be facing her outside, rather than inside. As soon as she had received message, she had gone to her secure port and downloaded the mission brief, details of which were sparse. She wasn't the team leader; she had been drafted in for liaison. As such, she had closed her art gallery and made her way to Paris as instructed. A one-time thief, Charlie had reached a position in her life where she was utterly comfortable. She didn't need money, so she could afford to retire and start an art gallery which she could operate when she felt so inclined. Every so often, a job crossed her path which intrigued her. A challenge, or a favour, but otherwise she was out of the game. She had built up her own little networks and contacts and no longer needed to do anything that required a great deal of personal risk.

And then she had been contacted by Kit. Kit was a woman, comfortably in her fifties, well dressed in tweeds, who was acting on behalf of someone known only as Flight. Flight had an intelligence network called the Doves, and Kit wondered if Charlie might be interested in joining the network, thanks to her unique abilities and skills. Charlie had laughed this off, but Kit had insisted they knew all about Charlie and her past. Kit even had some proof, which was disturbing to say the least.

But there was no blackmail, no threats. It was a simple request; to do some good, even ease a conscience.

In truth, Charlie didn't really feel guilty about anything, but Kit had a mission already and wanted Charlie to take part in it. That had been enough to tantalise curiosity, and so she had agreed. When she was asked to become team leader for a second mission, she knew she was part of the operation. Curiosity had definitely snagged the cat.

Though not particularly tall, Charlie cut an impressive figure in her perfectly tailored outfit – black slacks, black collared shirt, and a long white N Peal coat, and white high heel Hollie Cream boots. It was an outfit that made her look taller than she was, simply by being so striking. Alongside her deep red hair, and matching lipstick, she couldn't help but attract attention. Everyone looked twice, which was fine. Being noticed was never a problem.

She had been given images of this assignment's team leader, and had read his background. Michael Chen was former Australian SAS and an expert marksman. She knew the mission was to take out an Australian model, and was unsurprised that Chen had been the choice to lead it. By all accounts he would have no qualms about doing the job.

The arrivals hall was fairly typical of most airports, as a path had been created by steel bars, leading away from the sliding double doors that sealed off the baggage claim area from the rest of Paris. People stood around holding signs to get the attention of those that were arriving, but Charlie didn't feel the need to do that. She would be able to pick out her contact without any hassle.

Sure enough, strolling through the gate, wheeling a large suitcase behind him, and wearing a t-shirt, jeans and a long black coat with a white scarf wrapped around his neck, was Michael Chen. He looked around, knowing who he was meeting, and the pair simply made eye contact and nodded.

"Nice to meet you, Charlie. Charlie is OK?" Chen said as he walked up to her.

"Charlie is fine, Colonel," Charlie replied, and was rewarded with a raised eyebrow.

"Chen is fine for me. Or Mike. But not Colonel."

"Oh, no, of course. You're not," Charlie replied. She knew she was niggling, picking at the former soldier, but he was clearly determined not to get riled. She had to be a little impressed.

"I fell on my sword," Chen said. "But you can choose to believe what you want. As long as it doesn't get in the way of the operation."

"I just follow orders," Charlie smiled sweetly.

"The other two?"

"One should be joining us in a moment, the other is in Paris already. We can go and meet her whenever you want," Charlie supplied.

"Wait, was he on my flight?" Chen asked, surprised.

"No, no. He's arriving in about half an hour. Coffee?" Chen nodded his agreement, and Charlie pointed back to the Brioche Doree, and the pair walked over to get a coffee and wait.

It didn't take too long before they saw the third member of their newly formed gang. His sheer size made him stand out, and he walked through the arrivals lounge in his jeans, jacket and white scarf. When he looked around, Charlie gave a little wave and he smiled and made his way over to them. Once there, Charlie stood up and the pair embraced, though the size difference gave it a slightly comical feel.

"Mike, this is Ruvim Perič," Charlie smiled. Chen stuck his hand out, and the big man grabbed it and shook it enthusiastically.

"Did you want a coffee?" Chen asked.

"Nyet," Perić smiled.

"He doesn't drink coffee," Charlie said. She pushed forward the bottle of cola that she had purchased earlier, and Chen suddenly understood why she had done so.

"You guys know each other," Chen said, a little unnecessarily.

"We've worked together a couple of times. He's extremely reliable," Charlie smiled again, and the obvious friendship rankled Chen slightly. He wasn't a fan of pre-established bonds. Charlie had already proved she liked to stir the pot, and Chen wasn't keen on her having support in that.

"The weather is going to be good today," Perić said, holding up his phone to display the app. "We go and check in?"

"I don't know what Mike wants to do," Charlie replied, "but I have to say that we may want to act quickly. There's a reason we're meeting in Paris. Dana Spectra is already here."

If he were honest, Michael Chen would have to admit that he didn't particularly appreciate fashion. In fact, if pushed, he'd find it difficult to enjoy art, and he'd already been told more than once by Ash Frost that fashion was art. It was just a different sort of art, she insisted. Chen decided he and Ash probably weren't really going to get along that famously.

That said, he was beginning to understand why he had been given this particular team. Charlie Maxwell clearly understood the world that they were in, and spoke fluent French, which was a huge help. She also had contacts precisely where they were needed. Ruvim Perić was big and quiet, but he had an interesting ability to blend in, despite his size and beard. Even now, with the pair of them wearing dinner suits, Perić looked more comfortable in his than Chen felt. He had never been a suit and tie man at the best of times, but now, in a dinner suit, with bowtie, he felt more uncomfortable than ever. Perić, on the other hand, seemed calm and relaxed.

There had been little time for niceties as Charlie already had them on the guest list for the Paris Fashion week at the Palais de Tokyo. The building was a large, sprawling affair that looked beige, but definitely not close to boring. They were standing on Voie Georges Pompidou, the River Seine on one side of them, and the Palais on the other. There was a wide set of stairs leading between the two main wings of the building, and towards a set of columns that were closer to Av du Président Wilson, the street that ran on the other side of the building. The steps led towards the Fontaine du Palais de Tokyo, a large, rather beautiful pool that was currently filled with water that had somehow been coloured red and blue.

The stone steps that led from behind the Fontaine to the pillars had models making their way up and down them. They were all beautiful women, and all dressed in outfits that were also coloured either red or blue. Ash Frost informed him that this was an exhibition of the works of Mute, an artist that he had not heard of and wasn't particularly interested in getting to know more about.

Directly in front of the pillars, a beautiful woman with red and blue hair (presumably for the occasion) was singing, backed by a masked woman at a mixing desk.

"DJ Kabuki, and the singer is Luna Rochique," Ash said, presumably thinking she was being helpful, though Chen thought her hope was misplaced.

Ashley Frost was the fourth member of their team, and she was the technical expert. Chen had read a little bit about her, and knew that she was something of a prodigy at school, and used the school systems to hack into the CIA database as an exercise. She had been given a firm warning, and she learnt her lesson, though Flight's files suggested that Ash had continued to use her skills in a cleverer and more "under the radar" fashion from that point on.

"I quite like the outfits," muttered the other person in their group.

Unlike the other four, this woman was dressed far more casually in a long, non-descript dress. She had glasses and wavy, dark hair, and had a look of permanent distaste on her face, though Chen had discovered that wasn't entirely true; some things made her break out in a wide grin. Those things, however, were usually at the expense of other people. Hana Mortimer was their acquisitions contact. Chen had virtually no information on her at all, and Flight hadn't even included Mortimer as part of the team requirements. Charlie had informed him they would be meeting her at the Palais.

"So are you going in?" Mortimer asked archly.

"What?" Chen queried.

"Well, you can stand here marvelling at the architecture and the fashion, or you could actually go in. That's what the bits of paper are for," Mortimer added.

"I don't want to perform the action tonight," Chen said, and was annoyed he was on the defensive.

"I don't think you could if you wanted to," Charlie rejoined. She was wearing a long, black dress with a slit up to the waist, showing off a lot of leg. Of them all, she seemed the one who fit in with the crowd best, and passerbys were paying a little more attention to the pale thigh than they should.

"Come on," said Ash, grinning, and set off across the road, towards the steps. She was dressed in a white off the shoulder dress that sat came to midway on her thigh. She intrigued Chen as she didn't really seem the sort that would wear that sort of outfit. Whe she arrived, she was wearing a long black trench coat and was boyish in a number of ways, with short hair, an infectious grin, and glasses that gave her a very geeky appearance. But when she took the glasses off and removed the coat, all made up and in a very flattering dress, she suddenly looked like she belonged with the rest of the fashionistas.

This was good for a number of reasons in Chen's mind. With Charlie, Perić and Ash all clearly able to fit into the fashion world, they could go about their business without drawing attention. Only Mortimer didn't seem to be making the effort, but she had also made it clear she wasn't particularly interested in their problems. She would supply them with what they needed and then had to get back to her life.

Chen found himself standing on the sidelines with Charlie by his side.

"I know that you're all over this," she said casually, as though discussing the weather. "But just in case I'm wrong, that red-head girl over there is your target." Charlie casually inclined her head, and Chen looked in the direction she was indicating. There were a few blonde women, but the one red-head stand out from the others. She was tall, and was wearing an outfit that was both blue and red, unlike many of the others who were more monochromatic. Her dress was…unusual. In some ways it seemed to be a sheer of red over vivid blue underwear that highlighted the body of the model in question. When she walked, the muscles of her legs were clear, and she confidently strolled past people with a look that screamed she was the Emperor in her new clothes. When she walked past a light, the outfit suddenly became opaque, and was not a solid blue, with a casual red coat that had not been at all obvious.

"What?" Chen found himself saying aloud.

"Mute is a master of fabrics that look different under different lighting conditions," Charlie said. "It's quite impressive, to be honest. No light, and you get the red sheer dress, showing off everything the girl has to offer. Hit it at the right angle, and suddenly you're wearing a high fashion number with accompanying jacket."

"How much would that sell for?" Chen asked, curious in spite of himself.

"Oh," Charlie shrugged. "We're talking haute couture. That one is probably five figures, upper end, I'd guess. Nothing Mute designs would be less than 50G." Chen shook his head in disbelief.

"I don't understand fashion," he finally admitted.

"You're not the only one," Charlie grinned. "Most of these things will be sold to people who have a lot of money and don't know what to spend it on. If they ever get worn it will be the premiere of some event, or maybe the Met Gala. And it will only ever get out once. Twice would be gauche," Charlie smiled.

"What's the point?" Chen grumbled.

"We're not paid enough to understand what it's like for the rich and famous," Charlie said, her smile now a wider grin.

"How did she get this gig?"

"See the rocks on her fingers and around her neck? That's *Digné*. She's the brand ambassador. She's climbing the ladder and getting noticed."

"Well, she won't be climbing it much longer," Chen said.

"Can I say," Charlie said, placing a hand on Chen's arm, "just for the record. I'm not totally comfortable with this." Chen turned to look at her with a frown.

"What's that supposed to mean?"

"She's not much more than a kid," Charlie said. "I just find it really difficult to believe that she killed a CIA agent."

"You're saying she's not working on the Intelligence circuit."

"Have you seen her? She's a party goer. She's enjoying the high life and making the most of being young and rich. I know we're supposed to believe she's Bruce Wayne, but at least with him you could vaguely entertain the idea that he could have been Batman. Do you really look at her and think, yeah, she's an ASIS assassin."

"I don't think. I do as I'm told," Chen said.

"I suppose that's why you're leading the mission," Charlie said softly.

"I suppose so," Chen agreed.

There was a party atmosphere as Luna Rochique and DJ Kabuki continued their set, while people walked around admiring the outfits that the models were wearing. Somewhere in the crowd was Mute, but Michael Chen wasn't sure who he was or what he looked like. Or, come to think of it, if he was a he. There hadn't been enough time to read up on fashion details, and he was leaving most of that to Charlie.

Killing Dana in this public place would be unwise on a number of levels, and they simply weren't prepared to do it. Theoretically it could be turned into a scene of such monumental chaos that slipping away would be simple, but he had been bustled into this environment to do some groundwork. After his conversation with Charlie he was wondering if she had simply taken away an easy opportunity.

"You look lost," a voice came from behind him, and as he noticed a slight Australian twang, his heart sank. Sure enough, when he turned, he saw Dana Spectra. He could see why she was a model. She was very beautiful, but she had an energy about her that made her interesting. Her long blonde hair and green eyes were dulled slightly by the lights that changed her dress from blue to sheer. Seeing her in almost her underwear was distracting, as she had a gorgeous figure.

But he had no desire to engage with the woman, and now she was standing in front of him it would be almost impossible not to. Cursing slightly to himself, he glanced around to see if he could see Charlie, wondering if this was another step in a plan to spare the model's life.

"No," he replied, levelly. "Just a bit out of my depth."

"Oh, you're an Aussie," Dana said, a smirk on her lips. The lights changed and her body was on display. Chen fought to keep his eyes on her face.

"Yeah," he smiled back, slightly forced.

"Where you from?"

"Sydney," he lied. "What about you?"

"Brisbane," she said.

"Oh, welcome to the 2020's," he grinned.

"Oh, it's like that is it," Dana grinned back, and laughed. "We're not so bad. Plus, let's be honest, who'd want to live in Sydney?"

"Well, that's fair," he shrugged. "You're a model?"

"I am, hence the outfit. What about you?"

"Oh, nothing important. I'm here with a few fashionistas. Making up the numbers really."

"And getting the chance to look good in dinner suit?"

"I," he paused, and wondered if the girl was flirting with him. "No, just…" He waved his hand airily, hoping that it might contribute to something. "How does an Aussie get a gig like this?"

"By being a damn good model," Dana replied. "Some people have heard of me, and that helps."

"Right, right. And you are?"

"Dana Spectra," she replied, holding out her hand. Chen took it, noting the very expensive jewellery that Charlie had mentioned earlier.

"Kenny Boon," he said.

"What do you do, Kenny Boon?"

"I am an investor. Which is, before you ask, as boring as it sounds."

"But does come with the perk of being rich," Dana said, and for a brief moment she seemed to be judging him.

259

"Yes," Chen agreed. A waiter walked past, dressed in a white tuxedo, and held out a tray. Both Chen and Dana took a flute of sparkling wine, and the waiter walked on.

"I hate champagne," Dana confided, "But unfortunately in this sort of situation its hard to get the drink you want." Chen sipped his sparkling and noticed that she seemed as vacuous as he had been led to believe. Except when she had judged him. In that brief moment there was something more to her, and then she was grabbing a glass of bubbly and being silly. "You'll have to excuse me. I have to do a few more laps and be assessed before I go back to the Four Seasons. Such is the life of a hottie."

She moved away and immediately was seized upon by a woman in her fifties who was gushing over the outfit she was wearing. Chen watched her go, his mind working overtime. Another waiter strolled past, and he deposited his glass on the tray, heading back to the steps and Hana Mortimer. By the time he got to the car, Charlie, Ash and Perić were already there.

"I met the target," he announced, and the other four looked at him in surprise. "Do I think she could have killed someone?" he said, turning to Charlie. "She's cleverer than she likes people to believe. She's definitely hiding something. So, yeah, in truth, I absolutely believe she could have killed someone. She also revealed that she's staying at the Four Seasons, which might make our job just that little bit easier." He paused and then said (despite realising it was overly dramatic), "This time tomorrow, Dana Spectra will be dead."

Hana Mortimer outright laughed.

FOUR

The plan was simple and straightforward. They had booked a room in the hotel; the cheapest that they could get. From there, Ash Frost had set up her computer and was starting to *hack*. She just needed to get into the security systems, but not to actually do anything just yet. Ash assured them that a hotel of this sort – the Four Seasons – wouldn't have a bog-standard security system. But at the same time unless they did anything unusual, nothing would register on the systems. For the moment, then, all they were doing was getting into the cameras to keep on eye on who was coming and going. Dana Spectra was not in the hotel, Ash announced, giving a little smirk, that for a moment reminded Chen of Spectra's own.

Across the road at the Renoma Café, Ruvim Perić sat on the sidewalk under the black awning, enjoying a coffee with a cheeseburger and fries. His phone was out, apparently allowing him to play Candy Crush, but he kept a close eye on the entrance to the Four Seasons. Hana Mortimer's black Skoda Kodiaq was parked in the middle of the road. Once Chen had done his job, Perić and Charlie would get in and the three would drive away. Chen and Ash had to find separate ways home. Chen's plan was simply to get back to Charles de Gaulle and immediately leave the country. What the others would do was their own business, but once Dana Spectra was dead, his job was finished.

Not that he didn't enjoy working as a Dove. Having been unceremoniously removed from the SAS for circumstances that were literally beyond his control, Flight seemed to be the only person there for him. So when Kit appeared and made him the offer to join the Doves, he immediately accepted. He needed help, and help was there. The Australian government had put him out to dry, so he would go with the next best thing.

He wasn't an idiot, however. He immediately did some research to learn what he could about the Doves and their mysterious benefactor. However, to his surprise it was literally nothing. He then contacted an old friend at Interpol, and she had had just mentioned whispers. Criminal elements had encountered them and mentioned them when the police had arrested said elements. Interpol had been working with the various police forces around the world to try and connect dots, but it was proving to be annoyingly difficult. And as no crimes had been committed by them, wasting resources on searching for a, perhaps non-existent, organisation seemed a pointless exercise.

This was a definite positive, in Chen's book. And so when Kit found him for the second time, he agreed to join. He did ask why they trusted him, and Kit informed him that they had done some serious research into him, and considered him to be high quality. From there he was left to his own devices. You'll get a message, and then you'll do your job, Kit had said.

And he had. Several messages, all of which required his unique talents to permanently deal with someone. The first time he had been very cautious, but he had been given a great deal of information. Almost incontrovertible information, and when he had pressed to know why the police had done nothing, the response he had been given was enough to pull the trigger.

Most of the time the police were good. Sometimes, however, there was a bad apple that was spoiling it, and Chen was more than happy to carry out justice if said bad apple was getting in the way. He never used to approve of vigilante activities, but the fact was that the government and its law enforcement weren't always happy to play by the rules. Or they were more than happy to throw a sacrificial lamb to the wolves in order to appear clean.

To date, Flight had not led him astray, and as such he had no reason to doubt their judgement.

"She's back. Perić's just seen her walk past the café," Ash said, looking up at him.

"Is Charlie in play?" Chen asked. Ash looked up, her glasses reflecting the screen.

"I have them on camera. Charlie is making contact with her now."

"Good," Chen nodded, and with that he left the room. He didn't bother to say goodbye to Ash. It hardly mattered. He had to get to Spectra's room.

Within two minutes he had gone up the stairs to the floor above and was at the door to the room Spectra was staying in.

"Frost, open the door," he muttered, tapping on his earbud.

"Done," came the short response, and he saw the little red light turn green on the door handle. Chen pushed the door open and stepped into the room. Interestingly, Spectra wasn't staying in a suite, which surprised Chen slightly. He thought she would be spending on the company dime, but her room was a Deluxe, bigger than the one they had rented downstairs, but not that different in the broad scheme of things. The "living area", he supposed, was slightly bigger, with more room for the desk and lounge chair. The king-sized bed was still in place, and the large television directly opposite it. He was mildly curious about the bathroom, but he didn't have time to check it out really.

"They're almost…" Ash said in his ear.

Chen glanced around the room, making a rapid decision about where the best place to deal with the woman would be. He hesitated for a fraction of a moment, and then backed up against the wall beside the door. From inside his jacket he removed the Ruger Mark IV. It wasn't his personal choice of weapon, but Mortimer had given him limited options and of those, this was his preference. He raised the gun, and heard the door lock click.

"After you," he heard Charlie say.

"Oh don't be silly," came the Australian accent. "After you. I insist." At those last two words Chen realised something was wrong. His brain had registered Ash hadn't finished her sentence, and now there was something going on. "Your friend should probably make his way to the center of the room," Dana Spectra continued, and Chen silently swore.

Charlie stepped into the doorway, and the pair exchanged a

glance. They had the upper hand, Chen reflected. Charlie could stumble, he could get out of the window and escape. Except from the way Charlie was moving, she was being threatened, and so they were risking her life. Charlie gave a little shrug, but before she could do anything she was shoved into the room, and this lost her the advantage.

Chen moved quickly to the window, but then the pane of glass in front of him shattered outwards and he stopped, turning to the door. Dana Spectra, dressed casually in jeans, a t-shirt, and a pink, fluffy parka, was closing the door with her foot. In her hands was a golden Glock.

"I'm hoping you didn't miss," Chen said casually.

"I didn't," Dana said. "Drop the gun." He hesitated, and a second pane of glass smashed outwards. Instantly he threw the gun onto the bed. "OK, so, I assume you have a good reason for coming to kill me?" She wandered over to minibar, keeping the Glock trained on them both, and to Chen's surprise, she reached back and grabbed a bottle of sparkling wine.

"Got your priorities straight?" Chen sneered, but Dana just gave him the smirk. At that point, the door to the room was smashed open. Perić burst in, having barely raised a sweat, and Chen leapt up. However, in that moment he realised he had badly underestimated the Australian model. She fired her Glock, and Chen dropped to the floor in pain, as blood flowed from the new wound in his leg.

When he looked up he realised that Dana must have swung the bottle of sparkling straight into Perić's head, as the big man had dropped to the floor, moaning in pain, and the bottle was now smashed. However, Charlie had managed to get the Ruger and was pointing it at Dana. The two women were effectively in a Mexican standoff. Then, to Chen's horror, he saw Charlie throw the Ruger onto the bed again and hold up her hands.

"Why did you kill Mason Lemon?" Charlie said.

"What?" Dana said, not dropping her gun.

"Mason Lemon. Why did you kill him?" Charlie repeated.

"Why didn't you just kill her?" Chen snarled.

"I'm not good with a gun. And she obviously is, so there's a good chance the three of us would be dead and I'd have done nothing," Charlie replied evenly.

"I don't know who Mason Lemon is," Dana said.

"He was in Seoul when you were earlier this year," Charlie said. "You killed him."

"I didn't kill anyone in Seoul," Dana said, her voice full of disbelief. "I mean, there was definitely a killer in Seoul, but it wasn't me. And he…she…they didn't kill Mason Lemon. Unless Mason Lemon is the surprise name of a Korean pop idol."

"OK," Charlie said. "OK, can you put down the gun, and let's all agree not to kill anyone."

"I may look like a bimbo, but I'm not stupid," Dana snapped.

"How did you even…?" Chen said, but Dana just looked at him.

"There was something off about you at the event last night, Kenny Boon," Dana replied. "I mean, that was obviously not your name. Anymore than Caroline Sawyer is yours." Dana directed the last comment to Charlie, who nodded.

"Guilty," she said, with a smile.

"You were on edge, checking everything out, especially me. But not in a "she's hot" kinda way. Also your outfits. I mean, hers was quality, but the boys? A little too off the shelf. And then when I walked here and saw beardy here at the café, and ran into Caroline, well…"

"I do work better alone," Chen grumbled.

"Please, we're not going to kill you," Charlie said. "This is a complete disaster. Perič, come sit with us," Charlie instructed.

"Is there just one monitoring the cameras?" Dana asked. "I

mean, that's how you know everything, right?"

"Yes," Chen said, resigned to the fact he'd been beaten.

He sat down between Charlie and Perić on the bed, Dana still holding the gun on them. Chen suspected that Frost would have abandoned the mission, which was the protocol. Now they had to salvage the situation they were in. He was in enormous pain, and was going to need a hospital, though Dana hadn't objected when he started to wrap his coat around his leg.

"So?" Dana said.

"You don't know who Mason Lemon is?"

"No," Dana said as though talking to a particularly stupid child.

"What did you mean about a Korean pop idol?" Charlie probed.

"When I was in Seoul there was a Korean pop idol called Boom. He was murdered by…well, an assassin I guess. I think Boom was murdering K-Pop idols, and the assassin…" She paused. "Well, the assassin put a stop to that." Chen frowned at this surprise outpouring. For someone in the intelligence community she didn't seem particularly keen on holding back information.

"Can I use my phone to google something?" he asked. Dana looked at him with a raised eyebrow.

"Remember how good my aim is," she said sourly. Chen nodded and took out his phone, quickly googling K-Pop murders. There was a lot of rubbish results, but at the top was the murder of someone called Boom. Dana was in a few of the photos, and it was the same date as the murder of Mason Lemon. There were a few hours between Lemon's murder and the murder of the idol, so theoretically Dana could have done both, except… As he clicked on a few different articles, they made note of how Dana had apparently been celebrating with a group called G'Star. Again, there was nothing to inherently prove that beyond a doubt.

He flicked through some of the mission images he had brought with him, and finally came up with what he wanted. It was the blurry image of Lemon's murderer, according to Flight. It must have been taken by a security camera in the park where it happened, but the camera was on a building nearby and so wasn't really focussed on the park, mused Chen. He then turned the phone to Dana

"Convince me this isn't you," he said.

"I'm not wearing stockings," Dana said, handing the phone back. Chen paused and frowned.

"What do you mean?"

"If you must know, I have a scar on my thigh. From a childhood accident. It's not something I'm particularly proud of, so I tend to cover it. I do have a dress like that. I wear them a lot, actually. But I wear stockings because I don't like the scar. Besides which, I was wearing something totally different that night. Take a look, there's plenty of pictures."

"You could have got changed," Chen replied.

"Still would've covered the scar." She shrugged at him.

"Then who killed Mason Lemon?" Chen asked, annoyed.

"How should I know," Dana snapped back. "I don't even know who killed Boom. Or even why Boom was doing what he was doing. Or even if he was doing what he was doing. And I'm fine with that, OK? I've realised I'm not going to know everything, and if I keep on stressing about these stupid little back door secrets, I'm going to go insane. I'm not turning into you, or Justice or whatever. I refuse to." Chen realised he had a chance to turn the tables, as Dana had folded her arms in a huff, the gun now no longer on any of them. But in truth, she had been pretty convincing.

"Can I have my gun back?" he asked.

"No," Dana said acidly. "But you can get out of my room. If you've decided you're not going to kill me." Chen opened his mouth to say something, but then felt the pain stab in his leg. Cautiously he stood up, and Perić helped him to hobble from the room, Charlie following.

He didn't have to see her to know that Charlie was giving him an "I told you so" look.

FIVE

"I like her," Ash grinned. "You have to admit she has balls." Chen rolled his eyes as he put his head back on the pillow.

"You were supposed to abandon everything and walk out," he growled.

"Meh," Ash shrugged.

"What's the plan now?" Charlie asked. "Are we going to tell Flight we failed, and aren't going to carry on with the mission?"

"He'll send another team who will do it," Chen mumbled. "If we're going to get Dana off the hook we have to find out who actually killed Mason Lemon."

"You want to get her off the hook?" Charlie asked, somewhat surprised.

"I took this job for a reason," Chen said. "We do what we do because it's the right thing to do. Killing her isn't the right thing to do." Charlie sat quietly, though there was a new level of respect in her eyes.

"Well, it's funny you should say that," Ash said, and the three of them turned to her. "I was doing a little bit of digging on Lemon. Obviously there's not much floating around, right? But would you believe that someone recently turned up dead in New York. I mention this because he was found, not long after his father was murdered, execution style. Interestingly enough, there was an open safe at both locations. Why is this important?" Ashley let the question hang in the air as the other three just looked at her. "Well, I ran a facial recognition check on the people at Lemon's funeral. Don't get me wrong, there wasn't a lot there, right. No photos, all very quiet, etc. However, the house across the road has a security camera and it was pretty easy to hack. Most of the faces came back negative, except for Nathan Coulter, the guy who was found dead in New York, not long after his father was found murdered in Virginia. *And*, this is the exciting thing – there's pretty much nothing on Coulter. He's social media is a wasteland. Doesn't talk about his job, doesn't talk about himself, just boring old photos of dogs."

"He's CIA," Charlie murmured.

"I think so. Although it would appear, he also murdered his sister, and a stripper."

"That actually tallies with something I was told," Chen said, remembering his mission briefing. "You said empty safe?"

"It was a similar detail at both crime sites. You could almost think they were both home invasions, except that Coulter didn't live in New York, and you'll never guess who owned the house he was found in."

"Mason Lemon," Charlie offered.

"Bingo," grinned Ashley.

"So, question one, what was in the safes?" Charlie pondered.

"And question two, who killed Nathan Coulter?" Chen supplied.

"Question three, yes?" Perić said, and the other three looked at him, a little surprised to hear his deep voice. Now Chen thought about it, the man had barely spoken since they had met. "Is person who killed Korean singer involved in other two deaths?"

The foursome sat for a moment in the white hospital room

that Chen had been assigned to in order to recover. He was about to be discharged (there was no reason or room to keep him there), and that meant Chen had to consider what to do.

"I'm going to America," he said, after a moment. "Flight wanted Dana executed because of what she had done to Lemon. I think the spirit of the mission is to find Lemon's killer and exact justice. But it's not what you were signed up for, so I'll let you guys go your separate ways."

"Oh, no," Ash shook her head. "You can't just cut me out of the loop. I'm curious now. I'm invested. I have to know what's going on. Besides, I'm American, so it's a good excuse to go home and visit the family."

"I'm in too," Charlie added, to Chen's surprise. "My curiosity's also piqued. I have contacts there, I can be useful." Chen wondered if she just wanted to keep an eye on him, but he couldn't deny he could use her help. There was an awkward moment, and then Charlie turned to look at Perić.

"Oh," Perić looked up, slightly surprised. "Yes, I will go. Sorry. I thought it was understood." He grinned at them, and Chen nodded.

"Well, I appreciate it."

"Obviously I'm not," Mortimer put in, and they turned to the woman who was sitting in the corner. "I've got kids. I can't just go wandering around the world on a whim. But I'll put you in touch with US acquisitions. Good luck, though."

They'd probably need that, Chen reflected.

SIX

Michael Chen scowled slightly, as he stood out the front of number 16, 4th Street, deciding that there were so many things he didn't like about America. Yes, Melbourne wasn't perfect by any stretch of the imagination, but New York felt like a dump, and he didn't like it. This particular part of New York didn't do anything to remove those illusions. Quite aside from the constant sound of building, and the scaffolding blocking the entrance to Mason Lemon's apartment, there was the smell. A pervading smell of... well, he couldn't put his finger on it, but it didn't smell nice.

It was probably the bags of rubbish just lying around. Did they not have rubbish collection?

When he turned, he saw that Ashley Frost was strolling up the street towards him. She was dressed in a midriff jumper, and black bike pants, with a cap jammed on her head and a laptop bag over her shoulder. He wasn't certain whether he liked the woman or not, but he suspected he was leaning towards not.

This was the first time he had seen any of them in a few days, as they had departed Paris separately at different times. Chen had been the first to leave, and as such was annoyed to have spent more time in New York than he wanted to. He had no idea about the travel plans for the others, so wasn't sure what they had done before the decision to meet here at this time.

"Hey Mike!" Ash called out cheerily, and Mike was about to say something, but opted instead for just waving.

"This is the right address, yeah?" Chen pointed. Ash followed his finger and nodded.

"Yeah, why?"

"Well," Chen started and shrugged. "No police tape, no...

entry…"

"Oh, there's an entry. You can get in. And there's probably no police tape because it was a while back. There's not much chance the police spent a lot of time investigating. They were probably given the word to leave it. Call it something else."

"Call it something else?"

"Well, you read the files," Ash said with a grin. "Don't you think it was a bit odd?" Chen had to agree with her. Ash had successfully hacked into the NYPD database and retrieved the police investigation, and while the situation *could* have played out the way that the police reported, it seemed a little unlikely. Also, and perhaps most importantly, despite the two empty safes, there was nothing found. If Coulter had killed the stripper and then killed himself, what happened to the files? He couldn't possibly have taken them. Or, if he had, he had hidden them in the apartment.

It was a weak lead, but it was the only one they had.

A car drove down 4th carefully, before stopping and letting Charlie and Perić out. Mike was surprised to see Perić was wearing shorts and a t-shirt, while Charlie was wearing a light summer dress and a jumper. Quite aside from the fact it was quite chilly, the three of them looked so completely different in their everyday clothes as opposed to their finery for Parisian entertainment, Chen might not have recognised them if he hadn't expected them.

"Aren't you cold?" he muttered.

"Oh, it's a little chilly," Charlie smiled, "but it's not too bad. It'll get much worse in a couple of weeks. Let's hope we're not here for that."

"Is good weather for now," Perić said looking at his phone, and Chen pondered what his obsession with the weather was all about.

Ash was already walking up to the front of the building and she pushed on the door, turning to the others as it swung open, ending the various trains of thought that were going on.

"Nice to know that estates are the same wherever you go," Charlie grinned.

"Estate?" Perić wondered.

"Apartment block. Slum. Whatever," Chen supplied. The four entered and Ash led the way to the apartment they were looking for. When they got there, they found the door was bolted shut and locked with what appeared to be a relatively new lock. Perić pushed against it lightly, before looking around and then giving it a hefty shove, forcing the door open, and comfortably knocking the bolted lock off the door from where it had been screwed in.

Charlie touched his arm and pointed to a security camera, but Ash grinned at her.

"Don't worry. None of the security here works. It's in the police reports. No footage of any events, none of the cameras are operational." She walked into the apartment, followed by the other three.

There was a strong smell of bleach inside, and for the most part the few rooms in the apartment were empty. The kitchen still had an oven and a fridge, there was a single table and chair, and the stripped mattress was still in the bedroom, but everything had been cleaned and redressed, ready for a new occupant.

"So?" Charlie turned to Chen.

"It shouldn't take too long to search," Chen shrugged. "Shall we split up?

"I go to kitchen," Perić announced, and moved into the adjoining room where the kitchen and dining room were.

"I think there was a room off the hall," Charlie said. "I'll go there if you like."

"Bedroom or living room?" Ash asked.

"Bedroom," Chen said, shrugging again. He walked out of the

living room they were in and into the bedroom. The bleach smell was the strongest here, and Chen guessed that there was probably a lot of blood that needed to be mopped up. The safe had been removed from the wardrobe, so it was definitely empty.

If this was the room where the murders had taken place, then whoever came in to clean everything would have concentrated on this room. There wouldn't be a stone unturned. No, Chen mused, there would be nothing to be found here.

"Chen!" Charlie called out. There were two doors into the room, one that led from the living room, and one that went back into the corridor. He exited through that one to see Charlie standing near the door.

"Yeah?"

"Here," she tossed him something, and he caught it instinctively. When he looked, he realised it was a mobile phone. She pointed to a crack in the wall. "It was stuffed way down here. I think they probably spent a lot of time on those rooms, and forgot to look behind the door." Human error. Doesn't matter how professional you are, sometimes you cut corners, Chen reflected.

Ash had come out of the living room and Chen tossed the phone to her.

"Can you unlock this?"

"Yeah," she said, and pulled out a cord which she plugged into the phone. Awkwardly they waited for what seemed an eternity before she started to press buttons on the newly repowered phone. "Don't have to though. No lock."

"Burner phone?" Perić asked, appearing out of the shadows behind her.

"I guess." She clicked a few buttons on the phone. "Two calls, one message. I'd say Mr Coulter bought it to avoid being traced. "The calls were to the same number." Chen was about to say something, but realised

274

that Ash was already doing something.

"Good morning, Harreveld, Titman & Swindells Support, how can we help you?" came a friendly voice from the phone. Ashley looked at Chen slightly panicked.

"Oh, hi there, I'm just wondering if you guys do pest control?" Chen said.

"Sorry, sir, we do not. Is there anything else I can help you with?" the voice came back, without missing a beat.

"Nope," Chen said. "Thank you so much for your help."

"If you'd like to say on the line and answer a short survey, we'd greatly appreciate it," the voice said. "Have a nice day."

There was a pause.

"Please tell us how you learnt of our company. 1. Through a friend. 2. Through the internet." Chen shook his head and Ash rang out.

"What was the number?"

"Err," Ash pressed a few more buttons and then turned the display to Chen. He took out his own phone and dialled the number, changing over to speakerphone as he did. This time the answer was somewhat different.

"Yes?"

"I need help," Chen said carefully.

"Name?" There was a moment's pause as they looked at each other.

"Mason Lemon," Chen said. The phone immediately died. Chen hesitated, and then dialled the number again.

"Good morning, Harreveld, Titman & Swindells Support, how can we help you?" This time Chen disconnected the call himself.

"Who was that?" Charlie asked.

"Some intelligence cover," Chen muttered. "Not American, I'm guessing, if Coulter called. He would be hardly likely to give himself over to the Feds."

"So Coulter calls spooks and then he's killed," Ash mused.

"With a stripper," Charlie added.

"And an empty safe," Chen said.

"In Mason Lemon's house," Perić concluded.

"That can't be a coincidence," Charlie said.

"Do we assume that whoever killed Mason, also killed Coulter?" Chen said.

"What, we have to solve the murder of Nathan Coulter before we can complete this mission?" Ash said incredulously. "This is getting very complicated."

"Isn't it just?" Charlie agreed.

"You guys can tap out," Chen said.

"We're not going to," Charlie said. "But you have to admit this is no longer straightforward."

"And if the police shut this down because the Feds told them to leave it alone, how do we find out anything?" Ash said.

"And what is this with K-Pop and Australian model?" Perić piped up.

"I," Chen started, and then paused. "I need a drink."

Michael Chen walked into the Fairfield Inn & Suites where he was staying, paused for a few moments and then decided he wasn't going to go straight to his room. He and his team had opted to stay in different locations, and he had chosen something fairly straightforward. Yes, it was a Marriott, but it was low down on the food chain, was nicely located on W 40th St, and was relatively inexpensive.

He was quite impressed with the bar and restaurant, which was neatly spaced out, and was well set up. When he walked into the bar it was 3.30 in the afternoon, and was, for the most part empty.

"Hi, er," he paused to read the nametag of the staff member, "Lauren, can I please get an Old Fashioned?" She looked at him blankly and he closed his eyes for a moment. "Bourbon, bitters, sugar and orange?"

"Oh, right, sure," she smiled at him. "Did you want to take a seat and I'll bring it over to you?"

"Yeah, that's cool. Room 45 please." She nodded, and he turned away from the bar and headed towards the seating area.

The bar itself looked a little like a gold palace, thanks to the lighting behind it. However, once you walked into the seating area, it was more standard. There were a couple of tall tables near the marble pillars with the brown-cushioned stools near them, but in truth, Chen decided he was going to sit on the emerald wall sofa at one of the smaller tables.

The only other occupant in the room was a woman, probably in her late twenties or early thirties, with long dark hair. She was seated at a table towards the middle of the green couch, but he decided to take the one nearest the bar. Lauren had his drink to him quite quickly, and he nodded his thanks, and handed her a note. It mildly irked him that he had to tip, but he didn't want to draw attention to himself.

"So," the dark-haired woman suddenly said. "I was all set to leave this place, when I get a message that Nathan Coulter wants to talk." Chen's head snapped around so fast, he could have given himself an injury. "I meet him and give him the address he's looking for, and then I'm like, that's it. I'm out. Back home." Chen wondered where home was, given she had a strong American accent, but kept his mouth shut. "Anyway, it's all sorted, I'm fine, I'm ready to finally leave here, when, snap. Another call. Can you sort something out. There's this guy, he might be a problem." Suddenly the woman looked up from her phone and directly at Chen. "Are you a problem?"

"I think you have the wrong person," Chen smiled, amiably.

Drink your drink, then get up and leave. Nothing quick, just deliberate.

"You were right about the security camera. But there's one installed by, well by interested parties. It's much smaller, much neater, and it's on the inside. So, when you went in, you triggered it."

Shit.

"Also, you looked pretty shocked when I mentioned Nathan Coulter. First rule of business, don't lie about things that are obviously lies. I'm one of the interested parties."

"American intelligence?"

"No, but that's all you're getting. You?"

"I'm a Dove." The dark-haired woman's eyes widened slightly.

"Oh," she said. "Well. That's interesting. I was never sure if you guys were real or not. And you are. How exciting."

"We don't hide our existence," Chen pointed out. He casually got up and walked over to her table, sitting down in the grey chair opposite her. "Do you mind?"

"Not at all," grinned the woman. "You don't exactly advertise, though, do you? A world-wide vigilante group, backed by an unknown... well, billionaire, presumably. Is it Elon?"

"Fuck no," Chen laughed. "I wouldn't agree to that."

"So you've met him? Or her? Or they?"

"No. Talked, but not met. But let's just say, I know enough to reassure me it's all legit."

"That's a slight stretch of the meaning of that word." The woman sat back in her chair, crossing her arms.

"You don't approve, I take it."

"I've never been a fan of superhero comics," the woman drawled.

"We're not the Avengers."

"You definitely are not," she agreed, and Chen wondered how much of an insult that was. "What are you doing?"

"I'm assuming that you've investigated it all and decided that Mason Lemon's death wasn't important enough to be concerned about."

"Mason was killed by someone in Seoul. Who was found dead."

"You don't care beyond that?"

"I cared enough about how that happened. Mason, that is. That's why Nathan Coulter was dealt with."

"Because he set Mason up?"

"Yes," the woman took a sip of her drink.

"Why?"

"Why what?"

"Why did he set up Mason?" Chen planted his drink on the table and sat back in his chair, looking at the woman.

"Did you know about Nathan Coulter?"

"I understand he was a murderer," Chen said.

"Mason had that proof," the woman said, with a degree of finality.

279

"You're very open with that," Chen replied.

"What does it matter? The truth that the CIA want is already out there. You can be told whatever you like, it's not going to make a blind bit of difference in the real world."

"So why come to me? Obviously, you don't want people digging around further, so your truth is precarious?"

"I'm not CIA," the woman said. "But I gave a shit about Mason. His killer needed to be brought to justice. I was keen for that to happen."

"I agree. Except his killer hasn't been brought to justice."

"The person responsible for his death is," the woman pointed out.

"Is he? How long did Mason have that information? Why did Nathan wait so long to exact his revenge?" The woman took another drink of her drink and regarded Chen. He could see, however, that her mind was ticking over. "I was sent to kill the woman who killed Mason Lemon." The dark-haired woman frowned at this. "But I don't think I got the right information."

"Who were you sent to kill?"

"Dana Spectra, an Australian…" But he didn't finish his sentence, as the woman burst out laughing. "Do you know…?"

"Know Dana? Oh yeah, intimately," the dark-haired woman laughed. "God, honestly. I cannot get away from her. I mean, it definitely wasn't Dana."

"I agree." The woman looked at Chen again, frowning.

"So you're going to find Mason's killer? Having been convinced by Dana it wasn't her."

"Exactly. I want to know why this happened. I became a Dove for a good reason. I don't think you guys do your job properly. And can I say, everything that's been said today sort of proves my point. You took care of someone and think that justice has been meted out." The woman smiled when he said justice, and for some reason it irritated Chen. "I think justice is important."

"Oh, she's very important," the woman said, unable to stop grinning. Chen raised an eyebrow. "It's my name," Justice said. "Hence, I think she's important."

"Oh," Chen said, a little deflated.

"Look, I don't disagree with what you're saying. And maybe you're right. I think the CIA have solved the problem they wanted solved, and used that to say Mason's situation has been dealt with. But I'm not CIA, so…" She shrugged. "I want you to leave the US. I'm going to tell my bosses that your heart is in the right place, but I've convinced you to fuck off and leave it to the big boys. You leaving the US will make things much easier."

"Well I would, if I had somewhere else to go. We've sort of hit a dead end." Justice regarded him again, and then lent forward.

"You didn't hear this from me, but I can tell you that Nathan Coulter was murdered by an assassin called Man Garam."

"That name rings a bell," Chen frowned.

"It should do. They're the best in the business for sorting out problems. I would suggest that if you want to find out more, you contact Man Garam."

"That's impossible, isn't it?" Justice shrugged again, and then downed the last of her drink.

"I can't do it for you," she grinned. "Will you get this?" Chen rolled his eyes. "Thanks. Talk to your people. I'm sure somewhere in that big, scary organisation there's someone who can put you in touch with Man Garam's people." She got up and moved away from the table before turning back. "Nice to meet you, by the way. It's been sort of exciting meeting a Dove." She gave him a wink, and then turned and walked out of the bar.

Michael Chen sat back in his chair, drinking the last of his Old Fashioned, and then pursed his lips slightly. According to most people, Man Garam didn't even exist. How do you track down a ghost?

SEVEN

"I have bought us a little treat," the older gentleman said, before giggling slightly. "Or two, maybe. I've been a bit naughty." He sat down with the drinks tray and put it on the table. Ashley Frost regarded it with slight concern. "Burst your bubble," he giggled again.

There were two drinks in front of her. One did indeed have a smoky bubble on the top, and she watched as the gentleman opposite her popped his, the aroma of passionfruit and vanilla suddenly billowing out from the smoke. She did the same, poking at her bubble gently, watching it pop and the scents waft out.

"Wow," she murmured.

Wow, in many ways, really. After a great deal of discussion and conversation regarding Chen's meeting with Justice, Charlie had pointed out that the only real way forward was to try to get in touch with Man Garam, something which none of them really knew how to do. As such, Charlie suggested that they do the most obvious thing and get in touch with the person who should be able to provide them with acquisitions. One phone call later with a rather surly Hana Mortimer, and they were told to go to Barcelona, without any undue pleasantry.

When they arrived at Josep Tarradellas Barcelona-El Prat Airport, Mortimer was there waiting for them.

"You," she declared, pointing at Ash. "You need to get dressed nicely and get to a place called Sips. It's nice. Best bar in the world. You'll meet with Man Garam there."

"Man Garam is going to meet her?" Charlie asked, her blood pressure rising slightly.

"I don't know," Mortimer shrugged. "Probably not. But the contact or whatever. They'll find you. Just go there, where a white scarf, everything else will be fine."

Things seemed to be progressing at an unreal pace, and the next thing she knew, Ashley was walking into Sips, dressed in a Mystlemode black velvet tuxedo dress, with a white collared shirt and black necktie, as well as a white dress scarf. Charlie had also given her black over-the-knee boots, which made Ashley aware of how short the tuxedo dress was, and how short she herself was. Nonetheless she got out of the car, with Charlie snatching the cap off head as she did, and headed towards the glass door that led into the bar.

Truthfully, Sips' exterior didn't really stand out from the rest of the shop fronts. The Herbolari next door made sure to draw attention to itself with a large green sign, and the shuttered door on the other side was graffitied so much so it unintentionally drew attention. Sips, stuck in the middle, was barely noticeable, with its modest pink Sips logo on the window.

When she went inside, however, there was definitely a vibe. No one came to talk to her, so she looked around and found herself a seat. The bar was pretty small, and she felt slightly uncomfortable as she took a green seat near the wall away from the bar. The bar – an island in front of the shelves of alcohol – was attended by two middle-aged men in vests with big smiles. They were engaged in conversation with a man who was probably in his sixties, maybe early seventies, with a pale pink shirt, round glasses and grey hair.

When he came over to her, carrying a tray full of drinks, Ash had to admit she was a little surprised.

"Oh, it's vodka," she said as she sipped the drink.

"The vanilla and passionfruit gives it the flavour," the man said, his smile crinkling up his face. "I also have a Krypta. It's the signature drink of this place, and isn't it wonderful? I love it. I love coming here. There's such an ambience. I don't like bars usually, but this place just has my heart."

"I'm glad you like it so much."

"Oh, tish. I'm paying," he waved his hand. "These aren't that expensive, you know. Do you like whiskey? Port? We should try a Primordial. You're not driving, are you? I'm sure I saw you get out of a cab."

"You did?"

"My dear, even an old man like myself notices young legs like yours," he grinned again, and Ashley realised how wrong-footed this man made her. "Not that I would, you know. But I can't help but notice."

"Thank you, I don't usually…" Ashley indicated her dress, and then took another sip of the drink. "I thought I should dress up."

"For me?" the man said in astonishment. "Oh my dear, you are sweet. If they'd have known you were going to put in that effort, they'd have got someone those features would have been appreciated by. Not that I don't appreciate, you, you understand. You're gorgeous. But a beautiful thing like you is wasted on an old queen like me."

"It's fine, really," Ashley said, still feeling flustered. "I just need to."

"Krypta," the man said, pushing forward the other drink. This one was bizarre, Ash thought. A glass goblet, suspended on a tripod, with three green herbs stuck in the glass. "Thyme, Tarragon and, errr…" He paused. "Bay leaf! You breathe in the aroma as you sip on the gin and kiwifruit. It's quite amazing."

284

"Right," Ash nodded, taking the goblet. He was right, the smells of the herbs immediately filled her nostrils and she brought the drink closer to sip from it.

"They're not cheap, you know," the man said as she drunk.

"Sorry?"

"Man Garam. Not cheap. Very efficient, ruthlessly effective, definitely not cheap."

"You're not," Ashley started, and the man burst out laughing.

"Oh, lord no. No, no, no, no, no!" He giggled as he settled himself down. "Not my style at all. I'm just a go-between. Well, a go-between-go-betweens, really."

"You don't know where I can find him?"

"Them, no."

"I really need to talk to…them," Ashley said.

"What about?" The man looked at her over his glasses, as he drank more from him Bubble.

"I suppose I need to know if they killed someone."

"Oh, that's a definite yes," the man grinned. Ashley had to admit that the man was right; there was a definite vibe to Sips. She wasn't sure if she was starting to get a bit tipsy (surely not after two small cocktails?), but there was definitely a…vibe, was the perfect word. She felt calm and relaxed.

Oh.

"You didn't drug me, did you?" The man laughed again.

"No, it's the ambience of the place, trust me. I wouldn't do that. I don't like to bring attention to myself. Look, here's the thing. Garam is unlikely to confirm that they killed someone because it's not their thing.

They're terribly professional, you know." Ashley was suddenly struck by something she hadn't noticed before.

"You're English," she said.

"You're American, but I won't hold that against you," he said, grinning at her again. She found herself liking this man a lot, which was annoying.

"Do you live here?"

"Oh, no. I have no humble abode. I'm a transient by nature." He smiled benignly. "I quite like you, young lady. So I'm going to make you an offer that I don't usually. Who are you wondering if Garam killed?"

"Nathan Coulter," Ash said, scanning his face for a reaction, but there wasn't one.

"I'll get in touch with the chain, and see what they can tell me. If they can give me any information, I'll let you know in the next couple of hours. If not…" He shrugged. "So I suppose you can stay here and drink with me, or you can go back to your hotel. Where you will have to pay for some very bog-standard drinks. Unlike here, where I shall pay for you and I to enjoy a little something of everything."

"Well, if you put it like that," Ash grinned.

There is quite a large roundabout in L'Hospitalet de Llobregat in Barcelona, which is a feeder to a number of streets such as Avenue Mare de Déu de Bellvitge and Carrer de Jaume Ventura i Tort, and provides access for the Bellvitge campus of Universitat de Barcelona and Hesperia World and Hyatt Regency Barcelona Tower. The latter, despite being an impressive sounding 29 floors, and actually being quite beautiful on the inside, has a fairly drab exterior. Situation close to the El Prat Airport, it is really a businessman's hotel. Need to meet an important client on a stopover? Stay at the Regency. It looks amazing, and treats its guests well.

As the black and yellow taxi slid down the street that allowed access to the Hyatt, Charlie got out of the car, almost having to drag Ash with her, as the other woman was just a teensy bit tipsy after her meeting at Sips. A meeting, Charlie noted in annoyance, that hadn't resulted in anything.

"Whoops," giggled Ash as she got out of the car. "I think this dress is a little shorter than I anticipated. I may have given more of a view than I intended."

"I'm not letting you go by yourself to these things ever again," Charlie said coldly, as they started to walk down the walkway towards the entrance. However, even before they set foot on the surprisingly appropriate red carpet, a man walked up to them.

He had a shaved head and small goatee, and was accompanied by two others; a man and a woman. They had shaved heads as well, but the other man – a large brute – had a massive dark beard. All three were wearing suits and sunglasses, and even in her inebriated state, Ash's mind registered that something was not right.

"Excuse me," the smaller man said, shrugging as though he wasn't entirely comfortable in the suit. It was a slightly noticeable 15 degrees, so he shouldn't have been hot in his outfit. "I think you are friends of friends of mine." Charlie regarded him. He spoke with a thick European accent, that sounded Russian to her ear, though may have been from the area.

"I'd be surprised if we were," she said, cautiously.

"Yes, yes. You are friends of Nathan Coulter?"

"No," Charlie shook her head.

"Oh, but I am sure you are," the man said, and this time his associates turned slightly. The move was specific, as it made clear that they were concealing. They turned again, and the suits went back to their normal fall. "It's probably not my place to say anything," the man continued. "After all, we are just friends of friends. But, I feel, Barcelona is not an interesting city for you."

"That's what you feel?" Charlie said, testing the waters.

"No, it is not good. Very uninteresting. If I were you, I would just return home."

"Perhaps we are home," Ash said, forgetting they were standing out the front of a hotel. This elicited laughter from the three heavies. Someone walked past, and the speaker stepped back, apologetically, letting them through.

"Home is a much nicer place than here. Honestly, for you, I would strongly encourage going there. There is nothing exciting remaining her for you, I think."

"I'm assuming that something will happen if we choose not to?" Charlie said archly.

"No, no, no," the man raised his hands in surrender, a smile on his lips. "Nothing will happen." He paused and then added, "Ever again."

"I see."

"You are smart woman. Classy, intelligent. We will not meet again, but my loss, I believe," he smiled and bowed. With that he turned and walked up the sidewalk, heading to the entrance of the sideroad.

Perić suddenly appeared at their sides.

"Did you catch all that?" Charlie asked. Perić nodded.

"I got pictures. Was just over there," he jabbed a thumb over his shoulder, and Charlie nodded. In truth she had seen him when the cab pulled up, so had felt a lot safer when they were confronted. Ashley might not have. That thought made her turn, and sure enough, Ashley was looking very pale.

"Come on," Charlie said. "Let's go lounge by the pool for a bit.

Our glorious leader can tell us what he wants us to do."

"What will that be?" Ash asked.

"Well, you haven't had that dress on for very long. Would be a shame not to make the most of it," Charlie said with a grin. Perić smiled. "When she's a little more sober, we might get our princess here to do her thing around Barcelona."

"And then get Mortimer to do her thing?" Perić asked.

"Exactly. Hopefully he who rules will agree. I want to know how those guys are connected."

EIGHT

Ash swiped her iPad a couple of times, and sighed, leaning back in her chair. Now in a green one-piece swimsuit, with a big hat and large sunglasses, she sipped at her water, not feeling as good as she had an hour earlier.

Perić was doing laps of the pool. There were a number of pools at the Hyatt, but the group had decided to swim in the pool on the ground floor, virtually beside the Hyatt. The four of them had also decided to stay together, essentially because they hadn't thought they would be in Barcelona for a long time. And also because Mortimer had organised it quickly.

"Beggers," she had declared, "don't get to be choosers." Now she sat on a deck chair under a white umbrella, right beside the pool, with her legs stretched out, enjoying a drink of some description. The pool was surprisingly empty, so Perić was taking the opportunity to get in some exercise. Dressed in a black and gold bikini, Charlie, on the other hand, was enjoying the sun, and her own drink.

Only Chen seemed to be slightly on edge, sitting on the deckchair beside Mortimer, waiting anxiously for Ashley to come up with information.

"If they are going out," Ash said, a little petulantly, "we probably won't know about it until they actually mention it. If they do at all."

"Did you find their social media?" Chen asked.

"Yeah," she nodded. She swiped a couple more times and then turned the iPad around, wincing when it caught the light and reflected in her eyes.

"The guy who spoke was Vsevolod Fedorov. He lives in Kazan. The other guy, the big guy, he doesn't have social media, but he *might* be Borislav Fedorov, Vsevolod's…brother? Cousin? I'm not quite sure. They look similar, but it's hard to tell. The photographs are bad quality." She swiped across some photos, demonstrating her point. "The woman is Sashura Ilina. Believe it or not, she's a singer."

"What?" Charlie said, sitting up.

"I know, right? So weird. But, yeah, apparently."

"So, some KGB thug turns up with Russia's equivalent of Delta Goodrem?" Chen said in disbelief.

"That reference is lost on me," Ash said, pulling a face.

"Me too," Charlie agreed, and Chen rolled his eyes.

"Russia's equivalent of Dua Lipa," he said.

"There's no way that person you said is Dua Lipa big," Charlie objected.

"The point," Chen snapped.

"Well, not Dua Lipa big, but she'd be recognised."

"So, when she goes out tonight it will be news?" Chen asked and

Ashley's eyes widened.

"Oh, right! Good point!" She turned her iPad back and started swiping again.

"Genuinely like listening to a conversation my children are having," Mortimer muttered as she took another sip from her drink.

"Whiskey?" Charlie asked politely.

"Gin," Mortimer grinned at her. "Best drink to have when you're not driving."

"You're not driving?"

"Well, not yet," Mortimer smiled, closing her eyes.

"OK, so she hasn't put anything up," Ash said, "but DJ Kabuki is playing at Pacha Barcelona, and Sashura follows Kabuki on IG." She did a little more typing and then said, "Plus it appears that a few of her fans think that's where she'll be tonight. Should I get us tickets?"

"You have to get tickets?" Chen asked, astonished. "Isn't it just a nightclub?"

"Alright, granddad, slow it down," Mortimer said, unable to control her laughter.

"Whatever. Do it. Let's find these dicks and have a quiet word."

NINE

Perić shook his head and held up his phone.

"Could be rain," he said gloomily. Chen glanced up at the sky, almost involuntarily, and noticed that there were clouds rolling in. The app could well be right, he mused. They were standing in the line, waiting to get into Pacha Barcelona, and he felt distinctly out of place. The jeans and t-shirt weren't so much a problem, but he felt *old*. Everyone around him seemed like they were in their twenties, and it didn't help when Charlie pointed out someone who was older.

"See," she said unhelpfully. "That guy is definitely closer to fifty than forty, and he's ready to cut loose."

"You realise that every time you say that, all I'm thinking is that someone beside him is saying the same about me," Chen grumbled. "No wonder Mortimer didn't come."

"I think she may have decided to get plastered at the hotel bar, to be honest," Charlie admitted. She was wearing a blue sleeveless dress, quite short, but with a high collar. Perić was also dressed in jeans and a t-shirt, though he had opted for a Hugo Boss and looked much cooler than Chen felt. Ashley was back in her jacket dress and was blushing every time someone walked past and looked her over.

"I'm almost jealous of your attention," Charlie pouted. "I'm not used to being the one people aren't looking at," she grinned.

"Oh, you can definitely have the attention," Ash muttered.

"Look," Perić suddenly said, and he put his hand around Chen's shoulders and turned him as if to talk conspiratorially. Perić lowered his head closer to Chen's, but Chen had seen exactly what Perić wanted him to. The Fedorov brothers were a little further down the line. Both were dressed in suits, though their shirts were unbuttoned to reveal impressive gold chains, and Vsevolod had a particularly sour look on his face. Beside them was Sashura Ilina, though this time she was clearly the centre of attention. She was dressed in a metallic knit dress that had a long slit up one side, and underneath was wearing what seemed to be a black bikini. When she turned, it became more obvious it was a thong bikini, and both Perić and Chen turned away, feeling awkward. Charlie laughed at their discomfort.

"Oh come on, boys," Charlie chuckled. "You can't be that surprised by what she's wearing."

"Surely that's against the dress code," Chen muttered.

"People like her don't have dress codes," Ash replied, and Charlie nodded in agreement.

The line had begun moving, and they headed towards the small building with the glass front that they were lined up at. DJ Kabuki's mask loomed over them on a banner on the wall, advertising her appearance, and as they approached, Ash held out her phone for the tickets, which the woman at the door nodded at.

They moved into the pink glowing interior, a neon cherry hanging above their heads, and stepped onto the stairwell to go down into the club. To Chen it felt like they were descending into madness.

As they entered the dance floor, there were people packed into the club, writhing and squirming in time to a song that Chen distinctly remembered, but with a very different beat. They were standing on a raised platform, steps leading to the floor where the dancers were enjoying the music. Blue light bathed the room, turning everyone into so many aliens. All around were enclaves with seating, all roped off unless you had the correct pass, and every so often there was a bar. The club had a futuristic vibe to it, as though it had been designed by someone who had been told to create a bar that would be on the Starship Enterprise. The walls were white, and curved, and the tables were small and round. To their right was the DJ Booth, and DJ Kabuki was already there, dressed in a skintight white jumpsuit, with matching white mask.

"Our tickets are for over there," Ashley shouted, though it was barely heard above the music. She pointed across from them, to an area that was essentially across from the DJ Booth. "It's the Ciroc section," she continued. She opened her mouth to say more, but the shook her head, and grabbed Chen's hand, dragging him through the pit of dancers. Charlie and Perić genuinely seemed to be enjoying themselves as some of the dancers took an interest. Charlie politely laughed, and pointed to her friends, but occasionally Perić would turn to the person of interest and start to gyrate. As insane as it was, Chen reflected, he had to admit there was nothing sinister coming from these people. They were there just to have a good time. The end of the world could have been in just a few hours, but these kids didn't care. They just wanted to have fun.

He was almost envious of them.

Their VIP area was both behind and beside a bar; a barrier separating them from the bar on the dance floor, but giving them something to lean on as they surveyed what was in front of them. Chen was able to take in the lights hanging from the ceiling and, rather strangely, the rows and rows of LED lights that were hanging as well, adding to the blue. There were even old-fashioned chandeliers and a disco ball. It was an eclectic mix, but it gave the club the feeling of being out of time.

"We're taking a little risk, because we don't know where Sashura and the Federov brothers are going to be," Ash said, standing beside him, able to communicate slightly better now. "The thing is, I thought that Fedorov might want to impress and so get a ticket over there." She pointed across the room to their right, close to where they had come in. "That's the Belvedere suite. Very expensive. However, given that Sashura is the draw card, and she's here for DJ Kabuki, I'm guessing that she actually might want a ticket over there, in the Grey Goose area." This time she pointed almost directly across from them, but again, slightly to the right of the DJ Booth. It did look largely empty, Chen mused. Behind the booth itself was another area, and the people he presumed were DJ Kabuki's entourage were there, including a stunning Japanese woman, dressed in an outfit Chen guessed he would be unlikely to afford after a year's work.

"Looks like it was a good call, Ash," Charlie said, appearing beside the younger woman. Chen looked across to the Grey Goose area, and sure enough saw Sashura Ilina walking in, waving at some people as she did, and being met by the two men already inside the section. They talked animatedly, and then the beautiful Japanese woman left her section to enter the Grey Goose, and was introduced to Sashura Ilina. Curiously both Fedorov brothers were largely ignored. Chen realised that Ash was clearly right – this was Sashura's show, and not the men. "So now we wait?" Charlie asked, though it came across more as a statement. It had been the plan, after all. They would stay in the club, keeping tabs on the Fedorov brothers, and then follow them. When they had the chance, they would take the opportunity to ask some quick questions, which they would definitely get answers for, and then leave, following their next lead to... well, somewhere. Possibly Russia, given the brothers point of origin.

"Now we wait," Chen agreed, though he wasn't happy about it.

At midnight, Charlie decided it was time for a drink. Ash and Perić were on the dancefloor, having claimed that they'd be better on the floor rather than just sitting back and doing nothing, though Charlie smiled secretly to herself at the obvious lie. Both of them were surprising her, really. She had thought the dour Perić wouldn't have been interested in clubbing, and yet here he seemed completely in his element. Ash also had given the impression it definitely wasn't her scene, but then Kabuki had started to add G*Star to her mix, and the younger woman was immediately entranced. Charlie suspected it was a K-Pop thing, but decided not to get in Ash's way. Let her have some fun. Besides which, it certainly didn't seem like Fedorov was going to do anything while Sashura was entranced with Kabuki's beats.

She looked to Chen to ask if he wanted anything, but he was sitting looking relaxed and enjoying the ambience, which was impressive, because Charlie suspected that he was doing anything but. As such she just got up and walked across to the bar.

The bartender was serving someone else, and when she came back, she turned to the person who had just arrived at the bar – an Asian man in a black velvet suit with a white t-shirt. He started to place an order, and Charlie realised that she had been there before the newcomer and felt a slight irritation.

For a moment she wanted to say something, and then the British in her got the best of the situation and she kept her mouth shut. The Korean turned as he waited and immediately looked at Charlie, raising his eyes in surprise. She, however, was taken by just how dark the man's eyes were – almost black. She wondered if it was the lighting or if his eyes were actually that dark.

"Oh," he said. "I'm so sorry." He spoke with an accent, but it was very good English.

"Oh, it's fine," Charlie said dismissively. "It's OK. I'll still get served."

"But of course," the man said, and waved at the bartender. "Also a glass of Gaja Barbaresco, yes? Actually, change mine and make it two glasses." He turned back to Charlie with a smile that was very cheeky. "I'm sorry. I'm presuming a lot. Is that OK?"

"Ah, sure," Charlie replied with a grin.

"It's nice. Honestly. A really good red. I think you like red," he added with a smile. The bartender placed the two drinks on the white counter, and the man slid his card across the counter, and she took it to complete the payment. It was a power gesture, without a doubt, but it was rather impressive.

"Do you come here often?" Charlie asked, laughing slightly at her predictability.

"Only when I'm in Barcelona," he replied, his own smile never leaving.

The mysterious figure of DJ Kabuki moved her hands over the decks, twisting dials and pressing buttons, every so often looking up into the crowds. As she did, smoke machines blasted into the room, and Ash grinned as it engulfed her, the weight of their mission lifting from her as she felt like she was 18 again. Perič who was a little away from her, looked over and gave her a matching grin. For a moment Ash regretted why they were there and wished she could just be a tourist.

This made her glance across at the Grey Goose to check on their targets and she saw Sashura in deep conversation with Vsevolod Fedorov, the man not looking particularly happy. Borislav leaned across and spoke, but this just seemed to make Vsevolod more angry, and his face got redder as he shouted in annoyance at this flunkies. Curiously, though, Sashura seemed annoyed and turned away from Vsevolod, crossing her arms and clearly now ignoring the man. Borislav looked like he was about to say something more, and then he gave up as well and turned away. Vsevolod got up and moved away from the area, leaving his phone on the table, so Ash presumed he was coming back. She turned to find Perić but the larger man was no longer in her sight.

Ash twisted around, but couldn't make out either Chen or Charlie, and found herself in a quandary. Knowing what she had to do, but annoyed about it all the same, she started to make her way off the dance floor.

She pushed her way through the crowd and walked up the stairs through into the hall, and looked around to see if she could find Vsevolod. The crowd was a little thinner here, but there were still enough people moving back and forth, jostling one another and making it generally difficult to see anyone.

Mortimer had offered to get them earbuds, but Charlie had pointed out that the noise of the club would probably be so loud it would render them largely ineffective, but it meant that communication on the floor was very restricted. Ashley took out her phone and texted the others, but there was no response. Perić was probably still dancing, and presumably the other two weren't looking at their phones frequently. Ashley cursed slightly to herself, and the again when she saw Vsevolod Fedorov.

She eased herself behind a guy, who turned and smiled at her, before saying something in Spanish that she didn't understand. She smiled back and pulled him closer to speak to him, but at the same time took the opportunity to look over the man's shoulder to see what Fedorov was doing.

"I don't speak Spanish, I'm so sorry," Ash said, putting her arm around the man's neck, as if to hug him.

Fedorov was studying his phone intensely, before looking up and around.

"It's OK. I speak OK English," the man shouted back, not breaking the hug, though still remaining a gentleman. Ash tried to keep her mind on the job.

Fedorov looked at his phone again, and then looked up again, but this time he was suspicious and on-guard. Ash wasn't entirely certain, but she had fear in the pit of her stomach, and was worried that they had been made. Fedorov stormed back to the Grey Goose, coming within inches of Ashley, but she leaned back into her new friend's ear to talk.

"I'm Ash, what about you?"

"I'm Carlo, but I'm sorry, I have a girlfriend," he shouted back, and Ash felt a strange mix of relief and disappointment.

"Oh, I'm so sorry," Ash said. "You looked hot. Have a great night!" She kissed him gently on the cheek.

"Now you're making me regret my honour," Carlo grinned, and Ash touched him on the cheek slightly before turning back to go to the dance floor.

She needed to find Chen quickly, she decided.

They had been talking for a little while, and Charlie decided that her new friend was the archetypal man of mystery. He had given virtually nothing away while he talked with passion and wisdom about a range of topics, from the art of Joan Miró, to whether the political situation in America was going to be a problem for the rest of the world.

And yet, in that entire time, he hadn't given her his name.

Weirdly, he was probably the most feminine man Charlie had ever met, but there was definitely something about him. He had the androgynous look of a K-Pop boy band star, that was always beautiful regardless of what they were wearing.

"So I have to ask, what exactly do you do to have such a vast wealth of information?" Charlie asked with a smile.

"I think," her new friend said, leaning in so that they were so close their noses were almost touching, "that maybe you should consider coming back to my hotel so I could tell you more." Charlie wondered if he were going to kiss her, but then raised an eyebrow.

"That's very forward of you," she replied, though she didn't move.

"But you will come back, yes?" Charlie bit her bottom lip.

"I would love to, but I really can't," she said, and the regret was real. "I have a job to do."

"I think I can give you one really good reason to come back with me that would definitely make it worthwhile," her partner replied, and she could feel his breath on her lips.

"I mean," she whispered, "It would have to be incredible."

"I'll tell you my name, and then you can decide," he said. Charlie's eyebrows rose at this.

"Well, if your name is that impressive, I definitely will." The man touched her hand gently.

"My name is Man Garam."

TEN

By 1 am, Chen was bored beyond belief. Worse, he was slightly annoyed that his three associates weren't. Not that he lacked patience. There were times he had been forced to wait for hours before making a move. He just didn't enjoy it. Every time one of the Fedorov brothers left the section, he moved to the stairwell, ready to follow, but then he realised that the other brother hadn't left and so clearly they weren't making a move.

Now he had even lost the company of the rest of his team. He couldn't work out where any of them had gone, and trying to get in touch with them was proving problematic. In all, he thought, a bit of a shit show. And realistically, he really only had himself to blame.

So with that in mind, he looked across the room to see what was going on. DJ Kabuki had either finished her set or was on a break, and had joined the Japanese model in a conversation with Sashura. The three were talking animatedly, and Sashura was visibly laughing, though Kabuki still had her mask on, making it impossible to determine what she was going on in her mind.

With a shock, Chen suddenly realised that neither of the Fedorov brothers were in the Grey Goose VIP area. Cursing under his breath, he raced down the stairs and into the writhing crowd, forcing his way through to the opposite side of the room, until he was able to get into the Hall. There was still no sign of anyone familiar, and cursing again – this time definitely out loud – he raced for the stairs and the exit.

Once outside, he looked around to see that the line up into the club had died down quite a bit, but there was still no sign of…

He paused, suddenly recognising the hulking figure a little further ahead of him.

"Perič!" he called, racing over to him. The big man turned and gave him a smile, which seemed to be one of relief.

"Thank goodness you are here," he said. "Ashley is ahead of us. She is following Fedorov brothers. I was to try to contact you. I have been calling…"

"Yeah, fine, quick," Chen said, before suddenly stopping. "How?"

"Mortimer is driving," Perić replied.

"We need a cab," Chen muttered.

Ahead of them, Hana Mortimer eased her car through the streets of Barcelona, keeping a safe distance from the car ahead. Beside her, Ashley watched keenly, making sure she didn't lose sight of the Uber that was carrying the Fedorov brothers. There was a buzz on her phone, and she looked down, before answering on speaker.

"Hey," she said.

"We're going to follow you. He's pissed, I think," Perić's voice came from the phone.

"Did you tell him I was going to get him?"

"Well, I tried, but he was not in listening mood," Perić replied.

"Great," muttered Ash, throwing a glance at Mortimer, though the latter simply rolled her eyes. There was not a lot of love lost between their team leader and acquisitions operative, Ashley reflected. "I think they might be pulling over," Ash said, a little surprised.

"Definitely," Mortimer replied, but didn't follow. Instead she continued on up the street. Ash kept an eye on the rear vision mirror.

"We're on, er…di corsayga…" Ash started, stumbling over the name.

"Carrer de Còrsega," Mortimer said.

"Yeah, that," Ash added, wondering how Mortimer got the sounds from the spelling that she was looking at. "They've gone into a building called Seventy."

"It's a hotel," Mortimer supplied, as she turned left and almost immediately found a parking spot. "It's classy, nice place, not cheap."

"Perfect place for an aspiring Russian singer to hole up," Ash added.

"He says that you should wait for us, but wonders if you could perhaps find out what room they are in. Or rooms. Whatever."

"Oh, that's what he said, was it?" Mortimer said, dripping acid.

"Well," Perić replied, missing the sarcasm.

"I'll see what I can do," Ash quickly said. "But get here fast. We can't afford to lose them."

"I think he has a plan," Perić said, and then rang off.

"Would you like to have a shower?" Man Garam asked pleasantly.

"What, with you?" Charlie asked, curiously.

"No, no. I'm just," he paused. "It was quite sweaty. I feel like I need a shower." Charlie narrowed her eyes. Garam didn't look remotely stressed by the nightclub. With that being said, she did have to admit to having that "going home" vibe. She could smell the alcohol and sweat on her, and the idea of showering didn't actually seem that bad.

"Maybe I will," she admitted, and wondered what the hell she was doing.

"You're welcome to go first," Garam said, and opened the bathroom door. Garam had decided to stay at the Catalonia Catedral Hotel, which was a rather beautiful building on the outside, large panels of pink between the grey of the pillars and balconies, the latter of which had wrought iron railings. It was almost at the heart of the Gothic Quarter of Barcelona. In some ways the inside of the building had been painted to look like a cathedral, with an astonishing painting on the ceiling reaching up to a square that had been split with black lines and blue panels, totally destroying the goth feel with some modern art.

The room itself also lacked any gothic influence; a modern affair with wooden floor and a bed with a very large mattress. Noticeably the door to the bathroom was glass, which was moderately unsettling. It was a surprisingly small room. For some reason Charlie had assumed that Man Garam would be staying in something far more luxurious.

The glass door, though…

"You should go first," Charlie said. Garam regarded her for a moment, and then nodded. He slung his coat over the little table the room had, and then slid out of his shoes. Charlie was suddenly struck by how short he actually was. For some reason he had seemed bigger, and she wondered if it was the sheer force of his personality that had given that impression.

However, as he walked to the bathroom, the trousers slid off, and the shirt followed, revealing a toned, muscular body.

In a black sports bra and thong.

"Oh," Charlie said, her mouth dropping. Garam turned, and Charlie was confronted by the woman in front of her. Suddenly she felt enormously embarrassed, her brain retracing the evening, wondering how she had possibly assumed that Man Garam was a man. Was she really that shallow that a simple suit had made that suggestion?

Garam, however, had a small smile on his…her lips.

"I'm not what you expected?" she said.

"Oh, I just," Charlie started and then stopped. "I'm a fool," she admitted. "Ignorant. I'm sorry. I had assumed, for no reason, you were a man."

"If it helps," Garam said, "I consider myself gender fluid."

"Oh," Charlie said, not really knowing what to say. "I'm not…" she started, but Garam laughed.

"You're very beautiful. But I honestly didn't bring you here for sex. I felt very masculine when I went out earlier, but after meeting you… the feminine side of me kicked in. So now I feel very girly," she grinned.

"Why…?" Charlie started, and Garam climbed onto the bed. She patted beside her and Charlie obediently sat down. She was unsettled, but not uncomfortable around Man Garam.

"Hardly anyone knows anything about me, Charlotte Lily Maxwell," Man Garam said, and Charlie kicked herself, realising Garam was very well researched. "You could tell everyone that you know what I look like, that you know I don't identify as a specific gender…anything. But it wouldn't make a difference, because you aren't official, and you are just one person." She smiled again, and it was a beautiful smile, but with her dark eyes and white hair there was something disturbing about the image. "I wanted you to know that I did kill Nathan Coulter. I was paid to do it. But I'm a professional and I will not give you any more information than that."

Charlie opened her mouth to say something, but then closed it again. Finally, her brain kicked in.

"We had to come here for you to tell me that?"

"I killed Mason Lemon," Garam said, and this time Charlie stood up. "Sit down, Charlie," Garam said softly. Or rather, to be more accurate, more softly. Charlie hesitated, then did what she was told. She wasn't scared, not exactly. Garam was shorter than her, and honestly at this point looked far more vulnerable. But she (he? They?) was still intimidating all the same.

"Why?"

"The same reason I kill anyone," came the reasonable response.

"I was paid to." Charlie inwardly groaned. Chen's desire to pursue the actual killer of Lemon in order to get justice was admirable, but was starting to get less realistic. Trying to kill Man Garam would be nigh on impossible, if rumour was anything to go by.

"Who ordered the kill?" Charlie asked, hoping to find a way to steer Chen in a new direction. Garam's laugh was unexpected.

"I can't tell you that," she said, the giggle still in her voice.

"So why tell me anything at all?" Charlie asked, unable to keep the annoyance from her voice. Though she realised it probably sounded more petulant than she intended.

"You are Doves. I've heard of you. I suppose in my line of work I have a degree of respect for vigilante justice," Garam replied. "Maybe call it a professional courtesy."

"She's a professional," Charlie said drily. "He's? I'm sorry."

"Honestly, I don't fuss over pronouns," Garam smiled. She glanced at the mirror above the table on the opposite wall. "I suppose I definitely look she at the moment. But whatever." Charlie nodded, surprised by how accentless her voice was. "I'm going to shower. Then you should. Then…then we can do whatever. I won't be offended if you want to go. But please don't be worried. You are totally safe here." Garam slid off the bed and went over to the shower, pulling her underwear off as she did. For a moment Charlie was unable to take her eyes off the other woman, but then turned away.

She looked at her phone and noticed that there were messages. Ash was at Hotel Seventy, with Chen and Perić, about to confront Fedorov. They seemed to be about ten minutes away by car. They also didn't seem to need her help.

And she did quite want a shower.

Charlie laid her head back on the pillow on the bed and glanced at the shower, now steamed up.

ELEVEN

Seventy Barcelona, on the outside, is as far apart from Catalonia Catedral Hotel as could be imagined. Whilst the latter fits the Gothic Quarter perfectly, ten minutes away in Camp D'En Grassot I Grácia Nova, Seventy Barcelona looks more like a Lego building, with the rows on rows of windows looking like the studs on dark blocks. The bottom floor is glass, and the entrance has a red awning, with a simple white "Seventy" emblazoned on it. Even at two in the morning, a couple of motorbikes were still parked out the front.

Ash tapped her foot, anxiously waiting for Chen and Perič. Mortimer had opted to stay in the car, assuring Ash she was better as backup than as part of a frontal assault. Privately, Ash thought the older woman just didn't want to take any more instructions from Chen, and she could see that point of view, in all honesty.

To her relief, the yellow and black taxi pulled up relatively quickly, and Chen got out, followed by Perič with both of them looking ready for action.

"In there?" Chen asked.

"Yes, but what's the plan," Ash asked. Chen stopped and looked at her for a moment.

"You got the room number?"

"Oh yes, it's 2nd floor, room 5. But, I mean, what are we going to do? Just go in there and beat the information we need out of them?" Chen looked as though he thought it was a good idea, but before he could say anything, Perič spoke up.

"This is what I am here for, no?" This seemed to snap Chen into a semblance of common sense, and he shook his head.

"No, we…" Chen paused. "Well, I thought we could go in and demand to know who he's working for. But I suppose long term, that's not the best move we could make." He pocketed the phone he had out and looked up and down the street. "We need to follow the money," he said. Ashley looked at him, puzzled. "Look, you're right. If we go in, guns blazing, Perić punching, then we get the information, but we alert whoever is higher up the food chain. Probably the person we're looking for, really. But if we can find out who that person is without causing an issue, well…" Ashley nodded. "I don't suppose you could get his credit card details from the system."

"Not easily," Ash said. "It's encrypted precisely to stop that sort of thing from happening. And, yes, I could break the encryption, but that will take a fair bit of time."

"So we go ask him for credit card?" Perić asked, and Chen looked at him, wondering if there was sarcasm in his voice.

"Well, he's seen us, so that's unlikely," Ash pointed out.

"He hasn't seen me," Chen reflected, stroking his goatee. "It's old school, but it might work," he said, thinking out loud. "Come on."

With that he passed under the red awning and entered Seventy Hotel.

Vsevolod Fedorov was deeply unhappy. Dressed in just his jeans, he had stormed back into his room after his brother had left him, removed his shirt and decided he was going to get absolutely shit-faced. He had already a good start at Pacha Barcelona, but when Sashura made it clear that she was really only interested in meeting DJ Kabuki, and was definitely not going to go back to the hotel to get a hard fucking, Fedorov lost his temper. Stupid lesbian bitch.

By the time he had got back to his room, he had decided that he didn't care what Sashura Ilina thought was going to happen, the fact was he was going to fuck her hard in the arse. She could whinge and moan all she liked, but she needed to remember who the fuck she was dealing with. She had only got as far as she had with her minimal fucking talent thanks to the boss. And as he was the boss when the boss wasn't there, that meant she should be on her fucking knees sucking his dick to thank him.

As such he had gotten angrier and angrier, to the point when he heard a knock at the door he wasn't in the mood to give any real response other than: "*Chto?*" followed swiftly by, "*Ukhodite!*"

"*Servicio de habitaciones*," came the response and Fedorov lost his temper completely. After grunting, he flung the door open with enough force to shake the wall, and looking tired, exhausted and angry he stared at the room service clerk in his stupid black suit and shouted: "What?" this time clearly in English.

"*Champán*?" the waiter asked, proffering the bottle.

"What? I didn't order champagne," Fedorov snapped.

"Err, no it was a señorita Sashura who requested it," the waiter said. Fedorov looked at him, his eyes full of confusion.

"She did?" he said, the wind firmly out of his sails. Had she realised the mistake she had made? It would make sense. After all, he was quite irresistible. She would definitely want to come back to his bed. Perhaps he had been a little quick to explode. Borislav had suggested it, but Vsevolod wouldn't hear of it. And while she may have little talent on a microphone, her body was amazing, and her talents were definitely more in that direction.

"*Si*," the waiter said.

"Right, uh, ok," Fedorov stumbled. He looked around, frowning and then reached forward to take the champagne. "I will take it."

"*Señor*," the waiter said, and he held out a device, with a price and numbers on the screen, both below a logo for a credit card. Fedorov looked, and rolled his eyes slightly. Of course, she would make him pay for it. He looked back into his room, and grabbed the credit card that he had tossed onto the table as he stormed in. He was about to simply tap, when he reached forward and added 50 euro to the on-screen price. After tapping, it gave a satisfactory *ping* and Fedorov nodded.

Both mystified and happy by what had taken place, he closed the door and went back into his room to find two glasses. Maybe, just maybe, Sashura Ilina might be able to retrieve this disastrous night after all.

Back at the Regency, there was a general feeling of tiredness. After everything that had gone down, Michael Chen just wanted to sleep. Tomorrow they would have more to do, but he wanted to get some rest before they made their next move. At the moment everything seemed to be going at a ridiculous pace. He was getting too old for this, he decided.

Though not completely, because both Perić and Ash were clearly up past their bedtimes as well. Perić had actually crashed on the bed in Ash's room, and she was busy typing on her tablet, but every so often, she raised her glasses and ran her hands across her eyes.

As such, it was somewhat understandable that when Charlie walked into the room, the two who were awake looked at her with a degree of guilt, suddenly realising that they had forgotten all about her.

"Someone's burning the midnight oil," Charlie said with a smile, before wrinkling her nose. "Without having a shower."

"Where have you been?" Chen asked in surprise.

"Well, that's a story," Charlie admitted, looking around for a free chair. The room was rather uniquely laid out, in that the bed had a couch at the end, so that if you wanted to watch the large television on the wall opposite, you could either do it from the bed, or from the couch. However, the table that Ashley was working at was directly below the television, which meant that Charlie ended up on the couch, at the opposite end to Chen. She wondered briefly where Mortimer was, and decided that it didn't really matter. "While I was at the bar, I met Man Garam. Who took me back to their hotel and...we talked." Charlie shrugged, but even Ashley turned around at this news.

"You're not serious? What's he like?" Ash asked, gobsmacked.

"Ah, yeah," Charlie opened her mouth to say something, but then shook her head slightly. Garam was right. There was very little point in giving out any information. "They told me they killed Coulter."

"No surprise there then," Chen grumbled.

"They also killed Lemon," Charlie confirmed. She had wrestled for sometime over whether to actually admit this, but the truth was she wanted to test Chen, she supposed. She wanted to see what his reaction would be to the news. To her surprise, he did not react the way she thought he would.

"I suppose that make sense," Chen said. Charlie wondered if it was because he was tired that he remained so calm. "I'm assuming that whoever paid him to kill Lemon wasn't the same person who paid him to kill Coulter, though."

"No," Charlie nodded. "Two separate hits. Ironic really, since Coulter's death was probably because he passed information on that allowed Garam to kill Lemon." She sat back and waited to see what more Chen would say, but he remained silent.

"So where do we go from here?" Ash asked. Chen remained quiet for some time, his mind ticking over. "Why did Man frame Dana?" Ash suddenly said, turning to Charlie.

"Oh, just convenience. Apparently, she didn't think Dana would get the blame, but was a good scapegoat to force people to look in the wrong direction."

"That worked well," Chen finally said.

"It's not your fault," Charlie said kindly. "Flight put us on this path."

"And we see it through to the end," Chen decided. "Anything that can help with the credit card?"

"Not really," Ash admitted. "We need someone who has more experience in financial matters."

"Send Mortimer a message. Tell her we need a forensic accountant. We follow that money, then we find who is behind this whole thing." Chen stood up and sighed as he remembered Perić was on his bed. He grabbed the man's coat and reached around til he found a keycard. "I'm taking his room. You guys may as well get some rest. There's nothing more we can do tonight." With that, Chen walked out of the room. Ashley looked at Charlie.

"Don't ask me," the older woman said. "I don't know him any better than you do. Maybe he's always like this."

"I'll send the message," sighed Ashley.

"I'm going to bed," Charlie said, standing up.

"Hey, uh," Ash started.

"Yes?"

"Is there anything you aren't telling us about Man Garam?" Charlie looked at Ash and laughed.

"So much," she grinned, and then walked out.

TWELVE

Not that Michael Chen was particularly judgey, but he had to admit that if you needed an adjective to describe Kazan International Airport, basic would be that adjective. From the outside it looked like a concrete block with windows, and big yellow signs in Cyrillic, though in fairness, all signs were also in English, a degree of understanding that the world was a much smaller place than it had been in the past. With that being said, English did not come easily to those working there.

Although they had travelled on the same flight, Chen, Charlie, Ash and Perič had travelled individually. Before they had left, Mortimer had given them a set of instructions. She was going to ensure that Fedorov and his crew didn't leave Barcelona in a hurry. Had they been at Hotel Seventy, they would have seen the local police arrive with a search warrant, preparing to investigate one Vsevolod Fedorov for drug possession. They would find something, Mortimer assured them, and that would keep the crew in Barcelona for a few more days, buying them a little time.

She had also arranged a meeting for them with the Grey Knight.

"The Knight will get you all the financial information you need. Between Frost and the Knight, you'll be over that money trail before you know it," Mortimer had said, adjusting her glasses, before handing them each an envelope with their travel documents. Chen had to admit that Mortimer may have been a pain in the ass, but she was ridiculously efficient. Having made the decision to follow the track to Kazan, Mortimer's ability to expedite that had no equal.

They had left Barcelona on an Air Turkey flight that would take them directly to Kazan International, and once there, they had disembarked and made their way through customs. Perič had not been questioned; his passport given a simple glance and then handed back. Chen was surprised when they looked at his passport and then looked at him.

"Why are you coming?" the surly man said, as he shifted on his seat. Chen got the feeling he needed to be careful because his uniform might not have been able to take the change, struggling at it was to contain the man.

"Holiday," Chen shrugged, broadening his accent.

"Oh, you are real Aussie?" the official said, raising his eyebrows. Suddenly the long line that was behind Chen was no longer of concern to the official.

"Yeah, mate," Chen grinned cheesily.

"I like Aussie," the official said, handing the passport back. "You are good fun. Lots of laugh. I like *Neighbours*!"

"Proper export with our beer," Chen joked.

"I do not like Aussie beer," the official said, his surly face returning.

"Right," Chen muttered. The official waved him through, and Chen walked to the baggage collection point.

Mortimer had given him a ticket to catch the train into the city which Perič had assured him was relatively fast, and very convenient. Perič himself was going to do the same thing, though Chen was sure he had heard Charlie's voice asking someone if they were going into the city, and suspected that she and Ash were going to get an Uber. Perhaps this was Mortimer's punishment, he reflected ruefully.

The trains were fairly standard, though they stood out with their bright red and orange fronts. As he got on board the train, he had a brief moment of paranoia, convinced that there was someone watching him. He wondered if that was just a general feeling of being in Russia, a sensation given the situation they were in, or just something he had made up in his head. He twisted his neck as though stretching it, taking in the platform around him, but there was nothing sinister or out of the ordinary.

"*Ploshchad Tukaya*," Perič whispered to him, without looking at him. Chen was surprised, as he hadn't heard the big man appear, and yet suddenly he was standing there staring at a train map (surprisingly simple – a single line – sort of, it seemed to be split into two parts – with fifteen stations). Chen turned to see what had been mentioned, but the sign on the metro wasn't in English, and he had no idea what he was reading. "Five stops," Perić supplied, as though he had the ability to read Chen's mind.

"*Severny Vozkal*," came a voice over the loud system, and some people started to get up and prepared themselves to disembark. Chen considered sitting down, but then decided it was hardly worth it. He looked across the carriage and momentarily locked eyes with a gaunt man that had dark bags under his eyes. Chen frowned and looked again, but the man didn't look back.

He was definitely on edge.

When they alighted at *Ploshchad Tukaya* station, Chen had to admit he was very impressed. The white marble walls of the station might have been a nice enough change from every other metro station he had been in around the world, but it was the mosaics along the walls that really captured his attention. Opening his phone he quickly googled to see what he was looking at, and was intrigued to find that the station, and apparently the square it was on above ground, were named after a poet; Ğabdulla Tuqay, a legend, it would appear. Marvelling at the many things he didn't know about the world, Chen gave a small smile, and snapped a few of the mosaics.

Sometimes, he worried he was getting jaded and cynical in his approach to things, but when that happened, it was nice to open his phone and see a selection of photos that reminded him that the world was still full of wonders he had yet to explore. Certainly, he hadn't been to Pacha Barcelona before, but that was just a nightclub. He was too old to be blown away by that sort of thing. But art like this…well, it made it all worthwhile.

Someone bumped him heavily with a bag, and Chen turned to see Perić walking past him. Guessing that he was supposed to be following the big man, Chen pocketed his phone again and followed.

Perić left the station and began walking down Pushkin St, and Chen followed at a distance. His awe continued with the architecture of Kazan (or, perhaps more accurately, the district they were in), but had to chuckle as they passed a Burger King. He was struck by how the opposite side of the road had beautiful beige buildings with balconies and bay windows outlined in white, while his side of the road had more modern glass and concrete buildings. They passed Gabdulla Tukay Square properly, a copper statue of the poet dominating the greenery around him, and as they crossed the road, to his left, Chen could see a lake dominated by a fountain, and on the right was a massive building, with a pillared curved front and large open courtyard. Google informed him he was looking at part of Kazan Federal University. It was all both spectacular and beautiful, and Chen caught himself doing something he rarely ever did – act like a tourist. He was cautious enough not to take photos, however. Experience had told him you never knew what building you were photographing, and if you picked the wrong one, some governments would take great exception.

They crossed the road at a zebra crossing before the University, and turned right, so were now walking along Pravo-Bulachnaya St. Pushkin St had been wide, comfortably eight lanes, but this one initially seemed less, as there were only three lanes for each direction, but the street was split by the Bulak River running through it. The buildings were also less elaborate, more standard concrete high rise with lots of windows. More signs seemed to be in English as well, and at the Luciano Hotel, Chen guessed that this was a more touristy area.

At the intersection of Pravo-Bulachnaya St and Astronomicheskaya St, Perić stopped. They were out the front of a red brick building with off-white architraves, and Perić had paused to lean against the building as though catching his breath. They had certainly walked a little further than Chen had thought they were going to, but not so much that Perić would be exhausted from it. He wondered if he should stop and help his colleague, but as he looked across the road, he saw a bluey-grey building, stairs leading up to the entrance in a rather grand fashion. A red sign on the overhang had the word Ibis, and Chen realised that they had arrived at his hotel.

He walked on past Perić without acknowledging the other man and crossed the road, heading up the stairs and to his hotel. Once inside he went up to the check-desk where a man in a black suit and red shirt was tapping away at a computer. The interior was adequate, but not what anyone would call lush. A plain tiled floor, with dark mats at the door and counter, and a couple of little alcoves.

"*Privet*," the man said with a smile. "*Mogu ya chem-nibud' pomoch'*?"

"I'm sorry, do you speak English?" Chen replied. He did speak some Russian, but he certainly didn't want to get into a complicated conversation where he might miss something important.

"Of course," the clerk replied, the smile not leaving his face. "You are here to book in?"

"Yeah. I have a room booked under Barclay." The clerk tapped away at his computer a bit more, and then nodded.

"Jack Barclay?"

"Yeah, that's me." He handed his passport over to the clerk who took a brief look at it and then handed it back, largely uninterested.

"Do you have a credit card that we might be able to record for any later charges, Mr Barclay? Or we can take a deposit."

Despite the Doves having access to a great deal of information and experience, there was always an element of how to respond when you wanted to keep your identity a secret, without drawing attention to yourself. Handing over a credit card would avoid suspicion nicely, but required the creation of additional resources, which were not always possible when you were acting quickly. Handing over cash, however, could look dodgy in some countries. Fortunately, Russia was not one of those countries.

"I can just make a deposit," the newly christened Jack Barclay said, and reached into his wallet to pull out 20,000 rubles and put it on the counter. "Is this about right?" The clerk looked at it and nodded, taking it and then putting a piece of paper on the counter.

"If you could just sign this, Mr Barclay," he said, and then disappeared through the wooden door behind him. Hopefully to lock up the money in a safe, Chen reflected dubiously. The clerk returned and took the paper, barely giving it a second glance, and then handed a key over to Chen.

"Your room is 330," he said. "Third floor. I hope you enjoy your stay, Mr Barclay."

"I hope so too."

There was another step down in luxury once the elevator doors opened onto the third floor, and the tired green carpet with its red pattern (that immediately gave the image of a body having been dragged down the corridor, bleeding) didn't do anything to dispel it. Chen knew he was being unfair. The hotel was really no worse than any other average hotel. He had been lucky in Barcelona, but now they were to be more low-key. The Ibis was fine.

The room though, was very pine, Chen reflected. Pine floor, pine table, pine bedhead. The cabinet that had the television in it was walnut, and Chen decided that annoyed him more than the blandness of the room.

As he looked out of the window, he forgave the room completely. The view of Pravo-Bulachnaya St was impressive, but it allowed him to see the Bulak River much better, and it looked gorgeous. There were fountains in the middle of the river, spaced out and spraying little jets of water that the white birds flying around seemed to actually be playing in. The banks were a beautiful green, leading to the darker green of the trees lining them. Kazan was definitely a very beautiful city, Chen decided.

It was at that point his phone pinged.

Мега Казань. Now.

Chen stared blankly at it for a moment, wondering what the first two words could possibly mean. A destination he supposed.

317

Now might be optimistic, he thought sourly.

THIRTEEN

Chen got his first real taste of Kazan by trying to work out how to get to *Мега Казань*. The helpful man at the check-in desk at the hotel kindly explained how *Мега Казань* was the Mega Mall, a shopping centre which was about eight kilometres away. Getting there, it turned out, was going to be a challenge, not least because it was exceptionally busy traffic.

"It might take thirty minutes?" the clerk shrugged and smiled, and Chen gritted his teeth.

"Do I take a bus?"

"Oh, hold on, I give you…" The clerk trailed off as he looked around his desk, before finally coming up with a business card for a company called Lingo Taxi. "They speak English," he added helpfully. Chen nodded his appreciation and filled out the online form to book his taxi. There was a prepay option, which surprised him, but he opted to take it in the hope that it might mean his taxi wouldn't dismiss him out of hand.

Twenty minutes later, he came to the conclusion that he had wasted his money. To his surprise, however, his phone rang, and he answered it.

"Hello?"

"Yes, you are Mr Barclay?" The voice was deep, with a thick Russian accent.

"Yes."

"You are standing out the front of hotel?"

"Yes, I'm…"

"I see you." The phone rang off, and to Chen's surprise, a white four-door sedan pulled up in front of the hotel, ignoring the road rules. The driver's door opened, and a man got out of the car. He was in the process of growing a beard and wore a fedora, making Chen wonder if he was trying to accommodate for a lack of hair on top. "Mr Barclay?" he said with a grin.

"Yes," Chen said, trying to hide his surprise.

"I am Ralf," he said. "I am happy to be your driver for today. You are looking for the Mega Mall?"

"Absolutely. I have to meet friends there."

"Hop in, I'll get you there quick."

Chen hadn't really expected the journey to be quick, and so wasn't disappointed when traffic slowed them down quite early on and the clock kept on ticking. In truth he was irked that he had been summoned and told to be there "now" which was ridiculous, so his team had to expect him to be late. (Though he would be even more irked if Perić got there before him.)

Ralf, on the other hand, had proven to be delightfully entertaining company. He had talked non-stop since Chen had got in the car, which was not something Chen usually enjoyed, but in this situation it actually helped to pass the time, and Ralf was extremely enthusiastic about Kazan. He had talked at great length about Ğabdulla Tuqay (they were soulmates because Ralf was a poet himself, though it didn't pay the bills).

As they drove down Ulitsa Astronomicheskaya, Chen was impressed, not only at Ralf's enthusiasm for the buildings around them, but for the omnipresent and endlessly fascinating architecture. The buildings were different colours, mostly reds and greys, but sometimes a green one popped up to add a dash of variety. By the time they turned onto Ulitsa Maksima Gor'kogo, Chen had added the word Ulitsa to his vocabulary.

Ralf continued to talk, happy to give a narrative without getting too much in return, though Chen did actually try to inject something into the conversation.

"You have been to Kremlin, yes?" Ralf asked suddenly.

"The Kremlin?" Chen asked, a little shocked.

"Yes, you know we have one in Kazan?" Chen opened his mouth to say something, but Ralf was continuing. "It means fortress inside a city, you understand? So not just Moscow can have one, but obviously that is the most famous. It is where Putin runs everything. You should see ours, though, so much better. It was built by Ivan the Terrible in 1600. Is amazing. Looks incredible. The Metro can take you there directly, but you can walk from your hotel. Is not far. You should."

"I guess I have to see it," Chen smiled, sitting back in his chair.

"Amazing," Ralf replied, but drifted off as though lost in the beauty of the building he was thinking of. He remained in his thoughts until they were about to turn onto a very big highway. Across the road, Chen could see a large red building with white trim and gold domes on the top. Ralf swung onto the highway with what seemed to be either blind faith the traffic would let them in, or an arrogance that nothing was going to stop him.

"That is Cathedral for Holy Great Martyr Barbara," Ralf called back, and Chen closed his eyes as Ralf turned to him and pointed at the building, apparently oblivious to the fact they had just turned onto a ten-line highway. "Beautiful old church, rebuilt in the last twenty years because it was shut down in the thirties. You know I can do tours as well?"

"The road?" Chen asked, pointing ahead.

"Is fine," grinned Ralf, waving his hand like a magician.

The rest of the trip was more of the same, as Ralf would interrupt his driving to point out buildings of interest or anything that grabbed his attention. In truth, most of it was fascinating, and Chen decided he would love to return as a tourist at some point, and maybe get Ralf to take him on a tour. Though he would need considerably more guts to stomach Ralf's lax attitude to the roads.

Ultimately it took them a good half hour to reach their destination, and certainly not from want of Ralf's attempts to make it much, much sooner. Nonetheless, he finally eased the car off Prospect Al'berta Kamaleyeva. Chen noticed that there was a tram stop, but was glad that, despite the driving, he had got the taxi. Navigating the city was hard enough.

He got out of the car, giving Ralf a little wave, and reflected that the Mega Mall certainly earned its name. It was a massive, sprawling building, and Chen worked his way around it to find the main entrance, a rotating glass door underneath the enormous "Mega" sign, that was cleverly both in English and in Cyrillic. Once inside, Chen had to admit to being slightly surprised. Based on the height of the building, he had assumed that the complex would be two stories, and he was absolutely right, but the second floor was actually below ground. The floor he entered had a very high ceiling, and there was white everywhere, from the roof, to the floor tilings, to the pillars and lights.

It must be a nightmare to clean, he mused.

As he approached the railing that stopped him from falling to the floor below, he saw that below was a food court, and felt a hint of irritation when he saw Perić sitting at a table. On closer inspection he realised that Ash was sitting with him, along with another woman that he didn't immediately recognise.

In truth, Chen was never keen on out-in-the-open meetings, believing that they tempted fate. However, thanks to the people in the complex, and the distance it was from his own hotel (and presumably the others), if they were being noticed by anyone, this place was unlikely to garner any unnecessary attention.

Charlie looked up as Chen strolled down the escalator and over to their table, taking a seat between her and Perić.

"Ladies, Gentleman," he nodded as he sat down.

"You are late," Perić said with a grin.

"Well, no one told me anymore information other than "now", which didn't really help, did it?" Chen said petulantly.

"Sorry," said Charlie. "I thought it would be better to leave out long detailed texts in case…" She paused, realising she wasn't entirely sure if her paranoia had been justified. Chen just shook his head, dismissing it.

"This is the Grey Knight," Ash said, with a smile. She indicated the woman opposite her, who was dressed in what was effectively a black suit, though she was wearing shorts rather than long trousers. She was in her late twenties, had short, purple hair and elfin features. She was sitting close to Ash, as though the two knew each other.

The Grey Knight smiled and raised her hand to her forehead before giving what looked like a stylised wave. She then seemed to brush her palms before raising her index fingers and bringing her hands together, and then pointing at Chen.

To Charlie's surprise, Chen made a similar gesture, though he seemed to rub his hands, rather than brush them. She herself had been slightly taken aback when she had been introduced to the Grey Knight, and discovered that the woman was deaf, and communicated through sign language. To her surprise at that point, Ashley was fluent and the two conversed without hesitation. To learn that Charlie was also fluent was genuinely surprising.

"How many languages to you know, Michael?" Charlie asked, not trying to disguise the awe in her voice.

"Well," he shrugged. "I travelled a lot when I was with the SAS. I picked up a lot and, we had a few friends who lost their hearing." Charlie was impressed as he never stopped signing the entire time he was talking, ensuring that the Knight was kept in the loop. Curiously though the Knight turned to Ash and signed something, and Ash nodded.

"Not ASL, right?" Ash asked, her own hands keeping up with her.

"Oh, no Auslan. Sorry," Chen clarified.

It's all good, grinned the Knight. Charlie was still impressed that Chen didn't stop signing, despite the differences (and actually she could start to see a little how the Knight and Chen used their hands in a completely different manner), and her estimation of him went up.

"So you're going to trace the money for us?" Chen asked.

I already have, the Knight replied. *Once Ash was able to hack into Fedorov's phone I was able to start working through his accounts. Lots of payments from lots of different companies. Some of them are shell companies, but I worked back through them, and they all come back to one single name: Anisim Stepanov.* The Knight turned her iPad around and showed them a picture of a man who looked like he was in his late 60s, with thinning grey hair and a shambolic beard that might be kindly described as salt-and-pepper in colour. He was comfortable looking, his shirt struggling a little to hold in the belly. *Stepanov is a Russian businessman. And you were right, his headquarters are here in Kazan. He rose to prominence in the 2000's, but have a guess where he worked in the eighties and nineties.*

"KGB," Chen said, dourly.

And guess which colonel he answered to, the Knight said, her own face as grim as Chen's.

"So legitimate is probably a generous description," Charlie muttered. The Knight glanced at Ashley as she translated and then frowned.

That's the thing, she said. *He actually doesn't seem to have had any interactions with the President in the last fifteen years. If they are still in contact, it's very much on the down-low.*

"But why would a Russian businessman want to kill an American spy and pin it on an Australian model?" Chen said, his face furrowed.

"Assuming he did," Charlie added.

He did. Just follow the money, the Knight said. *There was a transfer made to a foreign account that was heavily encrypted on the day Lemon was killed. I mean, he might not have, but it's a hell of a coincidence.*

"So we need to get to him," Chen said.

"Do we want to know why?" Charlie asked, looking at Chen.

"Why he had Lemon killed?"

"I would like to know after all this," Perič sighed.

"Once we confront him, he'll have his guard up. We wouldn't be able to just shoot him," Chen said, shaking his head.

"Maybe you could," Charlie offered, and Chen looked at her. "We just need to get him to explain what happened. And yes, to do that we need to be vulnerable and he has to be in control. But if we are in the right place, and you are in the right place, then you could take him out, and we would just have to deal with the guards."

He has a small army protecting him, the Knight said, and the grimace on her face suggested that it was a terrible idea.

"Do we know where he is? Where he runs things from?" Chen asked.

I have a number of business addresses for him, but any information that might exist is probably in a personal office somewhere. Not in a building that the police can easily search, the Knight opined.

"Can you find that?" Chen asked, and the Knight shook her fist.

I'll need a little time, she added.

"Well, lunch is on me then," Chen said, with a smile that didn't reach his eyes.

In the end Perič had taken orders, but Chen did dutifully pay. He waited for lunch to return, slightly fascinated by the play tower in the center of the food court, where children climbed what seemed to be a white trunk, before settling on giant wooden leaves, all enclosed by a net, which several children used to climb, rather than the actual "trunk".

He was interrupted from his reverie by a gasp from the Knight, who looked up and turned to Ashley and started signing urgently.

He lives on Ulitsa Maksima Gor'kogo, she said, Ashley translating for them. Charlie watched as Chen frowned.

"Do you have a picture?" he asked, and the Knight turned her iPad around to show him. Chen's eyes widened in recognition. "I drove by that this morning to get here," he said, and the name of the street suddenly hit him. "Yeah, of course, yeah," he muttered.

The image showed a large, four-story white building, with red architraves, and double red doors at the front, with balconies on either side of the corner building.

That's his home, the Knight reiterated. *Not his business. He's celebrating his latest acquisition – an American car manufacturing company called AutoGold.*

By now all of them had their phones out, searching through them.

"AutoGold's stocks dropped and a number of the board dropped out when it was discovered that the owner – von Golde? – had connections to white supremacists, and was responsible for a terrorist act in Washington," Ash said.

Lots of people have been invited to the launch. It's very prestigious, the Knight added, but Charlie was already well ahead of her.

"So obviously the party is the easiest way to get to Stepanov,"

325

Chen said.

"And we might have a way in," Charlie said, looking up from her phone. "Guess who's on the guest list?" Chen leaned over and looked at her phone.

And then he rolled his eyes.

"Great."

FOURTEEN

"Can I help you?" the girl asked, not as pleasantly as Chen might have hoped for.

"We're friends. Just poking our head in to say hello," Chen smiled, though he suspected it looked a little like he'd drunk lemon juice.

"Friends?" the girl said dubiously. She was short, waifish and vaguely pretty, with long blonde hair, and a phone permanently stuck to her hand.

"Yes," Chen said, a bit embarrassed at the petulance that had crept into his voice. "Can we come in?"

"No," the girl said, looking pointedly at him.

"What?"

"I'm her PA," she said, just the wrong side of sweetly. "And also her sister. So obviously I know you're lying."

"Can you please tell her that the colleagues she met up in Paris with are here to see here," Charlie said. Chen looked at her and Charlie raised an eyebrow. "Obviously you're right, we're not her friends, but we need her help and she knows who we are. And I'm sorry he lied." The girl pursed her lips and then spoke.

"Hold on." Chen recoiled as the door slammed in his face and he looked at Charlie.

"Well it wasn't like your way was getting us anywhere," Charlie said, defensively. They waited a few moments, and then the door opened.

"Fuck," Dana Spectra said as she looked at them. "What do you want?"

"Can we come in, please?" Charlie asked. Dana narrowed her eyes at firstly Charlie, and then Chen.

"Guns," she said, holding out her hands.

"I don't have one," Charlie sighed. Chen shrugged, but Dana put her hand up and then held it out.

"I'm not an idiot, Michael Chen," she said, and Chen raised his eyebrows. "I've become people who know people," she added.

"I honestly don't have one either," he said.

"We get them supplied for us so we don't have to bring them into the country," Charlie explained. Dana regarded them for a moment, and then opened the door, giving them entry.

The Kazan Palace by Tasigo, is one of the most opulent hotels in Kazan. Somewhat away from the rest of the city, on its own little hill not too far from the Ibis where Chen was staying, it was in a completely different league, however. A massive red brick mansion with white livery, when the pair of Doves had been dropped off at the hotel, they walked through a set of double wooden doors, followed by another set, before walking down a flight of stairs into the lobby of the hotel. It was a curious style – on the outside suggesting old school opulence, but on the inside, a more modern façade in light grey, with lights hanging from the ceiling at different levels, and great archways along one wall. But it was the curious red sculptures of a box becoming a walking crocodile in different stages that really caught the attention.

A little bit of hacking from Ash had led them to the room they wanted, which allowed them to avoid any awkward questions. Thankfully they were also able to get into the elevators without a passkey as well.

When they had found that Dana Spectra was a guest at the launch of the AutoGold acquisition, Ash had done some digging and discovered that Anisim Stepanov had been keen to add legitimacy to the company after Jürgen von Golde had destroyed its reputation. Quite why that would be the case no one knew for sure, but Chen speculated it was probably political. Regardless, Stepanov had invited a number of fashion brands to represent at the launch, and a few had even agreed, including *Digné*, who had promptly sent along one of their ambassadors.

As they walked into the room, Chen supposed he should haven't been surprised to learn that Dana was staying in an attic suite, with jacuzzi. Pine floors afforded the only real colour in a suite that was predominantly black and white, and pop music with an Asian flavour was being piped around the suite. It seemed to be two bedrooms (one was a circular thing, but all had white spreads) with a bathroom (holding the jacuzzi) and a living room. The whole thing was open plan, and as they walked past the glass wall that separated the jacuzzi from the rest of the space, they also crossed two mirrors, and Chen caught a glimpse in one of them, of Dana, now holding a customised golden Glock.

They were completely at her mercy now, he reflected.

"Sit," Dana commanded, when they had entered the living room.

"Look, we know you didn't kill Mason Lemon," Chen said, but Dana waved the gun at him.

"Sit," she repeated. He shook his head and sat, Charlie following suit.

"We know who killed Lemon," Charlie said. Dana frowned.

328

"I wasn't lying when I said I don't understand what you're talking about. Who is Mason Lemon?"

"Look, cards on the table," Charlie said, and Chen buried his head in his hands. He was distinctly uncomfortable with Charlie's diplomatic approach to missions, particularly if she handed information out without too much prompting. "We are Doves. It's an organisation of… well private detectives. We get employed to investigate things that the authorites don't want to, or simply believe the case to be closed. When you were in Korea a man named Mason Lemon was murdered. The authorities believed they had sorted the problem out by killing a man named Nathan Coulter, who has passed information onto an assassin in Korea named Man Garam. Garam killed a Korean pop star that night, but after they had killed Lemon, dressed as you."

At this, Dana cocked her head, frowning a little.

"Wait, is Man Garam, like short, short blonde hair, androgynous, drives a black sports car?"

"Not sure about the car, but the rest is pretty accurate," Man agreed.

"They killed Boom," Dana mused. "I was never questioned," she started. "But I had a pretty good alibi, I suppose," she reflected, sitting down on the single chair, her gun not moving from the pair on the couch. "So you tried to kill me in Paris, and you came here…why?"

"We believe that the man who paid Man Garam to kill Mason Lemon was Anisim Stepanov. We don't know why, exactly, but we're trying to find out." Dana nodded to herself.

"So you want me to help you get to Stepanov, what…at the launch tomorrow night. Oh you want me to get you into the launch so you can do weird spy stuff, or whatever?"

"Pretty much," Chen nodded.

"I can only bring one," Dana said. "And basically you're telling me I have to let my sister down by taking you instead of her. Despite the fact she really wants a night out." Dana looked at them, without blinking and the Doves squirmed slightly. When Charlie turned to avoid Dana's gaze, she looked into the eyes of the young girl who had opened the door initially, and realised who she was looking at.

"You're going to ruin my trip to Russia, aren't you?" the girl said accusingly. Charlie continued to look awkward.

"What's in it for me?" Dana asked.

"We won't kill you," Chen said, and Charlie cringed.

"I could put a bullet in your head right now and get that," Dana pointed out.

"I meant," Chen hastily back tracked, "I meant we would go back to our boss and make it clear you are definitely on the side of the angels. If you ever needed our help we'd be there." Dana regarded them for a few moments, and the looked across the room at her sister, who glared.

"Dana," she said.

"You said you didn't really want to go," Dana said. "You only came because you thought G*Star might come as well."

"I," the younger girl started, and then stomped her foot. At this point, a young, good looking bearded man appeared behind Dana's sister with a wry smile.

"I don't know what all this is," he said, waving a finger around, "but very soon we have guests to get ready for tonight."

"You don't have to take us," Charlie said. "You just need to get us in. The front door is easiest, but if you can manage something else…" Dana looked between her and her sister; big puppy dog eyes desperately begging.

"Fine," growled Dana. "You come, and…I'll try to find another entrance for you lot to come through. And you owe me big time for this,"

Dana added, pointing the gun at Chen, and making him take a deep breath.

"You should stop waving that gun around," he said.

"You should shut the fuck up," Dana snapped in reply.

Charlie stood slightly nervously on the sidewalk of Ulitsa Maksima Gor'kogo, dressed rather fabulously in a Cham Cham gold stretch knit foil draped gown, while Ash was beside her in a black Showpo Emmary gown. They had both been sent shopping after their meeting with Dana, and were now in the results. Perić had also gone along and was dressed in a Charles Tyrwhitt tuxedo, though with no bowtie; rather he had a set of collar clips in gold. Both women had to admit he looked rather spectacular, and when Charlie pointed it out, they were surprised to find the big man go red.

Dana had made it clear that if they were to enter Stepanov's party, they had to look like they belonged, otherwise they would immediately be made. Chen had made it equally clear they needed information, and so the three would enter, with Ash attempting to determine the layout of the building and where Stepanov's office was. Charlie would then infiltrate the office by getting Stepanov to take her there, and once inside, hopefully Ash would be able to indicate where the office was, and Chen, who would be outside on the roof of a nearby building, would then execute Stepanov.

All they needed was a way in, and Dana would hopefully provide them with that. Dana admitted that it was her curiousity that got the better of her in the end; she was still curious about what Boom was doing in Seoul, and why he had been killing K-Pop idols, all of which was news to the Doves who had no idea who Boom was.

Now, in the fading sunlight, Dana stood in front of Stepanov's stately home as photographers from around the world snapped pictures, and called questions out to her. She was dressed in an Alamour red gown (which looked a little like she was wearing a red lacey dress over the top of a matching satin one), while her younger sister was dressed in an Alamour black Ayelet dress (a more glittery affair with an impressive slit). It turned out that the bearded man was a friend of Dana's who did her makeup, and while she smirked at the camera in all her glory, Dana's little sister Bella now looked as though she was in her twenties and was cutting quite the figure (though she seemed to be consciously trying to stay in her sister's shadow). A third person had joined them – a surprise guest, it seemed. This was the Korean singer Millie of the group G'Star. The tall, waifish woman was dressed in red Revolve Samba gown. Both Dana and Millie were also bedecked in *Digné* jewellery, making sure that they proved they were worth the money that *Digné* were investing.

Ash's initial research on the building had suggested that the best way of entering would be in the side street of Galaktionova. She had been able to pull down a floor plan of the building and showed Dana were the back entrance was, though Ash had to also admit that it was possible that the plan was wrong. Dana had rolled her eyes at this particular bit of information, but ultimately resigned herself to the fact there was probably not much more she could do about it.

As Dana, Millie and Bella entered the building, Charlie, Ash and Perić skirted around the paparazzi, heading down Ulitsa Galaktionova.

"Are you there, Chen?" Charlie asked, tapping the earbud that Ash had provided her.

"Loud and clear, Charlie," came the response. Ash nodded at her, but Perić tapped her on the shoulder. He had seen the red door that they were heading for, but there were two burly security guards standing there. Charlie grimaced, and they kept walking without breaking stride. The guards gave them a cursory glance, but weren't too interested in the trio.

"What do we do?" Ash whispered.

"I don't know," Charlie admitted.

"Problems?" Chen asked.

"More security on the back door. We should have expected that," Charlie replied.

"Solution?"

"I'm thinking," Charlie said neutrally. The truth was they couldn't do anything until Dana had opened the door for them, anyway, so she had a bit of time to think of something. She just needed inspiration. She took a little look at her phone to see how much time had passed, and wondered how long Dana would need to get to the back door. Assuming she decided not to leave them hanging.

To her relief, she saw the door open a little and caught a glimpse of red hair and green eyes, before the door was shut again. Dana had seen the security. Realistically they didn't have a huge amount of options, but the idea of fighting security on the street was going to make everything very problematic.

To her surprise she saw Perić walking up to them.

"What?" she whispered to Ash, who just shrugged.

"I thought he was still with us."

Perić walked up to the two men and spoke to them, pointing to the front of the building, and the two men looked at each other and replied. Perić said something more and the two scowled, but then nodded and turned and walked up the street to the entrance. Charlie and Ashley exchanged a look, but quickly raced up to join their friend, who was already banging on the door.

By the time the women arrived, Dana had the door open.

"Where's security?" Dana hissed.

"I told them there was a fight at the front and they need to go. I'd take the door here until they got back."

"When they get back and you aren't here they'll know there's a problem," Ash said, suddenly nervous.

"Is fine," grinned Perić. "I'll wait for them and tell them it must have been sorted, and then follow you."

333

"What if they push it?" Perič laughed at this.

"You forgot where we are and who they are?" He pulled out money from his inner pocket. "Trust me, this will solve any problems." He stared at them. "Go!" The two women quickly went up the step to the doorway and joined Dana inside.

"You're on your own now," Dana said. "I have things to do. Let me know what you find out, OK?"

"Sure," Charlie nodded. "Thanks," she added smiling at the younger woman. Dana paused and then smiled back.

FIFTEEN

Michael Chen stood on the roof of a building opposite Anisim Stepanov's house and reflected on just how clever his decision had been. Quite aside from the fact it involved jumping a fence and then scaling a building via its exterior fire escape (which had been, thankfully, very convenient), the truth was he wasn't entirely certain he had the right side of Stepanov's house in his sights. For all he knew, Stepanov's office was on the other side of the building, which would require him to then get off the building he was on, race from Ulitsa Galaktinova to Ulitsa Maksima Gor'kogo, and then get to the top of another building on that street.

However, there weren't an awful lot of options on Ultisa Maksima Gor'kogo to take position, and so Chen had put his money on the idea that Stepanov would prefer his office to look over the quieter Ulitsa Galaktinova.

There were only four balconies on the Galaktinova side of the building, and three of them were all on the same level. Chen used the sights of his rifle to survey the balconies, but all were dark and it was difficult to see into the rooms as a result. The windows were almost too reflective to penetrate, so he would need to concentrate on the doors that opened onto the balcony. He had suggested to Charlie that perhaps she might be able to get the man to step onto the balcony, and she had said she would do her best, but they both knew they were playing things very loosely.

Hana Mortimer had come through for him and sent a package to his hotel. Chen wasn't sure whether Mortimer was actually in Russia, or just using her contacts, but either way, he was impressed with the Proof Glacier Ti rifle that was in the box he had opened. It was a very new design (in fact Chen was surprised that Mortimer had managed to get hold of one in Russia, but he had to admit to himself, again, that she was *very* good at her job), and it felt surprisingly light in his hands; probably less than 3 kilos.

Attaching the sights back on the rifle, he flicked on the laser and aimed the gun at the door on the highest balcony, and watched as the little red dot appeared, firstly on the door itself, but then also on the wall behind. Perfect, he thought, and switched the laser off.

Now to wait.

The main lounge of Stepanov's house was where the party was going off, and Charlie caught a glimpse of Dana and Millie flitting around the room like two scarlet butterflies, catching the attention of people who asked for selfies and autographs. The room was very large and looked as ornate as one would expect based on the exterior architecture. Charlie suspected that the lounge occupied nearly all of the bottom floor, with the exception of the service corridors around it which they had come in through.

It was dominated by two formula one cars (though Charlie could only speculate how they had been brought into the house), both in gold, with the AutoGold logo on the side of each. Banners hung from the walls also proclaiming AutoGold, but also Shadow, a new energy drink and presumably another sponsor.

"I don't think the office is on the second floor," came Ash's voice in her ear, and Charlie remained silent.

"Try the top floor," came back Chen's voice. "There's a single balcony on the Galaktinova side which might be it."

"Which side is that?" Ash asked.

"The side you went in on," came back the slightly terse response. Charlie gave an irritated grunt.

"The voices doing your head in?" someone said, with a distinctive American twang, and Charlie turned back to see a woman of about average height with blue eyes and long dark hair. "Jokes, I'm sure you're not insane." Charlie stared at her, not sure what to say. "Don't I know you?" the woman continued.

"I don't think so," Charlie admitted. "Though I work in art, and have met a lot of people. I apologise if I've forgotten you. It's not intentional."

"Art, that would be it, of course," grinned the woman. "Charlie Maxwell, right?" Charlie opened her mouth to affirm, and then realised she had been caught totally off guard. Before she could deny it, the woman continued. "You're here incognito, right? I'll keep your secret. As long as you keep mine," she added with a conspiratorial grin.

"What's your secret?" Charlie asked, curious in spite of herself.

"Oh, I'm just trying to avoid her," the woman replied, and Charlie was surprised when she pointed across the room at Dana Spectra. "I need to be here, because I do like things wrapped up in a neat bow. But I also don't think I'm quite ready for that particular reunion."

"Right," Charlie replied, very puzzled. "Well, I'll keep your secret."

"Appreciated. And I'll keep yours." The woman turned to walk off, but then turned back again. "I did a quick search earlier, and I think what you want is on the top floor, Galaktinova side of the building. The only thing is, there's a biometric lock on the door. I think all of this," and she waved around the room as she said it, "is probably legit, which is odd considering who were talking about, but if by any chance you get in there, and you find something which suggests otherwise, I would love to have that information. A sort of, you scratch my back, I'll scratch yours type thing."

"Right," Charlie said, now utterly bewildered by the woman in front of her.

"Tell Chen Justice sends her love," the woman added. "Two Doves in as many months. I'm beyond excited." The woman turned and melted into the crowd. Charlie was about to follow her, and then changed her mind, tapping at her ear.

"Chen I just ran into a woman called Justice," she said, turning her face into her hand. "Ash, she says want we want is on the top floor."

"She's right, but it's got a…"

"Biometric lock?" Charlie finished.

"Yeah, how did you know?"

"That Justice woman told me," Charlie said.

"Did she tell you anything else?" Chen's voice came through the system.

"No. She was annoyingly vague," Charlie replied.

"That's spies for you," Chen said.

"You do know her?"

"Not really. She's the woman who pointed us in the direction of Man Garam," Charlie heard Chen say.

"This is quite the reunion, then, isn't it?" Charlie said. "Perhaps we should abort?"

337

"This is a big deal," Chen said. "I should imagine a few people are interested. You'll probably find there are a fair few Federal'naya sluzhba bezopasnosti Rossiyskoy Federatsii agents there as well."

"I assume you're just showing off your Russian skills?" Charlie said.

"KGB. Though that doesn't exist anymore. Sort of," Chen came back. "Have you found Stepanov?"

"*Zdrasti, zdrasti,*" came a deep voice with a thick Russian accent. Charlie looked around the room, and saw that everyone's attention was now on a makeshift stage towards the back of the room, at which a man was standing. He was older, probably in his seventies, but he was dressed in a black suit, and there was something remarkably handsome about the man. His hair and beard were surprisingly black, with distinguished grey streaks through them. He was in excellent shape, and the black suit, with the black shirt and tie settled on him stylishly. To his side was a younger man with ginger hair and beard, and a slightly pockmarked face. "I should probably speak English given that so many of us here do," the older man grinned. "Welcome to you all. And welcome to my humble home."

"Actually," Charlie said, "I rather think I have."

"So we're going to."

Charlie watched Stepanov as he continued to speak, waving at his audience and pointing out his celebrity guests, including Dana and Millie, and another man in a dark suit that Charlie didn't quite catch the name of because something suddenly caught her attention.

"Ash?" Charlie said. "We're going to what?" There was a singular lack of response and Charlie felt her stomach tighten a little. "Ash, respond please."

"Something's happened, I'm guessing?" Chen's voice came in, though Charlie noticed the slight pitch of agitation.

"Perić are you inside?" Charlie said, moving to a corner of the room so she could speak slightly louder.

"*Da*," came the response. "I'm going up now," he said.

"Quickly, Perić," Chen said. There was no response from the big man, and Charlie suspected he was biting his tongue. Feeling increasingly on edge, Charlie waited patiently, trying to ignore Chen's obvious agitation on the earbuds.

"Come on, come on, come on," he muttered. Charlie watched as Stepanov continued to speak, but was too distracted to pay attention to what he was talking about. Truthfully it would be largely unimportant to what they were doing, and there were enough people filming it for them to watch it in more detail later.

"She's been taken," Perić's voice finally came through. "I found her phone shoved under the office door. She must have known something was going on. I'm not sure where she is now though."

"Right," Chen's voice came through, agitation gone and a firm certainty replacing it. "Perić you need to see if you can find Frost. Do what you have to do. Charlie, make contact, get Stepanov into that office." Charlie nodded before remembering Chen wouldn't be able to see it.

"Understood," came Perić, and she echoed him.

Charlie made her way through the crowd to be closer to the stage.

"Obviously someone like me will have very little involvement in the day to day running of operations. We all know the real reason I keep Luca here is because he can change a spare tire," Stepanov was saying, and there was laughter, particularly from the pock-faced man beside Stepanov. "I'm delighted to say that Ted Hawley, who has been one of AutoGold's leading lights for some years will take over the racing side of the operation, while Natalie Vanda will take over the development side of the operations. We're still in the process of settling on our retail operations chief officer, but as soon as we do, I will tell you all. Where are Ted and Natalie? Not still at the bar, no?" More laughter. Charlie had to admit the man was charismatic.

"Find them, congratulate them, and continue to eat, drink and be happy. I'm sure Mr Moreau will be happy about one of those parts, anyway." This elicited laughter from the man in the dark suit. "Now I must have photos taken to make sure all our sponsors have spent their money well." Anisim Stepanov waved at the audience and turned to move off the stage, met by a tall woman with short dark hair dressed in a golden gown that seemed to be barely held together by the stitching on it.

And then Charlie did a double take.

"Shit," she whispered.

"What?" Chen's voice came back, and Charlie quickly melted into the crowd, trying to get back to a safer spot so she could talk. "Sashura Ilina is here!" she hissed, putting her hand to her face in the hope of concealing her speech.

"I thought," Chen started, but Charlie interrupted him.

"We thought wrong," Charlie snapped. "And if she's here…"

"The Fedorov brothers are here as well," came Perič's dour response. "I suppose we know what happened to Ash."

"We have to start moving quickly," Chen said. "Find Frost, get Stepanov to that office, and let's get the fuck out of here!"

SIXTEEN

Charlie looked across the room, mentally marking out the path that Stepanov was going to take across the room. She glanced around the room, watching the people move back and forth drawing a little map in her head, predicting where everyone would be in about two minutes time. It wasn't perfect – it never was; you couldn't precisely predict what a group of people were going to do in a room. But you could make a pretty good estimate, and as Charlie's mental map chartered the course of so many people, like they were microscopic particles moving through the air, she chartered her own path, and committed to it.

For the most part, she had made an excellent call, with people moving in the direction she expected them to. Some of the waiters not so much, but it didn't interrupt the plan too much. Within three minutes, she had walked half way across the room, and been hit by Anisim Stepanov.

"Why don't you watch where you're going?" Charlie demanded, having had her expensive champagne flute bumped, knocking just as expensive champagne onto her dress. Stepanov failed to respond. He seemed somewhat gobsmacked.

The Knight had sent them a file before their arrival, containing what little information they had on Anisim Stepanov. Most of it was what they had been told earlier, but there was one part that was interesting, and that was the rumour that he had a mistress, much younger than himself, with long red hair that was almost orange. It was Perić who had observed that the mistress looked not dissimilar to Charlie herself, though Charlie was a little older and wore glasses. Now decked out in a long orange wig and not leaving the glasses behind, the similarity between the two was clearly not wasted on Stepanov, which was the opening the group had been looking for.

"I am so sorry," Stepanov said, clicking his fingers for a waiter to bring something to help clean up the spill. "This is unacceptable, and all my fault. Please, accept my apologies. If there's anything I can do to make this up to you, please just say."

Score!

"Is there somewhere I might be able to take this dress off and try to soak up the spill?" Charlie asked, looking at the man, whose entire face suddenly became much more wolfish than it was before.

341

"My bedroom is on the top floor," Stepanov purred, his voice suddenly a lot lower. Charlie noticed that his PA, Luca, was looking a little nervous and glanced around.

"I think that's being a little optimistic, don't you Mr…?" Charlie said, and Stepanov seemed a little taken aback.

"I'm Anisim Stepanov," he blurted out, and Luca looked even more nervous as though he didn't like the attention that they might be receiving.

"Oh," Charlie feigned shock. "Oh, I'm so sorry, I didn't realise. But of course, you are. I'm so foolish."

"No, no," Stepanov said, smiling, "It's me, please, please."

"Of course, but appearances," Charlie said. "Do you have an office rather than a bedroom?" Luca reacted more to this than his boss did, but it clearly didn't matter. There was an order to things, and that wasn't going to be interrupted.

"What a good idea," Stepanov grinned. "Yes, I do. Yes, on the same floor. You are right. It will be much more appropriate. Please come with me. We can use my private elevator? Lift?"

"I've moved around so both words work for me," Charlie smiled.

"But you must tell me your name," Stepanov said, holding out his arm. Charlie slid hers through his and joined him on his walk, noticing that Luca was following them. She gave a little scowl to herself, trying to work out how she could get rid of the shadow.

"My name is Anya Collins," Charlie said.

"Anya? That is a good name. You must have some Russian in you," Stepanov said, laughing. He was annoyingly charming, Charlie reflected. Under any other circumstances, she would have absolutely considered spending some time with the man. There was a youthfulness to him that made him very accessible.

To her surprise, she saw Luca was no longer with them, and tried to work out where the PA had gone, as casually as she could. She was pleasantly surprised to see that he was in conversation with Dana and guessed the model had taken it upon herself to seize the man. She would have to pass on her thanks later.

Stepanov stopped at a set of elevator doors and summoned the lift.

"We should have a drink while we are there, yes? It might be nice to have a private moment," he added.

"It might indeed," Charlie agreed.

Ruvim Perić was not a man who was easily perturbed. He had watched his father been shot dead by soldiers in a situation that he didn't understand because he was far too young to. But his mother had held him tight, not saying a word. They had remained hidden until the soldiers had gone and then they left the house, without even looking at their deceased family member. Perić understood now why his mother had done that, and as he grew up he understood why she cried herself to sleep each night.

"Never show how afraid you are, Ruvim," she said to him on his first day of school. They were words to live by, and Perić did so.

Now he walked up the corridor on the top floor of Stepanov's home, pausing at each door to listen. A big part of him suspected that Fedorov had taken Ashley to another floor, but he had to be certain. He wasn't going to let anything happen to his young friend. But he would certainly make sure something happened to Fedorov.

The top floor checked out. Perić pondered on whether he should wait and see if Charlie made it into the office, but decided against it. Ashley was more important at this point. Perić hadn't worked with her very often, but on the odd occasion that they had, he found her very likable and the two had formed a bond. Nowadays he looked upon her like a little sister and was always happy to be assigned to a team with her.

He descended the interior stairs to the floor below. The layout was similar to the one above, in part dictated by the massive stairwell that linked the two floors. Interestingly there wasn't a matching one to go down to the next floor. Instead the stairs were located on the side of the building. Having the stairwell located in the middle of the floor meant that the surrounding rooms were all quite large, with some even having large double doors. Perić suspected that they were probably bedrooms. Double doors couldn't help but indicate opulence, and the fact that these were gold-gilded as well, didn't diminish the illusion.

Perić hesitated briefly before opting to simply start with the door in front of him. His routine on this floor was slightly different, dictated by the fact that he noticed the security cameras set into the wall. Clearly Stepanov preferred his privacy on the top floor as there had been no one there. Any lower and he wanted to know exactly what was going on.

As a result a more brazen approach would be needed, he decided, and he headed to the door and opened it, walking in.

It was a bedroom, with a four-poster bed at the centre, presumably for guests that Stepanov really wanted to impress. He crossed to one wall and put his ear to it, but there was nothing discernible on the other side. Equally when he crossed the room to try the opposite wall he got the same result. Annoying.

If he left the room and headed for another there might be a chance security would wonder what was going on. Logic suggested the best idea would be to take out the security room, but that would present problems on a number of different levels. Especially if Stepanov amped up his security, and in this little palace, he probably had.

He headed for the door and stepped out, straight into a burly security guard. The man was bearded with an ill-fitting suit, with a single brow that looked like it had been drawn on in crayon.

"What are you doing here?" he asked, his voice thick with a

Northern Russian accent. Perić weighed up his options and made two decision.

"*I was sent to help Fedorov*," he responded in Russian, rather than the English he was asked in. Mono-Brow raised his eyebrows slightly.

"*Who sent you to help Fedorov?*" came the reply, now in Russian.

"*His brother,*" Perić said, playing a gamble that was definitely high risk. Mono-Brow looked at him stonily, as if trying to read his mind. "*Apparently it was too much effort,*" Perić continued, deciding that he may as well go all in. Mono-Brow's facial expressions didn't change for a moment. Then he broke into a broad grin.

"*Of course. It is always too much for Boris, right?*" and Mono-Brow gave out a big belly laugh, which Perić joined in. "*You're new here, yes?*" and Perić nodded his assent. "*You want my advice? Don't hitch your wagon to Fedorov. He thinks he is a big wheel, but he is not as big as he thinks. One day, he will be let go. Next time you come here, you find me. You'll be on my team. It will be better for you. More consistent work, better pay. You won't have to do the dirty work.*" Perić gave a warm smile, and held out his hand, which Mono-Brow took and shook warmly. "*He's over there,*" he said, pointing to another door.

"*Thank you. Thank you. Next time, I come, I ask for...*" Perić left the sentence hanging.

"Koldan Kuzmin," Mono-Brow replied with a smile, and he turned and headed for the stairwell back upstairs, presumably to where the security room was. Worth noting, Perić reflected.

Then he turned and headed for the door indicated by Kuzmin. He paused briefly, then grabbed the handle and turned it, pushing the door open. He took everything in in just a moment. Ashley was tied to a chair, gagged, and her eyes wide with fear. She was in her underwear, and her upper arms and upper thighs had two cuts across each of them. Vsevolod Fedorov was wiping a carving knife on a cloth. He briefly looked up when Perić entered, but Perić didn't stop after he walked in, swinging the door closed behind him. Instead, he walked straight up to Fedorov, grabbing a chair on the way and swinging it into the man. It was a quick, short, sharp movement, Fedorov was caught off guard, uncertain how to respond.

He held up his hands to deflect the blow to the head, but failed to drop the knife, and Perić quickly lashed out after the chair strike, hitting Fedorov in his stomach and winding the man, so he was forced to drop it. Perić bent down to retrieve the weapon as Fedorov caught his breath to react, but the Dove was quicker, and his hand was around Fedorov's throat, pushing him across the room. Fedorov reeled, unable to get the upper hand in the fight, or even a simple opportunity to strike back. Perić's attack was quick, brutal and efficient, and as they approached the wall, Perić simply slammed Fedorov's head into the marble mantlepiece that was there.

There was an ugly thud, and blood stained the white marble, while Vsevolod Fedorov slumped to the floor. Perić wasn't sure whether he was unconscious or dead, but truthfully he didn't really care. He quickly released Ashley, an ungagged her.

"Are you OK?" he asked, grabbing a the cloth that Fedorov had been using to wipe the knife, and handing it to her.

"Yeah," she said, a weak grin on her face. "I'm alright. I've had worse." Perić raised an eyebrow, and she grimaced. "OK, well, this is pretty bad, I have to admit, but…I'm not dead. I would like my dress back, though," she added. Perić blushed deeply and turned away, causing Ashley to laugh. "Don't be silly, Ruvim. Just find my dress."

"It's funny the people you meet when you are holding these events," Anisim Stepanov said, as he poured two drinks from the drinks cabinet to the side of the room. Charlie was wandering around the room, and paused at the double doors that led onto the balcony. She looked through them and across the street, looking at the roof of the building opposite. She couldn't see Chen, but that didn't mean he wasn't there.

At least she hoped it didn't.

She reached up and tapped her earbud.

"Is security monitoring this room?" she asked Stepanov, but it was directed towards her team.

"Are we going to be interrupted, you mean?" Stepanov said, missing the point. "Well, there is always someone watching the door, and I have my panic button. But don't worry. I certainly have no desire to press it."

"I wouldn't want the panic button to be pressed either," Charlie said, turning from the balcony doors to her host. He held out a drink, and she took it. "I really don't want us to be disturbed."

"Can you hack into security?" Chen's voice said over the channels.

"I can try. I have my computer back," Ash Frost replied.

"Do it. Get that room offline."

"I'll try," Ash repeated.

"Don't try, Frost. Do it," snapped Chen.

"We are going to have a nice time then?" Stepanov smiled.

"Possibly," Charlie said coyly. There was a smell in the air, she suddenly noticed, and wondered if Stepanov had lit a candle. "I am curious about something, though," she added.

"I love to indulge curiosity," Stepanov said.

"Mason Lemon." Stepanov paused after she spoke, and then turned and went to his desk, sitting behind the large mahogany beast in a very beautiful chair. The office was nothing if not luxurious, and Stepanov clearly enjoyed being surrounded by comfort.

However, the two words she had just spoken seemed to utterly defeat the man.

"You're going to press your panic button?" Charlie said.

"I'm almost there," Ash said. "Just two minutes more!"

"Who are you?" Stepanov said.

"You don't seem surprised to see me," Charlie said, sitting down opposite him.

"The button is there," Stepanov said, pointing to his desk. "I suppose I could press it and summon help. But I also feel there might not be any point. I assume that this is my last day on Earth?"

Charlie suddenly felt very uncomfortable. This was not remotely the response she was expecting, and Stepanov's strange acceptance of his fate felt very awkward.

"Why?"

"It is a very sordid story," Stepanov said.

"Done!"

"I was once KGB," he continued. "A long time ago, when it was a powerful organisation, feared throughout the world. Three letters that struck terror into secret service agents everywhere. But all things come to an end, and when I had to make a change in career, I realised that power was still within my grasp. I knew the President after all. And people feared him, so in turn they feared me. Everything was perfect, because I had the President's ear. Until I didn't.

I didn't do anything wrong. There was no fight, no argument, nothing like that." Stepanov paused and looked around his table, before finding a packet of cigarettes. He took one out and lit it, inhaling deeply. "We just grew apart. But one can only be powerful if one has power. And power is knowledge, and I needed knowledge. What I needed was a direct line to the Kremlin. So, I needed someone who had the ability to give me that, and that's where Vitaliy Orlov comes in. He was a man who knew a great deal. But he had a vice. They all do, don't they? They all have something you can get hold of and twist to your advantage. I control a lot of gambling, and I have found a lot of gamblers that use my establishments end up paying me in different ways than hard currency. Orlov was one. Get me into the Kremlin computers and give me the information I need, I said. If you do that, your debt is cleared." He breathed his cigarette in deeply and then help the packet out as though his had forgotten his manners. Charlie shook her head and Stepanov nodded.

"Vitaliy did as he was told, but of course I needed more. Passwords change, encryptions change. I needed Vitaliy to keep me up to date, but I had cancelled his debt, so what else could I do? It turns out that Vitaliy has two sons - twins. One of them, heavily into drugs. So, I get my friend Fedorov to see them. Your father is in great trouble. He needs you to help him get out of debt. What can we do? they ask. Well, how about you make a dirty video, of the two of you. The drug one, he is given a little incentive, and says yes immediately. The other brother feels like he has to." Charlie's stomach lurched in revulsion and Stepanov nodded, his own face mirroring hers. "I told you is a sordid tale. I'm not proud of it. But tog et where I am you must do business without scruples. Is not a good life." He shook his head sadly before continuing.

"So, I take this video to Vitaliy and I show him. Do as I ask, or else these boys will do more of this degrading behaviour. Vitaliy is devastated. He is their only parent, but he has failed so badly. He cries, but he does as he is told. And it turns out that there are many people out there who like the idea of twin brothers having relations. So we make them do more, because we get good money for this." Stepanov paused to inhale again. Charlie wondered, now, if his acceptance of his fate was coming from a weariness of his life.

"When I was younger, we had a dog. My father would beat it repeatedly. All the time. The poor thing simply wanted love, but it got nothing except pain. Animals do one of two things in that situation. Some reach a point where they turn on their master. Others, well...they die. Not physically, but you can see it inside of them. My dog died. It just stopped moving. My father beat it to death, but the life had gone from those eyes long before that happened. I should have seen it with those boys. One of them – not the drugged one, the other one – the life died from his eyes. You would watch those pornographic videos, and there he was, having sex with his brother, or whoever, but there was nothing in those eyes. When we found out he killed himself, I wasn't surprised. The other brother then disappeared. I don't know where. But now we had no leverage on Vitaliy, and so he also vanished.

I was furious. How dare this man who belonged to me, suddenly think he could just up and leave? I had not given him permission to do that. And so I demanded that my people find out where this no one had gone. The arrogance of power." Again he shook his head sadly.

"It took some time but one day I get news. Vitaliy Orlov is working in Korea. This technical genius is working for a company called Moonlight. Unfortunately, I can't get to him the easy way, so I decide, well, I will bring down this company he is working for. I have my contacts, and they inform me that there is a man named Boom who is in the Moonlight company, and of course he is a gambler. Another one, huh?" Stepanov laughed mirthlessly at this. "So I tell him he has to murder a few people. Just one or two, here or there. Enough to make people start to get shaky feet about Moonlight. Shaky feet. Is that the phrase?"

"Cold feet," Charlie supplied.

"Cold feet, yes. But of course, this can't keep happening indefinitely, without raising some suspicion. It turns out that the CIA are curious about what is going on, so they send in this Mason Lemon guy. Now things are getting messy. So far, my man Fedorov has been organising all this, but it is not working, so Luca – he's my assistant – he tells me that we might need to get in someone who can clean up the operation. So we contact Man Garam. You have heard of them?"

"Yeah," Charlie replied evenly.

"Expensive, but effective. Luca has someone in the CIA compromised, so we use him to get information about Lemon, which we pass onto Man. Lemon is dead. Boom is dead. It is all sorted. But yet, I think, maybe not. Maybe there is a chance someone will find out about this. It will come back to bite me. And here we are." Stepanov drew the last drag of the cigarette and then stubbed it out.

"Why didn't you just get Man Garam to kill Orlov?" Charlie wondered, and this time Stepanov's laughter was more than empty.

"Have you ever been asked to solve a puzzle, and you think of a solution that doesn't work, but for some reason your brain refuses to open up and offer alternatives? All you see is that failed solution?" Charlie nodded, starting to understand. "I was a fool to rely on Fedorov. But my brain didn't think straight. Maybe I'm being too generous. Maybe the truth was I was desperate for Orlov to suffer. As if I hadn't made him suffer enough. Do you believe in God, Anya?" Charlie raised her eyebrows, before realising he was addressing her.

"I'm not sure," she admitted. "Maybe."

"There is a God," Stepanov said, conclusively. "Absolutely. I was hoping for a chance to seek forgiveness before I confronted him, but I feel that I will not get the chance. Perhaps that is justice."

"You've ruined a lot of lives," Charlie said, not quite as ruthlessly as she was expecting to, and Stepanov nodded in agreement.

"I'm not going to make this difficult," Stepanov announced. "You should go." Charlie stood up cautiously, but Stepanov was lost in contemplation, and she turned and headed for the door. She was stopped by his voice again. "Can I just say, that to be judged by an angel, I'm glad it was you."

Charlie left the room without looking back. She didn't really want anyone to see the tears stinging at her eyes. And truthfully, she wasn't even sure who they were for.

SEVENTEEN

Michael Chen trained his sights on the double doors to the balcony. He had heard the entire conversation, and his heart and mind were set, as immovable as concrete. He had no sympathy, no compassion. Just a ruthless desire to exact revenge.

When the doors opened, Chen saw the dark suited figure step through. He didn't even see the red dot already on his chest. Chen altered the aim of the gun, moving the red dot up to the man's forehead.

The trigger was squeezed, and Anisim Stepanov crumpled to the ground.

EIGHTTEEN

Ruvim Perić, Ashley Frost, the Grey Knight and Hana Mortimer stood gathered at Kazan International Airport's main enclave. People bustled around them, checking in, weighing luggage and keeping families together and happy. The Knight watched with mild interest before turning back to the group and signing something which both Ash and Mortimer laughed at. Perić was mildly irked that he had been left out of the joke, but said nothing, knowing that he would be rebuked for not having learnt sign language.

"Are we waiting for Charlie and Chen?" Ashley asked, but Mortimer shook her head.

"Nope. Charlie has already left, Chen is in a lounge somewhere ready to go. I don't think they wanted to talk to us, let alone each other." She took off her glasses and cleaned them before putting them back on again and giving Ashley a grin.

I'm guessing they didn't get on? The Knight signed, and Ash translated it for Perić.

"They are both very different people," Perić grumbled. "Very different ways of working. I wonder why Flight put them together."

"Convenience," Mortimer shrugged, disinterested in the personal relationships. "It doesn't matter, the situation has been resolved. We've done our jobs. We can rest until we get another assignment."

"I'm sleeping in all day tomorrow," Ash said with a smile.

"You need to after," Perić began, but then stopped, unsure of what else to say.

"It's fine," Ash said, touching him on the arm. "Honestly," she added, seeing the look on the Knight's face.

Perić said it was brutal, the Knight said.

He's worrying too much about nothing. Absolutely fine. Just some cuts that will heal, Ash replied. Neither Perić nor the Knight looked convinced, but the door was closed on the conversation.

"Come on," Mortimer said. "We need to check in and go. Let's get out of here. I'll miss you, but I'm glad I won't be seeing you tomorrow." She gave them another smile that was difficult to interpret, and led the way to the counter. The other three shrugged and followed her.

Michael Chen breathed in the smell of fish and chips and decided that he was quite happy to be home. He was never particularly comfortable with murdering people, but he wasn't overly upset about Anisim Stepanov. The man was genuinely horrible and his desire to prove how powerful he was had impacted on so many people and ruined too many lives. People like that, Chen decided, really didn't deserve a second chance. Sometimes you had to accept the evidence of your own eyes, and Chen's eyes were very clear on the fact that Stepanov was not a good person.

Unlike Dana Spectra.

He activated the computer and felt the room come alive around him. The connection was instantaneous and he could hear the breathing on the other end before any words had been spoken.

"Look, I know I didn't follow the instructions," Chen said, pre-empting his telling off. "And I should have got in contact with you earlier." He paused, deliberating on whether he should proceed with his prepared speech or err on the side of discretion. In for a penny, he reflected. "The thing is that sometimes you get tunnel vision and don't always see it from the coal face, if you know what I mean."

"You don't have to say anymore," the disguised voice came back. "I chose you for your ability to think for yourself and to make decisions based on the evidence at hand. I'm not upset with what you've done or why you've done it. However, there was no real reason you couldn't have kept me abreast of the situation, rather than make use of my operatives without my permission."

"I understand," Chen said, trying to sound obsequious.

"Do you? I bankroll this operation. I have to know where I'm supposed to be giving out money. I won't know that if I don't know what is going on."

"That's fair."

"I hope so, Mr Chen. You're paid to use your initiative, not keep me in the dark." Chen nodded before speaking.

"I apologise."

"You did a good job, though. Mason Lemon has been avenged and one of Russia's biggest crime bosses has been eliminated. Enjoy your weekend, Mr Chen. I hope to talk to you soon."

Chen opened his mouth to reply, but realised that the connection to the little room tucked behind the tiny shopping complex had been cut off. The computers had no more information on them scrolling, as window after window changed colour and the words "Complete" appeared on them.

Strange that despite the victory, he felt oddly hollow.

Michael Chen leaned forward and deactivated the computer, before standing up and walking out.

Charlie Maxwell knocked on the door and waited a moment, hoping that it was heard over the sound of the partying behind it. She was a little surprised to find that the door was opened, and a young man with a beard stood there, a smile on his face.

"Hi there," he said. "Uh, you were here the other day, right?"

"Yeah," Charlie said hesitantly. "I was wondering if Dana was available."

"Probably. I'll see if she's dancing," he grinned. "Come on in. Would you like a drink?"

"No, no, it's fine," Charlie said. The young man walked over to the interior door of the hotel room and opened it, calling out for Dana. He closed it behind him, and then a few moments later, Dana walked through. She was no longer wearing her beautiful gown, rather she was now in an oversized t-shirt and ripped jeans.

"Well, well, well. If it isn't a Dove," Dana said.

"I wasn't sure you'd still be in town," Charlie replied.

"Because the host of the party I went to last night was found dead? It's all good. I have contacts who have kept me from the authorities. I'm leaving tomorrow though. I don't think I'll be welcome in Russia for any great length of time."

"You don't seem upset," Charlie said, thoughtfully.

"I may seem like an airhead, but I know what's going on," Dana said. "Or, I know as much as I need to know in order to stay happy. Stepanov is dead, but his bully boy offsider is going to take over. Realistically, nothing will change. One thug is taking over from another." Charlie nodded, a little sad at her cynicism, though she appreciated the realism.

"I just wanted to come to tell you what had happened. Why Lemon was killed, why Boom was killed." Charlie paused unsure of how to continue, however, to her surprise, it was irrelevant.

"Don't stress it," Dana said. "I told you I don't want to know and I don't. I made peace with the fact that I'm not going to know everything that is going on in the world. I'm trying to learn to be content with being happy."

"You're not even curious?" Charlie asked.

"I'll tell you what," Dana grinned. "How about you email me everything and if I ever want to know, I'll open it and find out. But until then, I get to choose one way or the other."

"OK," Charlie nodded. "I mean, I don't know your email…"

"Call my agent," Dana grinned again. "Are you joining the party?"

"No, I'm going to head home. I was supposed to leave earlier, but I wanted to see you."

"It's a good party."

"I'm OK," Charlie smiled. "I'm glad you are too." To Charlie's surprise, the Australian leaned forward and hugged her, but then turned and went back into the room and the party beyond. Charlie sighed a little, her heart still heavy, and headed out.

Back to reality.

EPILOGUE

Vsevolod Fedorov straightened his tie and smoothed back his hair before taking hold of the handle to the double doors. Beside him, looking far less comfortable in the suit he was wearing, Borislav Fedorov stood attentatively. It had been a few weeks since the death of Anisim Stepanov, and in that time Vsevolod had made it clear that there was only one person that was going to succeed the deceased crime lord. Admittedly he had spent a few days recovering from the beating he had got by whoever the hulk was that was hunting for the girl – something he was fully intending to avenge the moment he found out who said hulk was and who the annoying brat was, but either way they were both dead – but once he was back in shape, he quickly had message sent to Stepanov's errand boy and that prick who ran security that he would be back to take the reins.

"*Are you sure we don't need a key to get in?*" Borislav asked, and Vesvolod shot his brother a look. He still hadn't forgiven the fact that his younger brother had decided to abandon the torture. Had Borislav been there none of this would have happened, and he wouldn't have the perpetual headache he seemed to have these days. But on the other hand, his rise to power would not have happened. No forgiveness, but Vsevolod supposed deep down he probably owed his brother something.

"*I told Kuzmin that the door was to be left open,*" Vsevolod said.

"*I don't trust Kuzmin,*" grumbled Borislav.

"*As soon as we have everything, I'm killing him. Maybe I'll torture him first and then kill him. Either way he's dead. As is Luca. Both of them. Neither will be in my empire.*" He turned the handle and to his annoyance, it didn't open. "*Yebat',*" snarled Vsevolod. "*Go to Kuzmin and get this door open and then tell him I want to see him, because he is going to learn a lesson he will never forget!*" Borislav nodded at his brother and quickly walked away.

Irritated, Vsevolod wiggled the handle repeatedly, and was a little surprise when it suddenly turned the full way and the door swung open. For a moment he wondered if he should get Borislav back, but then changed his mind. He could always pretend he had forced the lock.

He stepped into the office and paused, taking in the musky scent. He could see dust particles floating in the sunlight that was coming through the windows. In just a few weeks the office had become a memorial, feeling like it had been untouched by everything except time.

Vsevolod wanted to turn the lights on. Despite the sunlight, the room felt like it was sepia-toned and the details were difficult to make out. It was ridiculous, he told himself, but he had an unsettling feeling when this room was in the dark, and he didn't like it. He knew exactly where the light switch was on the wall beside the door, so he flipped the switch and the room was bathed in golden light.

Heading to the Stepanov's desk, he suddenly found himself forced to pause. There was a young man sitting at the desk. Young? Possibly old. He had bleached white hair, but was East Asian, and everyone knew that you could never accurately pick an East Asian's age. Vsevolod wasn't a racist, but he did dislike East Asians. They were untrustworthy. Chinese or Japanese, or whatever, Vsevolod had no interest in dealing with them. OK, so maybe he was a racist? Who cared?

However, he couldn't remember off the top of his head if Stepanov had the same thoughts. Had Stepanov been working with one of the Triads, maybe? Was that person here to take control of the business?

"*Who are you?*" Vsevolod asked in Russian, not willing to bend to the Asian. He didn't speak Chinese, Japanese or Korean or whatever, anyway. However, his brain did point out that he was unlikely to learn anything if they couldn't communicate. "Who are you?" came the repeat in English.

"Unimportant," the man said with a small smile. His voice was soft, and not as deep as Vsevolod would have expected.

"It is to me," snapped Vsevolod, "and that makes it very

358

important." The Asian man smiled a little more.

"My name is Man Garam," the man smiled. Vsevolod Fedorov was about to retort, but then paused. Somewhere in the depths of his memory the name rang a bell. Had he heard it before? Maybe yes, but only in passing, as though someone had said something, but…annoyingly he couldn't recall anymore.

And yet his brain nagged that the name was important.

"What do you want?" Vsevolod said, annoyed that his voice lacked the confidence it had started with.

"To be paid," Man said simply.

"I don't owe you anything," snarled Vsevolod.

"No, you don't," Man agreed. "But you are necessary for my payment." They stood up and shot Vsevolod Fedorov in the head. Man Garam walked over to the body and looked for a moment, satisfied with their work. Then they put their gun on Fedorov's body and pulled out a phone. They tapped twice and waited a moment before the lights went out around them.

Then Man Garam walked out of the room, and calmly exited the building, where a black Elemento Sesto was waiting. From a window above, a man with red hair and pock marked face watched the car pull away. Luca pulled out his phone and saw that the EMP that had knocked out the electronics in the building had also knocked out his phone.

Never mind, he reflected. He would transfer the payment later.

BOOK FIVE
BROKEN WEB

I

Dana Spectra was wearing premium Dreamsleep Australia fleece leggings, a Sherpa jumper and a Carol Women's double-breasted wool trench coat all in black, which meant that she blended into the shadows brilliantly. It also went some way to helping her in what was definitely 0 degree temperature, but not entirely as she still felt herself shiver a little. She was also wearing women's Harpy leather flat boots, which were surprisingly more comfortable than she thought they'd be. Honestly, it was an outfit that would zing if she was going out in Brisbane. She almost regretted wasting it now.

Cautiously she crept up the path towards the squat black house ahead of her, with its slightly darker roof. Everything felt like it was different shades of black, and the barren landscape of Árneshreppur didn't really make that much of a difference. A ridiculously flat terrain, except for the snow-topped mountains which seemed like they had been created by a kid in Minecraft who hadn't realised that you could build up to a mountain summit.

She kept her eyes peeled for security, and paused at a bush, waiting.

"I think there's a camera near you set up for infrared or heat, probably to your left. The interference signal is causing way more problems than I thought it would," came the voice in Dana's ear, and Dana reached up to tap the earbud, sending a signal of acknowledgement. She could have talked, but she didn't trust her teeth not to chatter.

Scanning the area to her left, Dana was able to make out what looked like a pole with a little globe at the top, and she guessed that was what would be doing the scanning. It wasn't easy to make out what was actually the camera, but suddenly the globe juddered and turned, and a small piece of glass was visible, glinting in the moonlight.

She could have taken it out with a single shot (or could she? Usually she could, but she didn't trust her hands, which were absolutely freezing), but she opted to wait for the camera to swing around and find another area to focus on. When it *brrr*ed into action, Dana hurried forth.

"There's definitely bound to be cameras on the building. You should be able to see them, but just be aware that there are probably a few. Trust me, we've been tricked before."

There wasn't an awful lot of coverage, and Dana pulled the hood of the Sherpa jumper over her head, and crouched down as low as she could, trying to make out what was on the building in front of her. The door was obvious, the path leading directly to it. There were no trees, or plants around the house, and no verandah or railings. It was just a block – which was pretty standard for the houses in Gjögur, so she wasn't surprised.

Deciding to risk it, she ran to the corner of the house and pressed herself against the wall. She looked up to the camera that she was standing under and then looked further down the wall to see the others. She was fine under the camera, as the other two were pointed away from her. Dana reached inside the coat and pulled out her custom golden Glock, and raised it, pointing it at the door. She wasn't sure how long she waited, though it felt like it was an eternity. She couldn't hear a sound and no one made an appearance, so she decided she was fine. Carefully she turned the corner, then paused, listening. Someone had opened the door and exited.

Dana screwed her face up slightly, weighing up her options. Making a decision, she reached up and twisted the camera, then turned her gun around and raised it. A man came into view, and before he had a chance to turn, Dana brought the gun down on the back of the man's head, wincing as she thought she heard a crunch. She felt a sudden stab of guilt as the man slid to the ground, and she reached forward and put her finger under the man's nose, relieved to feel breath. She tried to pull him back, but the man was ridiculously heavy, so she let him fall.

Hoping that whoever was watching the monitor was napping, Dana reached up and moved the camera again, this time pointing it up.

"God, I'd never be able to do something like that with my height." Dana grinned wryly, suddenly remembering that her choker had a small camera in it. She was impressed that her guardian angel could work out what she was doing. "I can send the drone if you want, and that might give us more information." Dana tapped the earbud twice. She'd given it a lot of thought and stood by her belief that a drone would actually be more noticeable than someone trying to go under the radar. "I wish you'd reconsider," came the plaintive response.

Dana slid across to the first window and risked a glance in. It was a small room, clearly heated, and two men inside were playing a board game that could have been chess. They were drinking, but it looked warm and dark, so Dana decided they wouldn't be losing focus anytime soon. She crouched down and continued her slide along the wall, standing up beyond the window, where she angled the security camera there up as well.

With that done, Dana turned to confirm that she was standing at a doorway. She reached forward and tried the door, thanking the stars that the door handle turned without resistance and opened. It was another risk, but again she was banking on the fact that if a guard had left, they probably hadn't turned on any alarms, waltliŋg for him to get back.

She stepped inside the corridor, which was dark, and after a few moments her eyes adjusted, and she was able to make out a side table and three doors, one to the front, and the others on either side of her. She put her hand on the table and ran her fingers over the top, but there was nothing except a set of keys. House keys? Maybe.

The door to the right would be the one that led to the room with the chess playing guards, which left two options. The one in front was probably another corridor. Dana gripped the handle to her left and carefully turned it, pushing it slightly so she could see what might be on the other side.

Bingo.

She eased the door open as carefully as she could and slid through the gap into the room beyond. It was dark, but illuminated by the light of several screens on a desk at one end of the room, seated at which was a man. Dana softly closed the door and pushed the lock in, before raising her gun and moving forward.

"Hello Dana Spectra."

II

When the email had first turned up in her inbox, Dana had glanced at it, seen the title "Broken Web", looked at the sender (whitebird@kingcharles.com) and decided it was definitely junk. Fortunately she hadn't bothered to bin it, as she was in the middle of work and was called back to the photoshoot – an exciting gig for the Shadow drink, and a shoot that she was covered in black paint for.

As a result the email sat there for a week, and it wasn't until she was back in Brisbane, had left the shower and was towelling herself down that she sat down at her actual computer and looked at her emails. There was the "Broken Web" email again, and Dana moved the mouse to delete the message. Except there was something about the email address. White bird at King Charles?

White bird as in dove? What had been the name of that Dove that was going to email her? Charlie?

Dana tapped her finger on the mouse slightly, wondering if she wanted to open the email in front of her. She had genuinely put to bed the notion that she would be able to keep track of everything going on in her life, and was content with that. But just because you knew there was probably no chance you could go through a door, did that mean that if someone gave you the key you shouldn't use it?

Her mother calling to say that she had prepared dinner, again made the decision for her, and Dana left it unopened. For the next few days, while she was free, she was able to spend time with Bella and Jeremy, catch up with Dr Prass for another session and generally kick back making pointless content that her followers on IG could like and not lose interest.

Actually she'd been doing pretty well with her socials, which was a miracle, and for once people were no longer nagging her to post more often. She'd even done a quick fire question and answer on a YouTube video. Except one of those questions – one that she hadn't read aloud – had simply been "Have you read the email?"

Dana guessed that whoever sent it knew that she hadn't. They'd have included confirmation of receipt, so Charlie knew exactly the status of the email. No, she was baiting Dana into opening it.

And annoyingly it was working.

Despite being in a world that many regarded as hedonistic and definitely substance-abusing, Dana was largely a good girl. She suspected that came from the fact her father was military, and so doing the right thing had been drilled into her from a very young age. While it was true, she had occasionally drunk herself stupid (OK, not so occasionally), and she was often quick to jump into someone's bed (though she was getting better with that that, wasn't she?), she hadn't succumbed to smoking and she didn't do drugs.

Aside from being a "party girl", Dana liked to do the right thing. As such, when she approached the ATM near the Myer center and put her card in to check her balance, the fact that it was displaying an eight-figure number didn't fill her with joy. In fact, she could feel the cold, icy hand grab at her stomach, and she found herself breathing a lot heavier than she usually did.

She had left Dr Prass' office and made her way along Queen St Mall, wondering to herself what she was going to do about lunch. She quite liked the idea of going to Korilla, a Korean BBQ restaurant, which was almost directly opposite Dr Prass' office, but it looked busy (as it often was), and she had no desire to just hang around doing nothing while she waited.

Beach House was another option, as was the food court in the Myer Centre, but Dana was struggling to even work out what she wanted for lunch. Food was a constant problem for her family, and Dana was one of the biggest contributors to the failure of the "where shall we eat" debate that they often had.

Regardless of what she had been going to choose, however, money was required, and that brought her to the ATM, which brought her to her present dilemma. She was now in a position where she could regard herself as fairly well off, but she had yet to reach a point where she would comfortably call herself a millionaire. Sometimes she thought she was close, and her asking price had increased over the past year or so, such that she thought a million might be within reach, if work kept going well for the next year.

There was no reason for eight figures to be displayed on her balance. She definitely didn't have that much money in her account.

Except apparently she did.

Something was very wrong.

She withdrew her card, and noticed with a shock that there was a slight tremble to her hand. She was comfortably aware that she was nervous, but she was a little disturbed that the nerves were manifesting themselves so physically.

As she turned to head towards the car park and go home, her mind raced. Would people know that the money had been deposited in her account? What should she do? Should she inform someone? She should inform someone.

Shouldn't she?

Her paranoia building, Dana quickened her pace, moving past the strip club tucked beside the donut shop, the car park getting nearer.

The she noticed someone walking behind her, a little to the left. Tall and dressed in a dark suit, he looked like a businessman.

Did he? Or did he look like a Fed?

Was he following her?

Grateful to hear the crossing button change its repetitive beep, she crossed with the rest of the crowd, heading towards King George Parking. Her shadow followed her across the road, and Dana was grateful to head into the parking complex, skipping past the tariff machines, and making her way to the concrete stairwell that descended to the lower levels. The escalators were useless, permanently taking people up, so the stairs were her only option.

The man in the black suit hadn't followed her.

She found her car – the McLaren 720S Spider she had bought in the town of Scullin the previous year – and slipped inside, feeling safer as she pulled the door closed behind her. She started the machine and guided it towards the exit, moving up the different floors slowly. By the time she pushed her credit card against the exit machine, she was feeling a little more relieved.

She would head home, talk to her father and contact Karam

Narogin, her ASIO contact, and they could make a decision what to do about the money. The man following her was definitely just a symptom of her paranoia. As the Spider slipped into the next gear, Dana pushed down on the accelerator, enjoying the feel of the speed. Now, she felt safe again.

Except, on the street corner, stood a man in a black suit, watching her drive away.

"Who was he?" Dana demanded petulantly.

"I don't know," Karam Narogin snapped back, irritated. "The way you've described it, there wasn't necessarily anyone following you at all. If you're asking was it us, the answer's no. And before you say anything, I'd have been informed." Dana glared at her phone, hoping that it would travel the internet and focus on Karam.

"ASIO, no. ASIS?"

"I don't know, Dana," Narogin sighed heavily. "I'm looking into it, but if they are, they possibly wouldn't inform us." Dana could almost hear Karam shrugging. "Most of the time we play nicely, some of the time we don't."

"What about the money?"

"Well, that's a good question," Narogin conceded. "And a little worrying if I'm honest. Bank transfers of that amount are usually flagged and someone would have been doing a check, but honestly, according to my information, that hasn't happened. Big Brother may have flagged it, but again, they don't seem to be playing nice. You could try your mates at Interpol, but aside from that, I don't know what else to say. Except be careful." It seemed even Narogin felt that was a fairly lame response, because he immediately filled the silence. "Look, honestly, I'm going to find out what's going on. Unless you've given us reason, we wouldn't just hang you out to dry.."

"So, I sit home and do nothing?" Dana asked pointedly.

"Do you have a lot on?"

"Actually, I have a bit of a break," Dana admitted.

"Hang low," Narogin advised.

"Thanks," Dana replied drily. As the call went dead, Dana paced around her room, before pausing at the window and pulling back. She peered out, but there was no one on the street, and Dana wondered if her paranoia was getting out of control.

There could be a camera on the window!

Maybe no more walking in front of the window.

Dana grabbed her phone and brought up another name, dialling it.

"Dana," came the delighted voice on the other end. "How are you?"

"Alan, I need your help," Dana said, and the panic in her voice registered with the man on the other end.

"Anything I can do," Alan said without hesitation.

"Does Interpol know anything about a massive money transfer to me? Have you sent someone to monitor me?"

"No, Dana," came the reply, hesitantly. "Are you alright?"

"I'm fine, I'm just…in the dark." There was a long pause.

"Well I can one hundred percent confirm there's no one monitoring you, according to our information," came Alan's response and Dana clicked her tongue slightly in irritation. Alan was high enough in the chain of command at Interpol so that if he hadn't any information, there probably wasn't any information to be had. "As for the money transfer…when you say big, you mean *bit*?"

"Tens of millions," Dana replied, and there was another pause.

"Very unusual. ASIO?"

"Karam Narogin is looking into it, but he says they know nothing as well," Dana replied.

"I see," came the measured reponse. "Well I'll get in touch with ASIO, though it's a bit unusual. Karam and I have come to know each other a little over the last year, thanks to you. Hopefully he'll be forthcoming. If I get anything I'll start making inroads elsewhere and maybe come up with something more useful for you."

"Thanks," Dana said, her heart heavy.

"Dana, stay safe. I'd hate for anything to happen to you." Dana nodded, before realising he wouldn't be able to see what she was doing, and so she said goodbye, though her voice made it clear what she was feeling.

Why would anyone transfer all that money into her account? Pursing her lips, Dana sat down at her computer but realised she didn't even know what she was going to type. Who would give me lots of money? Or maybe someone was trying to be nice to her, like the Doves.

Oh.

The mystery email was looking back at her from the computer screen. There was a file attachment. Glaring at the computer, Dana pondered as to whether she should open the file or not. With a hint of irritation, she moved the mouse and downloaded the file.

Fuck it.

"Anisim Stepanov blackmailed Vitaliy Orlov into providing backdoor access to the Kremlin to further his criminal empire." Dana mused on reading this; she had met Stepanov when he announced he was taking over AutoGold, the board having decided his was a good offer. Stepanov was an older guy, who didn't look it, dressed that night all in black, with hair that was obviously dyed, but suited him all the same. He was dead, now, of course, Dana knew that. Everyone did. AutoGold had gone into limbo for the second time that year, as a result.

"Orlov, though, had escaped to Korea after Stepanov had killed his family, and it was there Stepanov recruited Boon-Mee Sirisopa, the rapper nicknamed Boom, to essentially bring down the company that Orlov was working for, by miring it in scandal." A simple act of petty revenge that resulted in the death of Boom, which Dana had been present for. Dana suspected she had met the assassin, a curious figure with short white hair, named Man Garam, according to Charlie's information. According to Charlie, Man had killed twice that night, the first being a CIA agent named Mason Lemon. Lemon had been set up by a CIA analyst named Nathan Coulter, someone else in Stepanov's pocket. Lemon had been investigating…oh.

Lemon had been investigating the murders in Moonlight Entertainment, as she had been. And by all accounts Lemon had been murdered by Dana Spectra, hence the Doves had been sent to deal with Dana. All's well that ends well? That was Charlie's question, but to Dana, now it looked as though that might not be the case. Was she a loose end that someone wanted cleaned up?

III

Emails had flown back and forth, chasing each other across cyberspace so that Charlie Maxwell and Dana Spectra could communicate; though in Charlie's case it was definitely on the lowdown. Added into that mix was Ashley Frost, a computer expert. Dana's previous encounter with Charlie and Ashley – two members of the mysterious firm called "The Doves" – had not exactly gone well, but despite their initial attempts to kill her, Dana had decided the Doves were probably on the side of the angels, while Charlie and Ashley had both taken to Dana quite quickly, neither one of them actually believing that Dana had been responsible for the murder of Mason Lemon.

With no help from ASIO or Interpol, Dana had asked Charlie if she knew anything about a the massive money transfer, and Charlie had responded in the negative, which hadn't helped Dana, who was getting a bit paranoid, sitting around her parent's house, afraid to go out in case a mysterious man in a black suit suddenly strolled into view. She had spent her time glimpsing out the window, and though most of those glances were pointless paranoia, on one occasion she had definitely seen someone. Not in a suit; just normal clothes, but when she took the bin out the following day, a neighbour up the road was doing the same, and Dana could have sworn it was the same person she had seen loitering.

Her father, who had been spending a lot of time in Japan recently, looked as though he was making a permanent return to Australia, much to her step-mother's delight and when he arrived on the doorstep, Dana had embraced him perhaps with more enthusiasm than she intended to. She and her father had a close bond since the death of her mother, Alessia, and the subsequent disappearance of her sister Kimba, and whilst Dana had welcome Lily and Bella into her life with enthusiasm, there were times when a girl needed her Dad.

"Hypothetical question for you," Dana announced to her father, the afternoon after his return, and Indigo Spectra gave a vague response, trying not to fall asleep in the sunlight that was streaming through the window directly onto him in the lounge. Indigo was coming to the conclusion that it was a losing battle, but he wasn't that concerned about it. In fact, if his daughter hadn't just started a conversation, he rather felt like surrendering and accepting the beautiful defeat.

"If someone had acquired a small fortune, like, it just turned up in a bank account, what would you do?"

"Give it to your father," Indigo mumbled.

"I'm being serious," Dana pouted and Indigo opened an eye to look at her. He was well aware that his daughter was starting to get involved in some of the more questionable sides of espionage, and though he didn't entirely approve of the decision, he had to respect his daughter, safe in the knowledge that she wasn't an idiot and knew what was going on.

"You've acquired a small fortune?"

"No," Dana laughed it off, hopefully successfully. "But say a friend has."

"Oh," Indigo said, frowning. "Well. I'd tell the bank there'd been a mistake."

"The bank said there wasn't," Dana replied, circumventing the fact that she hadn't thought of that.

"I assume you think that it's an illegal transfer?"

"I can't see how it would be legal," Dana replied.

"We don't usually have that problem in the army," Indigo replied.

"The army doesn't pay people?" Dana said jokingly, and Indigo chuckled.

"If that sort of thing happened, it would probably be flagged somewhere and then there'd be an investigation. There're various security checks in, well a lot of jobs really, not just the army, but also there, of course. If you're flagged, questions are asked and actions taken. As a civilian, I suppose I'd inform the police, though if the bank thinks the transfer is fine, it's hard to know exactly what the police would do." There was a pause with both of them wondering how naïve the statement seemed to be, though Dana had a soft spot for her father who had an undying belief in the system. She knew her grandfather had been military as well, and she suspected her father was committed to the cause, but in truth, she doubted that governments were that straightforward.

"Well, as laudable as that is, Dad, it doesn't really help," Dana grinned.

"I would say you might be able to follow the money, but usually that sort of thing is heavily encrypted and difficult to do," Indigo shrugged. "I suppose on this occasion, maybe your friend got lucky. Shame it isn't you." Dana rolled her eyes and headed back to her room, disappointed at having gotten nowhere.

Although, she thought, as she sat in front of her computer looking at Charlie's "Broken Web" email, perhaps her father had made a good point.

AutoGold, Stepanov, Boom and Coulter…all part of the web Charlie had been talking about. Money was being sent back and forth between all of them, so if there was a web, there was probably a spider.

Quickly she fired off another email to Maxwell and Frost, a new idea suddenly striking her. If someone was coordinating finances for all these groups, then maybe that someone would be organising the finance for the would be assassin.

And maybe, Dana thought, if she could find that person she could hit AutoGold and Stepanov (or more accurately Stepanov's criminal empire, given the man himself was dead) where it hurt. Maybe even cripple them permanently.

On the edge of her seat, Dana kept refreshing her email over and over again, waiting for a response. After a few moments she came to the conclusion she was being unreasonable and that Charlie Maxwell had a life which didn't mean she was necessarily going to just drop everything because Dana wanted her to.

And then there was a new email from whitebird@kingcharles.com. Dana bit her bottom lip, and then clicked it open. There were just two words:

Chinggis Khaan.

"Hi," grinned the blonde behind the counter. She was, Dana decided, particularly bright and sparky, with a broad smile and glasses. "How can I help you?"

"I need to get to Ulaanbaatar," Dana said, and grimaced slightly, realising she was being a little vague in what she wanted exactly.

"Oh, right," the woman – Amanda, according to her name badge – said. She began tapping away on a computer, bringing information up.

With the little information she had been given, a quick search revealed two notable things about the name that had been sent (well, aside from the fact it was a more accurate version of Genghis Khan) – Chinggis Khaan was the name of a giant statue in Mongolia, a little outside Ulaanbaatar, the country's capital. With little else to go on, Dana packed a bag and headed to Brisbane International airport to try to get to her new destination. She hadn't given many details to her family, just telling them she was going to spend some time with a friend, and she would always have her phone on. Bella had pouted and her father had protested that he had just got back. Lily, on the other hand, smiled and told Dana to enjoy the last of her holidays before she was back at it again.

Once at the airport, Dana headed to the Flight Centre there in the hopes that they might be able to give her what she needed.

"Mongolian Airlines is what you need," Amanda said, still scintillating, "It's a 22-hour journey with a stopover at Incheon," and Dana felt her heart sink at the news. But when she heard a loud pop and almost jumped out of her seat, Dana realised she had no choice.

It was just a kid, stepping on a flavoured milk container, but it hammered home just how nervous Dana was about what was going on.

"Sure," Dana said, sliding her passport across the table.

"It's my favourite country," Amanda replied confidentially, her smile never leaving her face, and Dana wondered if she was just being polite. "You should try and see the statue. That was amazing." Within a surprisingly short time, Amanda had collated documents together and handed them over to Dana. "Enjoy your trip!"

Dana simply gave a grim smile in return.

Dana hadn't been particularly looking forward to visiting Ulaanbaatar, which, by all accounts, wasn't a particularly pleasant place to go. Indeed, flicking through a couple of guides online, the city was described as both the coldest and ugliest capital city in the world, which didn't exactly fill Dana with optimism. Not that she was going sightseeing, but all the same.

When she stepped into the streets, she thought that the city being the ugliest in the world was probably an exaggeration. It looked a little like most cities, Dana reflected, and the presence of such things as fast food shops and brands like Ikea made it more relatable. No, ugly was definitely an exaggeration.

Cold on the other hand, was fair. Admittedly it was February, and so the northern hemisphere wasn't likely to be forgiving, but Ulaanbaatar seemed to be delivering -9 degrees during the middle of the day, and Dana had a dread feeling of what it may be like at night. In truth, though, she wasn't that concerned about the night; her hotel, the impressive Blue Sky that looked a little like a giant blue sail in the middle of the city, was clearly aimed at ensuring tourists didn't freeze to death at any point.

However, she had determined that her goal was the Chinggis Khaan statue, and by all accounts it shouldn't have been that hard to get to. Her hotel was on Peace Av, and according to the map, that road led neatly to Tsagdaagiin Academi Av, then Gachuurt Rd, Tsaiz Gudamj....which was probably the road that went past the statue turnoff? Dana had put her phone back in her pocket, a little depressed at the realisation that getting to the statue was clearly a lot harder than she thought it would be.

Her room in the hotel wasn't particularly large, and was dominated by the curious blue carpet that looked like the swirls of waves crashing against each other. What Dana found most bizarre was the fact that the bathroom was part of the actual room – a glass cubicle that contained the bath tub, shower and sink – and given that the room itself had a wall of glass, Dana felt a little like she had become an exhibitionist when she was going to take a shower. Not that anyone would actually be able to see anything, but still.

Weighing up her options, she wondered if there was a way

she could get a taxi service to take her the distance she needed to go, and guessed her best option would be to go to the lobby and speak with reception. For once in her life, she was vaguely aware of how much money she was spending, given that a lot of her travelling recently had been funded by other sources. This time, she was relying on her own money, and she couldn't be quite as cavalier as she had been. She had been tempted to dive into the additional money she had acquired, but that seemed silly, so instead simply placed that in a new bank account and decided not to touch it.

In addition to that, there was the creeping concern that a global pandemic was just around the corner. People around the world seemed on edge that something was coming and the world was about to be turned upside down. Whatever Dana needed to do, there was an urgency that it should be done as quickly as possible so she could get back home if necessary. Truthfully, part of her thought she could rely on Karam to get her where she needed to be, if worst came to worst, but ideally she could do what she needed to do and go.

With the decision made, Dana took the lift to the lobby and exited into the vast space. While the rooms seemed to be quite small, the lobby was desperately trying to make up for it, an impressive open area where couches were scattered around, lit by ceiling lights that were rings. Dana found it hard to describe, but came to the conclusion that Mongolia was definitely not what she expected it to be. She wasn't sure what that expectation was, but it certainly wasn't what she was getting.

Fortunately English speakers weren't an issue, and though the pleasant lady with the round face at reception clearly had no idea what Dana wanted, she quickly summoned an older gentleman, dressed in the same uniform, and after a small discussion, he assured her that he would have a car at the front for her that would take her to Chinggis Khaan monument.

"Good price, and good service," he grinned, though Dana was dubious about what good price might constitute. Her answer was surprisingly quick – a 2010 silver Toyota Noah, which looked in quite good condition. The man behind the wheel, however, was, not quite as fresh as his car. She guessed he was in his forties, and was rugged up for the cold weather, but looked like he'd prefer to be anywhere other than driving an Australian to a tourist attraction. He had watery eyes and a sniffle, and Dana decided she wasn't getting too close in case he was actually sick.

The receptionist had joined her at the entrance and communicated something to the driver, who nodded his understanding, and then headed for the car.

"You go," the receptionist smiled, and indicated the car.

"Thanks," Dana said, but she was hesitant.

"No, no," the receptionist said. "He knows where to go. He will wait for you. Bring you back here, yes?"

"Yes," Dana replied, and felt more positive about the situation. At least everyone seemed to know what was going on. And yet, as she got into the car, she saw someone, dressed in a dark suit at reception. Dana moved slightly to get a better glimpse, but he had gone.

Surely not?

The drive out to Chinggis Khaan monument was largely uneventful, and Dana's driver seemed disinclined to become involved with her. Ulaanbaatar felt like a city that had been built decades earlier but hadn't bothered to keep up with renovation. Everything was bland and grey, the buildings all squat blocks that lacked imagination. All the writing seemed to be in Russian, which surprised her, as for some reason Dana had always felt that Mongolia should have been Chinese influenced, but clearly it was the Russians that had brought their culture to bear. She wanted to ask her driver about the history of the city, but his gruff manner didn't really invite conversation.

The further they drove, the more of a state of disrepair the roads were in, though the highway they were on seemed quite well maintained. And then it appeared they had left the city, with the flat, brown-green fields around them replacing the colourless habitats they had passed. The city itself, though, seemed surrounded by mountains, their snow-topped peaks now in front and to the sides.

Strangely the city seemed to come to life again, and Dana wondered if they were passing through an outer suburb or a small village.

"Ulaanbaatar," the travel agent named Amanda had said as she had been preparing documentation, "is pretty much the only city in Mongolia." If that were the case, then she was definitely still in Ulaanbaatar, but it obviously had room to expand if it wanted to. There were bus stops along the road, so that suggested they were indeed still in the city limits.

Once again, they entered open fields, with the power pylons looking like giant aliens marching relentlessly across the fields beside them. However, the fields themselves now seemed to have acquired scattered tents. Dana did a quick search on her phone, thinking they were yurts, though Google quickly corrected her, highlighting that Mongolians called them ger. On many, smoke billowed out from the top. The smoke reminded Dana of the cold and she shivered slightly within her Eliza winter jacket. She was rather glad she had got it in Khaki now, as had it been the bright red she initially considered, she would have felt very out of place.

The highway had expanded, rather surprisingly, into a fairly standard highway, with both directions having gained three lanes and the quality of the road, a high standard. This made Dana think that they had definitely left the city, now traversing the highway that linked the different towns together. Though, with that being said, little clumps of houses still appeared on the side of the road, and at one point Dana thought they passed what was called Orgil Supermarket, her attention caught not only by the sign in English, but also by the Pizza Hut proudly displayed on the front of the building in red. And yet, it was literally the only building around.

It was just after the supermarket her driver swung to the left and headed into what appeared to be a small town (or just another suburb? It was so hard to tell...). The road they turned onto was two lanes, and the village seemed to be mostly on the right of the car. Dana peered out the window to see it, and to her surprise, her driver spoke for the first time.

"Nalaikh," he grunted, and Dana wondered what the word was. The name of the town?

The drive continued, leaving the village (Nalaikh?) behind, though the pylons kept up. The clumps of houses became fewer and fewer, and Dana wondered how much further the journey would be.

And then she saw it.

Standing on a small hill in the distance was a white statue of a man on a horse. As Dana looked at it, she suddenly realised that the statue must have been huge, as, no matter how big it looked, it was still some way off. A stone archway came into view, and Dana knew that they had reached their destination.

Sure enough, her driver turned left to head through the arch, and the words Chinggis Khaan were clearly engraved at the top of the arch. A number of stone horsemen were also on the top of the arch, though even with the driver slowing the car down to follow the speed limit, Dana didn't get much time to make out the details.

They drove up the road, Chinggis Khaan's looming figure growing larger and larger as they did. The bitumen road gave way to paving stones, and Dana could see that there were a number of cars and buses parked around them. Her driver pulled up into a parking space that didn't actually seem marked, and he turned the car off. He turned back to her to her and simply said "I wait," before turning back and pulling up his coat around him.

He was asleep before Dana was even out of the car.

Dana headed towards the steps that led to the monument and once again was astonished by the size of the statue. It sat above an impressive building in its own right, and Dana counted at least fifty steps on the long path that led to it. The statue seemed to be made of steel, another surprise, while Khan himself – frowning but not angry – was holding a gold pole. Also, did he have a walking stick, Dana wondered? It looked a little like it…Strange...

She walked in through the main entrance, impressed by the large space she had entered. Mostly off-white, with light brown pillars and darker railings, what truly stood out was the giant red Mongolian boot that stood to the side of the stairwell that led to the upper level. Dana looked at it agog, suppressing a giggle. This place just got stranger and stranger. And then, as if to prove it…

"Hi Dana!"

IV

The three of them – Dana, Charlie Maxwell and Ashley Frost – sat down at the café, where it was moderately busy, but fortunately most people weren't speaking English so Dana doubted anyone would be interested in what they were talking about (though, now she thought that might actually be a possibility, it did suggest that perhaps she was getting a little paranoid).

"I was glad you called. And glad you looked at the email," Charlie said. Dana smiled a little, unwilling to give too much away. Beside Charlie, Ashley sat with a massive grin on her face, looking a little uncomfortable. Charlie clearly noticed this and elbowed the younger woman. "Ignore her."

"It's just nice to properly meet. I mean, properly meet you," Ashley said. "Such a fan. I think you're great. That whole cat thing was incredible." Dana blushed slightly, and wondered if she was going to be asked for an autograph which, if she were honest, she really didn't want to do. She had gotten used to signing autographs and it was becoming more and more of a thing, particularly on red carpets, but she still felt like a fraud.

"Do you want to see a picture of Dine?" Dana asked, hoping it was the right thing to say.

"Oh yes!" gushed Ashley, and Dana got her phone out, finding a picture of the kitten to show her. "She's so cute! She?"

"He."

"He's so cute."

"Anyway," interrupted Charlie (much to Dana's relief), "you wanted someone who's good with money trails?"

"My Dad said follow the money. It occurred to me that maybe there's someone who's coordinating the cash. Maybe Stepanov channels his money through different companies or…shell things…" She paused for a moment. "I just heard that on a tv show once," she admitted, but Charlie didn't seem phased.

"It's not that far from reality," the older woman said, pursing her lips. Dana wondered who did Charlie's makeup, because she looked perfectly put together. "And you think that it might be the same person working with…?"

"Wasn't Stepanov acquiring AutoGold? There was an AutoGold incident, you said."

"Justice Kennedy said, but yes," Charlie nodded, and both Doves noticed Dana's scowl at the name. Charlie suddenly remembered Justice making a comment about not wanting to be noticed by Dana at the Stepanov party, and she wondered exactly what the issue was between the pair.

"Stepanov had Boom create the problems at Moonlight Entertainment, and had Nathan Coulter assassinated in New York," Ashley mused. "There might be a money man that connects all the dots."

"But if there was," Charlie pointed out, "they'd be kept a long way from the business."

"But if there was," Dana repeated, "taking him down might be enough to sever the links between the different parts of Stepanov's empire. And I could find why someone decided to give me $80 million." At this both Charlie and Ashley sat bolt upright, their jaws dropped comically in reaction to the statement.

"It's just a thing," Dana said, regretting her words.

"Are you serious?" Charlie asked, and Dana nodded back. "That amount of money being moved would get the attention of a lot of intelligence agencies," Charlie responded, brutally. "Are you being followed?"

"Maybe," Dana said, guiltily. She looked around, as did the other two, but no one seemed out of place, or too interested in their conversation.

"Dana's right," Ashley decided. "Follow the money."

"Time to bring out our secret weapon, then."

Chinggis Khaan statue has a stairwell that leads to an exit from the monument towards the top. This exit takes you to the actual top of the statue, where you can walk up the neck (or mane?) of the horse and gaze across Mongolia in all its glory. Having done this, Dana had to admit the sight was incredible.

"The statue faces east," Charlie supplied. "Apparently, it's in the direction of where Genghis Khan was born. So, about a kilometre that way (and she pointed forwards from the horse's head) there's another statue of Hoelun, who is Khan's mother. Apparently, she's looking back." Dana peered into the distance, but couldn't see anything like a statue. There were definitely some buildings or something in the distance, but she couldn't see a statue – or at least a statue of the size they were in. "Tuul River is that way," and this time, Charlie pointed to their right. Again, Dana couldn't exactly make it out, but she suspected with binoculars, she might be able to see it more clearly. Annoyingly, there weren't any telescopes mounted for tourists, which was odd, because the place was tourist perfect in all other respects.

"I mean, it's incredible, but…"

"Allow me to introduce the Grey Knight," Ashley said, and Dana turned to find Ashley had joined them, along with another woman, about Ashley's smaller height, with spiky purple hair and glasses. She was wearing long shorts and a very big jacket, which Dana appreciated. The Grey Knight started moving her hands, and Dana immediately realised she was using sign language, and inwardly cursed at her inability to respond. It was something she thought she should have made the effort to learn, but time never seemed to be on her side.

"She says hi," Ashley said, and Dana smiled gratefully. "We've explained the situation and she agrees with you." The Grey Knight began to communicate again, looking both at Dana and at Ashley as she did, and there was a frown on her face as she did so. It ended with a shrug, and a strange gesture towards her head. When Ashley translated, this time it was directed to Charlie. "She needs me for some hacking stuff, but she thinks she can track the money."

"Should we stay?" Charlie asked, and the Knight nodded, before signing again.

"She has a room here," Ashley translated, though her voice was tinged with surprise.

"Lead on," Charlie shrugged.

They had gone down to the basement level, and the Grey Knight and Ashley had disappeared into a little room that for some reason the Grey Knight had access to. Dana hadn't bothered to follow them, suspecting that she would have little understanding of what they were doing anyway. So she wandered around, the basement level which was a curious dedication to Genghis Khan. She had little knowledge of the man, having been under the vague understanding that he was a horrific killer. She also thought he was the grandson of Kublai Khan. Or was it the other way around?

The museum had a lot of fascinating little ornaments from the first Mongol Empire, which seemed to be around 1200, and there were various portraits of Khan, and information about him. Dana was slightly surprised there was no information on how Genghis Khan died, but saw that he was succeeded by Ögedei Khan, and then Kublai established the Yuan Dynasty (so it *was* the other way round!)

Wandering back to the room with the portraits and the black door that the two women had disappeared behind, Dana found couches, and discovered that Charlie had appropriated as her own. She sat down beside the woman, and gazed around the room.

"I just realised I left my uber out there," Dana mused.

"Well, if he's bored he'll just go. We can drive you back to Ulaanbaatar," Charlie said with a smile. "Why are you doing this?"

"Sorry?"

"I don't get you," Charlie said, and turned to the model. "You have a perfect life where you can just be you and get famous and be flown around the world to look gorgeous. For me, and Ash…we've signed up to the Doves to…well to pay off a debt, I guess. Justice Kennedy is Interpol, but you don't have to be involved in any of this. Why not give the information to Justice or ASIO and let them sort out who's trying to kill you?" Dana looked at Charlie, a wry smile on her face as she thought about a similar discussion she had with her therapist.

"Maybe I have trust issues," Dana settled on. "Which is true," she added. "I don't think I'd trust Interpol or ASIO to stop someone assassinating me."

They settled back to silence, each thinking about what the other had said. Sometimes, Dana had to admit, she was worried that her continued involvement in these sorts of things was from enjoyment rather than from any genuine sense of justice, and that was more worrying to her than anything else.

Their reverie was interrupted by the black door opening, and the two women Dana had mentally decided were definitely pixie nerds, exited.

"Exciting stuff," Ash grinned, and the Grey Knight seemed equally hyped. "You were right. The Knight wove her magic, and I hacked systems left, right and centre for her, but in the end she discovered you were bang on the money, pun definitely intended." This broke up both women, and Charlie had a look on her face that suggested she wanted to put the pair into daycare. "Anyway, the money in all situations is funnelled through a number of different shell companies, payment made from no-name accounts in the Seychelles, all that jazz." Beside her, the Grey Knight was signing like crazy, and Dana couldn't tell if Ashley was translating or the Knight wanted to get to the next part of the story quicker.

"The thing is, there was a common factor once you started to dig really deeply. Like an electronic signature. That's the thing, right, the really smart people are also usually the really prideful people, and they can't help themselves but leave some sort of mark to identify who they are. And nobody was going to see this, except for," and at this, Ash gestured her thumb in the Grey Knight's direction.

Dana looked around the room, a little aware that they were starting to get looks from the other tourists.

"The point being?" Dana emphasized.

"So, they were all performed by the same person, because they all used a certain number sequence – 040131."

"What's that sequence mean?" Charlie wondered

"Who knows," Ashley shrugged, though the Knight grabbed her arm pointedly, and then started signing. "Oh, the Knight thinks it might be leetspeak. Like a word in numbers, like…blank-a-blank-i-e-l, or blank-a-blank-l-e-l."

"Or blank-a-blank-i-e-l," Dana murmured. She muttered to herself what sounded a bit like "ba…iel…da…iel…dabiel…dadiel," and then suddenly said "Daniel?"

"Could be," Ash said, and the Knight nodded enthusiastically, "but the truth is we couldn't identify a name at all. But we did a lot of digging, and I went through a lot of records, and we were finally able to trace all the transaction coding." She paused for exaggerated effect, but the Knight was already moving her hands, passing her thumb over her chin. Ash rolled her eyes, annoyed she didn't get the chance for a big reveal, before remembering the other two women couldn't sign. "It's Iceland!" she said, and this time the Grey Knight rolled her eyes.

"Where? Could you be specific?" At this the Knight and Ashley looked at other with broad grins.

V

As it turned out, they could be very specific, indeed. Once Ash had narrowed it down to Iceland, she had started to get more specific, realising it was outside of Reykjavik. Prompted by Dana's suggestion they might be looking for a Daniel, Ashley had done some more work, and eventually they had triangulated it down to a building to the north of Iceland that was apparently owned by one Daniel Logovik.

"Incidentally," Ashley had said at Ulaanbaatar airport, "the transfer details used that code. I don't think it's even a signature; I think it's just a force of habit. Like using the same password for everything, not that I think this guy would ever do it, but 040 131 might have been the last six digits of his mum's phone number, or his. You can bring that up with Mr Logovik when you meet him." At this, the Grey Knight had signed something, and Ashley nodded her agreement. "If that is even his name."

"Does he not have a cool online name, like the Grey Knight, or something?" Dana asked facetiously.

"No, actually nothing. Honestly if we didn't have a location, I wouldn't have assumed it was Daniel Logovik that was involved, but once you start to see if there are any signs of Daniel Logovik doing anything else in Iceland…well, it's the absence of information that gives it away more than an abundance of clues," Ash said. "Oh, by the way, if you ever need any computer help again, I can give you my number," Ash grinned, and Dana shook her head indulgently, handing her phone over. Hugging each of the three women in turn, Dana turned and headed to her gate.

"Be careful, Dana," Charlie warned, and Dana smiled back appreciatively.

It cost an absolute fortune, and a stopover in France, plus a change from Mongolian Airlines to Lufthansa, but after 22 hours, Dana was Reykjavik, and then there was another change as she waited for a flight to Gjögur Airport, which was the closest airport to where the women had identified Daniel Logovik to be (although the more they said the name, the more Ash thought it was just a front).

The plane was, of course, fairly tiny, and as Dana watched out the window, she saw that Iceland was definitely living up to its name, the mountains now just white, with snow covering the land. There was only one other person on the flight, but he was sitting at the back definitely disinterested in making conversation, absorbed in his phone.

The plane came into land at Gjögor Airport, and when Dana saw the ice on the runway, she closed her eyes and gritted her teeth, deciding that this was the last sort of flight she had wanted to make. Nonetheless, the plane hit the ground, bouncing only slightly as it did, and then the brakes applied, surprisingly without slipping at all. The plane came to a halt, and Dana opened her eyes, unsurprised to see that her fellow passenger hadn't even bothered to raise his eye from his phone; this was clearly standard fare.

She was invited to disembark the plane, and was soon in the tiny airport which presented no obstacles at all. Looking around, though, Dana suddenly realised she wasn't really sure how she was going to get to her destination. As she stepped outside, she looked around, shocked to see the cliffs to one side with their frozen waterfall, and the flat snowy wasteland to the other side.

And a spectacular lack of any sort of taxi service.

Dana, you twat.

Realistically, Dana thought, there was only one choice. She needed to walk to her destination. Fortunately, it seemed for the most part all she had to do was follow the *Strandavegur* highway, and though it would get considerably colder as the night approached, what other choice did she have?

Pulling her faithful Pacsafe Petite Econyl backpack on, she gritted her teeth, and stepped forward out of the airport. When she was grabbed by the arm, she swung around, ready to hit, but to her shock it was her fellow passenger, his hands raised in surrender and a weak smile on his face. He had long black hair and a black beard, and looked not only harmless, but actually quite nice. He said something that sounded a bit like Affsakith, though when he saw Dana's blank face he spoke again.

"Sorry, sorry," he said, his accent thick. "I did not mean to startle you. I think, would you like a lift? A ride? A lift, *já*?" He held out his hand in friendship and Dana narrowed her eyes.

"What's your name?" she demanded.

"Magnús Ásmundsson," the man said, and he looked at his hand, uncertain what to do.

Not Daniel Logovik, Dana mused, and she put her hand forward to shake his. Though, she thought, Daniel Logovik probably didn't actually use that name. Still, he probably wasn't Icelandic and didn't have the accent, so Magnús seemed a safe option.

"Sorry, I'm," Dana started but Magnús held up his hands.

"Please, I understand. But I can," and he gestured towards the only car that was in the small carpark.

"Thank you," Dana said, gratefully. She held out her phone, and pointed to the small part of the coast where she needed to go to. "Do you know this area?"

"*Já*," Magnús nodded. "I go past on my way to my home. I can drive you there, easy."

He led her over to one of the very few cars that were parked at the airport, a Toyota Landcruiser which Dana guessed was definitely older than her by a decade. The beige colour would not have come from today, but it was definitely a car that was used to the conditions that it found itself in, and Magnús opened it quickly and jumped in, encouraging her to do as well.

"Where do you have to go?" he asked, and Dana wondered what she should say exactly.

"Um," she opted for, and held out her phone, having taken a screenshot of the map earlier. This turned out to be have been for the best as Magnús studied it for a few moments and then nodded.

"Yes, I know this," he said with a smile. The car judded into life with a splutter (clearly a regular occurrence as Magnús didn't even raise an eyebrow) and as the smell of petrol wafted from the back of the car, it lurched into action, driving out of the carpark and away from the squat buildings of the airport, toward a road that looked distinctly rough. It wasn't a particularly rocky ride, but Dana suspected it had been worn down from cars driving on it, rather than any attempt to keep the road in top condition. It felt a bit like she was driving in outback Australia. Aside from the ridiculous cold, the vegetation being green rather than yellow, and the gloomy grey sky that loomed over them, it was identical.

OK, so felt as in vibe rather than appearance.

Dana was mildly concerned that the road was clearly one lane, but on the flat, barren, featureless environment around them, it was pretty clear that no one would be able to come towards them unexpectedly.

She took the opportunity to put a earphone in as surreptitiously as she could, and kept an eye on her phone, watching to make sure that her signal strength was strong.

"You are visiting friends?" Magnús asked.

"Er, yes," Dana said, not keen on getting into a lie she couldn't get out of. "You live here?"

"*Já, já,*" Magnús nodded enthusiastically. "Near *Árneskirkja II* church. Me, my wife, my kids. It's very quiet, very gentle, but nice. I think not your lifestyle, though," he chuckled and Dana smiled back, guessing that her clothes and backpack were miles away from the worn out suitcase Magnús had thrown in the back of the car.

Magnús had very little else to say on the journey, and Dana couldn't think of anything to fill the gap. Besides which, she was feeling the cold even through her coat, and she pulled it a little closer in the hope of more warmth. Magnús clearly noticed this, and turned up the heater in the car a bit more.

"There will be good warmth where you are going," Magnús assure her. "We fight the cold as well," he grinned.

After about ten minutes of driving, they passed a small road to the right, and then crossed a small stream. Then they were at another road, heading to the right, and to the shore. Magnús paused at this intersection, and turned to Dana.

"Down there is where you want to be. Should I drive you down, and you check on your friend?" Dana saw her phone had service and she hit the call button, having been ready to make the phone call. It was answered almost immediately.

"Am I in the right place?" Dana asked, before anything else could be said.

"Yeah, I have you," Ash's voice replied.

"I think I'm OK from here, Magnús," Dana said with a smile. "Thank you for all your help."

"No problem," he said. Then he paused and, after a quick look of apology, opened the glove compartment and rummaged through it, before pulling out a pen and a small card. He wrote a number on it and then handed it to Dana. "If you need a lift back to the airport, or there is a problem, please call."

"Thank you," Dana said, and slid the card inside her backpack. Truth be told, now she thought about it, she wasn't entirely sure how she would get back to Gjögur Airport, so this might be exactly the help she needed. She opened the door to the car and got out.

"OK," Ash's voice came from her earphone, "let's go."

VI

"I'm surprised you know who I am."

"I live my life online," came the measured response. "I've seen your picture a few times. You look more beautiful in real life, though."

"Thanks."

"You know at one point, they wanted you dead. The two heavy hitters in the world of assassination both said no to killing you? I can't believe it."

"You are Daniel Logovik, right?" Dana's gun never faltered as she took in the man in front of her. He was strange; she couldn't get a good sense of his height, and he had a full beard that made it hard to get a good sense of his age as well. She would have guessed in his forties, but wouldn't have been surprised if she was a decade out either side. He wasn't thin, but he wasn't fat, and he had a cheery face, a little like a garden elf's. Also, he was definitely wearing... "Calvin Klein, Eternity?"

"Yeah, very good. And in answer to your first question, sometimes."

"Not your birth name?"

"No."

"And you don't have a cool online identity?"

"You make it sound like an accusation," Logovik laughed. "No, I don't. When I was younger I did call myself "the Extra" because I thought I was a bit, but I soon realised that if you really want to be a good hacker, giving yourself a cool name is the quickest way for the authorities to track you down. So I became, nobody. And I deleted the Extra." He paused and then said, "But, you did manage to track me down."

"040 131. You gave yourself away." Unexpectedly, Logovik laughed again, but this time it was tinged with pain.

"People are always brought down by their own arrogance. I never thought it would be me, but there you go. I'm an idiot," and he seemed to genuinely mean it.

"I have a friend who's very good with computers. And another who's very good with finances. You're good, but you do actually exist," Dana continued. "So there has to be some sort of trail, somewhere."

"I'm assuming this is about the money transfer? I could probably get online and hack into a few systems, back track and create a new digital trail so the deposit seems proper legit. You're right if you think it was to bring heat down on you, and I know it sort of has, but I can help." He turned slightly, and then stopped. "Do you mind?"

"I think I do," Dana said, and Logovik sat back in his chair. Dana looked at the screens behind him, and saw that there was a wide array of things going on, from screens that had spreadsheets and pure code, to others that were showing security camera footage (live, presumably), what was clearly an episode of some television series from a *long* time ago (she remembered watching something with her father, and the fashions alone indicated that it wasn't from the last twenty years), as well as what seemed to be a countdown of some sort.

"Not about the money," Logovik observed. "Slightly surprised if I'm honest."

"We'll get to it," Dana said, cocking an eyebrow. "But you run money for more than just Stepanov's gang, am I right." Logovik smiled a small smile, and raised his hands.

"I do have a few clients," he said. "It's nice to be wanted. Oh, bad choice of words." Dana narrowed her eyes, and moved her gun, which took the smile off Logovik's face super quick. "Joke."

"You sorted out the deal to kill Mason Lemon?" Logovik looked blankly at her for a moment.

"May I?" he asked, but Dana shook her head.

"No keyboard for you."

"I couldn't tell you off the top of my head, then," Logovik said, quite reasonably. "I've funnelled money for many groups and many operations. Pick one out of a hat at random and…well, I'd need to check."

"The problem is," Dana said, "I feel like you could do something that I would be unaware of, and it would backfire badly."

"I have no reason to do anything to you, Dana," Logovik said.

"Dana," she murmured, and Logovik looked puzzled. "You knew my name."

"Sure," he said.

"But you funnel money for so many groups and so many operations." Logovik pursed his lips, his confidence slipping away slightly. Then he nodded slightly, accepting defeat.

"Yes, I paid Man Garam for killing Mason Lemon. And then Nathan Coulter."

"You could shut down Stepanov's entire operation, I'm betting," Dana said. "You could defund everything."

"Everything Stepanov owned I could bury," Logovik shrugged. "Even AutoGold now. But why would I?"

"So, I don't shoot you," Dana suggested and Logovik burst out laughing.

"Oh, come on, Dana. I've done some research on you." Dana

392

must have given Logovik a look, because he paused to explain. "When two of the biggest assassins on the planet turn down a job that has substantial bankroll, I'm curious to know why they don't want to move against you. Honestly I could find a reason for either, but there's so much about you on the internet. You saved that cat. You're not going to kill me, because you're not a killer."

"But I am," said a voice, and both Dana and Logovik turned in shock.

"Marcús?" Dana said, her mouth open in shock.

"Hello Dana," the Icelander said, with a smile, though his accent had completely disappeared, replaced by something far more familiar. He was standing near the door, a handgun covering...possibly Logovik, but also possibly Dana.

"Wait," Logovik suddenly said. "You're Úlfur?"

"Who's Úlfur?" Dana snapped, and Marcús looked equally blank.

"I was told if things got difficult they'd send Úlfur," Logovik snarled. "Why aren't you killing her?" His cool demeanour had slipped away quite dramatically.

"She's surprisingly difficult to kill," Marcús replied. "And very determined."

"A Taurus GX4?" Dana asked, identifying the gun accurately.

"Handles well, and it was given to me. Nostalgia means it's hard to replace."

"I get that. Are you actually Icelandic?" Dana asked.

"My mother is," Marcús said with a smile. "Turns out it's a small world after all. I certainly didn't expect to be coming here today. Obviously I don't live out in this hellhole."

"So, you're going to let her live?" Logovik asked incredulously.

"Oh you misunderstand," Marcús said, and Dana realised she was holding her breath. "You wanted to bring heat down on her with that money transfer, and you got your wish," and with this Úlfur raised his gun to point it

393

at Logovik. "But I overheard her some of her conversation in Mongolia, and it seems like she might be onto something. So, let's liquidate the Stepanov crime syndicate and AutoGold, and scatter that money around a bit."

"Úlfur is on his way," Logovik said, but the desperation in his voice was obvious.

"Come on. Úlfur is probably just another Russian bogeyman, made up to scare the likes of you." Marcús gave a grin, that was obvious through his beard. "The Stepanov syndicate is in tatters as they try to establish who is running it. AutoGold is suffering similarly. We have no desire for either of those organisations to continue running, and if you can sort that out, we'd be very happy," Marcús said. Logovik regarded them both and then turned to Dana.

"Might I use the computer?"

"Bearing in mind," Marcús said before Dana could reply, the warning in his voice clear, "Dana may not know what you're doing, but I have enough skills to see what you're playing with." Logovik nodded, accepting the warning, and turned to his computer. Suddenly the screens changed as apps opened up on them, with Logovik typing quickly and efficiently. Dana could see that there seemed to be some bank accounts being accessed, with money leaving some and appearing in others, each time the message was different, the names were different and the amounts were different. One screen displaying coding, suddenly scrolled through the code and then seemed to repeat, over and over, though again the numbers changed each time the code scrolled through.

"Make sure that AutoGold's employees have enough money," Dana said, and Logovik rolled his eyes.

"Maybe I should send money to their kids' accounts as well," he snapped, but suddenly his arrogance slipped away.

Marcús' Taurus was at Logovik's head. "Best put the phone down," Marcús said, and Dana mentally kicked herself for not noticing he had picked it up. "It makes me nervous. Though, for your information, you have no more security here." This made Logovik go pale, and Marcús pulled his gun back, letting Logovik got back to work. Dana felt a sudden chill as she realised what Marcús had meant by the comment.

394

Logovik continued to type, and Dana watched the code go up on the screen.

```
If ($access==false) {

foreach( $this->rules as $key=>$rule){

if ($details['id']==$rule['id'] && $details['id']){

$details['chalice'] = !$access;
```

"Wait," Dana suddenly said. "What's that?" Logovik put his fingers on the keyboard, but the Taurus was back at his temple.

"Answer her," Marcús said.

"I don't know what she means," Logovik said, but there was something in his eyes that Úlfur clearly didn't trust. Dana, however, didn't need to. She pointed at a screen where the word "chalice" had appeared.

"What's that?"

"It's just a point of transfer," Logovik said.

"Why is it called chalice?" Dana asked.

"Just a random name," Logovik replied, but both Dana and Marcús could see the nervousness in him.

"What's chalice?" Marcús asked.

"It might be nothing," Dana said. "But it's a name I've heard before and it wasn't good."

"I see I'm getting money," Marcús said. "You can undo that right now. One more slip like that and I will definitely end you. What's happened to the syndicate and AutoGold?"

"The syndicate has lost all its money," Logovik said. "AutoGold will probably go into receivership in the next week."

"Did you make another transfer to Dana?"

"Did he?" Dana said, and Marcús raised an eyebrow. "Don't do this to me again!"

"You're fine," Marcús said. "I'll be your advocate."

"I still want to know what's going on with that chalice entry," Dana said.

"You're being paranoid," Logovik protested. Dana set her jaw, ready for a fight, but before she could do anything a phone pinged, and Marcús took his out, looking at it.

"If seems everything you say about the syndicate and AutoGold is true. I think you've outlived your usefulness, then," Marcús said, and before another word could be spoken, he squeezed the trigger of his Taurus. Dana yelped as blood hit the monitors and some bounced back onto her.

"You didn't have to kill him," Dana protested, a feeling of frustration building up inside of her, alongside the hollowness of knowing there was no way to undo what had happened. "I needed to find out about the chalice entry," she said dully, not sure what else she could say.

"I don't know what this chalice is," Marcús said, a complete lack of care in his voice. "But I've what I was sent to do. You're in the clear, trust me. I have your back." Dana opened her mouth to speak, but nothing came out. What could she even say?

"Need a lift to the airport?" Marcús asked politely.

VII

"I mean, it's not ideal," Karam Narogin said, when Dana had completed her story.

"I said I didn't want money," Dana protested.

"I'll relay that to the upper management, I promise. It's just not going to look good if anyone goes through the money trail. Though when we ran it through Big Brother they didn't seem remotely interested" He was interrupted by a waiter putting down two drinks on the table in front of them. Neither of them were particularly exciting; both a standard soft drink.

"Are you saying Marcús was ASIS?" Dana asked.

"Obviously we were told there is no Magnús Ásmundsson working for ASIS," Narogin sighed.

"Great to see ASIO and ASIS work so closely together," Dana said, not remotely holding back on the sarcasm. "No one will be able to go through the money trail," she added. "Logovik, or whatever his name was, was too good at his job.

"You did," huffed Narogin.

"The Grey Knight did," Dana snapped back.

"Oh yeah. Those Doves," Narogin scowled.

"Why don't you like them?"

"It's not their job to do international espionage," Narogin grumbled.

"Because they don't hold an allegiance to a country?" Dana asked pointedly.

"Because they hold allegiance to a person, apparently," Narogin said. He lent back in his chair and looked around at the bustle of the Queen St Mall in Brisbane, and Dana wondered what it was he was thinking. "You'll be fine," he finally said, turning his attention back to her. He dusted at what seemed to be a piece of fluff on his jacket, though Dana had long noticed this was a nervous action, and it didn't exactly fill her with confidence.

"I won't spend the money," Dana offered.

"Honestly, it will be fine," Narogin said. "If it was from Stepanov's syndicate, it's not our problem anyway. I'll field it. Promise." This time there was no dusting, so Dana felt slightly more reassured.

"The guy had files on CHALICE, I'm sure of it," Dana said, and Narogin raised an eyebrow.

"Dana, I hate to be the one to tell you this, but the upper management don't think CHALICE is really a thing." Dana's jaw dropped for a moment, slightly surprised by this. The idea of an international clandestine operation was definitely like something from a Tom Cruise movie, but they had proof. Narogin had been involved.

"They don't believe us?" Dana asked incredulously. "What about the stolen virus?"

"You let Chandler go," Narogin said, and Dana pursed her lips. It had been over a year since Dana had encountered the thief named Tiffany Chandler and helped her to flee to Australia with a virus that had been stolen from a Japanese lab, only to discover Chandler had been working with a mysterious organisation calling themselves CHALICE. Dana had developed a soft spot for Chandler, not pursuing the thief when she disappeared in Singapore, and the Australian intelligence organisations had been less than impressed when Chandler didn't turn up. In fairness, though, Dana had made sure that Narogin had got the stolen virus.

"They don't trust me?"

"Of course they do. Otherwise, they wouldn't have asked for your help in Seoul. They just don't trust that you'll follow their instructions. And," he said, Dana sensing he was about to deliver the killing blow, "CHALICE hasn't been confirmed by anyone except you."

"And you."

"I don't know what I happened," Narogin said, and Dana glared at him.

"Thaks for the support." She put her phone in her clutch, and stood up. "This was obviously a waste of time."

"Don't be like that," Narogin said, running his hand through his shaggy hair in frustration. "You have to understand our point of view. If you'd have brought in this…Dan Logovik…maybe…"

"His name's not Dan Logovik," Dana said wearily. "That's just a name he created."

"Odd," muttered Narogin. "We found a Dan Logovik in Brisbane, but we guessed it wasn't him."

"Cool." Dana turned and started to leave the Pig & Whistle, where the pair had met up, and Narogin looked around flustered for a moment, and quickly jogged after her.

"Where are you going?"

"Home," Dana said. "Maybe you're right. Maybe I'm just a silly little girl, making things up. But when CHALICE does turn up properly, Karam, don't come to me. I'm not interested in helping you with something that doesn't exist." She didn't stop walking, unlike Narogin who watched her walk away. He noticed the looks Dana got from various people, and gave a wry smile. She was someone who definitely couldn't go unnoticed.

There was a storm coming, he noted. Both actually and metaphorically. Rumour had it the country could be heading for unexpected lockdowns.

He looked again to see the Dana's bright yellow dress fading into the Brisbane crowd. Let's hope Dana is wrong, he reflected. After all, hell hath no fury like a woman scorned.

ALSO AVAILABLE

DEATH ON ICE

by Ryan Alcock

"But diamonds…they were the most incredible. Hold them up to the light and the effect is transformative. I fell in love with their structure and abilities from the moment I saw them."

DANA SPECTRA'S FIRST AMAZING ADVENTURE!!!

Justice Kennedy: Interpol spy, hot on the trail of a gunrunner, ready to destroy his entire operation.

Librada Cisneros: brutal, wealthy and obsessed with diamonds at the cost of all else.

Dana Specta: stunning Australian model who has something that both Kennedy and Cisneros want.

Dragged from a beauty pageant into the deadly world of espionage, Dana finds herself facing death as she tries to stop a powerful millionaire from taking what he wants regardless of the price.

ALSO AVAILABLE

POISONED CHALICE

by Ryan Alcock

"Dana, things might get dangerous. You have to stay as safe as possible. I know this is a big ask, but in all the world, the only person I trust absolutely is you."

THE NEXT DANA SPECTRA ADVENTURE!!!

Shira Langlois: US Embassy clerk, she has stolen something deadly and needs protection to get it out of Japan.

Snake Eyes: a ruthless assassin dispatched to retrieve what Langlois has, with orders to execute anyone in her way.

Dana Spectra: Australian model and daughter of Colonel Indigo Spectra - the one person Langlois trusts to get her to safety.

When Dana is approached by Shira to get Colonel Spectra's help, she is instructed by her father to protect the American until he can get her safely into Australia. But with the secret services of Australia, Japan, Germany and the UK on their trail, as well as Interpol, Dana sets out on a journey across continents unable to trust anyone. And all the while, Snake Eyes has them in her sights...

ALSO AVAILABLE

SILHOUETTE

by Ryan Alcock

"I'm assuming you know something that we don't. I'll help you, but I really think this is a bad idea. A very bad idea. For the love of God, Dana, please be careful."

THE NEWEST DANA SPECTRA ADVENTURE!!!

Tom McAteer: eco-scientist, murdered in Canada at the launch of Shadow.
Shadow: the new energy drink from Silhouette Moreau, recycling entrepreneur.
Bella North-Spectra: younger sister of Dana Spectra; almost murdered when McAteer was.

Dana has become the brand ambassador for Shadow, but at the launch, her sister is almost murdered, and a scientist actually is. Spurred on by Bella's claim that the killer is one of her friends, Dana sets out on a journey that will take her to some of the darkest places on Earth, all to find who exactly put her sister in the firing line and why it was necessary for McAteer to die.